The Secret Sister

M. M. DeLuca spent her childhood in Durham City, England. After studying Psychology at the University of London, Goldsmiths College, she moved to Winnipeg, Canada where she worked as a teacher then as a freelance writer. She studied Advanced Creative writing with Pulitzer prizewinning author, Carol Shields and has received several local arts council grants for her work. Her first novel, *The Pitman's Daughter* was shortlisted for the Chapters Robertson Davies first novel in Canada award in 2001. She went on to self-publish it on Amazon in 2013 where it reached the Amazon Top 20 in the literary bestseller chart. Her novel *The Savage Instinct* was shortlisted for the Launchpad Manuscript Contest (USA) in 2017 where it was picked up by independent publisher, Inkshares.

THE
SECRET
SISTER

M. M. DELUCA

CANELO

First published in the United Kingdom in 2021 by

Canelo
31 Helen Road
Oxford OX2 0DF
United Kingdom

A CIP catalogue record for this book is available from the British Library.

Print ISBN 978 1 80032 329 2
Ebook ISBN 978 1 80032 328 5

Look for more great books at www.canelo.co

Printed and bound in Great Britain by Clays Ltd, Elcograf S.p.A.

1

To all those children who overcome unimaginable obstacles just to get to school each day.

No evil dooms us hopelessly except the evil we love, and desire to continue in, and make no effort to escape from.

George Eliot

Prologue

The lights around the giant Ferris wheel glow bluish-purple and the night becomes unreal. Like a scene from a fairy tale.

I decide it's time to lose my husband, Guy.

I slip into the shelter of an alleyway, between Cibo's Margarita Bar and Sin City Souvenirs. Watch him amble by the market stalls, still chatting as if I'm strolling beside him. He doesn't notice I'm gone until he stops at a leather stall to rummage through a case of tooled leather belts. Then he turns as if to show me one, his eyes wide with excitement, his head likely fogged with fantasies – my hair veiling my face as I kneel on the marble tiles of a hotel bathroom to undo that buckle. His hands grazing my shoulders, breath warm and tickly on my back. He loves me. Can't get enough of me. That I know. Have always known. I press my shoulder against the sunbaked wall, heart aching as he turns full circle, forehead furrowed, scanning the crowds with panicked eyes. The belt dangles from his hand. He throws it back onto the counter. Knocks down a rack of earrings. The pony-tailed vendor shrugs. Shakes his head when Guy staggers into the milling crowds and stands, arms outstretched, turning slowly like a creaking windmill. He reaches for his phone and fumbles with the thumbprint ID. My ringer is off so there's only an insistent vibration. Again and again he calls. Three, four, five times. Then the texts arrive.

> Where are you

> Anna where r u

> Where r u.

> Call me.

> Text me

> I'm still at the leather stall.

> I'll wait

> Where r u

> Come on Anna. Call me???

> R u ok Anna.

Back and forth he paces past the same three stalls. Past the busker with her plaid shirt, torn blue jeans and ruby lips. Past the rhinestone-clad showgirls posing with the drunken frat boys. He shoves his phone into people's faces as they amble by, jabs at the display, begging for information. I imagine his words. *Have you seen this woman? My wife? She's wandered off. Lost herself. Crazy, huh?* He holds his hand palm downwards and measures my height in the air. *She's five-six. Thirtyish. Shoulder-length black hair, slim, pretty, wearing a sleeveless white shift dress.*

His mouth droops at the corners and his hands move in freakish semaphore. Some people stop, shake their heads and move on. Others just walk straight by, brushing him aside as if he's a crazy, buzzing gnat.

When he slumps down on a garbage can and wipes his sleeve over his eyes, love and remorse swell in waves, clutching at my throat until I think I'll choke. I want to end this thing I'm doing, but then I remember Birdie.

How I have to fix everything for her. Make it all right again.

I made this promise and I can't go back on it now.

I won't betray you, Birdie. Ever, ever again.

Then I feel the pressure of a firm hand on my shoulder and it's too late to turn back.

Minneapolis

Eight months earlier

I knew all about Guy before I met him in person.

I checked out his Facebook profile and studied his photos closely enough to figure that his condo was in a newly built tower attached to one of the converted warehouse buildings in the Mill District overlooking the river, where penthouse apartments sold for a million or more. Luxury pads that boasted *"intelligent and intuitively designed condos with timeless finishes, sweeping views of the river and 24-hour concierge in a boutique style lobby."*

At that time, I was living paycheck to paycheck teaching English Lit at an alternative high school. Driving home every day from work, I crossed through the Mill District to get to my tiny upper floor, one bed, one bath on the other side of the river. The wrong side, next to the freight yards and abandoned cold storage plant. From my bedroom window I could see those golden towers in the distance, and I'd imagine exactly where Guy was. I'd picture him silhouetted against a wall of windows, the honeyed expanse of an oak-timbered, brick-walled room spread out behind him.

The heady promise of that vision kept me going, even though I was broke and barely able to scrape together next month's rent money. My only worldly possessions included a television on a ten-dollar Ikea stand, a bed, a second-hand patio table with two mismatched metal chairs, a floor cushion for a sofa, and a closet full of cheap, untouched clothes, their tags dangling in a neat row.

It was lunchtime when Guy and I met in person for the first time. The end of my grueling morning. My mouth watered at the thought of a peanut butter and banana sandwich waiting in the staffroom fridge. Then the intercom crackled into action and the principal announced there'd be an extended lunch period because of a high priority professional development presentation. Attendance nonnegotiable.

I slammed down the pile of student writing journals, scattering them across the desk. I'd rather spend my lunch hour having my wisdom teeth pulled than listen to some earnest academic blather on about the educational process. Often the speakers were remote, ivory-tower types – usually failed classroom teachers, totally unsuited to front line work – who'd retreated to the quiet sanctuary of a university education department to avoid a nervous breakdown. Once they'd escaped the real, gritty world of teaching, these academics thrived in peaceful isolation, cranking out research papers on student engagement, teacher charisma, self-determination, scaffolding, collaborating, integration or any other buzz worthy topic of the day. The result? All of us miserable frontline teachers lived in a constant state of flux, at the mercy of the latest research findings. Struggling to reinvent our teaching strategies like hamsters on a wheel forever trying to catch up to the latest fad.

But then I remembered. This presentation was different. Guy was today's speaker. Today I'd see him in the flesh instead of scouring all those Facebook posts.

Heart thumping, I gathered up the journals into a pile and grabbed a couple to take with me. If all else failed, they'd distract me from the hungry rumbling in my gut.

Robin, our principal, was British. An import from Cambridge. A dusty relic from the sixties hanging grimly onto the barest semblance of youth, with his diamond stud earrings, wispy strands of reddish-gray hair and musty checkered shirts that smelled of old laundry. He walked around the school wearing granny glasses and bedroom slippers and sported a shark's tooth necklace he claimed was from his surfing days at Zuma Beach. Unable to afford the California lifestyle and keen to dodge the draft, he'd drifted up to the Midwest in the late seventies and found his niche in teaching. He eventually moved up the system to head the team at our alternative school, which he ran according to liberal sixties educational strategies.

I'd been at the school for six years and loved it. It was a super-relaxed place. Teachers and students on a first-name basis, and courses that snailed on forever at the students' own pace. No deadlines, no lectures, plenty of interactive group projects as well as a big emphasis on music and the arts, and a whole lot of feel-good, self-esteem building sessions.

We took in the outsiders, the bullied, the disillusioned, and the disenfranchised. Kids would come into the classroom bruised, battered and alienated by the regular school system. Nervous aggression coiled like a tight spring in their gut. But once they realized there were no tight-assed discipline freaks around and they could work at a speed that suited their own individual needs, they usually settled into the calm daily routine without too much protest.

The door of the multi-purpose room swung open and Robin stepped out. He stopped dead in his tracks and held the door for me, grasping the metal bar. Dry, ropey veins stood out on the back of his hands. He glanced at the bare skin above my breasts. Everyone knew Robin was a bit of a lech but he was harmless. His heart was in the right place, especially when it came to the kids.

He leaned close. "Not coming in, Anna?" His breath smelled of liver masked by a thin veneer of mint.

I shrank back feeling like a mouse facing the exterminator. "I was gonna grab my lunch."

"No need, luv. Guy and Brian are bringing munchies."

"In that case I'll stay." Cringing inwardly, I ducked under his armpit, heading for the safety of the back row.

"Front row's all free," he called, encouraging me forward. "Let's make them feel welcome."

He scurried off as I slouched into the front row.

Since I was living from hand to mouth, I had no Kindle or iPad to hold discreetly on my lap while the *expert* burbled on about the latest evidence set to revolutionize classroom practices. My phone was a vintage flip phone with no internet capability so scrolling through Facebook was out. Instead, I flipped through the first journal.

Journal writing was part of my daily routine. Students would take ten or fifteen minutes to free-write in their notebook. Even if they spent the time doodling, the one requirement was that they keep their hand moving until they'd covered at least a page. And with every new intake of students, I'd stand at the front of the class, put hand to heart and make a solemn vow that I wouldn't report or censor anything written between the covers of those precious books. Once a week I did a page count and assessed accordingly. But I always lingered far longer than

8

necessary. The stories were just too damned compelling. Their painful, comical, sometimes deeply romantic details formed a vivid mosaic of the angst-ridden teenage mind. Not to mention, there was a whole lot in those journals that reminded me of my own sorry past.

I studied the first page. Written in pink Sharpie, the most recent entry described a hot tub party with Snoop Dogg and Einstein as guests of honor. When I burst out laughing at the image of a fuzzy-haired Einstein reclining in a smoke-wreathed hot tub, chugging a bottle of champagne, while scantily dressed dancers gyrated around him, an unfamiliar voice cut into my daydream.

"Haven't even used my best icebreaker and she's already laughing."

I looked up to see Guy – the first time I'd seen him close up.

In person.

Tall and lean with a head of cropped brown curls, his shrewd, caramel eyes glinted behind gold-rimmed glasses. His face was pleasing. A smattering of light freckles dotted the bridge of a slim nose with gently flared nostrils. Well-shaped lips with defined edges seemed etched into the angular face with its slightly pointed chin. And his clothes were immaculate. Black denim designer jeans and a gray tailored shirt with an expensive sheen to it. The edge of a chunky silver watch peeked out from under a starched cuff.

"Guy Franzen," he said, holding out his hand.

I shook it hoping my palm wasn't clammy.

"Anna Holt," I managed to croak. A tic or maybe a tiny smile played at the corner of his lips. He pumped my trembling hand up and down, seeming reluctant to let go. My throat felt suddenly dry.

A stockier guy appeared behind him. Thick black hair sprouted from his receding hairline, and he sported a full gray-flecked beard and striped acrylic sweater over saggy-assed chinos.

I looked down at the journals, now tucked under my left arm and in danger of slipping out onto the floor. "Creative writing. Kids have such great imaginations."

"And that's the kind of thing that really interests us," Guy said, fixing me in a confident stare. Close up, his eyes appeared paler. Amber in color. "Isn't that so, Brian?" His gaze was so unwavering I had to make a show of looking down and shuffling the journals into a neat pile.

His colleague hopped to attention, peering around Guy's back like a comic sidekick. "Absolutely. Untapped imagination and all that. That's the key."

The key to what? I thought but didn't ask. Instead I acted like a prom girl without an escort. Cheeks flushed, mumbling banalities, eyes avoiding Guy's cool, unswerving gaze.

The other teachers began to trickle in, defusing the electricity of the moment. Guy dropped my hand. "Oh, sorry – this is Brian – I mean Dr. Brian Metcalf," he said, remembering his associate.

I nodded at Brian, aware of Guy's constant gaze, just as Sabrina Melo, the Phys. Ed teacher, plunked herself down right next to me. Recently divorced, Sabrina spent her evenings and weekends alternating between the gym and the tanning salon. Her skin had the withered, orange look of dried clay, a sharp and jarring contrast to the blinding white of her bleached teeth. Norm Chandler, the Biology teacher sat in the row behind. It was no secret that he, a fortyish bachelor, was holding out for just one sign of encouragement from Sabrina. I could almost hear him panting, though she appeared oblivious to his noisy breathing.

"He's hot," she whispered, glancing at Guy. "I mean the tall one, not the hairy gnome guy. I'm gonna focus on his crotch. See if I can throw him off his script."

"Doubt it," I whispered back.

"Five bucks."

"Ten."

Half an hour later, Sabrina grudgingly handed me a crumpled ten-dollar bill.

"That guy was actually enjoying the attention," she said, throwing back bleached blonde curls. "He's a real horn dog."

I stuffed the money into my jeans pocket. I had money for supper now.

Sabrina grasped my arm, her eyes narrowed. "Don't play the innocent, Anna. You were eyeing him up like you'd mentally undressed him. Never seen you so turned on."

"You kidding? You're imagining it."

"Wonder if he's single."

I tucked the journals under my arm. "I thought you always checked that out in the first few minutes."

She shook her head. "In the summer you can check for tan lines, but in winter you just gotta do it the old-fashioned way. Watch and learn."

Lunch was pizzas in open boxes, strewn across the counter. A couple of Hawaiian, a bacon and mushroom and a double pepperoni were the extent of the choices. Nothing green in sight, not even a limp piece of onion or a sliver of green pepper. I wondered what the die-hard vegetarians would eat.

I picked away pieces of ham from the Hawaiian and watched Sabrina in action. In a high-pitched jabber she gushed about the amazing presentation and how careful adherence to student-generated goals already guided her teaching methodology, or some other generic theoretical garbage. Sabrina didn't just breach your personal space, she invaded it with her sharp, minty breath. But even as she moved closer to Guy, he held me with that wry smile of his.

After Robin had rescued Guy from Sabrina's clutches, she lunged at me.

"He's single and he's got money," she hissed in my ear.

"How do you know?"

She shrugged. "Well-honed instincts and a nose for expensive cologne."

But she didn't need to tell me. His Facebook status had been set at *single* for the last three months.

As soon as Robin was in a heavy discussion with Brian, I made my move. As Guy stuffed some papers into his briefcase, I moved forwards and touched his shoulder.

"I'm interested in learning more about your homeless outreach program," I purred into his ear. "Like to go for a drink?"

He knew I'd ask.

I knew that from the way his eyes had zoned in on me the moment he entered the room. And I'd made sure to stand out with my jet-black hair, milky skin and gray eyes. *A back-alley Snow White*, someone had called me in my dim, distant past. Besides, I was an ace at non-verbal cues, and I liked to act on them. That skill had helped me survive a nightmarish childhood.

I also favored the direct approach. Truth was – I was incapable of making small talk.

"Love to," he said, those amber eyes staring as if he couldn't quite believe I was giving him my number.

I felt strangely lightheaded and my hand seemed disembodied – guided by unseen spirit forces while my head reeled with the tangy citrus scent of his cologne. Tongue-tied, I thrust my business card at him just before Robin swept him away to his fusty office. I stood, slightly stunned as if blindsided by a fresh gust of wind from a lemon orchard.

2

I rarely felt that pulse-quickening, breathless feeling when I met a man. In fact, I'd actually laid off men after dating a string of losers, con-artists and narcissists. The pharmaceutical salesman hiding a pregnant wife and twins. The cute art student who, in the drunken haze of a New Year's party, looked twenty-five but turned out to be eighteen. The hotshot lawyer with commitment issues and mega-debts, and the undercover cop with a poker problem.

I didn't really give a crap. It was way easier to be alone. Less demanding. And I hated all the obligatory first date chit-chat. Where'd you live, work, party, hang out? Vegan or carnivore? Favorite series on Netflix? Exercise nut or couch potato? How do you feel about politics, weed, gay marriage, dogs, the weather? Second dates were worse because things usually became way more personal. Your family? Your past? Your home? Your feelings? Who are you? What makes you tick? What's your essence? Duh? That's when I clammed up. "I have no clue," I wanted to say. "Who the hell am I? A closed book that nobody cares to open. A lone survivor huddled behind a wall that nobody dares to breach, clutching all her hurt and sadness so close that no one could ever really know her." So, they inevitably drifted away and left me to my own solitude and to my constant thoughts of Birdie, my beloved twin sister.

Later that day, I didn't even have to sit around agonizing about whether Guy would call. The phone rang about half an hour after I got home from school. Supper was on the table. A steaming bowl of macaroni cheese and two *final demand* utility bills to accompany the meal.

Guy invited me to meet him in the restaurant of an expensive downtown hotel. Living alone on a teacher's salary I'd never set foot in the place, so I launched into a frenzy of dragging dresses from their hangers, trying them on, then flinging them into a heap on the floor. Too flowery, too short, too long, too matronly, too cheap, even though many still had store tags on them. But I couldn't think about that now.

Finally, I settled on something slim, black, and plunging, brushed my hair, cleaned my teeth, and applied a coat of deep red lipstick before heading out the door.

I'd done my homework. Seems Guy loved vivid lipstick. He stared at my lips right through dinner. When I shaved a thin slice of filet mignon, lifted it to my mouth and bit into it, a thin dribble of something ran down my lips. I couldn't tell whether it was blood or juice, but Guy reached over and wiped it off with his fingertip. Then, with eyes locked on mine, he slowly licked the juice from his own fingertip. A familiar fluttering started up in my stomach. I wanted him so badly I squirmed on the chair, unable to settle myself. And when he reached over and ran his fingertips across the tender skin of my wrist, I knew it was time for a sudden and urgent exit from the restaurant. He threw a wad of bills at the waiter, then guided me to the front desk, his hand firm at the base of my spine. He arranged a room and we were locked in a hot, visceral embrace by the time the elevator doors swished open onto the third floor.

Next afternoon, a bouquet of roses with pink, fleshy petals arrived in the front office. Daphne, the school secretary and chief architect of the jungle telegraph that disseminated gossip throughout the school, was already ogling the gift card. She held her glasses over the scrawled handwriting.

"For you, Anna. *For an unforgettable evening.* G. Who's G?" she blurted.

"Do you mind?" I grabbed the gift box, the soft petals grazing my nose. *What a jerk. Delivering them to school.* Then I remembered he didn't have my home address. Sabrina swooped in behind, alerted by Daphne.

"Someone got lucky last night," she hissed. "I can sniff out the pheromones."

I walked away trying to shake her off. Memories of Guy's naked body and the gorgeous feel of his sinewy legs entwined around mine had clouded my vision to the point that I almost walked into a closed door.

"Got it real bad with Professor G," said Sabrina, pushing the door open. "Watch out, little Anna. He's an operator. That man will eat you up and spit you out. Seen men like him before. It's all in the eyes."

I pretended not to hear. I'd enjoyed a night of mind-blowing sex and the guy had sent me flowers the next day. This was cause for celebration. Time for a shopping frenzy.

–

I dropped the roses off at my apartment and drove straight to the mall. My happy place. I got high on the ambient scents pumped into the place. Like a drunk at a cocktail bar, I needed a fix of tropical citrus or vanilla lotus flower.

I have only a few vices. A healthy appetite for good sex, and the ability to maintain a stone face when I tell lies, but first and foremost I'm a compulsive shopper. Combing the racks is my shot of nicotine. Grazing the stores for deals, my release. Not for high-end goods. That wasn't until after I met Guy.

Back then I was after end of season bargains. A red sales tag was akin to Pavlov's bell. I salivated at 80% off the original price, while an extra 20% off the sale price gave me heart palpitations and sweaty palms.

I'd lined my closets with cheap tops, pants, dresses and jackets. Bought sandals at the end of summer for the next year, boots in March for November. My drawers burst to overflowing with bras, panties, nighties and socks. My dresser was strewn with piles of cheap, glittery earrings, bangles and necklaces. I'd buy three of some things. So when one wore out I'd have two or three replacements.

At least that was my rationale. Mostly the red tags remained attached, dangling in a bright row, a reminder of my expanding credit card balances which had taken on a life of their own, compounding at bloated interest rates. I'd grit my teeth and pray when I swiped my Visa, fearing the dreaded *your card is declined* message delivered by a haughty sales clerk before a line-up of restless customers, who'd dart meaningful glances and raised eyebrows at each other. Then I'd mumble lame excuses like *it's new and not activated yet* or *this must be my old one*, while everyone's expressions clearly read *utter baloney*.

Sometimes I bought things only to take them back two days later just to clear the card for more purchases. It was the act of buying that delivered the charge, the carrying of the bags out of the store that thrilled me. Back home in my cramped closet with its crystal chandelier I'd run my hands along the line of new, untouched clothing and feel a sudden rush, a temporary sense of triumph.

As a semi-rational person, I had an explanation for this instinct to stockpile material goods. My intense drive to buy things and gather them in a comforting hoard around me stemmed from a deprived childhood. A history of intense and painful loss. An erasure of childhood memories. A complete lack of belonging to any place or person.

For the first sixteen years of my life, I was deprived of good clothes, decent food, safety and security, permanence and a home to call my own, but I finally lost something more precious than any of those.

I lost my sister, Birdie.

3

My sister, Birdie always hated her name.

"What kind of dumbass name is Birdie?" she'd say. "Why couldn't they call me Laura or Jacqueline? Or even a classic name like Anna?"

Birdie was my twin.

When we were old enough to understand, Dennis, our dad, told the story of our birth.

Almost thirty years ago on a sweltering summer day, I burst into the world head first, plump and rosy, fists clenched. Birdie slid out like a wrinkled prune twenty-four minutes later.

From day one I looked after her, circling baby arms around my tiny sister in the crib, her pale cheek pasted to mine, our breath mingling in sleep. Birdie was the runt. The scrawny kid with no meat on her bones and a fuzz of black hair that stuck out like a wispy brush from her large head.

"Like a cute baby crow," Dennis always said, chuckling and pinching Birdie's cheek. "Just cracked through the shell. That name was a given."

Dennis was our real dad. An ex-hippie from a commune near Eureka who'd driven across country, dumped his ailing VW van and settled further north. I couldn't remember anything about our mom except long, black hair and a soft voice that belonged to a wispy figure floating past the bedroom door. She OD'd on heroin when we were toddlers and Dennis tried to hold things together. Straightened himself out and struggled to keep us fed and clothed as well as work his job as an ice road trucker.

But it didn't last.

Birdie and I were joined by blood, sorrow and loss. Ripped from our home, our family and all we knew about love and belonging. All those years we clung together for protection in the belief that we could never be separated and evil couldn't touch us if we only had each other. But reality was a dull-edged knife, shearing away the bond between us, until later when we split apart and Birdie drifted away.

I spent long hours trying to figure out how it all happened. Going back over the events that led up to her leaving. Recounting, revising over and over again until I couldn't distinguish between truth, imagination and drugged-out fantasies. I just knew I had to find her. She was the only family I had. The only one that knew the story of how they, the trusted adults – the people in charge – stripped away every part of our identity until we couldn't speak about our pain.

I survived it all. Sorted myself out in the end. Guess I was the lucky one. But if I was that smart, I figured I could work out a plan to find my unhappy, unlucky sister.

Up until Birdie and I were eight we lived with Dennis in the white stucco bungalow with the sloping floors. Dennis was always trying to fix the place up. Never could get ahead of the old house that was always shifting and settling when the weather changed. Doors that worked one day were jammed the next and cracks spread like spiderwebs across the ceiling and all the way down the walls.

I have only a few memories of life with Dennis.

One time when I was four, Dennis was slapping white paint on the baseboards, his hair tied back with a red bandana. The sickly paint smell made my head ache. I cried to go outside in the fresh air but the windows were fogged up and the rain slashed across the panes.

I lay face down on the couch, head in my hands, my stomach heavy and sick. I was covering my mouth and nose to escape the chemical stink of oil paint. Then Birdie, dressed in the Snow White cape Dennis bought at the thrift store, flitted across the room carrying a basket of loose Cheerios. Slipping my hand into her sticky one, she pulled me down onto the kitchen floor. Her hair stuck out in a fluffy halo and her eyes shone as she linked hands with mine and leaned forward to brush my cheek with hers.

"My name is Princess Skylark," she babbled. "A tiny fairy gave me a special name and magic powers." Then she made whispering noises and stroked her fingers across my eyelids until the pain dissolved away. Her breath was cool and wispy like butterfly wings.

We'd watched the Snow White song from the *Disney Singalong* video at least a hundred times and Birdie knew it off by heart so she sang it in a silvery, tinkling voice. *With a smile and a song.* The one where the deer wander out from the forest, the rabbits stop their scampering and all the bluebirds line up on the trees just to hear her sing. Then, when the song was over, she placed a finger on each corner of my sulky mouth and pushed upwards until I smiled. Until I felt better again.

Dennis stopped his painting to watch. Then he put down his brush and swept Birdie up into his arms, smacking her cheek with kisses.

"This girl's got a big heart. Got happiness in her blood and she wants to share it."

"What did I get?" I asked.

Dennis put Birdie down.

"You're the thinker, Anna. Always mulling over every little thing. But together you got the best of both worlds. That's why you got to stick together. Sunny and Sulky. You'll always look out for Birdie because she sees the best in everybody. Feels their pain, but she's got her head in the clouds. And that's a recipe for sorrow."

And he was right. From the moment we scampered out into the garden to play on the rusty swing set, I was the one who tested everything out first. Picked up insects, poked around in mud puddles, lifted up beer crates to explore the teeming insect life underneath. I was the brave one who checked under the bed for monsters or shut the closet door when it creaked open in a draught, and I was Birdie's protector when Dennis slept most of the afternoon after a long shift at work and left us alone to roam the streets for hours on end, way beyond our junk heap of a yard. Birdie believed the world was an enchanted kingdom waiting to be explored. But I knew that just outside the gate and down the street were burned-down houses with rotten floorboards, wild dogs straining at rusty chains, and scary strangers lurking in darkened alleyways.

We ate fake food. Noodles – chicken, beef, oriental or mac and cheese. And those foil envelopes of juice. Starch, sugar and salt. Filler food that left us shaky and hungry. Longing for more.

Birdie laid noodles out on colored paper plates and called them royal feasts. Made me drink juice from a cracked teacup, holding her pinkie finger upwards because that's how the Queen of England did it.

We got by all right until Dennis couldn't do it any more.

One bitter January day when we were eight, we couldn't go to school because we'd grown out of our jackets and the wind chill was -40. Birdie cried because Dennis wouldn't let her go out with her bedspread tied around her like a cloak, which meant she'd miss the rehearsal for the winter concert where she was supposed to wear a snowflake costume and sing 'The Icicle Ball' solo. She cried herself into such a state her throat swelled, then lost her voice so she wouldn't have been able to sing anyway.

Dennis had an important delivery to make so he left us alone in the house.

The front door was tied shut with rope and the laundry piled so high in the window I could only glimpse a ribbon of cold winter sky. The house was full of noises. Floorboards creaked, radiators hissed, hot water pipes clanked until I was sure they'd all explode and bring the house crashing down around us. Birdie fell asleep then woke up, her face damp with sweat and her skinny ribs shuddering with fever. I sat by her bed ladling fruit punch into her mouth, which she promptly threw up in a bright, red stream.

Dennis wept when the lady from Children's Protection Services showed up to sweep us away in her clunky Ford Taurus, our few possessions stuffed into garbage bags. He crouched on his knees and said he loved us more than any other girls in the world and he'd come as soon as he could to get us back. Once he was on his feet again and found a decent place where we could all live together. I hugged him, afraid to let go for fear I'd never see him again, but Birdie curled herself into a tight ball in the corner of the couch, her fists pressed against her eyes.

The social worker lady had a puffy red parka and a soft voice but she couldn't get Birdie to move. Her face became sweaty and red like her parka when she tried to drag Birdie out. She'd flopped to the floor and twisted her body around the legs of the kitchen table. Dennis tried to sweet talk her but she kicked at him with boot-clad feet. He backed away from her, tears running down his cheeks. I lay on the rug and pressed my face against Birdie's hot cheek. Made those babbling, whispering sounds until she uncurled herself and plastered her body against mine. I limped and dragged her to the car while the social worker lady lugged the garbage bags and mumbled under her breath.

We heard from Dennis a couple of times after that. Postcards from Alaska and the Yukon with mountain backdrops and frosty pine forests. The last one promised he'd never forget his two sweet girls. I still believed him, but Birdie was done. Never forgave him.

Never ever mentioned his name again.

Later, in my university years I grew my hair long and wild, and dabbed patchouli oil on my hair and body in honor of Dennis. Something about that spicy, nutty smell kept him close. I even got a tattoo behind my left knee. A small "D" for Dennis and Dad. A reminder of the man who'd tried so hard to love us. Big, gruff, grizzly Dennis who let me sit in the cab of his truck and turn the steering wheel. Who'd given me the gift of reading. He read to me every night and every day when he wasn't working. Read anything and everything.

All words are worth saying aloud whether they're on a cereal box or in the world's greatest literature he'd say. And so we read old *Superman* comics, Harlequin romances, car engine manuals, the *Farmers' Almanac* and my favorites, the Narnia stories.

But Birdie wasn't interested. She preferred playing with dolls. Said reading gave her a headache and all she wanted was to be pretty first, then an actress, dancer and singer so she could make more people happy.

Too bad she hadn't focused more on her own happiness.

She might still be with me now.

4

On our third date, Guy discovered the "D" tattoo and instantly wanted to know all about it. I shrugged it off. Lied and told him it was in memory of my first dog, Dmitri.

I never had a dog. Ever. For years, Birdie wanted one desperately. When we were still with Dennis, Birdie made a lumpy little fake dog out of ripped up sheets tied together to make a head and body. She painted eyes and a snout on it and called it Prince. Then she dragged it around the garden on a piece of string until it was black and shredded. We buried the bundle of rags under a tree and said prayers for the poor thing's soul.

But I was determined not to open any part of my childhood to Guy. I muttered something about how my parents died in a car accident. It wasn't so far from the truth anyway since my mother had faded away into a tragic death. And Dennis and Birdie might as well be dead for all I knew. So I claimed no sisters, no brothers, no baggage. It was easier that way. Starting with a fresh, blank page made it easier to steer the conversation towards the details of his life instead.

Besides, all those years in foster homes had left me damaged by profound grief and burdened me with a chronic sense of loss never acknowledged by anyone in charge. I was a troublesome weed to be ripped from the ground at a moment's notice, my identity wiped out with every new placement – every new start. My childhood was dominated by a series of hasty, careless decisions that left me feeling so uncertain and so insignificant I withdrew into a state of cold impassiveness. I trusted no one. Except Birdie.

Impermanence had been the guiding factor in my life and always would be, as far as I could see at the time.

Guy and I went to the theater on our third date. The grand old Orpheum Theater in all its red and gold glory. I loved musicals, but usually couldn't justify dropping a hundred bucks or more on a night's entertainment. Especially when every spare penny was going towards keeping my credit cards afloat.

With Guy there was no question about whether we'd go or not. He simply chose the best seats and booked them. This new experience of taking what I wanted without asking *how much* was a heady one that gave me a rush so intense it felt sexual. Voluptuous. With Guy I could reinvent myself. Live from one hedonistic moment to the next. Indulge like a glutton in everything I craved. The pre-theater gourmet dinner, cocktails at intermission, a nightcap at a plush nightclub, all concluding in a comfy ride to his place, cradled in the soft leather upholstery of his black BMW. I'd seen my share of bachelor pads but Guy's was a male boudoir. A sandalwood-scented corner penthouse with a wall of floor-to-ceiling windows that revealed a glittering panorama of city lights spread out below. The space exuded masculinity with its cinnamon and gray painted walls, gleaming walnut woodwork and king-sized bed piled high with embossed silk pillows. Nudity felt natural among all that sumptuousness, so I slipped off my dress and fell naked across the gray silk sheets. Thoughts of rent and bills and microwave dinners slipped away as Guy fed me glass after glass of fizzy champagne from a fragile crystal flute, then turned me over to kiss my back from head to toe. We made love and fell asleep in a state of alcoholic bliss.

"Move in with me," a voice whispered in my ear sometime during the night. "I can't get enough of you."

In that half-sleep, curled under silky sheets, I peered at the eggshell gray of the morning sky and a city I now looked down on from above. I knew I could never leave this place. This kind of world had always been beyond my reach, but Guy would be my passport to a new and lavish lifestyle.

I wrapped my legs around his lean body, stroked the smooth skin of his back and said *yes*.

–

Next morning I woke with only a vague memory of making a life-changing commitment. Guy was propped up against his pillows watching me rub my eyes and come to.

"You look like a kitten," he said. His eyes, large and vulnerable without the protection of glasses, searched my face. "Did you mean it?"

"Mean what?" I rolled over and buried my face in the pillow. "I have a sick hangover."

"You know what I'm talking about."

"And I have to be in class in less than an hour."

"Forget class. I'll pay you to stay away today."

Propping myself up on one elbow I traced a finger down the feathery hair of his chest. "Are you soliciting favors, Mr. Franzen?"

"Can't you see I'm trying to become your exclusive customer."

"I'm a teacher, not a hooker."

He flipped himself on top of me and smoothed my hair back from my forehead. "Stay, Anna. You won't regret it."

"I'm very expensive."

"Money no object."

"In that case, pay up," I whispered.

He reached over to the bedside table and opened the top drawer. When he turned round, he was holding a wad of twenties.

"Enough?" he said, grinning.

I lay back, spread-eagled. "Shower me."

The bills floated down onto my skin. Twenties, fifties. At least a thousand dollars. I was so turned on I could barely get the words out when I called in sick. We spent the rest of the day in bed.

Since I was already in arrears with the rent, the landlord was only too happy to get rid of me. Even forgave half the outstanding rent when he rested his greedy little eyes on the wad of bills I offered him. He lined up a new tenant in a matter of days.

Guy offered to rent a van to move my stuff but I told him not to bother. Years in the foster system had taught me the art of the hasty move. Back then all my belongings were stowed in one garbage bag. Toys, clothes, treasures and all. Now I could barely get it all into a couple of suitcases.

So I purged. I wanted to leave all the cheap stuff behind. That junk had no place in Guy's upmarket condo.

I went through every closet, drawer and cupboard to empty the place and felt no regret when I bagged about three quarters of the discount clothes, in preparation for the shopping frenzy I had planned. Since I'd be living rent free with very few expenses, I'd have a whole lot more spending money. I'd finally hit the big one.

It didn't seem to matter that we'd only known each other little more than a week. I was an old hand at impromptu new beginnings and this new home looked way more promising than some of the other sketchy hell-holes that Birdie and I had been dumped in by harried, stressed-out social workers trying to cover their caseloads. And yet doubt still needled at my brain when, for a brief moment, I imagined Guy shopping for a live-in partner like he shopped for his shirts.

Would he tire of me when the novelty faded? Would he move on to a fresher, more current replacement?

But I reminded myself that I was a survivor – an old hand at dealing with rejection. I'd hop on this glorious ride as long as it lasted and get as much as I could out of the deal. That's why I took those bags of brand-new clothes and donated them to a charity clothing bank for destitute women trying to get jobs. Since most were unworn, I was sure they'd be overjoyed at my generous donation.

The pastor at the Holy Springs Mission, a sandy-haired guy wearing a faded corduroy jacket over eighties-style blue jeans, opened up the twist tie on the first bag and stared at the labels in disbelief, fixing me in a gaze that made my insides shrivel.

The room stunk so badly of musty, unwashed clothes I couldn't breathe. I thrust the bags at him, mumbled a hasty *you're welcome* and he replied with a polite thank you, watching me closely when I stopped in front of a large poster that declared:

> *The wealth of the rich is their fortified city;*
> *they imagine it a wall too high to scale.*
> Proverbs 18:11

When I glanced back at him, he raised his eyebrows, as if urging me to run to him and beg forgiveness for my shameful avarice. Fling my wretched body at his feet and allow him to bludgeon me with some guilt-inducing sermon delivered to ease my misery. But he just turned away and started pulling out all my cheap new dresses from the first garbage bag. I could swear he shook his head and made that disapproving *tutt tutt* sound. I wanted to swoop right back in there and slap his self-righteous face. He reminded me of Luke and Esther Penner, our first foster parents. People who felt it necessary to display their core philosophies of life on our bedroom wall.

God's wounds cure, sin's kisses kill.

Luke and Esther were patronizing do-gooders who professed to be guided by holy laws and preachings, yet failed to actually live according to them. Who owned a porcelain doll collection they paid more attention to than us. Who braided our hair so tightly our eyes would water and locked us away in our room. Who beat me when I took fruit punch from the fridge to lift Birdie's fever.

Our placement with the Penners only lasted for three months. It turned out their emotions were as bland as their food.

They believed they were saving us, but they messed up Birdie and me.

I still bear the scars.

5

I'd been driven from one life to another so many times, never knowing where I was headed or who I'd end up with, but when I moved in with Guy the leaving was different.

I sat on the steps of my apartment block, two suitcases stacked next to me. It was a chilly morning, frost on the grass, trees in early bud, gritty swathes of sand the only remnant of winter. The perfect time to make a new start. I'd simply shed my old life and take on the new dream life. The thought of it pulsed through me like a drug. Sex and luxury and money had all become tied up with Guy. He'd slipped into my addiction and become the ultra dealer. The more I saw him, the more I craved him. And he wasn't like the other losers. No agonizing wait for texts or phone calls. No sign of commitment phobia and broken promises. No hidden monster just waiting to leap out and show his true colors when we were alone.

Not yet.

When Guy's car pulled up, the sun slid out from behind a cloud and I squinted my eyes against the light. The outline of his car seemed edged in rainbow flecks. A magic chariot driven by a mythical prince. I stood up waving like a kid, until I remembered to press my arms to my sides and curl my hands into fists. Eagerness could be a dangerous trait. I'd learned long ago that my best defense was to appear detached and aloof. That way you didn't have so far to fall.

Guy wore a snowy, white shirt under a tan leather jacket. Mr. GQ. Crisp and well groomed from his designer jeans to his pale buff leather shoes and well-cut hair. The prince had chosen me. I could barely contain myself as he got out of the car. *If only Birdie could see this*, I thought to myself over and over, but I vowed he'd never know anything about my past. Or about Birdie and all the other hidden stuff.

"I would've carried these out for you," he said, reaching for the cases.

"Didn't want you to see the dump I was living in. You might've changed your mind if you'd seen the state of the fridge. It's like a biology experiment."

"I try not to stand in judgment," he said, lifting the trunk cover.

I tapped his shoulder. "You should know I'm allergic to housework."

"No worries. I have a cleaning service coming in once a week."

"I'll make an effort, I promise," I said, trying not to remember the harsh, gray mornings at Luke and Esther Penner's home. The hours spent, head down, knees aching, bladder full, scrubbing the bathroom floor with a sponge that left big soapy puddles that wouldn't be soaked up. Esther standing above me, chewing her thin lips and tapping her feet on the linoleum.

"You're so earnest," Guy said, smiling as he held the passenger door open and feigned a mock bow. "Lighten up and have some fun."

A sob caught in my throat. Birdie always said that to me.

I could've crumpled up in tears, but instead I nestled into the soft leather seat, ready to be properly taken care of for the first time in my life. My eyes were fixed on the road ahead. I wouldn't look back at my old life. Ever. Now was all that mattered.

Once the car pulled away from the curb, Guy reached his hand across the seat and took my hand in his.

"Happy?" he asked.

I nodded. I wasn't lying this time. I really meant it. "But it's all happened so fast. Maybe too fast?" I glanced up at him, trying to catch some weird flicker of malice, some lying twitch of his eyes. But it was too late for second thoughts. I was already homeless.

"You have to grab happiness when it comes along. Don't deliberate too much. If it feels good, go with it."

"Is that what you tell all your girlfriends?"

"I haven't had that many," he said, an edge creeping into his voice. My insides scrunched a little. "You'll soon discover I'm not that kind of guy."

The sun etched his profile in gold. I hadn't realized how handsome he really was. "Then what kind of guy are you?"

"I can be impulsive." He turned and smiled a closed mouth kind of smile. "But don't worry. I don't go asking every girl I meet to move in with me."

"You mean there isn't a secret drawer full of toothbrushes and tampons for last minute overnight stays?"

He shook his head, still grinning. "Promise. Check my dresser."

"Why me, then?"

"I have this feeling about you. You looked at me like you really wanted me and I like that."

If only he knew the truth, I thought, staring so hard at his profile it blurred against the passing trees.

He placed my suitcases just inside the front door of the condo. Against the gleaming woodwork and furniture, they appeared cheap and shabby. I had the strongest feeling they'd be put away in a closet and never opened. That the next time I checked they'd have mysteriously disappeared. That I had to shake off every bit of my old life to become part of his.

He took my hand and pulled me towards the bathroom. I'd never showered in anything more luxurious than a plain, white tub shower with a plastic curtain, so Guy's bathroom was a revelation. A haven of oyster-colored marble with a glassed-in shower complete with dual rain showerheads and a massive jetted tub lined with jewel-colored bottles.

He ran a bath, undressed me and once I was immersed in the scented water, he soaped my body down from head to toe and gently washed my hair, kneading at my scalp with expert fingers. I lay back as if receiving a ritual baptism. I'd never felt such gentleness – had no memory of anyone touching me so tenderly, even as a child.

Once my hair was rinsed, I opened my eyes. He was watching me. Suddenly I felt too naked and vulnerable. I tensed up and hugged my knees to my chest.

"You can trust me," he said. "I'm a gentle person."

I slid down into the bubbles. "That's rare in my experience."

"Mine too," he said, the corners of his lips drooping slightly. I realized then how little we knew about each other. How easily I'd assumed he'd lived a carefree life.

He rubbed me down with a towel that felt weightless as a carpet of feathers. Once I was warm and tingly, he led me into the bedroom.

"A surprise for you," he said, pointing at the bed. "Think of this as a welcome gift."

The bed was covered with boxes and bags from stores I'd looked at from the outside but never set foot in. The ones with bored-looking security guards in navy blazers stationed at the door. Lingerie, cashmere sweaters, silk camisoles and crisp cotton shirts. Pants, skirts, dresses, a pair of tan leather boots and finally a glorious coat in soft camel wool. My hands trembled as I sorted through the pile. There were no sale stickers, no red clearance tags. I could barely imagine what he'd paid for them. I clutched the coat to my face and tears filled my eyes though I tried to hold them back.

"You said you liked to shop. Well so do I." He watched me closely, chewing his bottom lip.

"I can't accept all this. It's too much." But I was lying. An army of bodybuilders couldn't have pried these gorgeous garments from my clutches.

He placed his hands on my shoulders. "I loved buying these things for you. Just indulge me. Put the coat on. See if I guessed your size right."

The coat slid on like a second skin, its slippery satin lining chilling my body.

"It's perfect," I said, tying the belt and twirling around. "I love it." I threw my arms round his neck and nuzzled into the citrusy scent of his neck.

"You'll always be safe here," he whispered as the coat slipped from my shoulders.

—

36

At first, going back to work was like crossing from heaven to hell. Mornings in the condo I'd struggle from warm, silky sheets into the glorious shower. Guy's citrusy cologne combined with the bitter tang of espresso carried me through into the muted lighting of the kitchen and the view of the waking city with its blinking streetlights under a gray dawn sky.

We'd sip coffee, nibble on fresh fruit, bagels and smoked salmon and chat about work. He loved my stories about the kids and the crazy things they wrote in their journals. Made me promise to bring a couple home so we could look at them together. Then I'd head off from the underground parking lot past the renovated warehouses, chic artisan bakeries and brew houses, until I crossed an invisible line into grim streets lined with tenements, laundromats, pawnbrokers and beer stores, which led to the school whose corridors lingered with the stink of mildew and damp paper.

The first morning after I moved in with Guy, Sabrina zoned in on me, her eyes all over the camel coat. I'd taken care not to use all of the new clothes, but I couldn't resist the cozy comfort of the coat on a chilly spring morning.

"That looks like it's worth more than my month's rent," she said, her hand lingering over the fine wool. "You found a sugar daddy or — no…" Her hand flew to her mouth. "The prof's buying favors. Don't tell me."

I pushed past her. "I won't."

"You can't hide it for long," she said, touching the side of her nose. "I have that sixth sense. Remember."

By now her shrill voice had lured Robin from his dingy, book-cluttered lair. He stood, red-rimmed eyes blinking as if he'd just blown in from an all-night party, his wispy hair still flattened from crashing on some bug-ridden sofa.

"Did I miss something?" he said, scratching his left armpit.

"Anna's become a kept woman," said Sabrina.

"Bullshit," I hissed and left them both standing, open-mouthed at the swish of satin lining and the click of my tan leather boots on the asbestos tiles.

We'd just had an influx of new students that week. A group of seventeen-year-olds who spent their nights turning tricks on the downtown riverside. They sat at the back of the class, their faces vampire white, their bleary eyes edged with smudgy black liner. The hems of their dusty black trench coats brushed the floor and each sported crazy manga style mops of hair dyed to inky blue-black. Two of them had silver and brass rings piercing their ears, while the other two wore eye shadow and blood red lipstick. Like weirdly beautiful Pierrot dolls, they sat glowering beneath their mantle of hostile silence. The other students had turned away as if they didn't exist. Evidence, from my experience, that the new kids had viciously staked out their territory, establishing a no-go zone around themselves before I'd even entered the class.

"Morning everyone," I said, throwing my coat onto the chair to reveal the glistening lining.

"You win the lottery or something, Anna?" said Hailey, a blonde girl with a half-shaved head.

"Just a gift," I said, piling the daily journals into my arms.

I handed them over to Clarence, a pudgy guy with a red Afro.

"Great gift," he said, distributing them to the class. "Some dude must really be into you."

"Or maybe it comes at a high price," said Viola, a muscular girl with a buzz cut and a broad smile.

"Okay. Enough speculation about my private life. Let's welcome our new students," I said, glancing over at the back of the classroom. "Would you guys like to introduce yourselves to the rest of the class?"

My request was met with pursed lips, scowls and shaking heads.

"Okay," I backtracked. "Maybe when you're feeling more comfortable we can try. In the meantime, we'll do our daily journal writing and follow up with novel study groups."

It took a while to convince the newcomers that I'd scan their journals but wouldn't comment on any of the content, so they were free to write about anything they wanted without stopping to think too hard or censoring themselves.

"The idea is to fight your inner editor and tap into your most original, unfiltered ideas."

"Does that mean we can write any swear words we like?" asked Dane, the guy with the most hardware on his ears. The other three covered their mouths and tried not to snicker. Obviously they thought laughing was uncool.

"I said *anything* and I meant it," I repeated.

They grasped the glossy scribblers and pens as if they hadn't been given anything new in years and immersed themselves in the task for the next half hour, stopping every now and again to suck the end of their pens and conjure up images from their young lives they thought I could barely imagine.

At three thirty I slipped out of the school, keen to avoid another grilling from Sabrina and not ready to tell Daphne about my change of address. I didn't want the whole world to know about my new living arrangements until I was sure living with Guy was more than a temporary stopover. I'd had too many of those in my life. Flying under the radar was my style anyway. Low-key. Proffer the least possible amount of personal information and don't confide in anyone. I'd learned this from an early age. Birdie was my only confidante. I'd never had a best friend to pour my heart out to.

Not that I didn't socialize. I'd gotten into the habit of going out for drinks with Sabrina and her buddies at least once or twice a month. But a noisy bar or nightclub is no place for sharing intimacies when there's electronic music pounding out at a thousand decibels and everyone yakking so loud you can't hear yourself think. That kind of setting suited me just fine. Besides, I'd learned during my university days that nobody really listens to each other anyway. They're just waiting for a lull in the conversation. The moment when you stop filling them in on your boring life and basically shut up so they can jump in and talk about themselves.

That's why most people gravitate to the good listeners, the empathetic people who nod and sigh and shake their heads at just the right time. At college I'd become popular without anyone realizing I wasn't actually listening to them. That all the time they were pouring out their inner-most secrets, I had a whole other dialogue going on in my head.

Perhaps that's a testament to human superficiality. Because when all is said and done, we're alone. No matter where we are or who we're with. We come into the world alone and leave it the same way, only I didn't. I came in with Birdie right behind me.

I thought I'd be with her until the end, but it didn't happen that way.

I'd found out that one of my new students, Dane, was living at the group home where Birdie and I were sent after the Penners'. Now I'd moved to Guy's it was on my driving route home, so I drove there and pulled up to a stop on the narrow street, shaded by its arch of ancient elm trees. The house was a three-story brick structure, its front porch cluttered with broken bicycles, spider plants, boxes and an ancient refrigerator. Though spring buds were sprouting on the two lilac bushes by the front steps and the front lawn was freshly mowed, the house had seen better days. Someone had tried to scrub graffiti off the walls and abandoned the task halfway, two broken front windows were wrapped in dingy plastic sheeting and propped against the sidewall and the rusty metal gate hung off one hinge.

I sat back in the car, watching skinny, hunched kids come and go through the battered front door. I knew what it was like to be one of them. Tired, permanently hungry and pissed off. Our room had been on the top floor. I looked up at the tiny window and remembered gazing down onto the street on frigid winter mornings before school, my eyes sore and dry, nausea twisting my gut because Birdie had jerked around the bed all night drifting from one nightmare into the next.

Birdie and I landed up there after the Penners because there was no suitable foster placement available for two siblings. At nine we were much younger than the twelve-to seventeen-year-olds living there. But we were soon lost in the cloying disorder of the place, supervised by a succession of nervous twenty-one-year-olds who spent more time on the phone talking to friends rather than to us. But despite the nuisance of hair pulling, mild bullying and petty thievery it was still preferable to Luke and Esther Penners' frigid charity. Birdie and I enjoyed our roles as the unofficial mascots of the place. We were petted, cossetted and fought over by neurotic teens who pinched or slapped us one minute, then hugged and cuddled us the next. We grew tough there and learned more than a few survival tricks.

Birdie recovered some of her perkiness when she discovered it worked like a charm with the other kids. She became the cute little performer and I her sulky sidekick, lurking in her shadow, lank hair hiding my face, lips drooping at the corners in a permanent huff. One of the older workers had grown-up kids who'd left home so she took a real shine to Birdie. She brought a massive bag of clothes for her. Some were dated from the late seventies and early eighties. Lots of plaid and neon pink and green, but Birdie didn't care. She wore a different outfit every day. Danced and sang and kept up my flagging spirits with her endless energy.

Be pretty, twirl your skirts and pull a silly face. Hop around on one leg and play silly monkey tricks. That's how she collected pockets full of Bazooka gum, licorice and sour peaches. We went to bed sucking on Ring Pops, Tootsie Rolls and red licorice. No wonder I had a mouth full of cavities when I got to university.

I shuddered at the thought and pulled away before Dane showed up. Didn't want him to think I was stalking him. I just had this sudden urge to revisit places I'd been with Birdie. It seemed odd that since meeting Guy, the past was seeping into my consciousness like water through cracks in a wall. And I thought I'd barricaded my emotions in so tight that nobody could touch them, which put me in a cold sweat. I'd lost touch with those feelings long ago. They hurt too much.

Guy taught at the university two nights a week, so when I got back to the apartment, it was empty. I shucked off my clothes at the door and wandered round the place in my underwear. Pressed my body against the rough honey-colored brick wall, lay my cheek and breasts across the cool granite counter top, traced fingertips down the length of the stainless-steel fridge, threw myself onto the pale leather sectional and rolled onto the white fur rug where I made snow angel movements and looked up at the chrome chandelier. Then I pulled myself up and padded to the bathroom for a long, hot bath.

I didn't feel fit for Guy's place until I'd washed off the dirt from school.

Finally, I stood in the bedroom looking at myself in the lavender lace bra and panties Guy had bought me. It occurred to me that he was a very trusting man to leave me here with all his things. That's when I went to his bedside table and slid the drawer open. Maybe I'd learn something about him from his personal stuff. Some quirk or weird habit or obsession. But the top drawer was filled with briefs and boxers. All neutral colors. Arranged in neat little rolls. Opening the drawer had shifted the rows so I tried to get them back in perfect order. The bottom drawer was filled with socks in the same arrangement. The chest of drawers revealed the same story. Sweatpants, T-shirts, shorts, gloves, each with their own exclusive drawer. All in pristine order.

So he was anally obsessive. I liked that about him. I'd lived among chaos and disarray for far too much of my life. I could actually breathe in a tidy place like this.

I decided to leave the closet for another day since I was starving. Throwing on my robe, I poured myself a glass of chilled Pinot and arranged a plate of olives, Reggiano cheese, Prosciutto, cantaloupe and focaccia. I was just about to set it in front of the TV when the phone rang. I lunged for it hoping to hear Guy tell me he'd missed me all day.

"Hello."

"Who is this?" said a voice that sounded like Guy's but deeper.

"Anna."

"You Guy's cleaner?"

"Not exactly."

"This is Gord, Guy's father. Tell him I called, Mandy. Oh – and tell him to call me ASAP."

The phone clicked, leaving the dial tone purring in my ear. *Who actually says ASAP? And gets my name wrong immediately after hearing it?* It hadn't even phased him that I was a stranger, alone in Guy's apartment. Maybe there'd been many women here. But then I'd had other boyfriends too. *Hey, who was I to have a double standard?* Then it occurred to me that everything had happened so quickly I hadn't even thought about Guy's family. I hadn't been a part of a normal family life for years. In fact, I was so used to being alone I assumed everyone else was free of all ties like me. There was nobody left in the world that gave a damn about me. Dennis was long gone and Birdie was lost.

I was sure Guy's hand trembled when I told him his father called. He slung his briefcase down and poured a large glass of wine. When he sat on the sofa, he glared at the crushed rug that still bore the evidence of my snow angel antics. His brow knit for a brief moment.

"He asked if I was the cleaner."

"Sorry he can be a bit undiplomatic at times," he said, gulping down the Pinot and wiping a hand across his mouth.

"You mean he's a dick?"

"Whoah!" He frowned and smiled at the same time. "I get on with him well enough but he has his flaws."

"Doesn't everyone? Do you see him much?"

He leaned an elbow on the sofa arm and propped his head on his hand to direct a weary expression my way. "Okay. Since we're living together, I guess you should know something about my parents."

A slight fluttering of panic whirred in my ears, a hangover from childhood and too many foster homes that seemed perfect the first few days but then the world tilted and turned upside down and they became scary, nightmare places once the doors were closed, the curtains drawn and the social workers safely back in their offices.

Guy reached over, touched my hand and laughed. "I scared you. It's nothing bad. It's just that we're more than a family, we're a business as well."

"Like one of those soap operas," I said, thinking of last year when I'd sworn off guys and gotten into the habit of binge-watching *The Young and the Restless*. "The overbearing patriarch or matriarch and the gaggle of beautiful but parasitic children fighting for Daddy's attention and a share of the family fortune."

I regretted the words as soon as I'd uttered them. He almost choked on his wine.

"You're so brutally honest. That's why I like you so much," he said, stroking my arm. "Dad – or Gord as he likes me to address him – is the prolific author of multiple textbooks on educational methodology, now standard reading in university faculties all over the world. He's a consultant to government and business, a keynote speaker with a year-long waiting list, and now he's developed a series of remedial software that's taken off beyond his wildest dreams. In other words, he's a driving force in the field of education."

"And you're following in his footsteps?"

"I'm the heir apparent."

"You like that?"

He sat back and surveyed the glossy room with its designer lighting and polished surfaces. "I like *this*," he said with emphasis. "You don't get this on a prof's salary."

"He wants you to call him. He said ASAP."

He plunked the wine glass on the table, spilling a little over the side. "Guess I'd better do that then."

I could hear the low murmur of his voice from the bedroom where he'd taken the phone. It was strange he hadn't talked about his mom. I made a point to ask him about her. *ASAP.* His dad, Gord, had talked in clipped tones as if reading the contents of a memo. Suddenly, I was sober. The heady buzz of the wine had receded into a dull headache and I remembered I had to be up early for a staff meeting the next day.

On the way to the bedroom I stopped at the windows and looked down at the city spread out below, twinkling like a field of stars. Beyond the magic of brightly lit shopping areas and glossy skyscrapers was the black gleam of the Mississippi River, snaking its way round shadowy, deserted banks and side streets where faceless men in dark cars cruised back and forth preying on the young and lost and vulnerable who'd trade their bodies for money.

Shivering, I went into the bedroom where Guy had fallen asleep, the phone still clutched in his hand. I covered him with a blanket and tucked myself in beside him, trying hard to forget the sick sense of fear that always crept in with memories of the past.

6

Birdie had been my sister, my confidante, my other self, my all.

She could feel what I was feeling and I could sense her every change in mood. It was all down to twin telepathy. I'd done some reading on that phenomenon. Hard-line scientists liked to dismiss it as merely anecdotal. No proof that it exists. Others were more open to the idea. They described it as a kind of coupled consciousness that is particularly strong in identical twins.

Birdie and I were fraternal twins but one study I read claimed that female fraternal twins have almost as close a bond as identical girl twins. I believed it. We'd spent nine months next to each other in the womb, our cells budding, then dividing at the same pace. Breathing in unison like two tiny frogs, our limbs brushing against each other, separated only by the membrane of our own amniotic sacs. This absolute closeness meant that once we wormed our way into the outside world, we were still interconnected, no matter how far apart we were. If Birdie's electrons spun, mine did too. It was known as a *field of interconnection*. Crazy stuff, but I happened to believe it.

After she was gone, I'd been pretty much a loner. No close friends or confidantes. Plenty of drinking buddies and party pals, but no intimacy. No ties. That's why I preferred eating lunch alone in my classroom. Mainly to get away from Sabrina, Daphne and the gossip crew that met every noon hour in the staffroom to tear apart friends, husbands and celebrities while sharing the latest dieting fads. But since Guy had told me we'd been invited for dinner at Gord and Nancy's the following weekend, I couldn't settle down to work alone. I squirmed on my chair, my heart trilling with barely controlled panic. How could I carry this off? I wasn't good around other people's parents. I had no childhood anecdotes or blissful family experiences to share. My background was a jumbled mess of hazy memories. Now and again I'd reach in to retrieve a tangled thread and try to tease out the memories and sensations. Most times I gave up. The truth was, I didn't want to remember most of my past. Monotony, hopelessness and fear don't make for good memories.

Restlessness drove me towards the staffroom that day where a large pink and white celebration cake sat on the center table. Fran Kuzyk, the Math teacher, was pregnant. Quick work considering that only a year and a half ago I'd accompanied Sabrina, Fran, Daphne and Kate McAllister, the Work Ed teacher, on Fran's drunken bachelorette rampage through craft breweries, a strip club and several downtown clubs. We'd all piled into a taxi and taken turns throwing up out the window. The driver finally kicked us all out at Fran's place and we'd crashed on her floor. Her fiancé, Tom, a lawyer, made us bacon and eggs next morning. I was the only one able to eat it while the others groaned and sipped at cups of black coffee. I was never one to waste free food.

Now Fran sat, pink and glowing, at the center of the group and announced the baby was due in five months. The other girls took turns patting her stomach before digging into the cake. I wished her a quick congratulations before jabbing my plastic fork into a large slice. Maybe the sugar rush would calm my nerves.

"How's the prof doing?" asked Sabrina, picking at her wafer-thin slice of cake. She'd recently taken up body-building and ropey sinews bulged through the tanned skin of her arms. I pointed to my mouth, which was crammed with cake.

"Careful," she said. "This crap is poison. Don't want your new guy looking elsewhere." Her eyes wandered over my gray cashmere sweater. One of Guy's many gifts to me.

"He's good," I said, licking the crumbs away from the corner of my mouth.

"That's it? That's all you can tell me? We need to go for coffee. Have a real heart-to-heart. I can give you some sisterly advice or something."

I felt the color drain from my face. My shock reflex was so immediate I crashed the plate down onto the cutlery. Sabrina's hand flew to her mouth.

"Jeez I'm so sorry, Anna. I forgot."

"It's okay. No worries," I croaked as I stood up and fled the room, feeling my way through a fog of tears along the nubbly stucco walls.

A year or two ago – after a few B-52s at a nearby sports bar – I broke down and told Sabrina that my sister had disappeared without a trace. After that, she'd tried many times to pry more details out of me, but even with her free booze, sly questions and her sixth sense, she didn't get anywhere. I wouldn't let her.

I sat down at my desk, rested my head on my hand and flipped open the daily journals. Anything to distract myself. Birdie was in my head again. That jerky little puppet figure with the scrawny arms and legs turning around and around like a wind-up doll. I pressed at my eyelids as if I could squeeze away every trace of that image.

The first journal belonged to Carla, the only female in the new group. She looked like a vampire child. Dainty, white face, limpid kohl-lined eyes ringed with violet shadows. Blood-red lipstick. At sixteen she was the youngest and smallest and always kept herself at the center of the boys, shielded by their vast black trench coats. Her printing was square and large like a child's. I read, letting the pictures form in my head.

> *I love the outdoors. I love nature and pine trees and camping in the summer. I love my family. I once went in a canoe. I'm a good dancer. My Dad drowned when I was a baby. My Mom gets tired. She has problems with alcool. When she drinks there's no food for my bruthers and baby sister. I try to get food from the food bank but she says she dusn't want any charity. When the soshul worker comes I make sure Mom's hair is brushed and she's drinking tea. I don't want to go with those people. They're all liars. Did you know judges and other types of rich people pay for us to do things to them. You wouldn't believe it if I told you wot. But the boys get it worse. That's really gross. That's why I'll do everything to keep us together.*

I shut the book. If only she knew how much I understood about her life. How her writing brought me even closer to Birdie. I groped around in my mind for a clue, an image of my lost sister. Then it came to me in a rush. So vivid she could have been right there in my classroom.

I remembered her standing on a chair in the group home kitchen, wearing a monkey mask, a striped sweater and a pair of boy's blue shorts so baggy they flapped around her skinny thighs. She curled her stick arms gorilla style under her armpits and hopped up and down, tilting her head from side to side, making dumb chimp noises. My stomach clenched with shame. She looked pathetic. But she was so into it she didn't care about the kids who were chanting, egging her on and laughing at her. Then she stumbled forward on the chair edge. It tipped over, sending her tumbling off, arms flapping in panic, the monkey mask slipping over one ear. On the way down she smacked her face on the corner of the kitchen table and split her lip. Her face crumpled up in tears as a stream of blood dribbled from her nose into her mouth and down her chin. I ran to her, folding her bony body in my arms. A surge of love and fear almost knocked the breath from me. Then I yelled and screamed at those asshole kids to *piss off and leave her alone.*

The buzzer for afternoon classes blasted like a ship's horn, sucking away the horrors of the past and leaving me so shattered I threw on *The Shawshank Redemption* and had a Friday film afternoon. It was early dismissal so I was out of there at two thirty before Robin could collar me with some phony claptrap about professional development or curriculum review.

My insides churned as I drove home. Worry about meeting Guy's parents next weekend and memories of Birdie had sent me into a tailspin. I had to stop and think somewhere quiet. Carry on delving into the past. Testing the waters. Guy wouldn't be home for at least three hours so I took a detour off the freeway and paid a visit to one of my old stomping grounds. The place I'd been happiest. When I lived with the Levines.

I pulled up by the playground near their place, a long, suburban street of shabby seventies-style bungalows. The playground gave off a neglected vibe. Rust bloomed on the swing set, graffiti on the edges of the slide, a cracked steering wheel on the playhouse. Maybe I could channel some of the old memories. Remember growing bolder. Laughing again as the swing flew high and the good, clean air blew the demons away until I could actually look someone in the eye without frowning. But I couldn't conjure up anything specific.

Empty playgrounds in the afternoon are the loneliest places on earth. Filled with memories of laughing children and muddled, sleep-deprived parents. Or maybe ghosts of ragged kids with hollow eyes and pale, undernourished faces like my student Carla's brothers and sister. I'd been one of those kids when I was in the foster homes. Kids who ran wild on the streets all day with only a bag of chips or a pack of dry noodles to chew on. Back at dark and mind out for the creeps and perverts. Go to sleep in the clothes you stood up in. No time to brush your teeth.

But not with the Levines. It was different with them. I spent two years there from when I was fifteen or maybe sixteen, then Marty Levine got sick and Rachel couldn't manage to look after me as well as him. But by that time I'd stabilized, and was old enough to go into a dorm at university.

I looked over at their place. The front of the house had polished brass carriage lamps beside a painted turquoise door. I thought it was beautiful when I first saw it. And Mrs. Levine was cooking shepherd's pie with real grated cheese on the top. I was in paradise.

Except Birdie wasn't there with me.

By then I didn't know where she was.

The previous four or five years spent bouncing between temporary placements was a shadow box of formless impressions I was afraid to open. Linda Martin, my social worker at the Levines', always said I could come and talk to her about the particulars of that time. When I was ready.

I still hadn't talked. Because during that dark period of constant change, Birdie disappeared.

And now the Levines were long gone.

I owed so much to Rachel. She took a traumatized teenager who glowered like a demon from beneath heavy, black bangs, who called her foster mother a stupid bitch and worse, until the endless supply of love, patience and good books broke through the tough shell and I became human again. Years later, I heard Marty had died and Rachel moved to the country with her sister, a bee farmer. I made a mental note to visit as soon as I had time. Maybe in the summer holidays.

A steady drizzle had started up, so I pulled up my collar and ran back to the car. I drove straight to the mall and plunged into its cinnamon warmth. Once there I bought a giant latte and began to loosen up a bit. Credit card in hand, I slipped into one of the pricier stores. The kind that doesn't have a dollar sign on the price tags and the marble floor is so polished it feels like you're walking on water. Normally I'd slide right out again when one of the wraithlike sales clerks fixed me with a *what the hell are you doing here* look, but the camel coat was now my membership to this exclusive club.

I exited the glass doors an hour later after purchasing a strappy little dress in floaty gold material as well as drop earrings and a gold pendant. My heart thudded in my ears when I paid the equivalent of my rent money for it. Thanks to free lodgings and Guy's generosity, that extra cash was burning a hole in my pocket. I'd felt a momentary dizziness when the purchase went through, followed by a rush as if I'd drunk three shots in a row. Carried along on this euphoria, I stepped into the first lingerie shop that had a deal on panties. I bought twenty pairs, vowing to throw away all my old ones except the gifts from Guy. Scented candles were going three for twenty dollars at Bath and Body, so I bought six as well as four bottles of body lotion and two car deodorizers in the shape of daisies. Afterwards, I pushed through the mall doors into the late evening sunshine, breathless and elated. The past was a distant and nagging memory, the weight of the shopping bags a comforting reminder of my new good fortune.

–

Guy was home early.

"I need to get you a better cell phone," he said, folding me into a warm hug as soon as I came through the door.

"What's wrong with my trusty old LG?" I said, nestling against his shirt. I could feel the beat of his heart through the thin cotton. It was unfamiliar, this sense of belonging to someone. This closeness that sent a little dart through the place where my heart was, chipping away at the wall I'd built around it. It felt weird that suddenly someone actually cared where I was and when I'd be home. For a moment that thought made me stiffen up and draw back, but I caught the sparkle of wine glasses and the reddish glow of a good vintage, so I relaxed into him.

"It's probably got a five-minute battery life. I called you a couple of times and you didn't answer. We're going to a retirement party at the faculty club," he said, handing me a glass of wine that slid down my throat like velvet fire.

I neglected to tell him I didn't answer the phone because I'm oblivious when I'm shopping. Instead, I held out my glass for a refill.

He poured the wine, but before I could lift it to my lips, he caught hold of my wrist.

"I've got a bone to pick with you."

He looked dead serious. Unsmiling. I had this sudden urge to shove the glass in his face and run, but just as quickly as the picture formed in my mind, his face broke out into a grin. I slammed the glass onto the table.

"Never ever do that to me again."

His face flushed. "I was just kidding."

"You scared me."

He reached his arms out to me but I turned my face away. My insides were churning.

"C'mon, Anna. I just wanted to ask if you found anything interesting in my sock drawer."

Now it was my turn to look sheepish.

He touched my shoulder. "It's okay. I don't have anything to hide."

"Except that you're totally, insanely anal."

"Inherited from my mom. You'll understand when you meet her."

"I guess she's one of those *don't use the decorative hand towel* types."

"Not exactly, but close," he said, holding my wine glass out to me. "But now you've snooped into my personal life I want to know something about yours."

56

I slugged the wine back. His eyes were wide. Expectant.

"I don't like to talk about it."

"Something. Anything."

My mind raced through memories. I had to give him something. Anything. As long as it had nothing to do with my sister. That wasn't a conversation I was ready to have.

"My family loved dogs. My father and I trained Dmitri to fetch the mail, play dead, walk on his back legs and everything. We were going to enter him in a talent show."

"What kind of dog was he?"

"Gray and white husky."

Guy's face fell. He sipped his wine and gazed through the window. "I envy you. I always wanted a dog. Mom and Dad said they couldn't cope with the smell or the hair shedding."

"They're a whole lot of work," I said, reaching for the wine bottle again. "Not a word of a lie."

We made love in the shower. I'd just soaped myself down when he slipped in and held me, studying my face in the bright lights of the bathroom, stroking every part of my body until it quivered. For the first time ever, I actually looked into a man's eyes as he pushed inside me and I had a vague sense that this was the nature of true intimacy – all that sentimental stuff about being joined as one.

Before Guy, sex was just a mechanical release. Nothing more than furtive, sweaty groping in a dark bathroom or anonymous bedroom with some guy whose first name was the only thing I knew about him – and even then, I couldn't be sure if it was a fake one. Now I had this urge to let go.

"You're incredible," I said, nibbling at his earlobe. Driblets of water ran from his hair down his cheek and I wondered if the wetness around my eyes was from tears or shower water.

"I knew you had good taste," he said later, his eyes lingering over the filmy, gold dress. I twirled around letting the skirt flutter around my legs. Round and round until my vision blurred and I remembered Birdie in the monkey mask, her spider arms held up in the air, a thin thread of blood dribbling down her lip. Pinpricks of light danced in front of my eyes and I stumbled. Guy seemed oblivious as he pulled the scented candles from their bright checkered bag.

"But these candles have to go. I'm allergic to this cheap junk. Give them away to your students. An incentive. Research shows that kids work way harder for entice-ments."

"What are they going to do with scented candles? Some of them don't have enough food to eat," I snapped, stuffing them back into the paper bag. "I mean you were there. You saw the kids."

"Are you saying I'm insensitive to poverty?" His brows knit. I'd never seen him look annoyed. "Or are you saying the poor don't deserve pretty, frivolous things? That it's all about survival. Isn't that just a little bit condescending?"

"I guess you have a point," I said, grabbing my purse. I didn't want a fight. It was way too early for that. "I'm sorry I overreacted. You can help me think of a classroom contest while we're driving."

"Apology accepted, but I don't talk shop on the weekend," he said, patting my bum and grinning as he held the door open for me. "Besides, the contests I'm likely to conjure up now would hardly be suitable for classroom use."

"Let's give them a whirl later," I said, standing on tiptoe and kissing his freshly shaved cheek. Then the world tilted upright again. Balance and harmony restored. For now.

7

To prepare myself for dinner at Guy's parents' place I did some research on Gord. I collared Sabrina during lunch. She'd made the rounds of educational conferences and, at numerous drunken post-conference parties in garish Holiday Inn hospitality rooms, had ended up on the knee of more than a few eminent keynote speakers. There was a good chance she'd met Gord during her travels.

She scratched her insta-tanned cheek and thought for a moment, checking her nails for telltale orange stain. I imagined her flipping through a mental catalogue of paunchy, gray-haired guys in navy sports coats and tan Fortrel slacks.

She chewed at her lower lip, then nodded. "I'm so glad you asked, Anna, because I do actually remember him. It was at a Westin. High-end place just outside of Denver. Artificial lake out front, monogrammed robes in the bathroom, wrapped truffles on the pillows. Definitely a cut above your Super 8 motel."

She stared out into space then held up her French-manicured index finger with its little arc of white nail. "It was a major national conference – he was the keynote speaker." Frowning, she searched the staffroom wall for inspiration. "It's hard to explain. He was weird – different. Kind of like Jimmy Swaggart channels Dr. Phil at a kindergarten concert. I can't remember a goddamn thing about his speech, but at the end he asked everyone to close their eyes and concentrate on strengthening their personal auras. Then he played Joe Cocker singing 'You Are So Beautiful' and stood in front of us all with his hands held up like some modern-day messiah. Let's say there was a whole lot of whispering and speculation about what he was on and how we could get some of that good stuff too."

I nodded my thanks and got up to leave the lunch table, but she grabbed my wrist and held on tight.

"Oh my God. That's the prof's dad. Is your honey finally taking you home to meet Mommy and Daddy?"

I nodded, wishing I'd kept my mouth shut. "Sunday. For dinner."

"They'll probably make you link arms at the table, sing 'Kumbaya' and become one with the cosmos before you can take a bite." She laughed, tipping her head back exposing the sharp line where her fake tan ended.

"And who says I don't want to?"

"What?"

"Get in touch with the cosmos? Be one with the universe?"

"Sure. Why not? Especially when there's a big payoff involved. I'd wear a sheet, shave my hair off and dance a jig for a ticket to the good life."

"Maybe he's changed since you saw him."

"I doubt it," she said, lifting the lid from her cottage cheese salad. She'd put walnuts on it instead of the usual raisins. Her fork stopped in mid-air and she smiled at the now-distant memory. "Oh God, *now* I remember. He was holding court in the hospitality room. Sipping on mineral water and icy as a frozen log when it came to the old Sabrina charm. Barely lifted an eyebrow. Even when I showed a bit of thigh and squeezed in tight during a toast. That guy was oblivious to everyone except himself and his ego."

"Well I guess I'll find out on Sunday," I said, getting up. I didn't need any more revelations to prejudice my first impressions of Guy's parents.

–

I distracted myself from the upcoming family dinner by reading my students' daily journals, which were becoming more revealing day by day. I couldn't just scan them. I had to read them from front to back, cover to cover. Their contents drew me back to a time and place I thought I'd put behind me.

As I read them, I'd start to feel all my old outrage about the powerlessness of marginalized kids. How they're invisible to the rest of the world, until some creep murders one of them and the papers run a story on society's seamy underbelly and its disenfranchised victims. Usually, there's an immediate burst of moral outrage from a few charitable do-gooders and opportunistic politicians who make all the right promises to clean things up. To name the johns, tighten up the foster system, and clean up the policing, but all too often these kids disappear and nobody cares until the next body washes onto the riverbank or turns up wrapped in a garbage bag in some back-alley dumpster.

Dane, the oldest of the new group of students, had raw talent. His writing was punchy and showed a weary kind of wisdom too old for his years. I read it at the end of the day. The words swam in and out of my vision, competing with memories of Birdie and me.

Carla's got a real job. Tell the world and the universe!! Her aunty hooked her up. She's a mall cop with connections. It's at Victoria's Secret of all places. Now our sweet Carla gets a huge discount on all that sexy, lacy lingerie. Me and the guys are glad she's off the street for now. She's too tiny. A baby bird. Some thug is gonna crush her. The rich, powerful ones are the worst. Those people have layers – the outer, respectable layer that everyone sees. Nice clothes, sweet cars, manicured nails, designer cologne, a good job, wallet full of cash and plastic. Peel that back and you find the inner layers. The bad-boy layer that drives them to look for a quick hand job or feel up behind the garbage cans of some stinky restaurant. Beneath that is the rotten, evil layer. Not everyone has this, but you can't tell from the outside. These sickos pay good, but at night, when the sun goes down, they just shuck the outer layers off and let their real evil selves shine. Make their victims do gross and vicious things you couldn't imagine, mostly to helpless and scared and poor people. But I can't write about this any more. I don't want to think about it.

I'm just glad about Carla. I hope they like her at that snob store.

I closed the book, my hand shaking. Maybe Birdie was wiped out by one of those creeping sickos in a brilliant flash of pure, dazzling evil. I'd never thought about it in that way. I'd always imagined violence lurked in foul, smoke-wreathed rooms or murky alleyways, but this was the first layer that Dane had talked about. The scary stuff

63

was sharp and blinding. The point of a needle piercing a vein, the glinting edge of a knife blade on soft skin, the flash of a bullet slicing through muscle and sinew. Was this how I'd lost Birdie? I held tightly to the edges of my desk, my eyes swimming, and in the nick of time bent my head over the garbage can and puked up my entire lunch.

-

When Guy was doing one of his late classes that week, I took a trip to the mall again. I drifted towards the Victoria's Secret store. I'd maxed out many a credit card there. Had drawers full of lacy panties and bras. Usually bought during the two-for-one sale or the *five panties for $25* event.

Fuchsia pink signage lured shoppers to the store's black marble entrance and banks of spotlights flooded the place with dazzling light. Like a pink pleasure palace that sold sanitized sex in frills, lace and satin. Birdie had always been a sucker for anything feminine and girlie, while I slobbed around in jeans and hoodies. She hated looking ugly.

The time after she fell and smacked her eye on the table, she had to wear a bandage wrapped around her head and couldn't wash her hair for a week or two.

She was a pitiful sight. A one-eyed runt with greasy hair, dragging herself around the group home, refusing to look anyone in the eye. Finally, one of the young supervisors took pity on her and brought her a Cinderella dress and wand from home. Once she was wearing that ivory lace dress with its stiff taffeta petticoat, she instantly morphed into the Good Fairy. Flitted around night and day, laying the wand on everyone's head and doling out angel dust to make them happy. Even the back-door stoner kids joined in, running around the yard whooping and flapping imaginary wings after getting the Birdie treatment.

After a month or so we had to bribe her with an extra helping of mashed potato to get the dress off her so it could be washed. Once she wore it for a whole week to the playground and caught it on a nail sticking out of the wooden climbing frame. It hung in filthy ribbons and tatters round her legs and then just disintegrated around her.

She cried like a baby when we finally had to throw it away. So I rescued the wand and the plastic Cinderella pin from the bodice and pinned it to her jacket, telling her she was still a member of the Cinderella club. When I was done pinning it, she lit up, placed her palms on my face and tried to twist the corners of my mouth into a smile.

"I love you, Anna," she said, placing her face against mine and making butterfly kisses on my cheek with her eyelashes. "But don't be so angry all the time or nobody else will like you."

It occurred to me as I trailed my hands along the pink corsets with feather accents, the tiny French maid outfit with its bum-skimming frills, and the white garter belt with pink rosettes, that this was the "princess gone naughty" look girls like Birdie were urged into. A slick segue from the innocence of childhood to post-pubescent sexuality. *You're all grown up now, little girl, but you can still play dress up. Only it's different now. Way different. Prince Charming doesn't just want a kiss now. He wants payback or he turns into a poisonous toad.*

I shuddered. Walking around this store made me miss Birdie even more, but I stayed, circling the displays. Sampled the hand cream and body spray. Found a negligee made of the same lace as the Cinderella dress. It was like scratching a scab that wouldn't heal, coming to this place Birdie would've loved. Or maybe more like gouging an open wound.

After minutes of aimless drifting, I remembered Carla. I'd come here to see her. She wasn't among the other girls on the floor. Tiny dolls with perfect makeup, running back and forth, talking into headsets, bras slung over their arms. Polished, pretty, perfumed and young. Striving to emulate the exquisite and untouchable angels that strutted their sparkling wings in the everlasting lingerie show that flickered on the bank of screens at the far side of the store.

I finally found her behind the cash desk, wrapping undies in pink tissue. She looked fresh and young, her shiny cheeks and lips scrubbed clean of the thick coat of makeup. I waved and she glanced up at me, smiling like a kid who's just performed a dive and then emerges from the water pleading for praise. I saw that look on Birdie's face so many times, I wanted to slap her sometimes when she performed like a trained dog for idiots who didn't care or who were just winding her up.

On instinct I grabbed a couple of lotions and a body spray and lined up at Carla's counter.

"You like it here, Carla?"

She glanced around to see if anyone was listening. "Yeah. I love it. I like all the nice things."

"I'm proud of you. You're getting on track here. Let me know if you need any advice."

She nodded and wrapped my purchases in tissue paper. "Thanks," she whispered but her eyes were elsewhere, darting to the person behind me. I moved aside. Hope was so tenuous for kids like Carla and Birdie. Everything stacked against them. Like tiptoeing barefoot along a slippery balance beam. One wrong move and you fall off. Back into the old life and all the dangers that come along with it.

I watched her for a few minutes longer, then left with a sense of dread. Like my head was being held under icy water. Birdie's shadow was everywhere, crowding into my new life until the feeling was so heavy it took on a weight of its own.

In a weird trance I drifted to the coffee shop and bought a small butterscotch-flavored latte, then sat down at a table to purge the sense of loss that seeped under my flesh like the creeping chill of a winter graveyard.

I had trouble sleeping the days before we met Guy's parents. Lying in bed late at night, I grilled him about his mother, Nancy. He told me she'd been a kindergarten teacher. According to him, a good one, even great. Hands-on, inspirational, dearly loved by all who enjoyed her *Bring Your Teddy Day* and her legendary *Kindergarten Cooking Fun* class. But it seemed that all her little victories paled in the shadow of Gord's colossal empire and, naturally, when his business grew too large to manage on his own, she retired from her job and became his full-time sidekick and Girl Friday, excelling in her role as the guru's wife.

"I guess you could say she sacrificed her own ambitions to help Dad make a success of the business."

I rested against his chest, calmed by its steady rise and fall. "Do you think she resented that?"

He kissed the top of my head. "She made me her project instead. Homeschooled me for kindergarten and first grade."

"What was it like?"

His arms pulled me closer. "Amazing. Being the only kid with the best kindergarten teacher ever. We read so many books, made puppets, did science experiments in the kitchen, baked Halloween cookies, painted murals, carved, sculpted, had our own grocery store with play money, went to museums, art galleries, plays."

I thought about my own early childhood in Dennis's garbage-filled backyard. Alone there with Birdie for hours on end.

"What happened in second grade?"

I sensed his heartbeat quicken. "Dad said I should go to school and learn about the real world. Said he needed Mom's help with the business. Said I needed to toughen up."

"That's harsh," I said, propping myself up on one elbow to look at him, but he turned his face away. "Must've been a shock."

"At first it was like torture. I guess I've blocked most of it out."

I couldn't think of anything to say after that, so we lay there, quiet until Guy finally drifted off, his eyelids flickering then staying shut.

I wanted to know more about Nancy. Anything that would give me a feel for this woman who'd been the center of his universe. But he looked so vulnerable, I couldn't bear to wake him. I kissed the corner of his mouth then lay back and stared at the ceiling, willing myself to sleep.

I counted sheep, lost track, then ran over my lesson plans for the next day. Then I pictured Guy in second grade. Hair brushed, shirt buttoned up to his chin, glasses perched on his nose. A timid, pampered boy, alone and motherless among all those other kids. They must have eaten him alive. Birdie and I survived only because we were a team. If she couldn't charm them with her sassiness, I was ready to step in and smack the bullies and meanies, to pull their hair and hoof them in the butt. I wasn't afraid of anyone. Neither was Birdie with me by her side. Not at first, anyway. We were a team. Just how Dennis predicted.

Gradually, the safety of darkness and the steady sound of Guy's breathing allowed me to get back to Birdie. To remember of all things, a door. A wooden door with a smashed lock and a rope tied through a hole in the doorpost to secure it shut. The walls in the room were papered with sickly orange flowers and a sour smell hung heavy in the air. Someone's finger touched my swollen eye. Birdie's finger?

Squeezing my eyes shut, I pushed the thought away, my heart racing so fast I thought I'd pass out. I slid out of bed and put my head between my knees. When the dizziness passed, I padded out to the kitchen, poured a glass of water and gulped it down, my throat catching at its cold bite. Staring down at the city below, shrouded by night, the reflections of lights flickering on the river, I thought of Dane and his buddies out there. So young and vulnerable. I could give them food and money, then maybe they'd go home and not have to cruise the riverside for tricks. But Robin, our principal, had always told us never to get involved with the kids outside of class.

> *If you're not prepared to be a friend for life, then don't be a temporary buddy. These kids have been let down too many times before by well-meaning do-gooders who float into their lives, raise their hopes and then drop them when their demands become too inconvenient or when the next cause of the moment presents itself. Our job is to help our students help themselves. Not patronize them with charity.*

I took that lesson to heart.

Placing my palms against the glass, I felt a sneaking sense of claustrophobia, a longing to get out into the open air, so I grabbed my shoes and coat, slipped out the door and headed down to the underground parking garage.

The dash display glowed green telling me it was a few minutes past midnight. I had to be up at seven the next day. Not to worry. I'd managed on a couple of hours sleep before and if Guy woke up wondering where I'd gone, I'd tell him I went to buy aspirin at the drug store.

I nosed the car through the garage doors into dimly lit streets, then turned right towards the river, past burger joints and late night coffee bars still filled with night owls and late night stragglers. The riverside was so close to Guy's place. The area now gentrified with towering loft-style condominiums, quaint boutiques, artisan bakeries and coffee bars that could have graced any chic New York street. Further along, the apartment buildings became grimier, their few lit windows revealing broken blinds and dusty spider plants, and beyond that, unseen chaos. Cluttered kitchen sinks, teeming ashtrays, stained cushions, unwashed laundry and the stink of neglect. I knew it well. But I screeched to a sudden halt, narrowly avoiding being rear ended by the guy behind me who sped past, burning a whole lot of rubber, mouthing profanities and sticking up a stubby middle finger.

I was oblivious to the insult. All I could do was stare at a lit window on the third floor of the redbrick apartment block. Beyond the row of empty beer bottles, sickly yellow and orange blooms snaked their way across the wall. My head spun as I checked out the front doors of the building expecting a wooden door with a broken lock, though logic told me it would've been replaced by now. I exhaled at the sight of a pair of large glass doors. For at least five minutes I sat staring at the flowered wallpaper, trying to remember being in that place, but I either couldn't or wouldn't come up with anything other than a sour smell, like stale beer mixed with fried bacon, rotting milk and the chemical stink of burned cleaning fluid.

A tap on the passenger side window almost sent me through my sunroof. Someone large and pale loomed out of the shadows and I fell back against my seat hyperventilating until I recognized the face and rolled down the window.

"Jeez, Dane – you almost gave me a heart attack."

"Why are you here?" he asked, his glance darting from me to the street. "Or are *you* trying to get lucky?"

I could only manage to croak an answer through parched lips. "I was on my way home from a party. I stopped because I thought I recognized this place," I said, nodding towards the grungy apartment block.

"Hope not," he said, putting a cigarette in his mouth and cupping his hand to protect the lighter flame. "Unless you're into crack."

His head swiveled when a sleek black Lincoln edged by, slowing down for a moment beside us. I tried to make out a face through the tinted windows, but the car accelerated off leaving a silvery exhaust trail.

"You're scaring off my regulars," he said, flicking the cigarette away.

"I saw Carla at the mall. She looks happy."

He jammed his hands in his pockets and tried not to smile. His eyes were brown liquid under the thick eyeliner. "Got my fingers crossed for her."

Next, a charcoal-gray SUV sidled past and stopped just ahead of us. This time I caught sight of the driver. White collar with silver, Ken doll hair. Tiny silver goatee and gold-rimmed glasses. Like a bank manager, real estate agent or accountant. A regular white-collar guy. He looked familiar, but I couldn't place where or when I might have seen him.

"Who is that guy?" I said, feeling my world tilt to the side and then back again. He looked like every TV commercial image I'd been programmed to trust.

Dane shrugged and raised his eyebrows. "Customer confidentiality assured," he said, touching his finger to his lips. "Gotta run."

Chills crawled across my skin when I watched him saunter over to the car, hands jammed into his pockets. I wanted to go after him, bash on the driver's side door, rip it open and smash that smug pervert across the face. I'd scream *I'm a teacher and I have to report you to the cops and the Child Protection Services or maybe I should give your poor, unsuspecting wife a call. I'm sure she has no idea that you're a predatory creep.*

Instead I watched, powerless as Dane climbed in and the SUV inched away, bound for some dark alleyway snaking down to the river.

-

I woke with a jolt the next morning, shivering with a cold that spread from my core. Nestling closer to Guy's warm body I tried to make sense of the dream I'd just had. In it, Birdie had been trying to climb up the orange wallpaper. She was wearing a hoodie and underwear and was chattering like one of those speeded up audiotapes. *See, Anna. It's just like Jack and the Beanstalk.* Over and over again. Limbs spread crablike across the wall.

Pushing my face into Guy's shoulder, I tried to breathe deeply, to make the image go away. Guy's arm reached behind him and found my face.

"You okay?"

"Just a bad dream."

"I can help you feel better," he said, turning around and wrapping me in his arms. Then he stroked my hair and neck and the demons flew away. I fell asleep cocooned in his warmth.

9

Gord and I were doomed from the start. I disliked him the moment I walked up to his house, an architectural monstrosity consisting of four white concrete cubes linked together with narrow walls of white brick. It resembled an alien space pod docked amongst drooping willow trees and a gray wasteland of pebbles. Several larger rocks sat strategically around a huge abstract metal structure that spouted a stream of water from somewhere in its twisted mass. Behind this display, three massive bronze plaster balls of descending size sat on the grass.

I looked up at Guy, unable to stop my eyebrows knitting together.

"His new landscaper is into astrology," he said as if that explained the balls. He'd been silent in the car and edgy that morning at the condo, chewing his lip while I paraded back and forth in front of him wearing various outfits until he'd nodded in approval.

"I want them to like you as much as I do, babe, and Dad can be a judgmental bastard if he wants. Believe me, I'm giving you the best chance."

I'd call the final look he'd approved *private schoolgirl meets Brit royal family.* Gray dress pants and crisp white blouse, topped with a fine black cashmere sweater. The ensemble was completed by pearl studs, a heavy silver pendant and hair caught up with a silver clip.

Nancy met us at the door. I'd expected a petite brunette in a flowered skirt, not the tall, willowy, brown-eyed blonde wearing a pure white tunic and black slacks. Her short cap of hair was slicked back to reveal a tight, flawlessly made-up face that barely moved when she hugged Guy and kissed him on the cheek. I recognized the perfect mask of the botox addict whose wrinkled throat betrayed the truth.

She turned those warm brown eyes onto me. They were Guy's eyes.

"Mom this is Anna," he said proudly.

"How exquisite," she said, taking my hands in hers. "Gray eyes and black hair. I'm envious." She leaned forward and pecked my cheek. I felt awkward. Unsure if I should present the other cheek, but the moment passed and she slipped her arm into Guy's and bustled us into an enormous room. A cavernous space, painted clinical white except for a broad gray stripe that ran from the floor, across the ceiling, and down the opposite wall. She noticed the drift of my eyes and smiled.

"Gord's idea of drama. I know it's a lot to take in. We don't like clutter, you see."

As far as I could see there wasn't a single surplus item in the entire place. A large white leather sectional, a chrome and glass coffee table with one square red plate on it, large-screen TV on the wall, below that, a curved white entertainment unit bearing wafer-thin speakers. On top, three wicker balls. *What was it with this guy and his balls?*

"Are you guys talking about me again?" boomed a carefully modulated radio voice.

I turned round to see a tall, broad-shouldered man enter the room. This was him. This was Gord. Father of Guy. Face to face with me for the first time. For a moment

I thought the floor shifted beneath my feet, but I painted on a smile and breathed deeply.

He was slim except for a slight paunch that strained the waist of his tailored charcoal silk shirt. He strode towards me, his hand extended. Polished. Practiced. Professional. But though he tried to fix his pale blue eyes on mine, I couldn't stop staring at his hair. It had a rusty, dyed hue from those *cover the gray* products, and was combed back from the high dome of his forehead so perfectly it appeared to be sprayed into place. With his manicured sideburns, salon-tanned skin and shaped eyebrows, he was a walking TV evangelist. Just as Sabrina had described him.

I snapped my eyes away from his hair and moved in for a handshake, only to be completely surprised when he hugged me around the waist, dug his fingertips into my flesh and planted a damp kiss on my cheek. I tried not to recoil, but my body stiffened.

"We're an affectionate lot," he said, stepping back to check me out so boldly my insides withered. "At least my side of the family is. You'll get used to me. Nancy's lot tend to be a bit standoffish. I hope Guy's not holding back. Takes after his mother."

He clapped Guy on the shoulder and I had the urge to blurt out something like *no, you ball-obsessed jerk, your son is gentle and tender and loving, and maybe you don't know him as well as you think*. Instead, I pasted on a smile – the type I used for ingratiating myself at parent-teacher meetings – and slotted my hand into the crook of Guy's arm.

"He's been wonderful," I said, smiling up at Guy whose face relaxed into an expression of relief. As did Nancy's.

"Come on, you two lovebirds," he said, directing us towards the pristine leather sofa. "I'm sure Nancy's fixed some cocktails for us."

Nancy had been silently hovering in the background. Now she snapped to attention and bustled into the kitchen.

"Can I help?" I said, moving to stand. Gord motioned me to stay put.

"She doesn't like anyone else in there. It's her *exclusive domain* shall we say." He winked at Guy. "Eh, son?"

Guy jolted into action. "What – oh yeah. You'll probably get a tour later. Then you'll understand. Mom's a perfectionist when it comes to cooking."

"Damn obsessed, I'd call it," said Gord, rolling his eyes upwards and twirling a finger by his temple.

Nancy appeared carrying a tray of tumblers filled with colorless, sparkling drinks stuffed with limes and greenery. "I hope you like vodka," she said, placing the tray on the table.

"All young people like it," Gord snapped. "Guy's bar is stacked with Grey Goose."

Guy took a sip and wrinkled his nose. "Actually, I just bought a bottle of Alize Limited Edition. Way smoother taste."

Gord held his glass mid-air, his upper lip curled in disdain. "Well, sorry if our discount brand doesn't stack up to your champagne tastes."

"Try it next time you're over," said Guy, picking up his glass.

Gord winced. "I'll hold you to that, kid," he said, downing his drink in two gulps.

Nancy and I were virtually silent for the entire pre-dinner exchange. She kept flitting in and out fetching perfect little nibbles on stark white plates. Wafers of prosciutto coiled around tiny cubes of melon, shrimp curled in miniature white cups with their own white dipping sauce, and little squares of melba toast spread with cream cheese and a dollop of pale caviar. I sat listening to the back and forth between Guy and Gord, relieved on the one hand that Gord wasn't probing into my murky past, but puzzled that he'd barely addressed me since our initial, awkward greeting.

When Nancy finally announced dinner was ready, we all filed towards the dining table, an enormous slab of black granite flecked with beige. The edges were rough and unfinished.

"Custom order," said Gord, pulling out his chair at the head of the table. "Quarried in Italy according to my exact specifications. Incredible what you can get nowadays."

"They say quartz is the new thing now," said Guy, settling himself at the other end of the table. "I'm thinking of refinishing my kitchen with it, then working in some metal or natural wood."

He'd never mentioned the idea to me. His kitchen was already high-end as far as I was concerned.

"Well, good luck trying to get it custom quarried like I did," said Gord, a noticeable quaver of irritation in his voice.

"You don't quarry quartz, Dad. It's man-made," said Guy, reaching for the bread. The barest flicker of arrogance distorted his face, transforming him for an instant into a stranger I hardly knew. I shivered as Gord placed both hands on the table.

"Always trying to make the old man look like a moron. Never misses a trick." His eyes finally rested on me.

"Watch out, Mandy, he'll be tripping you up on your misplaced modifiers before long."

"It's Anna, Dad, not Mandy," said Guy with a sigh, placing a hand over mine and smiling with such affection I realized I'd been holding my breath for the last thirty seconds. I exhaled and let the warm cocoon of intimacy wrap around me once again.

Gord sat back. Tension shimmered in the air. Then Nancy swept in with a platter of white fish garnished with asparagus and tiny roasted potatoes.

"I hope you're not allergic," she said, nodding towards the fish.

"Well, it's a bit late to ask that, isn't it?" said Gord, offering me the plate. "That's the kind of thing you'd find out in advance."

I shook my head. "It's fine. No allergies here." If they only knew there were times in my life I'd have eaten potato peel I was so hungry.

Entertainment during dinner was the Gord show. He treated us to a complete rundown of his educational theories, only pausing his lecture to insert a piece of fish, chew on it, then start up again.

I'd seen people like him plenty of times before. Self-proclaimed gurus who sold a *quick-fix* solution to harried school boards struggling to raise standards to keep up with students in Finland, Korea, China and all the other top ten countries. *At last*, they pronounced, gleefully rubbing their hands together, *the answer to every problem that ails our faltering education system. The golden key to unlocking unlimited potential. We can sell this dream and we've found the right person to do it.*

He regaled us with anecdotes about his many keynote addresses. In my short career I'd sat through plenty of those forty-minute speeches that left everyone feeling good but empty-handed. With nothing that could be translated into real, concrete classroom practice.

When the plates were empty, he stopped abruptly and turned to me. "So Guy tells me you work in an alternative program."

I blinked myself into full consciousness, understanding why I'd seen Guy and Nancy do exactly the same thing earlier. "I do, that's where I met Guy." I smiled over at Guy. He smiled back and I felt an immediate urge to make love to him.

"I think they're in love, Gord," said Nancy, her eyes smiling but her face strained.

"Ah – the joys of youth," said Gord, sighing and stumbling to his feet. He'd downed at least three glasses of wine over dinner. "But I'm afraid it's time for some shop talk if you'll excuse us, Anna. You girls can take the time to get better acquainted."

Guy gave me a hurried peck on the cheek, then father and son took off into a teak-paneled office lined with bookshelves. Before the door slammed shut, I saw a heavy wooden desk surrounded by framed photographs and certificates.

I picked up my dinner plate and followed Nancy into the kitchen, which resembled the interior of a space pod. Glossy white surfaces everywhere. Chrome accents. The fridge and stove concealed into recessed walls. A gleaming white island with three white pendant lights dangling above three white candlesticks of varying heights each topped with a perfect lemon. There'd be no spaghetti and meatballs cooked in this kitchen.

Nancy bustled around, stacking dishes into the dishwasher.

"Gord talks a lot at first, but he's just insecure meeting new people."

Insecure was not a word I'd ever associate with Gord Franzen, but then I remembered she'd been a kindergarten teacher, a position requiring a saintly level of empathy and patience.

"It's okay. I found him interesting. Stimulating actually."

"You *are* a diplomat," she said, turning from the sink with a candid expression that quite disarmed me. This was not the person who'd sat like a dutiful robot during dinner while Gord did his turn.

"I did – I mean I really enjoyed…" I stuttered.

"Don't worry, Anna," she said, drying her hands and turning towards me. "Gord and I are delighted that Guy's finally hooked up with someone like you. Someone who understands what we're all about."

I wasn't sure how to respond since I really hadn't figured them out at all, but somehow, she'd decided I was *the right fit*. That I belonged. Maybe because I sat like a statue and let Gord do his thing. Maybe because Birdie and I had learned to throw our lot in with anyone that showed an interest in us. We were chameleons, changing our skin to suit our surroundings and *fitting in* was the way we survived one lousy foster home after another. I mastered the art of blending in till I was almost unseen. It was safer that way. But Birdie clamored for attention, praise – connection. She twirled like a wind-up doll, begging for anyone to *look at me, see me, I'm cute, loveable. Want me, notice me, love me.*

Too bad it would eventually be her undoing.

It was almost mine, too, because later when Birdie disappeared, I was too broken to care about *fitting in*.

"How about some grapefruit sorbet?" Nancy slammed the dishwasher shut, rousing me from my thoughts. She opened the fridge door revealing stacks of perfectly arranged Tupperware containers. I gulped my wine too quickly and coughed.

She laughed. "I know. I'm a little obsessive. But order calms me."

"Now I see who Guy takes after."

She spooned the pale lemony ice into white glass bowls. "He was always a lovely boy. A gentle soul." She stopped for a moment, the spoon held in mid-air and looked at me with steely eyes. "Be kind to him, Anna."

"Of course," I said, taking an extra slug of wine to steady my nerves, then excused myself to use the bathroom. The tone of her voice had felt like a warning, which made me wonder just how many times Nancy had stepped in as Guy's protector. Maybe the two of them still enjoyed a mutual alliance against the power of Gord.

But any misgivings I had about fitting into Nancy's world flew away when I stepped into their bathroom. Compared to the sterility of the other rooms, this was a haven of sensuality. Tears sprang to my eyes when I estimated that 99.9 percent of the population would never set foot in or even glimpse a room as exquisite as this one. Two white tapers in large teak candlesticks flooded the ceiling and walls with a pale honeyed glow. One side of the room was a continuous wall of windows looking out onto a forest of birch trees, their slender trunks so perfect it seemed an artist had created the exquisite arrangement of silvery saplings.

In front of the window a perfect shell of a tub sat like a modern sculpture on a freckled marble platform. A long marble and wood vanity ended in a shower enclosure as large as an average bedroom. Lined with the same honey-colored marble, it boasted four rectangular showerheads. My fingers itched to switch on the water. To strip off my clothes and get inside. It would be like standing in the middle of a forest during a warm rain shower. I stood open-mouthed like a child in a toy store, my fingertips resting on the glass enclosure.

My mind swam back to all the bathrooms I'd ever used in my life. Cracked white tubs with scum lines and mildewy grout. Hairs plastered on shower walls, the eggy stink of sewer gas, toothpaste splatter on mirrors, moldy vinyl shower curtains streaked with soap scum. Danger lurking in every grimy corner, behind every cracked and fingerprint-streaked door. A wave of nausea rushed into my throat.

Sabrina was right. I wanted this world. Wanted it so bad my stomach ached. If I could live in safety, surrounded by such pristine perfection I'd learn to listen to Gord and never interrupt. It was worth it at any cost. I'd give up my soul just to stay here.

–

"They loved you," said Guy on the drive home. He patted my knee. "I'm proud of you."

"Really. I hardly opened my mouth."

He shook his head, his eager glance flitting to me then back to the road. "Not at all. You were polite and interested. That counts for a lot with Dad."

I focused on the rear lights of the car ahead, my vision blurring in a fog of red. "Easy to see why," I murmured.

"Meaning what?"

"He likes to hold court. I mean he's probably always the one that grabs the mic at parties or family gatherings. The guy you have to drag offstage with a metal hook."

Guy's shoulders slumped. "Mom and I both know it's easier to let him have his say. He's used to taking charge and having the last word."

"No offense meant," I said, picturing the forest scene from that glorious bathroom window and swallowing any further acid comebacks. "I enjoyed listening to him and I really liked your mother."

"She's a special person. Glad you liked her."

I leaned over and nestled against his arm. I really didn't want to hurt Guy.

Curb your wicked tongue I told myself, wondering who on earth had uttered that strange, archaic phrase to me. Or did someone say it to Birdie? I couldn't remember. Or perhaps I knew perfectly well and wasn't ready to confront the awful truth yet.

10

Just before spring break, I stayed late one night looking over the student journals. Carla had been absent for more than a week and no one had heard from her. I scanned the last few entries in her notebook. A garbled story had begun to emerge.

> *I hate people basicly. People are crap. I don't like it when people do and think and say evil things. Things that show they don't give a shit.*
>
> *What is life? What is love, Mommy? What is life? What do you really know about life? I know everything about it. People are rotten perverts. Hey I can write anything here. I can say anything my little mind wants to say. Ha ha. Ha ha. LMAO.*
>
> *I'm scared of the dark. The closet door sucks. There's sumthing inside that I don't want to see. It's the sharp-clawed boogeyman! Go to hell and back. Stay away.*

The next few pages continued – half-mocking, childish but with an ominous undertone. Reading those words revived another thread in my memory. A memory of fear rising into my throat like undigested food. Sharp, tingly, acidic. I swallowed it back and checked the last pages for more clues about what could be going on. I'd have to alert Robin if there was reason to be concerned. We'd been diligent about that since a fifteen-year-old kid had committed suicide last year after throwing down a bunch of hints in his journal. Too bad I hadn't checked it until after he'd downed a bottle of pills.

Carla's last entry was bizarre. Even cryptic in its way:

> *I opened the closet door and let him in. I laughed in his face cos I'm not afraid of him. He's real close. So close I can smell his colone, and he's got money. Lots of it. LOL. But I can slit his throat when I'm high. I can do anything. I can climb the wall on my hands and feet. Like a super hero. Carla the Conkerer. Is coming to a place near you. Watch out.*

I closed the book, wondering when the room had grown so cold and silent. I switched off the classroom light and tiptoed down the hallway towards the entrance hall. The light was on in Robin's office so I did an abrupt turn and rushed out through the back exit instead. Something had set my blood racing. That image of Carla climbing the wall. I remembered Birdie trying to clamber up a wallpaper-covered wall, her hair sticking out in clumps from her scalp as if someone had shaved bits of it off. I was watching her, my left eye throbbing with pain. Who would shave her head? Her lovely wavy hair? I fumbled with the ignition, my hands trembling and sweaty. I needed to go to the mall. Needed the bright lights and fake air. Needed to buy something.

The engine pulsed into life and I pulled out of the parking lot. No matter how hard I blinked my eyes, I could still see Birdie. Thin and bony, like an insect, her arms and legs splayed like a daddy longlegs as she tried to clamber upwards. Pulled herself up onto a crocheted wall hanging – a black silhouette against the throbbing mess of flowered wallpaper. And someone nearby was laughing. Gut-wrenching laughter. More than one person giggling and snorting. Then she slid downwards, fell and cracked her head. Her skin split like a melon, spilling red juice onto the floor. My throat was paralyzed. No voice.

A screech of brakes and a screaming horn told me I'd strayed into the next lane. I snapped to attention and swerved back. *Pull yourself together.* Gripping the wheel, I took a deep breath to steady my jangling nerves. Maybe it was time to talk to Linda Martin, my ex-social worker, before the visions consumed my newly discovered happiness.

My phone rang and Guy's voice flooded the car. I let out a deep sigh of relief.

"Are you OK?" he asked.

"Of course. Just happy to hear your voice."

"I've got a surprise for you."

"Tell me, tell me," I begged like a child.

"You have a decent bikini?"

I had to think hard. I hadn't been swimming in eons. "I used to have a one-piece. Think I left it in the change room last spring when we took the kids swimming."

"Then go buy yourself something brief and sexy. Get two or three. You'll need them."

"For what?" I'd never needed swimwear since I'd never been anywhere on holiday except the lake. Nowhere hot or exotic. No all-inclusives to Mexico or the Caribbean.

"We're going to Vegas next week. Dad's treat. A suite at the Bellagio. Five days of sin under a sweltering sun. It is your spring break isn't it?"

I couldn't restrain a squeal of excitement. "You mean five days together. No work. No phones. No worries."

"That's what I love about you, Anna. You're so enthusiastic. So easy to please."

If only he knew how easy. My blood was already racing at the thought of scouring the mall for swimwear. I couldn't wait to get going, but had to stop off at the condo where Guy said he'd left another gift for me. It turned out to be a credit card in my name with a staggering limit of twenty thousand dollars. A handwritten note propped beside it on the table said:

> *All yours, I'll take care of the monthly balance.*
> *Shop your heart out.*

In the past I'd had to beg for a two-grand limit, which I'd somehow wheedled up to four. Now this card burned like fire in my hand. I raced down to the car, buzzing with apprehension, and I barely noticed the rain slashing across the windshield when I pulled out of the underground garage.

-

I chose three bikinis in the end. Pale pink edged with black, a strapless gold confection with tiny triangular bottoms and a stark white two-piece with halter neck and scalloped edges. I was on an all-time high when I found the last one and just had to buy the sheer white cover-up with its turquoise beaded trim, and the black fringed wrap as well as the tiny pink robe with the flounces. Five days in Vegas also meant I'd need some suitable hot weather clothes, so by the time I was done scouring the stores, I'd bought cut-offs, strappy tops, and a different dress for each night out. My favorite, a cream, silk sheath, just had to have a chunky, gold necklace to match.

When I added up the cost, I realized I'd dropped close to seven grand. My heart thudded at the enormity of the amount until I convinced myself that Guy had given this gladly and I had to learn to accept his generosity instead of acting like a guilty kid. All those years of deprivation had convinced me I didn't deserve to enjoy luxury. That somehow, I always had to fight, cheat, lie or sleep my way into enjoying the good life. But now I was determined to give it a damned good try. I clutched the Visa in my palm like a lucky rabbit's paw and made a beeline for the exit. Whatever Vegas had in store, I was ready for it.

Or thought I was, considering what actually unfolded there.

11

By the time I got to school the next day, I'd forgotten all my worries. Guy had ordered in sushi then made me model all my swimwear purchases, making sure to peel each one off with intense attention to detail. Then we'd eaten supper washed down with a bottle of champagne and staggered into the bedroom to make wild, tipsy love. I'd woken with a slight headache but a warm glow from the amazing sex and the dizzying list of shows Guy had booked for our trip.

My mind was so occupied I barely registered the empty corridors. Floating into the staffroom I stopped dead at the sight of everyone gathered there, grim-faced like guests at a wake.

"What's wrong?"

Robin stood up, his face leached of color. "I guess you didn't get the message," he said.

"What message?" I realized I still hadn't told them about my move.

Daphne shuffled the folders in front of her. "I tried her number, Robin. It wasn't in service."

"Sorry. I changed it." The color rushed to my face. "What's happened?"

Sabrina's eyebrows almost hit her hairline, but I glanced away. Robin cleared his throat. His foot tapped a frantic tattoo under the table.

"Carla's gone missing. Her mom called last night. Said they haven't seen her for the last ten days."

I sank down onto a chair. Sabrina reached out and squeezed my shoulder.

Robin cleared his throat, his sallow cheeks flushed at the sudden attention thrust on him. "The new job was going really well. She was helping out at home with groceries but then apparently, she left work one night and never showed up at home. Mom's tried all her friends. Carla's never stayed away for longer than two days at a time. She's protective of her little brothers and baby sister."

"I bet some asshole picked her up in the parking lot," said Sabrina. "Weirdos hang out there late at night, just waiting for someone like her to show up."

The other teachers nodded in agreement. Norm even patted Sabrina on the back saying *right on, tell it like it is.* She shook off his hand as if ridding herself of an irritating insect.

Robin coughed into his palm. "You're probably dead on, Sabrina. But if we want to find out what happened to her, we need information. Facts. So if any of you know *anything*. Names, contacts, places that could help in any way, talk to me. Come to my office. Don't hold anything back. I'll pass it on to the authorities."

"You think the cops will actually do anything?" said Fran, leaning forward and looking round at all of us. "Tom says these kind of cases get low priority."

"Too right," said Sabrina. "Especially if her parents don't make enough noise about it."

When the meeting was over, I staggered back to the classroom. The after-effects of last night's champagne caused a steady buzzing in my head. My excitement about the new clothes and the trip had faded, sucked away by a nasty current of danger.

Robin had canceled classes for a prep day, so I looked around my empty classroom and began to wonder if it was time to pack this job in. Find work in a bank or a real estate office or the perfume counter of a chain store instead of coming here day after day to dive back into the seamy lifestyle I'd fought so hard to escape. Staying here would always remind me of Birdie and my old life. I'd never put the memories to rest.

Then it occurred to me that now I'd met Guy I could join the family bandwagon. Contribute to Gord's education super-dynasty with some practical, usable ideas. The image of that perfect bathroom on the edge of the wild forest flooded into my head. I wanted that. I wanted the pillowy towels, the marble walls, the perfumed lotions, the four-headed rain shower. All of it.

I told myself perhaps I had to stop trying to change these kids' lives. That nothing could drag them out of the scum. Only luck had got *me* out in time, otherwise I'd have been lost like Birdie. But why me? How had I survived?

I folded my arms and lay my head on the table trying not to think of Carla. Thoughts of her only led me to Birdie. I closed my eyes and saw that orange wallpaper, still heard the laughter, still felt that sense of being frozen – powerless to stop a pair of disembodied hands from grabbing Birdie's skinny arms and yanking her upwards. A hand tapped my shoulder and I almost jumped out of the chair, swinging my arm outwards and catching Robin on the jaw. He staggered backwards, holding his chin, his mouth saggy and trembling.

"What the hell, Anna?" he gasped. Faced with violence, Robin crumbled into a gibbering mess.

I settled him down with plenty of heartfelt apologies. Finally composed, he asked for Carla's journal.

"After the last time, we need to be vigilant," he said in a clipped tone.

I handed it to him. His eyebrows lifted at the massive spiderwebs drawn in black ink spread across the cover.

"Someone's come into her life. A man who scares her. It's pretty clear from the last few entries."

"The cops might know what to make of it," he said, taking it and scanning the cover, the tip of his tongue moistening his upper lip. He looked up at me with red-rimmed eyes in a pallid, jowly face.

"I should tell you, I've been thinking of retiring, Anna. Things are really getting to me now. I'm not sure how many more tragedies I can take before I realize that this job – maybe my whole life – is an exercise in futility. Pretty sad for a lifetime devoted to kids on the margin. I want to travel again. Maybe go to California and enjoy the sunshine for a while. These frigid winters are freezing my soul."

I felt a sudden stab of pity for him. The cute surfer boy was long gone. Instead, a faded, disillusioned old man looked back at me.

"You'd be missed, Robin. Give yourself some credit. We've had plenty of victories along the way and every one of them counts."

"Thanks for the kind words, Anna," he said, bowing his head as he left, sucking all the air from the room and leaving behind him a vacuum of negativity. I couldn't breathe, so I grabbed my bag and rushed out of the classroom.

Guy was still at work and I didn't relish sitting alone in the empty condo. Not the way I was feeling. So I drove towards the riverfront. Time on my hands meant time to remember. And the memories flooded in, menacing and dark. Thoughts of people and places from my past crowded up against images of Carla abducted by some crazy stranger. I glided past the whole food delis and the designer accessories stores. Past the patisserie with its trays of brightly colored macaroons until I reached the sandstone arches of the old Stone Arch Bridge.

The wind whipped my hair across my face as I climbed up the steps to the bridge. Birdie and I came here when we were still at the group home. In the summer holidays there were long days to fill when the staff were stretched to the limit with laundry, cleaning, and dealing with the older, troubled kids. They were only too happy to let us run off and play. I leaned against the stone parapet and remembered.

Birdie and me running through the park, scrambling up the grassy slopes, kicking up the nighttime debris. Crushed Styrofoam burger boxes, empty wine bottles and aerosol cans, used condoms like puddles of wrinkled skin among the tufts of grass and syringes scattered everywhere. A single mud-covered sneaker with no laces, a striped red silk scarf that Birdie wanted to drape round herself until I told her it might be infected with smallpox and that's how the Indians had died, catching it from contaminated blankets brought by the European settlers. She burst into tears and said I was lying but I told her for sure I read it in a history book at the library. Then she covered my mouth with a grubby hand and said I should stop reading so many books because they were turning me into a mean, cruel witch.

We ran back and forth across the bridge, past the joggers and the cyclists, trailing sticks along the red metal railing and making a loud *clunk clunk* sound. Louder than the rushing of the Saint Anthony Falls. Louder than the noise of cars and trucks roaring through the nearby city streets.

I held on to Birdie's hand and pulled her along so fast I could hear the chesty rasp of her breathing. She was whining, complaining her tummy hurt. But I knew it was only hunger because I felt the same gnawing in my own stomach. Ahead, the city skyline rose, shimmering in the sun, rich with the promise of food and relief from the never-ending ache.

Sometimes in the summer when the tourists thronged the river walks, we stood by the hot dog vendor until he threw us a bag of chips or a hot dog just so we'd move on. We loaded them with ketchup, mustard, sweet pickle and onions. Then we sat on a bench and wolfed them down, our hands, mouths and faces sticky with ketchup, the mustard dripping down our shirtfronts.

We watched the families stroll by, the happy kids holding ice-cream cones in one hand, the other clutching the hands of their parents. Sometimes they pointed and stared at us, but I just stuck my tongue out until they started crying. Birdie placed her hand on my arm and told me to stop being so rotten. I said I was only trying to protect her and she leaned her ketchup-smeared cheek against me and kissed my shoulder. Told me she loved me more than anyone in the world, which was easy because no one else cared about us. Then she made me play *Pick the perfect family* and together we studied each cluster of kids and parents and decided which we'd like to go home with if they asked us. Birdie always picked the families with only one child.

Our first placement after the group home was on the other side of the Stone Arch Bridge, with Rosa Flores-Rivera, a tiny dark-haired woman who lived alone above a launderette. Her children – two sons and a daughter – were grown and lived in California. Rosa had a heart full of love to give and we were the beneficiaries.

Too bad it couldn't last.

12

Over steaming cups of hot chocolate and a full plate of cinnamon buns Rosa told us she was lonely and missed being a mom. Birdie and I devoured the whole plate of pastries between us and Rosa didn't say a thing.

At first, it was like heaven living there. Stretched out on the blue flowered sofa, bowls of popcorn on our laps watching *The Fresh Prince of Bel-Air*. Breathing in the clean, soapy smell that wafted upstairs from the washing machines below. Vinnie, an ex-marine, lived in the apartment next to us. He had a bad case of the shakes. Rosa said he'd seen men tortured and killed in a war in some Far Eastern country and couldn't get the memories out of his head. He ordered pizzas or Chinese takeaway all the time. We heard the delivery boys ringing the doorbell at six o'clock every night.

Rosa cooked us food we'd never tasted before. Corn tortillas filled with beans, chicken tacos seasoned with lime and cilantro, omelets studded with red peppers and sprinkled with jalapeno cheese. Birdie and I sat at the kitchen table mouths wide open like a pair of baby birds, while Rosa's nimble fingers conjured up dish after dish of tasty food. Sometimes she'd leave a covered dish of leftovers outside Vinnie's place and next day he touched his hand to his forehead in a salute of thanks, but he never spoke or looked us in the eye.

I felt a strange sort of bond with him because even at that early age I understood how tough it is to look right at people – to meet their eyes. You can't unless you've had many people cheering you on in your life, loving you enough to wipe the snot from your nose, or cherish the cute way your face wrinkles up when you eat a pickle. To care about your cuts, scrapes, bruises, fears and nightmares or pat your head and tell you it doesn't matter when you wet the bed. A whole, sound person needs all of this to build up enough confidence to look a person in the eye. Looking away means you've already accepted your own insignificance. You don't matter. You trust nobody. Because you've already realized nobody gives a damn about you anyway. Vinnie understood that. He'd already seen what humans can do to each other. He knew how crappy life could really be.

Within two months of arriving at Rosa's, Birdie and I filled out until our cheeks were pink and chubby. Rosa scrubbed and mended our clothes, took us to the thrift stores to pick out pretty dresses that she altered on her sewing machine, and threaded ribbons into our clean, braided hair. At our new school Birdie was in her element. All the girls wanted to play with the chatty, smiling new girl. Not with me, the silent, brooding sister standing on the sidelines, waiting to pounce at the first hint of trouble.

Our newfound happiness and contentment lasted all of six months until Rosa's estranged husband, Perez, came back.

The tiny, neat apartment wasn't big enough for his husky, square-shouldered frame. He swept in like a great thundercloud, blocking the sunlight that streamed through the kitchen windows and making the walls tremble. Muscular arms loaded with packages, he stomped across the floor to shower Rosa with chocolates, cookies, underwear, perfume. Gifts for the wife he'd missed so much. Then he took one look at us, scowled and carried on as if we were invisible. Birdie was crushed. She batted her eyelashes, tilted her head and even did a couple of twirls, believing her cuteness was enough to win him over. Enough to guarantee her an instant father. But Perez wasn't buying any of it. He didn't even watch when she recited a poem we learned at school, and then performed the silly dance that went along with it.

My hands curled and uncurled into fists at my sides. I even told her she looked stupid but she didn't listen and shook my hand away. That's when Perez's large fist crashed down on the kitchen table, sending Rosa's frog salt and pepper shakers tumbling to the floor. Birdie froze and dove down to rescue them, but Rosa's chirpiness vanished, replaced by white-faced panic as she grabbed Birdie's arm and chivvied us off to the bedroom. I had to drag Birdie there, her heels skidding along the floor, the salt shaker clutched in her hand.

Once the door shut, Birdie started to gulp in air as if she was going to cry. *There's a monster inside that man*, she said. I slipped my hand into hers and together we crept close to the door. Our ears pinned to the wall, we heard him tell Rosa stories about his stint in the North Dakota oil patch. About the fortune he'd made then lost. The poker, whisky and cocaine that devoured his money. Now all he had left was his dear, sweet Rosa and maybe she didn't even want him, now she has two foster kids. Little brats who weren't even Latina. *What does she take him for?*

Before she could even answer that question, he burst into loud sobs, calling himself a loser, and a worthless bum with no right to live. The sobs escalated until the loud, scraping noise of chair legs dragging across the floor was followed by the screech of the kitchen drawer being yanked open. I peeked through a crack in the door. He'd taken out a kitchen knife and he was jabbing at his chest yelling *Madre de dios me destruya*. Rosa was plastered against the wall, her hands clamped over her ears. Birdie and I sucked in our breath as he lunged forward, grabbed Rosa's hand and forced the knife handle into it, screaming, *I'm a worthless piece of shit. Cut my throat. Stab me through the heart.*

She screamed and wailed *no no te amo te amo* as she tried to yank the knife back.

Birdie was frozen to the spot, pee dribbling down her leg. I had to get her out of there even though I was scared for Rosa. Then someone started banging on the front door. Grasping the knife again, Perez threw Rosa against the wall, charged towards the door and threw it open. On the other side Vinnie stood, muscular arms bulging from a baggy wife beater shirt, his red hair sticking up at all angles and his whole body shaking. He reached up with one meaty hand and clamped hold of Perez's arm. They faced off like battling rams. Rosa pulled herself to her feet and staggered over to them. She grabbed at Perez's arm trying to pull him back from the door, but he swatted her like a bug with one heavy blow, and sent her crashing against the kitchen table.

That was my signal. I grabbed Birdie's hand and we ran. We tore out of the apartment without even putting on our shoes and slid down the stairs. I called emergency from a nearby convenience store and we ended up at the cop station, eating licorice sticks and Krispy Kreme donuts. We started in on a whole box. A dozen sugar dipped. Birdie threw up in the garbage can, then sat back and stuffed more into her mouth, scared someone would take them away. We swung our shoeless feet against the chair legs and waited to see who'd come to get us. Three hours later the emergency social worker, a pale, spindly thing in a beige trench coat and plaid scarf, woke us up. She drove us back to the group home, barely exchanging a word. After that we never saw Rosa again or learned what happened to her or Perez or Vinnie.

-

I snapped back to reality and realized it was raining, so I started back to the car. Rosa's was not the nightmare place with the flowered wallpaper. Her walls were painted pure white. I knew that because I remembered bright red blood spattered across the white expanse, like a string of tiny flowers sprayed in a diagonal line.

I decided to go back and check out the riverside apartment from the previous evening. As I drove, I wondered if Carla might have been picked up from the same spot I met Dane. The place where the Ken doll guy prowled back and forth in his glossy SUV with the tinted windows. But it was noon now and the nighttime's menace was gone, replaced by the lively bustle of office workers sitting on benches or sprawled on the riverbank eating lunch and enjoying the rush and sparkle of the water.

A couple of blocks further north was the in-between place where you might get mugged walking home from the theater or meet a glassy-eyed glue sniffer staggering towards you begging for a quarter. I stopped outside the apartment building where I'd seen Dane. It was a three-story block of red brick with zero architectural merit. No doubt doomed to come under the wreckers' ball and make way for yet another swanky riverside condo block. I scanned the windows for the wallpaper room. In the sunlight, the panes appeared dirt-smudged, with broken blinds hanging askew.

Then I saw it again. A faded square of orangey yellow flowers. The sickly expanse that always appeared in the image of Birdie, climbing upwards, hair sprayed out in a static fuzz. Me looking on, my eye throbbing, swollen and painful when I touched it. Then the laughter. A smoker's hoarse laughter. More than one person. Men and women. A chemical smell, like burning plastic and dried piss.

I closed my eyes, pressed my face on the steering wheel and tried to think of Vegas though I had no frame of reference, no picture to conjure up the place in my mind. I tried not to think of Birdie climbing or Dane getting into the stranger's SUV or Carla being lured by some creep in the mall parking lot.

When I finally got my breathing under control and dared to look upwards, a parking meter guy was pulling out a pen ready to ticket me. I revved up the engine just before he could plant the ticket on my windshield and screeched away in a cloud of burning rubber. Two hundred bucks could buy me a nice pair of sandals and besides, I'd taken down the number of the apartment block. I had to get to Linda Martin's office and tell her I'd remembered something. Maybe it could help us find out what happened to Birdie.

13

Linda Martin had been my social worker when I was placed with the Levines. I hadn't seen her since then. Hadn't needed to. Or maybe hadn't wanted to.

Her office was plastered with posters. One was a super-hero decal with a big purple SW and the words *Super Social Worker* emblazoned across. Above her desk a bright green poster declared, *There can't be a crisis today, my schedule is already full*. But the best one featured a trim fifties lady and read, *As a social worker, doing a good job is like wetting your pants in a dark suit. You get a warm feeling but nobody else notices*. I was chuckling at that when Linda's trilling voice interrupted my thoughts.

"Anna – I had to do a double take when I saw you there. I barely recognized you."

I blinked my eyes twice and looked at her. She was wearing a turquoise jacket I'd seen last year in the clearance section at the Gap and she'd cut her hair in a short, choppy style that emphasized her sagging jowls. Her attempt at pleasantries left a sour, flat feeling in my gut.

I tilted my head away and concentrated on the fifties lady in the poster. She was stylish in a neat Audrey Hepburn suit and Gucci pillbox hat.

"Did you pull my file?"

"Well it's been a while, so I had to dig deep to access it."

I turned to watch her shuffling through a green folder. "Did you read my email?"

Red blobs flared across her cheeks as she lowered her eyes away from me. "I did."

"And?"

She glanced over some papers she'd taken from the file. "You mention an address."

"And I told you about Birdie climbing up the wall? The laughter? My swollen eye?"

She sighed and picked up a printout. "I'll read your statement: *I remember seeing Birdie climb up a wall with flowered wallpaper. There was a stink of burning plastic in the air. It felt like my eye was injured*," she recited, her eyes flickering over the paper. She looked up at me, her eyebrows lifting. "Shall I go on?"

Yellow light buzzed around her head. I blinked my eyes. There were penciled-in gaps on her sparse eyebrows. I shook my head. "And what do the records say about that placement?"

She sighed, her face settling into a martyr's smile. Rainbow letters above her head spelled out the words, *I'm a social worker. I do my own stunts.* What was with this hero fixation?

"The records show, Anna, that Birdie wasn't with you at that particular placement. Before the Levines." She pursed her mouth so tight, her lips disappeared. She stared at me, tapping the desk, waiting for me to talk.

I didn't.

I knew silence was poison for people like Linda, so she kept on babbling as she pulled out a dog-eared paper and waved it in the air. "This report shows there's nothing to connect that particular place with her disappearance."

I brushed aside the desk magnet with all the little pins sticking to it. "I happen to know she was there. I keep remembering her there. And I remember other placements. Rosa Flores-Rivera. The cop station. The donuts. After that the group home, then some other useless placement, *then* the place with the wallpaper."

She sat back, her eyes crinkling with the semblance of pity. "I don't mind going over this with you, Anna. The system didn't give you what you needed at that time and yet you've done so well for yourself. Overcome chronic instability, neglect as well as unbelievable trauma. Some kids never recover from the horrors you've been through, but you've triumphed. Look at the way you're dressed. Gorgeous," she said, her watery eyes devouring my camel coat.

"Anna, I understand how trauma and chronic grief can change the way you remember events in your life, so I'll clarify it all for you. You were taken from the Rivera place after the double stabbing."

"What stabbing? We left before anyone was hurt."

She shook her head. "Mr. Vincent Cavallo, an ex-marine suffering from PTSD, fatally stabbed Rosa and her husband Perez. You and Birdie witnessed the whole thing. Luckily, Mr. Cavallo spared the two of you and took you out onto the street just as the police arrived."

I vowed I'd never cry again but the tears started to trickle down my cheeks. "That's not how it happened. Vinnie was protecting Rosa. Perez stabbed her then attacked Vinnie."

"That's not the story that the jury heard, Anna. Cavallo was found guilty of killing Perez and Rosa."

"He wouldn't do that. He was trying to save her."

"At the time you said you didn't witness the incident, Anna."

"I was a kid. My head was mixed up."

"They decided not to press you for information in view of your age and the traumatic circumstances."

"He's in jail?"

"Not exactly. He was found to be suffering from severe PTSD."

"But he's locked up?"

She nodded. "Probably for life."

Her voice became so soft I could barely hear her through the buzzing in my head. "The emergency social worker took you back to the group home on Ardis Street. During that period you turned thirteen, a kid hanged himself there and Birdie got involved with an older crowd. There was substance abuse involved and she ran away several times after that until she finally disappeared later at the age of fifteen."

"No – never. Not without me."

She reached across the table and took my hand. I ripped it away.

"That all happened before my time, Anna, but the documentation is all here. There's even a picture of her at an ATM machine with one of the older teens, withdrawing money on a stolen card."

She pushed a grainy black and white picture towards me. Two hunched grayish shapes in a glassed-in space. Formless blobs that could be anyone. I looked away.

"This is all a mistake. Why do I keep seeing her in the wallpaper room?"

Sympathy dripped from Linda's eyes. "Like I always tell you. Almost fifteen years ago, somebody did a sloppy placement job. Failed to conduct a thorough background check. You were put into a house of substance abusers. They gave you drugs. Bad drugs that messed with your head. The memories are probably hallucinations, Anna. Distortions of the truth."

I pulled the picture towards me. It was hard to make Birdie out from the mass of gray-white pixels, but a hunched form slowly materialized, her hair a shock of black static. I shoved it away.

"I have to go. Get ready for a trip." I stood up, tipping the chair over in my haste.

She moved around the desk, a turquoise smudge. "Are you sure you're feeling okay, Anna? You can wait here. I'll get you a coffee. I'll get our psychologist to go over some of the difficult stuff."

I had to get air. That office was squeezing the life out of me.

"Gotta go," I mumbled and flung the door open. I strode past the cubicle offices, avoiding eye contact with anyone and stopped at the *Missing* posters. Grainy, smiling faces looked out at me. A row of them. But where was Birdie's picture? The one that said, *Have you seen this girl? Disappeared without a trace.* Her face. My face. The fuzzy dotted picture of her at the ATM.

Tears welled up in my eyes and I looked back. Linda stood at the far end of the hallway watching me, her arms folded, her eyes filled with pity. The elevator doors swished open and I dove inside. Guy could never know about any of this. I'd always looked out for myself. Didn't need anyone sharing my private pain, so I wasn't about to let anyone else into that world. Especially Guy. Too much was at stake. Besides, I'd come this far in my life by treating everyone as an outsider.

I burst out into the open air, longing for the calm anonymity of the mall. I was drained. Sucked out. Only the flowery coconut warmth, the tinkling music and the glitter of new things would soothe me. And I could also check out the shoe stores that I'd forgotten to even glance at the day before. After all, we were going to Vegas for five days. I'd need sandals for the pool, and some strappy, glitzy evening shoes. Hell – maybe I'd buy two or three pairs or more if the mood struck me.

14

When the plane took off for Vegas on Sunday evening, I lay back in my seat going over the visit to Linda Martin. She was dead wrong about my memory being distorted. Since I met Guy my thoughts had been more lucid. No worries about money meant more time to piece together our story – Birdie's and mine – if I could just stay focused.

She'd been right about the group home. When Birdie and I were placed back there we went to KC's funeral. KC was a sixteen-year-old boy who'd hanged himself in the bathroom with a chain of sneaker laces. We didn't want to go but the staff said we had to pay our respects, even though Birdie said she'd faint if she saw a dead body. But I said I'd be right there for her, so she clung to me the entire car ride there.

When we entered the funeral chapel with its sweet stink of formaldehyde and flowers, Birdie clasped my hand so hard she crushed the bones of my fingers. Karen and Addie, young staff from the home, pushed us forward through the small crowd, herding us ever closer to the wooden casket at the front of the room.

Everyone from the group home was there as well as a few others who looked like KC's relatives. His mom, a brassy blonde in red stilettos, tight jeans and a skimpy black leather jacket over a pink tank top, sobbed into a spotted handkerchief, her wails soaring up and over the hum of voices. A bald man with an eagle tattoo across the back of his head gathered her into his arms and kissed her hair.

Too late for that show now, whispered Karen.

She never had two minutes for him when he was alive, said Addie. *Chose eagle head over her own kid.*

When we reached the casket, Birdie and I were nose level with the body. Birdie pulled back, but Addie was unyielding.

He looks so peaceful, said Karen.

As if he's sleeping, said Addie.

He just looks dead, said Birdie and I had to agree. There was no life in that stiff doll with its waxy, bloated face. No sign of KC, the crazy kid with the Minnesota Wild hat, scooting along the street on his skateboard. The joker who used to slurp the milk from his Cheerios, then Birdie would watch as he speared each soggy piece with the tip of his tongue like a lizard.

Birdie started to sniffle, rubbing a fist across her eyes. Then to cry. *He's dead and gone*, she chanted, over and over until the sobbing mother stopped her wailing and directed a red-eyed glare at us. I glowered back at her, narrowing my eyes and folding Birdie against my chest. And I asked myself, why did his mom desert him? Abandon him so many times he felt worthless, ashamed – not good enough to be wanted or loved. A stray dog – no home to call his own.

"You scared of flying?" a voice said. I blinked my eyes to see Guy staring at me. "You looked like you were gonna burst into tears."

"It's my first time," I said. I couldn't share my pain with Guy. I hadn't even told him about Carla. Didn't want to burden him with all my worries.

His face split into a broad grin. "You're a strange one, Anna. You should've told me this is your maiden voyage. Let's celebrate," he said, kissing my cheek.

We were in business class so, within minutes, we were both nursing a glass of chilled Prosecco and nibbling on a succulent turkey and cranberry brioche.

"We're flying in at night so you get to see the Vegas lights and skyline. You're gonna love it."

I took a drink and cuddled against his shoulder. "I know I will."

Five days of freedom lay ahead. No work, no worries, no memories. And Guy would be away from Gord and all his demands. Gord was in the habit of calling Guy at the same time every night. Nine on the dot. Holding Guy hostage for at least half an hour. And there was no way to give him the brush-off. Guy would lean back in a chair and close his eyes as if all he wanted to do was sleep after a long day at school, not to mention he hadn't even touched the briefcase full of student term papers. Sometimes he rubbed his eyes so hard, his glasses slipped off his nose onto his cheek and I felt a pang of pity for him.

Once, I asked him why Gord called so much.

"I'm a vital part of the business. Being a consultant with a PhD behind my name lends a certain gravitas and credibility to the entire operation, but Dad still gets a bit riled that he only has a Masters."

I just hoped that Gord would lay off the calls while we were away. I wanted this to be a real escape for both of us.

Guy was right. I loved Vegas. The town was one giant mall. We walked from one hotel to another, from one glossy shopping area with its fake, painted sky, marble walls and granite-tiled streets to another expanse of premium outlet stores. Cruised entire blocks where fake European monuments from Rome, Venice, Paris and Florence rubbed shoulders with karaoke bars and yard-long margarita stands.

The only time we ventured outside during the day was to the pool, a glassy turquoise expanse of water with a gushing fountain at one end. Tall cypress, drooping palm trees and cone-shaped shrubs in cream ceramic pots surrounded the pool area. White umbrellas shaded plump couches inside luxury cabanas and the massive towers of the Aria and Cosmopolitan hotels rose like glittering monoliths in the distance.

We lounged on the daybeds, sipping on mojitos until we were so tipsy we slid into the water to cool our heads. We nibbled on sushi, shrimp ceviche and buffalo wings, then dragged our feet past the clanking slot machines to shower and get dressed for the evening show. Our room was a fountain view suite with the dancing waters directly below. I stood watching them at the window, Guy's arms round my waist, his warm breath on the back of my neck.

"Anything you ask for, Anna. I'll give it to you. I want to make you happy," he whispered.

"I've never seen anything so beautiful," I said, thinking this moment was the closest to perfection I'd ever been.

The tightness of fear almost slipped away from me when he carried me to the bed. If I could just let go. Let that warm, supple feeling take over my body. Say I loved him. Trusted him. Felt safe with him. Would climb inside him if I could. But I couldn't find the words, couldn't rid myself of that tiny thread of doubt. Instead I concentrated on the way he thrust himself into me, clutching him closer, faster, harder until we both shuddered to a sweaty, trembling climax.

He rolled onto his back and trailed a hand across my breast. "Hell, Anna, you're on fire."

At the Cirque show, I soaked in the music, the dazzling costumes and the rainbow spectacle of dancers, aerialists and gymnasts, while coasting on a perfect buzz from two giant gin and tonics stuffed with fresh lime. I'd never seen anything so magical and had to bite my lip to stem the tears when I remembered all those years of deprivation. The grinding monotony of poverty, the total absence of love and care from anyone after Dennis. The gnawing uncertainty and suspicion about every person in my life.

No wonder I'd buried myself in books.

Maybe that was when Birdie began to turn away from me.

Maybe she had good reason to run away when I lost myself in a fantasy world that didn't include her.

The weight of grief pressed down on my chest until I thought I would suffocate, then the waitress arrived with our drinks. Another sweating gin and tonic chilled my hand. I gulped it down, thankful it tasted more like a double or triple. By the time we hit the casino I was flying high. Guy bought me a thousand bucks worth of chips at the roulette wheel and within half an hour I was up to eight grand. He laughed when I gathered up the chips and hurried away from the table towards the cashier.

"Keep going. You're on a roll."

"No chance," I said, pushing the chips towards the cashier. "I'm keeping this." I'd never even seen this much cash, let alone held it in my hands. Wasting it on stupid games seemed like a crime.

He shrugged. "Taking risks, Anna. That's what gambling's all about."

I couldn't get far enough away from the jangling machines and flashing lights. "Let's eat. My treat."

We sat at the restaurant overlooking the fountains and ate scallops and steak washed down with never-ending bottles of wine. Guy chatted about his research project over dinner. Something about a special outreach program for homeless kids that he was absolutely committed to seeing through until the end, but the sound of his voice soon merged with the hiss of the fountains and the tinkling of background music. Sparkling lights reflected on the water, making the night so magical I felt free for the first time in years. I could be anyone in this make-believe place. History and substance were irrelevant here. Guy didn't seem to notice my distraction. Just kept talking while I continued drinking, my head becoming foggier with each glass of wine.

When Guy suggested we go dancing it seemed like the best idea ever. I'd never been one for dancing or letting loose but in Vegas I felt like I could fly.

The night was a blur after that. We swept into a rooftop club, high above The Strip. A crush of scantily clad bodies milled around us and music pounded so loud the floor shook. Somehow, I always had a drink in my hand, garnished with pineapples, mint sprigs, cucumber, olives. We wandered by floodlit palm trees and illuminated hot tubs, where the smells of sweat, cologne and perfume mixed with booze and the musky tang of weed. Guy pulled me onto the dance floor and I threw my head back to gaze up at the stars, then ground my body into his until he kissed me so hard I gasped for air.

Next, I remember speeding down The Strip in an open-topped car. I stood on the seat and stretched my arms towards the sky, screaming and whooping at the top of my lungs. Guy clamped his hands around my hips and pulled me down just as we sped towards a low-hanging tree branch. I fell back onto his lap, nuzzling at his ear, whispering I loved him more than anyone I'd ever met. After that, the stars seemed to swoop down towards me and I passed out.

–

"Morning, Mrs. Franzen," said a voice in my ear. I tried to open my eyes but the iron band that gripped my forehead forced them shut. Dim memories emerged from the night before; standing under an arch of fake pink and white flowers; a man in a gray suit reading from a white book; people laughing around me; a bunch of flowers shoved into my hand. My hand. I touched the left ring finger. Felt the smooth rim of a metal band.

"We're married?"

I felt Guy bounce onto the bed beside me. "We are, my darling, sexy wife."

"You proposed to me?"

He shook his head. "I said *yes*." A sharp intake of breath. "You don't remember?"

"I think I have to throw up," I said, pulling myself upright as waves of nausea rolled through my body, sending me in a headlong dash to the bathroom where I sat on the floor, my head poised over the toilet bowl.

After the purge, I splashed my face with cold water and took three aspirin, then stood under the shower trying to understand exactly what I'd done. Had I really proposed to Guy? The memories were fuzzy. Maybe it happened in the back of that limo? Why had I done it? A catalogue of reasons clicked through my mind. If I married him, I'd be safe. He'd take care of me forever. I liked being with him and the sex was mind-blowing. Besides, maybe this was the closest I'd get to that feeling other people with a normal past called love.

The only person I'd ever truly loved was Birdie, and when she'd gone my heart was torn in two.

Afterwards – if I believed Linda Martin – I'd descended into a kind of hell, drifting into homes where I was entrusted to a bunch of weirdos, drunks and drug addicts.

But Guy offered the ultimate sanctuary. He promised permanence and belonging.

What was there to think about? I'd never have to go back to my old life. I could have everything I wanted. The money, the gorgeous home, that bathroom, endless guilt-free shopping. I'd be protected, pampered, loved like I always should have been. What the hell was I worried about? I'd try – I mean really try – to love Guy the way he loved me.

When I burst out of the bathroom he was sulking on the chaise longue.

"So, Mr. Franzen, Mrs. Franzen wants breakfast," I said, smiling as widely as I could. "Let's phone room service for the biggest wedding breakfast ever."

"You got it," he said, jumping up like a child who'd been pacified. "Your wish is my command."

–

Later, Guy insisted on taking a walk along The Strip. I held onto his hand, jarred by the suffocating heat and a nagging hangover. Guy chattered on as we pushed our way through the crush of tourists – the knots of young guys swigging beer, the micro-skirted bachelorettes and their bridesmaids teetering in nine-inch heels and sucking at yard-long frozen margaritas. We made our way past the sunbaked Mexicans in T-shirts emblazoned with *Girls Girls Girls*, snapping their handfuls of escort cards and trying to push one into Guy's hand. He swatted the guy away and kissed me on the cheek.

"They're crazy. My wife is the hottest chick around here. No need for a cheap hooker."

At one time I thought Birdie might have come here, drawn by the tinsel and lights and glamor. I searched for her face among the girls in thigh-high skirts, even on the billboards of vans that cruised The Strip offering *Hot Babes Direct to You*.

Guy's arm circled my waist, propelling me along, past a faded looking Elvis with ratty toupee and sideburns dripping blackish sweat. He posed next to a hollow-eyed Marilyn Monroe in white halter-necked dress. It cost ten bucks to pose with both of them, but tourists passed by without a glance.

The pulse at the side of my temples throbbed. I breathed mouthfuls of hot, dusty air. Riding the escalators that led to the overpass, I could barely touch the sunbaked rail. At the top, a row of panhandlers begged for money. One with a soft-eyed lab puppy sipping from an ice-cream carton filled with water. At the bottom of the escalator an old woman lay beside the scrubby hedge, head thrown back, a frothy stream of spittle dribbling from her mouth. Two calloused feet stuck out, one bare, the other dangling a broken sandal. A crowd had gathered, staring, wondering if she was dead, until her husband, a stringy-haired old guy wearing a stained T-shirt and ragged, plaid shorts rose from his sleep behind the bushes and started to yell, *Whaddya want? A picture or something?* With his hands clenched into fists, he began to dance around like a boxer.

Guy propelled me away. "Low life panhandlers," he hissed.

A sour taste filled my mouth. "Don't judge. You don't know what circumstances brought them to this," I snapped. But I didn't want to start a fight. Not on my first day of marriage.

His hand slipped into mine. "You're such a sensitive soul and I don't appreciate you enough for it, Mrs. Franzen."

Head buzzing and aching to get back into the cool sanctuary of a hotel or mall, I forced a smile and held out my cheek for him to kiss. A trio of topless showgirls, their nipples topped with shiny red tassels giggled at the sight of us. Guy insisted that he get his picture taken with them. They stood, one foot in front of the other, one hand resting on a tiny hip, the other held up in a dancer's pose. Guy grinned as I clicked the camera and I imagined that his hand slipped low enough to pinch the pert bum of the youngest one. I snapped the picture again and decided it was just a trick of the sunlight.

Birdie always loved to pose. If she wasn't pirouetting on a table, she'd be standing in front of a mirror practicing poses. In the group home she'd steal lipsticks from the older girls' rooms, plaster it on her already pink lips then turn her face sideways and pout at her reflection. I'd tell her she was just slapping stinky whale grease on her mouth and besides it was toxic and carcinogenic. She'd just shrug and tell me not to be such a grouch. *Why don't you just try to enjoy yourself*, she'd say, *live your life instead of griping all the time and picking out the bad, scary things. That's how you get to be popular.*

Remembering those words coming from her smudgy lipstick mouth made my throat catch. I swallowed hard.

"We done?" said Guy, his smile looking strained. I snapped back to the present, but not before a blurry impression flashed across my mind. The white glare of a camera flash illuminating Birdie's swollen, red-rimmed eyes. A crudely tattooed hand trying to wipe away smudged mascara. I gasped at the impact of the vision.

"Anna, snap out of it," said a voice on the periphery of my consciousness. Then, just as my legs threatened to give way beneath me, a pair of strong hands held me up.

"Must be the hangover," I said, feeling Guy's arms grip me tightly. "Or maybe the heat."

–

At the airport, Nancy towered like an elegant giraffe above the knots of friends and relatives. Chic and untouchable in a white windbreaker, she provided a glaring contrast to Gord's shiny, spray-tanned face hovering above the bunch of white roses clutched to his chest. He thrust them at me, then grabbed me round the waist and kissed both cheeks as if we'd known each other for years. Nancy swooped in on Guy, kissing his face, stroking his hair, and clinging to him as if he'd been away for weeks. Then, as if she'd just remembered I was standing there, she turned and gathered me to her, crushing my face into her narrow bosom.

"I've always longed for a daughter and now here she is," she said, tears misting her eyes as she held my shoulders to look at me. Jarred by her scrutiny of my naked face, I looked away. My mouth felt like sandpaper and tasted like stale airline coffee.

"Don't be shy now. Show me that ring."

I held out my hand in the way I'd seen the girls do it on TV, arching my wrist to allow the diamond to twinkle and catch the light. It was a beautiful stone. Probably the most expensive item I'd ever owned. We'd shopped for it in the mall at Caesars Palace once my hangover had receded.

I wiggled the finger, loving the tiny rainbows of light that sparkled from each facet of its perfect surface, even though a niggling voice in my head kept saying this could never last. That somehow, I'd aimed too high and would eventually get my come-uppance. But I knew I'd wanted this. Wanted it so badly, and for a long, long time.

Nancy held on to my hand long enough to glance from her own diamond ring to mine as if comparing their size. "Quite, quite lovely," she said, pasting on a furtive smile and dropping my hand. "My son always had great taste."

Gord slapped Guy on the back. "It's a rock, son," he said, winking. "You must've woven some kind of spell on our boy, Anna."

They acted like Guy and I had been dating for years, but fake familiarity wasn't new to me. I was raised on it. The shallow type of interest that flares briefly in people you've just met, then quickly fades when reality sets in. When you realize you have absolutely nothing in common and you actually dislike the things you do know about each other. Would this be the case with Guy's family?

I hadn't felt that kind of boredom or insecurity with Guy. I like to think the way he cared for me was solid and real. That he appreciated me for who I was, or who I wanted him to *believe* I was. But he'd never know the real me. I'd make sure of that. The real me was private – strictly off-limits. Only Birdie knew me inside and out and I still had to try and find my way back to her.

She was the only person in the world who could see through all my pretense, who could know what I was thinking just from the expression on my face or the tone of my voice. Who could stop my breath with just a look or a word.

So, being the chameleon I was, I went along with Gord and Nancy and smiled in a modest and daughterly way. "Actually, I think your son enchanted *me*." I latched onto Guy's arm. "It was the most romantic getaway. Thank you both so much for your generosity."

Nancy clasped her hands together. Tears pooled in her eyes as she tilted her head and let out a long sigh. "So sweet. But you must allow us to have a little celebration this weekend. Just a few close friends and relatives to mark the occasion."

A sudden gust of air conditioning chilled my skin and somewhere in a far corridor a muffled voice announced final call for a flight to London. I briefly imagined dropping everything and running until I found that departure lounge and stormed my way onto the plane. Instead, I leaned in closer to Guy, resting my face against him.

"We'd be delighted, Mom. Wouldn't we, Anna?" He nudged my shoulder.

"Absolutely," I said, already dreading the thought of a day in the Franzen family spotlight. "We'd really appreciate it," was all I could muster.

All I wanted was a nap in the back seat of the car but Nancy chatted nonstop the entire journey home about wedding cakes, canapés and champagne.

"I must come with you to buy a dress, Anna. We'll find something white, floaty and exquisite – I mean, not a formal wedding dress, but maybe a little retro number with a pillbox hat and veil – or perhaps you'd prefer a circlet of flowers and something long and lacy. A touch of Pre-Raphaelite romance."

I supposed if it meant another shopping trip, I'd accommodate her. "Late closing on Thursday. We'll do it then," I said, reaching for Guy's hand.

"Perfect," Nancy said, turning to look at Gord and stroke the side of his face. "I can't wait."

"Of course, sweetheart," he said, "go out and buy the most beautiful dress for our new daughter-in-law. No expense spared."

"That's too generous," I protested.

"Money no object for family," he said, glancing into the rearview mirror, and as the sudden glare of streetlights illuminated his face, the knot of dread in my stomach twisted tighter.

15

When school started up again, all the female teachers clucked around me like predatory hens. At lunchtime, Sabrina grabbed my hand and studied the ring. It blazed like a sparkler in the bright lights of the staffroom.

"You conniving little bitch. I've never known such a smooth operator. You go out with this gorgeous guy maybe two, three times, then he's begging you to move in. He showers you with expensive clothes, whisks you off on holiday and *boom* you're a fricking item. The two of you. Mr. and Mrs. Franzen. How did you do it? I mean, you could sell your secret to all of us lonely, aging singles knocking ourselves silly trying to get a date."

I tucked my hand into my jeans pocket. "I didn't do anything." Which was technically true. Though the events of that drunken night in Vegas still weren't exactly clear in my mind. As far as I was concerned, I'd let events unfold and allowed myself to be carried along on the Franzen family juggernaut.

"Wish I could believe that. You must be giving some fantastic blowjobs or something. You realize you've landed the motherload here. You're now entitled to half of all he owns and that will eventually include Daddy's empire." She leaned forward and grasped my hand, her eyes wide. "You didn't sign a prenup, Anna. Tell me you didn't do anything stupid like that?"

I shook my head. "You want to come to our wedding celebration?" Her eyes lit up. "It's at my in-laws. I don't have anyone else to ask."

"You have just made my week, babe," she said, enveloping me in a minty hug. "I'll be your unofficial maid of honor. Hey, maybe there's a rich relative or family friend who's into mature women. Maybe I can strike gold too and we can have our mani-pedis and spa days together."

Though the prospect of lounging with her in a tanning booth or nail salon was possibly the most sickening idea ever, I was relieved there'd be someone there to talk to among all those Franzen relatives and friends. "You can borrow one of my dresses," I said and her eyes went all misty and wide.

I drove home that day thinking Sabrina was a poor substitute for Birdie. Birdie should've been my maid of honor like we'd always promised each other. As kids we'd linked pinkies, nicked our palms, swapped blood and vowed there'd be no one else in the wedding party. Even though we never talked about what it might be like to be married, because in our world marriage was a fleeting experience. Something chaotic, painful and potentially fatal.

That sobering thought drove me back to the group home on Ardis Street. I parked outside and tried to picture Birdie sitting on the front steps, hands dug into the pockets of her hoodie, hunched over a cigarette. She started smoking when we came back to the group home after leaving Rosa's place.

After the murders.

Her hands shook so badly she could barely brush her hair or clean her teeth. Maybe it was the stabbing – the sight of all that blood spattered across the wall. Some pimply loser kid offered her a drag of his Marlboro and she never looked back. The smoking calmed her down. We were only twelve and she was already on a pack a day by the time she was thirteen. It was the smoking that got her involved with the bad kids. The step out back was the domain of stoners, dope heads and budding criminals.

Loni was the first one to take a shine to Birdie. She was sixteen, the daughter of an alcoholic father and meth addict mother. She was also a chronic shoplifter who spent the day cruising drugstores stealing flu medication, toothpaste, razors, shampoo, soap and other small items. Once she'd collected enough, she'd head out into the seedier parts of Hennepin to sell them and make enough to buy her daily weed. The first time we went out with her was the beginning of the end between Birdie and me.

I was hunched up in the corner of my bed reading. Birdie rushed in, eyes sparkling, arms flapping.

"Loni wants us to come shopping with her."

"I'm busy."

"She says she needs me. I'm a star actor. And she's really popular. She doesn't even *have* to ask us, but she did. She *chose* us."

"To do what?"

Birdie shrugged. "Who cares? It's better than staying in. And she promised me lipgloss."

I went grudgingly. Mainly to protect Birdie who was so gullible she'd do anything for attention.

Birdie brought me to Loni as if taking me into the presence of a visiting queen. A huddle of older kids stood around the step outside, slouching and smoking. At the center was Loni. An imposing figure with a spiky red buzz cut, flinty garnet eyes that gleamed from a hollow-cheeked face, and a barbed wire bracelet tattooed around her wrist. I'd thought I was tough, but Loni towered over us with her sinewy, muscular body. Rumor had it she could bench press almost two hundred pounds. Nobody messed with her in the group home. She was at the top of the pecking order.

Birdie pushed me forward. "This is my sister, Anna."

I took a deep breath. My stomach turned a somersault. "We're not stealing anything," I squeaked.

"Did I just hear some little lowlife back talk me?" said Loni, pulling herself up to full height and looking at me with such disdain I felt my insides shrink.

Despite my defiance, she dragged us both to a shabby strip mall. Drugstores and convenience stores next to pawnshops and instant cash stores. Loni said we'd hit the drugstore first, and our job was to cause a diversion by dropping something, asking a lot of questions or crying so loudly the clerk would leave the cash desk.

"They won't suspect skinny little white girls like you," she said, jamming her red spikes into a green, knitted cap.

I was about to open my mouth to tell her that actually we weren't sure if we were totally white because Dennis told us we came from a big mixed-up set of folk from some small town in the north of the state, but Birdie nudged my shoulder hard and I shut up. After two stores, Loni told me to wait outside.

She pinned me up against the wall with one hand, her face so close I could see the pimples on her chin. "Your sister's cool, but your sourpuss face is gonna rile them up in there. Park your skinny ass out here and don't move unless I tell you to."

I stood out in the cold, seething. I'd promised not to let go of Birdie and now here we were, hanging out with shoplifters. Accessories to a crime. And no one gave a damn about where we were. No mom meeting us from school in her SUV. No milk and cookies waiting back home on the kitchen table. Nobody reminding us to get our homework done or be home early from a friend's house.

The other kids at school always complained about how their parents pissed them off with all their questions and interference. I wanted to scream at them – tell them how lonely it is to know that no living person has you on their mind. No mother, father, brother, grandma, grandpa. Nobody. Only Birdie. We had each other and that was that.

When Birdie burst out of the front door of the store, red-eyed and swollen-cheeked after a successful sobbing session, I was so mad I grabbed her arm to drag her away before Loni came out.

"The cops are gonna catch you and then what? You'll be in juvie."

But she dug in her heels and refused to budge.

It was the first time she'd ever disobeyed me.

I yanked her arm, my heart bursting at how light and skinny it felt. She shrieked and pulled back, so I wound up and slapped her face so hard her head snapped sideways. She slumped against the wall, a frail bag of bones, hand plastered to the side of her cheek. I froze. I knew I'd gone too far.

"I didn't mean it, Birdie, I swear," I screamed, at the sight of the red, raised welt swelling across her cheek.

"I hate you, you bitch," she shrieked, lunging at me and smacking her skinny hands against my chest. "Nobody likes you. You spoil everything. You're evil and jealous and pissed off all the time."

Her fingers were hard and bony like bird claws scrabbling across my skin. Passers-by glanced sideways at us, then averted their eyes and rushed by. That's when Loni swooped out and waded in between us.

"Cut it out, you crazy little fuckers," she yelled, yanking my arms away from Birdie. "Someone's gonna call the cops if you keep this up."

Once she'd separated us, she grabbed Birdie's hand.

"You can come with me but your bitch of a sister can fuck right off." She glared at me then turned back to Birdie. "Her or me? Your choice."

Birdie scowled at me, her hand cradling the welt on her cheek. "Yeah – she can fuck right off."

Her words were knives stabbing at my heart. The ground tilted underneath me, only this time it wouldn't straighten itself. They walked away, but I tagged along behind.

"Where are you taking her?" I croaked, running alongside them.

"Did I hear someone talking or was it a pig grunting?" said Loni, turning her head to smile down at Birdie.

"Oink, oink," said Birdie, giggling. She slipped her hand into Loni's and I started to cry, tears burning down my cheeks.

"Don't go with her, Birdie. Don't leave me. I'm sorry."

Birdie just looked round at me and pursed her lips. I'd never seen her look through me like that. "You have snot bubbles coming out of your nose. Yech," she said, then trotted away with Loni.

I drifted back to the group home, barely noticing the rain that drove against my face. Nobody noticed me coming in drenched. Maybe Birdie was right. None of them liked me. The night supervisors didn't even look up from their Mario Kart game and the assistant had her nose buried in a pile of schoolbooks. The other kids were gathered round the TV watching *Survivor*. I ran up to my room and flopped onto the bed, stuffing the pillow into my mouth to stop anyone hearing my howling. Not that they'd care anyway.

Much later, when Birdie returned, my eyes were sore and dry and my heart was a chunk of ice.

I turned to the wall and concentrated on the weird orange-peel texture of the paint. A sweet, skunky stink floated in with her. Just like the weed smokers at the back of the house. My stomach heaved at the thought of Loni giving Birdie weed, but I bit my lip and pretended to be asleep. I felt her standing above me, breathing lightly. The air hung heavy and hot in the room.

"Sorry," she said in a small, slurry voice.

I stared at the wall.

"I said I was sorry."

I chewed at my lower lip and stayed silent. I'd make her pay.

"Suit yourself," she said. When she finally left the room, I was paralyzed with regret. I wanted to run after her and tell her I forgave her, but my voice was trapped inside my body.

Later on, when I calmed down and was really ready to forgive her, I wandered into the lunchroom. But it was too late.

A cluster of older kids stood in a circle, kicking off at Birdie who was shoving fistfuls of chocolate raisins into her mouth.

"I've got the munchies," she chanted. Over and over. Then she filled her mouth again, chomping on the candy and letting the chocolate dribble down her chin. When she smacked the side of her bloated cheek a stream of chocolate pulp shot down her chin and T-shirt.

Anything for an audience. That was Birdie. I hung around on the outside watching, my legs paralyzed, unable to step forward and pull her away. When she started drinking milk and shooting it out from her nostrils, I looked away, sick to my stomach, then drifted back to the bedroom.

I woke up much later. The moon shone through the window. Birdie was sleeping behind me, snoring, her arms wound tightly round my waist. She stirred and mouthed *sorry*, her lips sticky with chocolate.

Guy was teaching a night class so I left the group home and drove by the mall. My mind settled the moment I stepped into the scented warmth. Glassed-in elevators swished up and down, escalators hummed from one white-balconied floor to another, sunlit evening sky glowed through the skylights. I passed all the familiar stores as if I was walking down my neighborhood street.

Nancy had called earlier to excuse herself from our shopping trip. Apparently, the PowerPoint for Gord's new keynote address needed work and she couldn't be spared. I was relieved. I preferred shopping alone anyway. Company always broke my concentration and prevented me from getting into the "zone" of maximum satisfaction. Besides, they'd never put up with my idiosyncrasies. I'd go down a row of garments at least three times, pulling out the clothes, turning them around and around, checking out the place of origin, the washing instructions, etc. I'd try on armfuls of dresses, tops and pants, then go through them all again to ensure I was making the right choice. Then I'd get to the front of the checkout line, spot a cute little jacket or fancy belt hanging nearby and give up my spot to go rooting through the racks again. Nancy's patience probably wouldn't stretch that far.

After three hours of circling the best boutiques, I found the perfect dress. Creamy white with a lace trimmed bodice, wide straps that wrapped under the bust line and a long, floaty skirt. I swirled around in front of the mirror knowing Birdie would have loved it. It was a dress she could only dream about.

Then I stopped in at the lingerie store, mainly to see if Carla had shown up again or if anyone had seen her. On the way in I just had to pick up the white lace corset with pink bows and the matching bra. Guy would get a kick out of it.

My husband, Guy. I'd hardly let myself say it. *I had a husband. Someone who'd worry about me.* It hadn't really hit me until then. I actually had a family. Husband, mother-in-law, father-in-law and — what's more — they were loaded and they seemed to like me. Or at least they put on a good show. I could live with that. But the weight of the dress in the white and gold bag and the armful of sinful lingerie I'd accumulated under my arm were enough to allay any misgivings I might have about my new family. Besides, if they turned out to be total shits, I'd always have the mall. Forever. It was legal and official. Half of everything he had was mine. Maybe that's why Sabrina was the only person I tolerated. She didn't mince words and she always spoke the truth.

Carla wasn't there. Not at the cash desk or working the change rooms or circulating the floor. I asked one of the other girls. She frowned and took off her earpiece.

"Who?"

"Carla. She was in cash."

"Haven't seen her for a couple of weeks. She didn't show up and never called or anything," said the girl, plugging in her earpiece and flouncing off.

Next thing I knew I was driving along the riverfront to see if Carla had drifted back to the streets. It was so easy to be pulled back to that life. In the mall she was under the lights. Had to struggle to be accepted. But the streets didn't judge you. They were always there, waiting to suck you back into their darkness. There were no interviews, no deadlines, no judgments. You just wandered right back as if you'd never left, regardless of all your flaws and weaknesses. Birdie always said that. Or maybe I said it to her. Years after the group home. My head ached. I couldn't remember exactly when or where those words were uttered.

It was dusk. Streetlights flickered on along the riverside. I cruised past the Whole Foods Market and the French bakery. Headed towards the narrow, deserted area shaded by trees where the bridge crosses the road, creating a quiet shadowy enclave. A perfect place for doing things you don't want anyone else to see.

It wasn't dark enough yet for the kids to be out, so I pulled over to the side and waited. That's when I saw the guy again. The Ken guy with the perfect hair and goatee who'd picked up Dane at the riverfront. He drifted by in his SUV, slowing down when he passed me. His sunglasses glinted like small mirrors, my face reflected in them.

His car pulled up, maybe a hundred yards ahead and the door opened. I shrank back against my seat and watched. He wore expensive shoes. Shiny, tan loafers, a gray polo shirt and a black zip-up wind jacket with a Vikings insignia. I tapped on my steering wheel, my breath fogging the windshield. I wanted to march up to him and ask him why he was crawling around here picking up vulnerable kids.

He stood around for a minute until his phone rang. Then he started walking back and forth past his car yakking. He had one of those Bluetooth headsets on that make you look like a crazy person talking to yourself. I shoved on my sunglasses and shrunk lower in my seat even though he'd already checked me out. He stopped and glanced once again in my direction, shook his head and got back into his car. He was still talking when he revved up his engine and drove off so fast he sent a spray of gravel into the air. Maybe he wasn't really a sick creep. Or maybe I'd scared him off and saved one kid for tonight at least.

It was a start.

16

I locked myself in our bathroom the day of Nancy's wedding "do". I'd popped a zit, made a mess of my chin and my eyes had dark hollows under them after three nights spent running the events of Birdie and Loni's first shoplifting trip through my brain. I viewed the day from every possible angle, agonizing about how I could've done things differently. If only I'd run faster or straightened up my sour face and gone along with them, I could've stopped Loni from getting Birdie into drugs. Instead I'd sulked like a brat and sent Birdie off into the streets where creepy men lurked around in their shiny Lexus SUVs. Now they were probably circling around Carla like vultures sniffing a fresh kill.

Guy knocked on the bathroom door. "Are you ready, Anna?"

"I can't go. Call them. Cancel it."

Shuffling feet, clearing throat. "Open the door, Anna. Let's talk."

"Nothing to talk about. Your relatives will hate me."

"I love you, Anna. That's what counts. Let me in."

"What happens if I don't?"

"I have a key. I can get in anyway."

I opened the door and sat back down on the toilet. Guy came over and folded his arms round me. "You're a prickly little thing, Anna. That's why I love you."

"I forgot what it's like to be around family. I don't know how to act."

He folded me into his arms and rocked me like a child. I nuzzled his scented neck and wondered how Gord could've spawned such a gentle, empathetic son. It must've been Nancy's influence. The nurturing kindergarten teacher treasuring every silly utterance, every childish sketch, every stumbling step of his growing years. Teaching him to *share, use your words, don't bully, be kind.*

Unless there was another side to Guy that I hadn't seen yet. I couldn't help remembering Dane's words, the first time I read his journal.

> *Those people have layers — the outer respectable layer that everyone sees. Nice clothes, sweet cars, manicured nails, designer cologne, a good job, wallet full of cash and plastic. Peel that back and you find the inner layers. The bad-boy layer...*

I felt Guy's hand stroke my hair. "Earth to Anna."

I blinked my eyes. "Sorry, it's just last-minute nerves."

"You were like – in a trance."

"I have a lot on my mind."

He turned my face towards him. "I told you already, if you ever want to talk to me about anything to do with your past or your family, I'm here to listen. Maybe it'd help to share it with me."

I shook my head. I couldn't let him in. Not now. Not yet.

"When you're ready, then."

I nodded. "Okay – but how should I act around all your family and friends?"

"Imagine you're at a parent teacher meeting."

"We don't have them. The parents of my students are either at work doing their second or third job or out partying."

He sighed. "Okay. Imagine they're all naked and that'll put just the right kind of smirk on your face. Drink plenty of champagne. Eat. You'll be fine. It's only a few friends and a couple of aunts and uncles. Oh and some cousins."

"You'll stay beside me the whole time?"

"Promise I won't let you out of my sight," he said, stroking the curve of my jawline and planting a kiss on my lips.

I let him carry me to the bedroom and dress me in the floaty dress. After I touched up my makeup, he appeared behind me carrying something that glittered like fire.

"Hold still," he said, draping a necklace of tiny diamond-encrusted feathers round my neck. "Every bride needs something old. This was my grandmother's. Mom told me to give it to you."

He reached into his pocket and took out a small crocodile skin box. "And something new."

I flipped it open to find diamond drop earrings in the shape of flowers. While I was fastening them on, he gently took hold of my foot and raised it so he could slip the cream and blue lace garter around my ankle and up my leg.

"You forgot the *borrowed* part," I said, holding his face and kissing him. All the bad stuff went away when Guy was around me.

"Hmmhh," he said, stroking his chin. "What can you borrow?"

Then I had a brainwave. A brilliant flash of light with Birdie standing in the center of it. "It's okay. I have something. Wait right there."

I ran to the closet where my old suitcase had been pushed into a corner, still packed. I dragged it out, careful not to touch its dusty surface on the perfect silk of my dress. I'd borrow something of Birdie's. I'd kept a few things of hers that I'd get out every now and then to remind me of her.

A waft of musty air hit me when I opened the case. A fusty mix of mold, damp and rancid cooking oil was a powerful reminder of my other life – debt-ridden and miserable in a run-down apartment. Under all the cheap, creased clothing a black velvet box was tucked into the corner. Inside was a silver ring with a square green gem flanked by two pale blue stones. She'd lifted it from Kmart on one of her jaunts with Loni. Afterwards she'd get that ring out every night and put it on, then move her finger up and down so it sparkled and caught the light.

From the moment I saw it I wanted that ring. I remember lying on the frayed pink bedspread at the group home and watching her as she twirled around in front of the mirror, pouting and holding it to her face. But no matter how much I pleaded to try it on, she shook her head. A spiteful smile twisted the corners of her lips as she stuffed it in the inside pocket of her ratty green parka.

When Guy called to ask if I was ready, I snapped the suitcase shut. Next time he was teaching evening class I'd throw it in the garbage. Now I was married with an unlimited supply of money and credit I had no need of any of that cheap stuff from my old life.

But first I twirled around in front of the mirror looking at myself. I pouted and fluttered my eyelids like Birdie used to. The ring flashed like green fire under the halogen lights. So pretty. So shiny. Now I would sparkle for her. The way she always wanted to. Wearing her ring would bring her closer to me. As if she was with me at my wedding reception.

–

The long driveway up to Gord and Nancy's place was a gallery of Porsches, BMWs, Jaguars, Mercedes and a smattering of SUVs. I always shivered at the sight of them. Large silver ghosts drifting through the night, their drivers concealed by a shield of tinted glass.

"You cold or scared?" asked Guy, reaching a hand over to steady me.

"Just spooked," I said, chewing my lip.

"Smile and be gorgeous. You'll enchant them," he said, pulling up to the front door. "Just let them have their day."

By this time Nancy, luminous and sleek in a shimmering, gray gown with a choker of large pearls, had appeared at the open door waving frantically at someone behind her. Guy held the car door open for me and I stepped out like Cinderella from her coach. I said to myself *Birdie are you watching* as I glided up the driveway on the arm of my handsome husband. Three little girls dressed in crisp white party dresses burst out from the house carrying silver baskets and throwing pink rose petals at our feet.

"My cousin Ronnie's daughters," whispered Guy. "They're sweet kids."

Silver pots of white hydrangeas filled the foyer with a sweet, heady smell and we entered the living room to a sea of faces. Maybe it was the flickering candles that cast long shadows across the walls, or maybe it was the fact that I hadn't eaten a thing that day, but I was so lightheaded I almost fainted. Guy caught my elbow and someone dressed in a white shirt and black skirt thrust a drink into my hand from a silver tray. Gord's voice boomed out, *The bride and groom, Mr. and Mrs. Franzen*, and champagne bubbles fizzed up my nose amid a loud burst of cheers and applause.

Soon people I'd never met were hugging and kissing me, wishing me a long, happy marriage. I mumbled out a few "thank you's" and tried to fix a smile on my face.

Guy eventually rescued me, steering me towards the food table.

"Eat something before you pass out from starvation." He fed me some creamy little confection made of mushroom, cheese and garlic. I ate two, followed quickly by a couple of skewers of spicy satay chicken. Gradually the dizziness receded and my head cleared enough to take another glass of chilled champagne, then follow Guy around the room to be introduced to friends and family.

I made passable small talk, mostly chatting about my job and dodging any questions about family or the past. In return I got the usual tilted head and simpering smile together with stock comments like *teaching must be such rewarding work* or *how wonderful to actually make a difference*. All of which really meant, *I wouldn't be caught dead working for peanuts with reprobates, lowlifes and dropouts but someone has to do it and I'm glad it's you*. I put my hand to my heart, Oprah style, and pasted on a glowing smile. My career was a guaranteed conversation stopper so they invariably moved on. Eventually, I receded into the background, content to let Guy do the talking.

At one point we ended up near Gord who was holding court with a bunch of friends and colleagues. Impeccable in an expensive navy suit and sharp white shirt, he was talking up his latest app designed for struggling readers. I gazed in awe. He had the gall of a Wild West snake oil salesman. Gord's heart didn't just bleed when he talked about his work, it gushed a stream of saccharin platitudes and stale clichés. Words like *differentiation, rigorous core standards, data-driven instruction, action-oriented, forward driven, relentless pursuit of excellence, stakeholder involvement, enhanced observation guidelines, synergistically accountable, raise the bar, close the gap and reap the benefits* poured from his mouth.

His audience stood, glassy-eyed. I couldn't tell whether they were awestruck or bored. My face must have reflected that thought because he glanced at me and the stream of words faltered for a minute. He looked like a kid caught with his hand down his pants. Under the tan, his face flushed and he threw back his drink, then shot a quizzical look my way. I didn't want to cause any waves at this early stage of our relationship and lowered my gaze.

"Bathroom," I said, patting Guy's arm.

"You okay?" he said, kissing my forehead.

I handed him my glass. "Great."

Gord started up again after I'd left the circle and all I could think of was how much I wanted to snoop around the beautiful bathroom.

A section of the massive mirror turned out to be a medicine cabinet containing a large collection of pills. Vicodin, Valium, Percocet, Xanax, Klonopin. And all for Mrs. Nancy Franzen. Seemed life with Gord wasn't exactly a picnic. I'd suspected as much. I tipped a few from each container into a Kleenex and stuffed them into my underwear. If the dreams about Birdie got too real I'd drop a couple to get past the pain.

The bathroom led into a walk-in closet as large as a bedroom. Lit by three crystal chandeliers, its walls were lined with ribbed aqua-blue silk. A long row of tailored suits, plastic-wrapped shirts and sweaters took up one side and on the other, Nancy's monochromatic wardrobe of well-cut jackets, silky shirts, pants and sheath dresses. Two towering shelves were filled with designer shoes – Gucci, Comme Des Garcons, Saint Laurent, Prada. I pulled a few drawers open. Perfectly folded scarves, gloves, neutral underwear. Then I lifted up the stack of beige and gray undies and found a fat cache of frilly, lacy panties. Red, pink, cream, leopard print. So Gord and Nancy did have a little fling every now and again.

Someone tried the door handle so I slipped out of the closet, flushed the toilet and opened the door. I was just about to paste on a smile again when I came face to face with the SUV man from the riverfront. He stepped back smiling.

"Excuse me," he said. "Have we met?"

I stepped aside. "Don't think so."

He stroked the silver goatee. "I'm sure we have. Wait. It'll come to me."

"You must be thinking of someone else," I said, pushing past him.

He held up both hands. "Sorry, could be mistaken, but I swear I thought – anyway – congratulations," he said, pushing the washroom door open. I stood in the hallway, my heart slamming against my chest. I needed to know why he was here tracking in sludge from that other secret world of mine.

Guy appeared from around the corner.

"You get lost in there?" he asked, holding out his arms. I ran up and caught him around the waist.

"Who's that guy?" I said, as the man left the washroom and swished by, patting Guy on the shoulder.

"Why – you got the hots for him?"

I shook my head. "I've seen him somewhere but I can't place him."

Guy led me back into the packed living room. "That's Peter Karrass. He's some kind of social worker. Works on Dad's projects a lot."

I remember thinking that might explain why he might have been hanging around the riverfront, but it didn't totally satisfy me. I decided to keep him on my radar and follow him next time I saw him cruising the dark side. But Sabrina had just arrived all decked out in a figure-hugging orange dress that clashed with Nancy's carefully placed hydrangea posies. And she was talking loud enough to drown out the rest of the guests. I swept across the room to rescue her from my mother-in-law's purse-lipped platitudes.

17

After the wedding party Sabrina treated me in a whole different way. The pushy, ballsy woman morphed into a humble devotee who stared at me awestruck.

When she finally pounced on me in the staffroom at lunchtime, she couldn't restrain herself another minute. She leaned towards me, her fork hovering in the air above her kale and quinoa salad, and spoke in a confidential whisper, as if we were members of an exclusive club.

"That place was to die for. Right out of a soap opera," she said, checking that Daphne and her crew hadn't heard. "And the bathroom. Like a luxury spa. I was afraid to pee in their fricking toilet."

When I told her Nancy had a spray in the washroom that neutralized poo smell she almost fell off her chair laughing. "But your father-in-law. Sorry to say it, he's a tool. Said he didn't remember me from that conference I told you about, when I know for sure I had my knee against his crotch for at least thirty seconds."

"Can't say I know him well enough yet to make a judgment," I said, munching on the smoked salmon bagel Guy had made me. He'd been so sweet since the wedding. "Besides, I'm not married to *him*, am I?"

"You marry someone, you're married to their family. Believe me. I know. I've turned down a couple of hot, ripped guys because their parents were major assholes."

"Sometimes you gotta put up with shit to get shit," I said, pulling a container of fresh raspberries from my lunch bag.

Sabrina lowered her fork and narrowed her eyes. She smiled a slow, knowing grin. "You, Anna Holt, are one materialistic little bitch," she said, her face cracking into a blinding smile. "But don't you forget to introduce me to any eligible relatives or friends of the family. Single, widowed, newly divorced, weird, nerdy. Don't matter. I'm very flexible."

I smiled, knowing with absolute certainty I had no intention of allowing her near Guy or any member of his family. "Will do," I said, spearing a plump berry and watching the juice spread like fresh blood onto the white plastic.

–

Carla still hadn't shown up at school. Only Dane and two other buddies of his came to class every day. Sabo with the sable-black Mohawk and ripped trench coat held together with safety pins and Martin with the purple tipped hair and tongue piercing.

But Dane was the only one who actually talked to me. The others drifted in, wrote their journals and read a lot.

I asked Dane if he'd seen Carla.

He shook his head. "Nah – but some kid said she might've met some guy at the mall who promised to get her into modeling."

A wave of nausea rolled through my gut. That was the oldest con trick in the book. "Which guy?"

"From the mall. Downtown. He owns a record store. Told her he'd seen her around and thought she'd be great for promo work."

"You know where?"

"I think it's Toonz. By the gamer store. But like I said – I haven't seen her. It's maybe just a rumor."

"Thanks, Dane. I appreciate the info."

He shrugged and took his journal from my desk.

–

On the way home I drove towards the downtown mall. News about Carla was a swift reminder that even the mall wasn't a safe place for lost kids. One time, Birdie told me about the guys who hung out there trying to pick up kids nobody cared about. They'd drift up with their crooked smiles, hands stuck into the pockets of their fake leather bomber jackets, paunch straining the front of their polo shirts. They'd offer cigarettes or chocolate and tell little girls how pretty they were and ask them to model for some photo shoot or video.

At first Birdie said she'd gotten all starry-eyed and almost fell for it, thinking it would be the way to launch her dream career as a famous movie actress, but Loni put her straight. She barreled right in between Birdie and the middle-aged loser and told him to *go screw your dog instead*. For once I said a silent thank you to Loni for protecting Birdie who, left to her own devices, would probably hold out her hand and let any weasel-faced perv lead her away to porn land.

I parked the car in a side street and sat nursing my coffee and gazing at the dark brown buildings linked by glassed-in crosswalks. Some city planner had introduced fancy streetlamps and colored street banners in an effort to brighten the place up, but all I could feel was a sense of brooding darkness. An absence of sunlight and air.

This place was very important to Birdie and me. Bad things had happened here. I knew because I felt that familiar sense of dread squeezing my gut. We'd started coming here when we were still at the group home. A place where we'd begun to feel settled. But as usual, nothing was ever permanent in our lives. Some well-meaning person always moved us on, whether we wanted to go or not. I remember the day they took us away from there. It was a muddy spring afternoon. Dirty, half-thawed snow flecked the sidewalks and I'd skipped school, faking a stomachache.

Tammie, the supervisor didn't care if I stayed away from school. She was in her final year of nursing and exams loomed on the horizon followed by the prospect of a raunchy spring break week in Fort Lauderdale if she passed. She came around and checked on us every few hours, mostly to see we weren't shooting up or hanging ourselves from a coat hook. But she was a major pushover. We were into our teens by then, and didn't give a damn. If we didn't want to follow orders, we just got right up into her face and lipped off at her. She usually shrugged and backed down.

I was enjoying a rare moment of peace and quiet, lying on the couch in the TV room, sipping tea and polishing off a pack of white chocolate chip macadamia nut cookies. *The Young and the Restless* chugged along at a snail's pace. I loved that show. The expensive clothes, every room with a giant arrangement of cut flowers, every woman made up to the teeth and sporting chunky, glittering jewelry and rhinestone encrusted earrings that they only took off to answer the phone. People fell in and out of love, plotted, connived, cried, died, got possessed by demons, ran away then returned to big, comfy fortunes. It was all there in glorious color. An hour of pure escapism every day.

I was just nodding off to sleep when the front door burst open and Marian, our social worker of the moment, marched in holding Birdie by the arm. Birdie mouthed *I'm fucked* to me and I jerked upright, spilling the last of the cookies on the floor.

"Shit," I said, reaching to catch them.

"Sit," snapped Marian, pushing Birdie towards the couch and reaching into her black briefcase for her notebook. She flipped through it and directed her pale blue eyes onto me. "Why aren't you at school?"

"I'm sick," I said, wondering how the irises of her eyes could be almost the same color as the whites. It gave her face a weird, zombie look.

"Well at least you aren't out committing felonies like your sister. I guess that's something in your favor." She bustled around the place, looking for staff, finally spotting Tammie, hunched over the pile of books at the kitchen table. She marched over leaving Birdie and me alone.

"Pass me one of them macadamia cookies," said Birdie. "I'm starving."

"*Those*," I said. "And they've been on the floor."

"Don't care." She reached for them. "Haven't eaten since yesterday lunch."

"Where'd she find you?"

"At the mall. I went with Loni and Duane. Loni jacked some lipgloss in the drug store. Cameras caught her. I wasn't doing nothing."

"*Anything*," I said, taking a cookie and chewing it slowly.

"'Scuse me. *Anything*," she said, sticking her face into mine. "It was an ugly color anyway. Some black color. Squid Ink they called it."

I pushed her away. "You stink. Why don't you go take a shower?"

"Bathroom's gross. I found pubic hairs on the tub."

"Clean it."

She shrugged and I tried to concentrate on the TV again.

Nikki and Victor were getting dressed for a big dinner dance. Victor zipped up Nikki's red satin dress and kissed the back of her neck.

"Horny old perv," said Birdie, reaching for another cookie.

"He's what you call suave or distinguished. Doesn't matter that he's old. He's got money and nice clothes and he smells nice. Unlike you."

"Yech. You can keep him. I like them young and smooth. Old ones are too hairy."

"What do you know about that?"

She nibbled round the edge of a cookie. "Enough. I kissed Duane and Loni told me about the old ones."

"What does she know?"

"They pay her to do things. You'd puke if you knew so I'm not gonna tell you."

I was just about to twist her arm back until she told me, when Marian stormed back in.

"Go upstairs and pack your stuff. I'm taking you out of here. Supervision's too slack for minors like you."

Birdie sat back on the couch, mouth filled with cookie, tears flooding her eyes. "I like it here. I have friends."

Marian's eyes flared, her lips pressed together and she threw back her shoulders. "You call them friends. Taking you on shoplifting trips, feeding you drugs. It's in your best interests that you're removed from their destructive peer influence."

I hated it when Birdie blubbered. Her nose got all snotty, strings of saliva dripped from her mouth and her face turned red and puffy. She looked way worse because she'd plucked all her eyebrows off. Me, I just sat there mute and still, a frozen lump of ice where my heart once was. I didn't care about anything. Even Birdie had turned away from me since she met Loni. But I felt a faint tremor of hope. Maybe this move could be a chance to win her back – to rip her away from Loni. I touched her arm.

"She's right. We have to go," I whispered. "You can call Loni and Duane from wherever we end up."

Her thin body still shuddering, she allowed me to lead her up to our room and help her pack our usual garbage bags. Marian patted my head and said, "You're a calm and positive influence, Anna. I see a bright future for a girl like you."

I smiled and said nothing.

Marian drove us to a small bungalow on a street about half a mile away from the mall. A foster home run by Donna Inglewood, a single mom in her mid-thirties, gaunt-faced and squinty with a cascade of curly black hair and a headful of manic ambition that would eventually send her to jail.

But Donna introduced me to the real wonders of the mall.

It was a seamless transition from the soap operas I gorged on at the group home. A perfumed world of plenty where everyone smiled as they strolled up and down the gleaming hallways, their eyes filled with the promise of bigger, better and nicer things to buy. I learned that the mall promised everything. Magic, plenty and perfection. Time was erased here. Poverty wiped out. My edginess gone.

Too bad Donna never had enough money to satisfy her shopping habit and Dayton's just happened to be crawling with undercover security the day she decided to lift a pair of diamond earrings that turned out to be cubic zirconias.

–

I finally left the safety of my car and entered the mall, but felt no urge to buy more clothes. Thoughts of Donna had dampened my enthusiasm and my closet was full to bursting, the overflow spread to the guest room. Instead I lingered at a jewelry store, picking up a pair of over-priced turquoise earrings and a sleek Scandinavian watch. I followed up with a couple of weightless silk scarves and a pale beige handbag from another store. Soon I was on a roll again, memories of Birdie, Donna, and Carla gradually receding from my mind with the thrill of each new purchase.

Two doors up from there was Essentique Salon. Hair, makeup and nails all in one sparkling beauty palace. Suddenly the idea of a mani-pedi was the most appealing idea in the world, so I grabbed a smoothie from a nearby health food bar then surrendered myself to the sharp chemical cocktail of shampoo, nail polish and hair spray.

As I leaned back and set the massage chair to full back rolling and gliding motion, I vowed to treat myself more often. My mind had been racing lately, buzzing like a fly from one strand of thought to another, and since the wedding I'd barely had time to consider my new status as a married woman.

The tiny, ponytailed girl filed away at my toenails and I closed my eyes, drifting into thoughts of Guy. How he held me at night, one arm wound around my waist, the other cradling the top of my head. How he remembered the way I liked my coffee – three sugars, light on the cream. How he always stopped his work to turn his face and kiss me, even when I interrupted him. How he never pressured me with questions about my past.

I supposed that having such an overbearing father had made him a more sensitive man. One who waited patiently for the right moment to intervene, who never bullied or dominated, who truly listened and never feigned interest.

A warm glow of happiness spread through me and I must've drifted off into a half sleep, dreaming of Guy's lean body silhouetted against our sunlit window, stretching his arms upwards to yawn, his back arched and his head thrown back. Only the dull rasp of the pumice on my heel kept me hovering at the edge of consciousness. Aware enough to hear a sudden wave of giggling. Squinting through lowered eyelashes I spied a knot of girls crowding into the empty spa. Most likely a bachelorette party, I thought, judging by the high intensity shrieks, giggles and chatter. They settled down on the opposite side of the salon and soon the *plinking* of text messages and the fractured music of YouTube videos accompanied their nonstop babble. My neck muscles tensed up again, the calming effects of the foot massage wasted.

"You wait five minutes for drying," said the girl and I blinked my eyes open to view my freshly painted tangerine toenails. I thanked her, glanced over at the girls and did a double take. Carla sat in the center of a group of girls at least five to ten years older than her. Her hair was cut, styled and expensively streaked, her face barely recognizable with its mask of thick makeup. The hoodie and jeans were gone. In their place a tight, pink top and designer jeans. I recognized them as mid-priced clothes. Not H&M or Forever 21. I sat forward and tried to catch her eye, but she caught one glance, then turned her head and body away so her back was all I could see. She wanted nothing to do with me or what I represented. I ached to rush over and confront her, but I feared she was already lost. Gone. Moved on.

I felt a rushing in my head that forced me up and out of the chair. I'd been through this with Birdie. Had the same helpless feeling that she was slipping away from me. I threw on my shoes, oblivious to the protests of the tiny manicurist who kept repeating *Careful, don't wreck the polish*.

I flung on my jacket, grabbed my purse and packages, then shoved a few twenties at the receptionist who arched her brows at the sizeable tip and tried to offer me change and a receipt, but I was gone. Out the door where I almost mowed down the guy standing directly outside, leaning against the window talking into his phone.

"So sorry," I gasped. He looked straight through me with eyes that were cool and green against his coffee-colored skin. His full lips curved sweetly. It was a mouth made more kissable by the small mole at the left corner of his upper lip. And the way he kept glancing back into the spa, I was absolutely certain he was waiting for Carla and her friends. That he was the person who'd paid for the beauty treatment.

But something deeper was stirring inside me. I already knew this man. Birdie knew him. Somehow, somewhere, we'd met him in that messed up time fifteen years ago.

He put down his phone, stared at me, then shrugged. "Got a problem?" he grunted. I shook my head and pulled my coat around my shoulders, then ran off in the direction of the parking lot.

18

I had my first row with Guy a week after Gord and Nancy's do.

I knew his perfect husband act would eventually crumble. It was simply a matter of finding the right trigger to set the destruction in motion. To start the rot that revealed the cracks in his perfect façade.

It was inevitable. So much so I was almost willing it to happen. Then I'd be alone again. Back in my hard little shell. Immune to all hurtful feelings. Protected from human contact. Comfortable in my isolation.

Familiar territory for me.

It started off as most married spats do – with an innocent question on my part. At least it seemed innocuous to me.

It was a sunny Sunday morning. Beyond the window, blue spring skies were dotted with patchy white clouds. A half-empty pot of coffee sat on the bedside table and croissant crumbs littered the duvet. We were sprawled out reading the papers. I'd just finished reading an article about foster kids living in unsupervised hotels and had lingered over the paragraph that described an entire family of siblings, aged two to fifteen, forced to live in a grungy motel room rather than split the group up between foster homes.

The Carla incident was still making me irritable and edgy. Maybe she was shacking up in one of those places. I felt the stirrings of anger. How many kids were living in dives like that? As far as I could tell, way too many. Nothing had changed in a system that was already broken when I passed through it.

Birdie and I saw our share of grimy motel rooms after the Donna fiasco. That was one reason I hated traveling. I had no idea why anyone would choose to pay big money to sleep on mattresses that thousands of random strangers had slept, dribbled and screwed on. And just because you choose an expensive hotel doesn't make it any better. Rich people sweat and screw just the same as everyone else. For all I knew, the thick mattress cover in our luxury Vegas hotel was probably hiding a multitude of gross stains. Not to mention bedbugs.

I'd rather buy a tent and go camping. Any day.

I put down the paper and curled my arms around Guy's waist, resting my head on the silky skin of his chest, tracing a finger down the faint line of hairs below his navel. "How's your inner-city drop-in project going?"

"What's that?" he said, casually.

"You know. The drop-in school for homeless teens."

He sighed and I sensed the tension as the muscles shifted in his shoulder.

"We put it on the back-burner. Dad needs help with his new app, so I'm cutting down on my university teaching for now to give him a hand."

"You're kidding." I sat up and grabbed my newspaper, holding it up like a trophy. "I just read this feature. It says there's way more kids living in seedy hotels and motels. They barely have any supervision. Nobody checks that they go to school. They just drift from one house to another, sleeping on couches or mooching around malls during the day, which basically makes them easy pickings for all the predatory weirdos and perverts out there."

Guy looked bemused. "Don't you think I already know that?"

A buzzing started up in my head. I raised my voice to drown it out. "Apparently you don't if you can just cancel your project like it's an inconvenient hair appointment."

He raised his hands up in a gesture of surrender. "Hold on. Did I say cancel?"

By that time I didn't want to listen. I was on a roll. "You don't understand. There's no time to waste. We're raising a whole generation of illiterate kids who'll gravitate towards a life of crime and addiction. I'd say there's a massive demand right there."

"Won't you just back up a bit here." He took off his glasses and wiped them. His eyes appeared vulnerable and unfocused without the lenses to sharpen them. He squinted at me and I sat back against the pillows, shaking.

"Okay." I nodded.

"I want you to work on it with me. But first, we need to do something about your job."

"What about my job?" The hairs on the back of my neck bristled.

"Maybe it's time to quit that place."

"Says who?"

He reached his hand out to touch mine. I jerked it away into my lap. "I do – well, Dad mentioned it. He thinks maybe you could come to work with us for a while and then, once you get some experience, we'll go back to my project."

"I barely know your father and he's trying to organize my life." My voice rose as the thudding in my head started up again. Even though I'd flirted with the idea of working for him, I balked at Gord's arrogance. I wouldn't be a pushover like Guy and Nancy.

"In case you hadn't realized, he's now your father-in-law. Not some random stranger."

I sat up, feeling the familiar sense of panic that set in when other people tried to steer the course of my future. To send me away, take me in, uproot me and rip me away from everything I knew. I'd vowed long ago I'd never be at anyone's mercy again. "He has no right to tell me what I should and shouldn't do without talking it over with me first."

The newspaper slid off the duvet onto the floor. Guy's shoulders stiffened. "It's not like that, Anna – just listen."

"Maybe he's ashamed of his new daughter-in-law. He thinks I should be doing something more acceptable to his upscale corporate friends."

"What the hell are you talking about?" Guy's eyes widened. "He's just trying to be helpful. So am I for that matter."

I pulled the sheets up to cover my nakedness. "You call it help. I call it interference. And just because he has you tucked into his back pocket doesn't mean he can do the same thing with me too."

As soon as the words were out, I wanted to bite them back. How could I say those things when *I'd* actually crawled into Guy's pocket like some greedy parasite, consuming everything he had to offer?

"I'm sorry," I said, my hand flying to my mouth. "I shouldn't have said that."

"I don't get it," he hissed. "I don't get you."

I tried to backpedal. "I mean I appreciate everything he's done for you – for us."

It was too late. Guy threw the sheets back and moved far away from me. "I share my money, my home, my family, *my love* with you. I don't pressure you about your past. God knows what you've been through. But I don't care. I respect your privacy. No questions asked – and you dare to say I'm in my father's pocket because I'm in business with him, and a successful business I might add." He clambered out of bed and began to gather his breakfast dishes. "You certainly don't mind reaping the benefits of it. In fact, if I took a look in that closet, I'd say you were pretty much reveling in it."

My breath came in short bursts. I wanted to go back in time and replay the past minute. I tumbled out of bed, dragging the covers with me. "I've got a wicked tongue. I swear I don't know when to shut up. I didn't mean it."

He dragged his sweats on, his face tight and pale. "Sure you didn't. Take a good, long look at yourself, Anna, before you start preaching to me." Then, pulling on his sweatshirt and shoes, he slammed out of the condo before I could say another word.

I sank back onto the edge of the bed, black dots dancing in front of my eyes, nausea swelling my gut. Why couldn't I keep my stupid mouth shut? I'd promised myself to stay calm this time. Keep my thoughts to myself. That's how I'd managed to escape the streets. By being the one in control. By keeping a low profile and waiting for the right moment. It'd worked for me time and time again and I'd vowed it would work this time with Guy and Gord. I needed it to work. The stakes were too high and I couldn't jeopardize everything I'd planned just for a job at a lousy school. This was what I'd wanted. Surely it wasn't too late to get things back on track.

But the first thing I had to do was apologize to Guy. Make it right.

I gulped down three cups of coffee then tried his phone but he wasn't answering. I figured maybe he needed time to cool off. I'd touched a nerve with my comment and now he wanted to make me pay for it. He was just like all the rest of the people in my life – vengeful, vindictive. Not happy unless they could get back at you in some mean, spiteful way.

Like Birdie.

After she started hanging out with Loni, she did a total one-eighty. The little girl who'd clung to me and made all the hurt go away, suddenly took pleasure in making me suffer. And each time the pain was worse.

But I couldn't think about that. My head was in turmoil. One minute I was agonizing about how Birdie and I had drifted apart and the next, I was longing to make things right with Guy.

I picked up my keys. A drive would clear my head. Help me think.

I drove towards the Stone Arch Bridge again, parked the car and sat watching the falls. The scrappy spring breeze gusted in through the window, bringing with it the faint sulfurous stink of the river. I closed my eyes and tried to think. Back to Birdie and what eventually happened at the end of the Donna placement.

Birdie and I started going to the mall by ourselves. Sometimes at night. Donna was in such a dark phase she'd forgotten we lived there. As long as her girls were locked in their bedroom, she didn't worry about us.

At first, I was glad Birdie asked me along with her until I spied Loni and Duane slouched against the wall by the Lego store. I grabbed Birdie's sleeve.

"I don't wanna go with them."

She rolled her eyes. "Piss on Donna and her loser friends. I'm starving. You want a burger, fries and onion rings? So tag along and learn. I'm sick of begging."

Loni looked different. Nice hairstyle, silver earrings and wearing a white quilted jacket with gray fur trim. Her eyes lit up when she saw Birdie.

"If it ain't my little sister, Birdie. Babe, you gone skinny like a weasel," she squealed, hi-fiving Birdie. A massive grin cracked my sister's face. The first genuine one I'd seen in months. I felt a stab of jealousy. I wanted to punch Loni in her big, wide face. And she could see right through me because when her heavily lined eyes rested on mine, her mouth drooped. "Pick up your face, bitch, or Duane and me'll give you a whooping."

Birdie whispered something in her ear and Loni glanced back at me. "Okay, she can come, long as she stays back and don't cause no trouble."

I trotted behind them, salivating at the thought of a juicy burger and hot, salty fries. And when Loni, Duane and then Birdie took turns stealing clothes and makeup from the stores, I pretended to be looking through the racks. They'd go into changing rooms, rip off the tags and then saunter out with T-shirts, underwear, pants and sweaters hidden underneath their coats. I always made sure to leave the store before them. I wanted the burger so bad, but no way would I let myself get caught jacking stuff. Loni and Duane might think I was a just a stupid, dumb loser, but unlike Birdie who was a *grab it while you can girl*, I had a clear view of the way the world works and the future I wanted, and it didn't include getting a criminal record. Even at thirteen, I knew you could kiss the soap opera fantasy life goodbye if you tarnished your name in your teens.

A tap on my window brought me back to the present. A parking guy was motioning me to move along. The sun had retreated behind gray clouds and a fine drizzle misted the windshield, blurring the lines of the downtown skyline. I checked my watch and realized I'd been parked there for at least an hour and Guy still hadn't called or texted. I needed to keep moving – go somewhere or else I'd drive myself crazy, so I started driving. I passed by the apartment with the orange flowered wallpaper and pulled up outside the building. The harsh spring sunlight bleached the graffiti scrawled across the brick frontage. A couple of ragged looking junkies sat on the front steps fighting over a bottle. And the windows were so grimy I couldn't see that wallpaper.

How had we ended up there? Was it after Donna's or was there some other place in between? I kept thinking of those words I'd said to Guy. *Curb your wicked tongue.* I knew they were associated with this place but I couldn't remember who had said them and why. I stared so hard the junkies got up and wandered towards me, so I drove away leaving them waving their arms in the air. Then it came to me. A vivid memory of a strip of cheap hotels just blocks away.

The Sunday traffic was light. I drove almost on auto-pilot, wondering if I should call Guy, but I had no idea what to say. No relationship in my dating history had ever lasted longer than a week, so I had no words for making up with someone. I'd never done it in my life.

Except with Birdie. I'd begged her like a dog to let me back. And it didn't work.

I drove up and down the strip of cheap motels, trying to find the place Birdie and I had lived. A long row of crumbling brick and concrete cubes built in the sixties. Painted yellow or pink, with rusted stairwells and fancy names like Capri, Palm Court or Tropicana Bay. I circled round each block, checking out the flickering neon signs.

Finally, I settled on the Capri Motel, a pale pink cube with open balconies on each floor and a dried up, cracked shell of a pool surrounded with wire fencing. It sat next to the offices of Godfather Bail Bonds, a sooty brick structure with broken shutters, the mustard yellow block of Kaiser and Siegel, Attorneys at Law and the Hidden Treasures Pawnshop. Finally, three pickup trucks were parked outside a long, low one-story white building with red shutters that boasted, *Strippers Nude Daily. Every hour. Girls, Girls, Girls.*

I remembered. There'd been no placements available, so after Donna was arrested, we ended up at the Capri just half a mile from the mall.

"I'm hungry," I'd said, staring at the faded forest scenes hanging on the dull yellow walls. Birdie glared at me. She was back hanging out with Loni a lot more, and had picked up her language and her *screw you* attitude.

"For crying out loud, now you're whining too. I told you I'll go get us some food. Just sit tight and keep quiet."

After she stomped out, I took stock of the situation. I had a dollar in my pocket, so I went down to the vending machine in the front lobby and bought a chocolate bar. I filled a plastic water cup and sat down on a flea-bitten plaid couch to eat my supper. As darkness fell, people emerged. Night creatures afraid of the sun. A man opened a door on the second floor and shoved a girl inside by the scruff of her neck. Two drunk guys staggered up to the third floor and almost fell backwards down the stairs. My stomach felt queasy. This was not a safe place. I had to get back up to our room and barricade the door.

I let myself in and switched on the TV. At least we had entertainment. Half an hour later someone bashed on the door. I froze. Until I heard the faint sounds of Birdie's voice and a whole lot of giggling in the background.

"Pizza delivery," she squealed, breaking up into a fit of laughter. I could tell from her slurred words she'd been drinking. She burst in with Loni and Duane. A couple of other older kids I didn't recognize slouched in behind them.

"Pizza *partay*," shrieked Birdie. She was drunk or high, sashaying around the place, pulling open drawers and flicking the remote.

Loni opened a pizza box and a fragrant scent of cheese flooded the room.

I was so hungry I'd have turned somersaults and begged on my hands and knees for a slice of that pizza, but when Loni slapped a huge piece of pizza onto a napkin and took a big bite, that was the signal for us to dive on the three boxes and stuff our faces. I dropped a piece on the carpet and lunged for it too late. When I picked it up the cheesy side was coated with hairs and dust. I was about to throw it in the garbage and reach for another piece when Loni slammed the box shut and stuck her face into mine.

"Don't think of wasting it, bitch," she spat. "Clean it off and eat it."

I looked over at Birdie, but she was helping Duane open a twelve pack of beer, so I picked off the hairs and tried to forget what might really be lurking among the fibers of that disgusting carpet.

Then Birdie said she was thirsty, and Duane fed her some beer from his bottle. Everyone laughed when she guzzled too fast and it fizzed out of her nose, but she was so thirsty she wanted more and soon everyone was chugging beer except me. I sat watching them sling beer over the carpet and bedspread. At one point Birdie puked into the garbage can and Duane passed out under the coffee table. I slunk into a corner and helped myself to more slices of pizza.

After all the food was gone, Loni said it was time to quit this shithole and find somewhere more chill to spend the evening. Birdie piled up the empty boxes and said she was going too. By that time, I was too full and tired to object, so they grabbed Duane by his jacket collar and dragged him out. Besides, I had the luxury of my own bed and I was soon curled up in front of a movie.

When I woke the next day, Birdie wasn't there. The place stunk of stale beer and the door had a hole in it where someone had tried to punch it in from the outside. My eyes burned and my head pounded. I couldn't deal with any more crap so I called our social worker and she showed up an hour later to drive me back to her office. Birdie arrived an hour later, picked up at the mall for panhandling visitors at the entrance.

19

Guy still hadn't called so I drove to the mall and headed to the older section. During the week the downtown office workers crammed in for lunch or afternoon shopping, but at the weekend you could've thrown a boomerang the full length of the hallways and not clipped anyone's head. The stores were empty. In their place drug dealers, junkies and burnouts sat by the fountain or huddled on the benches and balconies as if they finally had room to conduct some serious business. Occasional groups of shell-shocked tourists wandered through, checked out the scene and soon scurried towards the nearest exit doors, barely taking a second to look behind them at the sad human circus that cranked along from morning till night.

Fifteen years ago, I'd been one of those dull-eyed dropouts. Birdie, Loni, Duane and I hung out there all the time. Or rather Birdie, Loni and Duane hung out and I sloped along behind them like an outsider.

Loni had an intense hate on for me. Jealous of my relationship with Birdie, she'd test Birdie's loyalty any chance she got, forcing her to choose her or me. Eventually she drove a wedge between us that finally splintered any solidarity or love we'd ever shared.

Now the sight of a uniformed mall cop pacing around the fountain, talking into his handset, set my stomach rolling. I wanted to turn and run and I knew damn well why.

After the motel debacle they'd placed Birdie and me with Lester Flatt, a sleazy mall cop and his obese wife, Patti. I remembered him clear as day.

Lester was a pasty-faced asshole who strutted around the apartment whistling and polishing his gun. He'd stop once in a while, drop into a crouching position and whip the gun out, aiming it at one of us. We'd freeze, our hearts slamming against our ribs until he burst out laughing, revealing a row of mossy gray teeth.

"Put that freakin' thing away, Lester," yelled Patti from the living room. Patti had been a supermarket cashier until she supposedly injured her back lifting a heavy crate of canned tomatoes. When the workers' comp ran out, they applied to be foster parents.

"They'll take them kids away and then what? I'll have to go out to work and you know how my back is."

"Consider it done, my lovely," he crooned, licking his lips, grinning at us and rubbing his crotch with the gun before he stuck it in the holster. "My weapon is now concealed, darlin'."

A couple of weeks later we cut school early to hang out at the mall.

"Duane's gonna get one of his friends to give Lester a scare," said Birdie. I limped along behind her because my backpack was so heavy. I was carrying three books: *Madame Bovary, Crime and Punishment* and *Great Expectations*. Estella had become one of my personal heroines.

Beautiful and with a heart of glass.

Nobody could ruffle her icy composure. I'd even begun to cultivate a kind of haughty, superior stare that challenged anyone to try and mess with me. But it didn't seem to work with Birdie.

"Christ's sake. Did you hear me? Snap out of it, Anna. We're gonna mess up creepy old Lester. Then afterwards, he'll have the shakes so bad he won't be able to hold his damn gun, let alone play with that shriveled up pecker of his."

Birdie was manic. She'd ducked outside with Duane and Loni and probably sniffed glue because the sharp chemical stink was all over her. And they were acting so goofy, hopping up onto the fountain walls and walking like tightrope walkers. I cursed myself for not watching Birdie more closely. All the kids at the Capri Motel were doing it – glue, aerosols, hairspray – anything to take them out of the miserable hellhole they were stuck in. Me, I had my books. They were my fix. My escape. I thanked God for Dennis and the reading we did together.

So the three of them started going over a crazy plan to ambush Lester when he checked the men's washroom on his rounds. They'd jump him, stick him a few times in his paunchy gut and leave him to bleed.

I was stone cold straight. Anyone with half a brain could spot the gaping holes in their wacko plan. "And what if he identifies you? I mean you do happen to live at his goddamn house. That means you'd have to kill him."

Birdie ignored me and kept on babbling, her whole body twitching like she was having a seizure. "Then we're gonna crush his nuts and snap that pathetic pencil dick of his."

"Ew! Gross," screamed Loni and Duane, doubling up with laughter.

"You junkies couldn't jump a drunken bum lying in his own puke," I snapped, surprised by the venom in my voice.

Birdie jerked upright, her eyes red and watery. "My own sister's such a bitch," she said, looking at me like I was a stranger. "Can you believe it?"

Loni made a quick move and smacked me across the side of my face with a closed fist. Stars flashed into the blackness, my teeth clunked together and my feet skittered underneath me as I tried to stay upright. Instead, I swayed and dropped to my knees.

"Now you've done it," I heard Duane say.

"Yeah, knocked some sense into her thick skull," said Loni. "Bitch had it coming to her. Thinks she's better than us."

Birdie was silent. I tried to look up through the circling fog in my head to see if she was still there. If she felt sorry for me. If she still cared. But I could only see the shifting shapes of the other deadbeats edging forward at the prospect of a fight. My eye throbbed, swelling like a ripe plum.

"Fuck off," I heard Birdie say, waving her arms and sending the gawkers scurrying back to their perches. She was agitated, banging her foot against the wall and wiping her sleeve across her nose. "We can't just leave her here. She's all messed up. I'm gonna get her some ice."

Loni's voice pounded like a hammer in my sore head. "You go do that, you forget comin' with me. We're gonna get some good stuff over at Toonz."

"What stuff?" said Birdie. I heard the hunger in her voice.

"My good buddy Earl's there, he's gonna give us smack and a free tattoo. Real good price."

"You sure?"

"Cross my legs and hope to die," said Loni.

I felt across my face to where a swollen lump was swallowing up the vision in one eye. I opened the other eye to see them rifling through my backpack. Birdie cast nervous glances back at me.

"My books," I croaked, the effort sending a fresh wave of pain down the side of my face.

They'd already ripped them out of my backpack. Loni waved *Madame Bovary* up in the air. "Woohoo we got us one prissy little nerd here. Thinks she's too good for us with all her fancy books. Teacher's pet. Hey, Duane, maybe we can get a couple of bucks for these."

He shook his head. "Good for wiping your ass. That's about it."

Loni lobbed them all into the fountain, laughing as each one landed with a loud splash, bobbed around on the surface, then sank to the bottom.

"Let's go," said Birdie. "Leave her be."

"You feeling sorry for your sister?" crooned Loni, taking hold of Birdie's ear. "But I'm your real sister, Birdie, and don't you forget it. *Capiche?*"

"I know," said Birdie in a tiny voice. "But let's go now."

I felt the toe of Loni's shoe thunk at my side as they left. "Keep your goddamn mouth shut next time. Nobody gives a damn about you. Nobody in the world. Not even your sister, cos now she's got me instead."

They took off, leaving me to scrabble around in the slimy fountain for my books. Two old drunks helped me out until a pile of wet pages sat on the mall floor. I thanked them, but I was crazy with anger. Birdie's absolute betrayal was a searing knife in my gut. I'd wiped her nose, cleaned up her puke, held onto her hand when she lagged behind, suffered other people's wrath to keep her safe. And now she'd stood by, not lifting a finger and let Loni abuse me. I stumbled to my feet, jarring my knee on the concrete edge of the fountain pool. My left eye throbbed with pain and my insides seethed with a thirst for vengeance that terrified me. I staggered out promising myself that I'd kill all three of them. I'd slit their miserable throats. I'd hold their heads under water until every bubble of air sputtered out of their bodies and their lungs burst.

Birdie had left me totally alone in the world and I could never forgive her. Ever.

—

I'd been drifting around the mall for over an hour and still not a word from Guy. I felt a nagging sense of fear. Would this be the argument that finally broke us? Just then my phone buzzed. I grabbed it.

"Anna?"

"Guy?"

"Where are you?"

"I went for a walk."

"Anna, I'm sorry."

"Me too. I said a whole lot of things I shouldn't have. I gotta learn to keep my mouth shut."

There was a moment's silence. "No, Anna. It's my fault. I overreacted. I'm a pompous idiot. You're the one with the moral principles. Come to Mom and Dad's for supper. I'm there right now but we're just talking shop and you'd be bored. See you in a couple of hours."

"Okay, sounds good," I said, feeling the brief elation of victory that soon fled when I spotted the old fountain with its gray scum line and usual rag tag group of junkies hanging around its perimeter. My hand stiffened over my purse. I wasn't ready to be here, near the place I'd been laid so low. The site of my betrayal. So I veered a sharp right in the other direction.

"You okay, Anna," I heard a faraway voice ask. Then I remembered Guy was still on the phone.

"I'm fine. Just out of breath. See you later," I said, heading east towards Toonz. Maybe I'd see Carla there, though I wasn't sure what I'd say to her.

The record store was in a grubby corner of the mall next to LA Nail Palace, Kreatures, a pet store with some listless guinea pigs on a wheel in the window display, and DB's Comics, a gamer and comic-lovers' paradise frequented by a stream of slouching, greasy-haired post-pubescent boys who hadn't seen the inside of a shower stall for at least a month.

When I spotted a couple of kids in hoodies walk hand in hand out of DB's, I felt a sudden jarring of my consciousness as if time had shifted backwards and once again I was the ratty kid with the musty clothes and black eye that still smarted from Loni's beating. This corner hadn't changed in fifteen years. This was the place I first felt the stirrings of adolescent lust.

20

After the Birdie betrayal I stopped hanging out with her. Instead I came to the mall after school to look out for Colby, a guy from my English class who loved reading as much as I did. He hung out all the time at the comic store because he collected *Batman* and *Green Lantern* comics. He was a skinny, quiet kid with a hank of dark hair that covered his eyes and shielded him from the rest of humanity.

I'd become the only other member of his reading group the second day of English class and listened in awe as he let loose with his take on Raskolnikov, the consequences of alienation and the merits of nihilism. We were the only two reading Dostoevsky. The other kids in class – the cheerleaders, jocks, stoners and car fanatics – were still stuck on books with one-word titles like *Busted*, *Ripped* or *Slammed* or teenybop series like *The Baby-Sitters Club* or *Goosebumps*.

Miss Potter, our teacher, hadn't even read *Crime and Punishment*. Her eyes bugged out when she read the first page, a look of incomprehension creeping over her doll face. But she shrugged and smiled, happy to let us sit together in the corner and keep a daily journal of our observations and discussions.

I liked her. At least she didn't pretend to be something she wasn't. Sometimes I sat on the floor in the hallway outside the classroom talking with Colby about the isolation of intellectual superiority and the concept of a human Superman, while the other kids made character posters, composed acrostic poems and created media collages that they plastered all over the classroom walls. Colby and I watched from our intellectual fortress, finding much to identify with in the solitary agonies of the tortured student, Raskolnikov.

I waited by DB's every day after school, until Colby ambled out, jamming a new comic into the pocket of his denim jacket. Then I fell into step alongside him. He always ignored me for the first few minutes until I said something that piqued his interest.

"I know exactly how he felt," I said, panting to keep up. "Raskolnikov, I mean. I looked up the meaning of his name. It means schismatic, dissonant, dissenting. He feels separate. Apart from the common mass of humanity."

Colby nodded. "Hmmh. Good." He darted a sideways glance at me through the curtain of hair. "Who smacked you in the eye?"

"Just some inferior louse from the mediocre masses."

"Well rats like that need to be exterminated."

"Exactly what I was thinking. Only I wouldn't feel the same guilt as Raskolnikov. I'd take extreme pleasure in squashing this particular parasite," I said, picturing Loni's painted face with a broken nose in its center.

The first time Colby held my hand, I thought I'd faint. He pulled me into the narrow corridor that led to the washrooms and pinned me against the wall right beside the coat lockers. My insides melted when he placed his palms on the wall, enclosing me in his shadow. When he bent over and placed a soft kiss on my sore eye I almost burst into tears. It had been a long, long time since someone was that gentle with me.

"You ever had sex?" he said, his breath warm on my cheek. He smelled of greasy hair and gum with a faint note of something sweet and spicy.

I shook my head, not daring to speak in case I made a fool of myself.

"Me neither," he whispered into my ear. "But you'd be the first if I was going to. Would you let me?"

"Yeah, I would." My voice was so hoarse he had to lean closer to hear me.

We stood there for a while, bodies trembling with the urge to touch and kiss each other, until he suddenly broke away. "Gotta go home. My old man'll be pissed if I miss supper."

I felt a twinge inside. Patti barely roused herself from the TV to make meals and usually expected Lester to bring in KFC, or Subway. Birdie and I waited for the leftovers, though Birdie had barely been home for supper since the incident at the fountain. Not that Lester or Patti noticed.

"Yeah, better get back."

"See you in English class?"

"Sure," I said, aware that we'd crossed a line and couldn't step back even if we wanted to.

—

I checked my watch. I was due at Gord and Nancy's in just over an hour. But something held me there, compelling me to stand in front of DB's Comics' window. Maybe I still believed Colby might walk out, head down, chewing a piece of hair, but the place was quiet. Only a few bedraggled looking kids sat round a trestle table playing

Magic Cards, a game I'd never really understood even though Colby tried many times to explain it to me.

Time was short so I forced myself to move past DB's and the tattoo parlor to Toonz, the music store.

I wondered if I'd see Carla there. Persuade her to come back to school. The electric blue sign flickered on and off and I was suddenly short of breath as if a weight was pressing on my chest. I had history there. Long-buried history that stopped me from pushing open the door and crossing the threshold.

I leaned forward trying to see beyond the posters to the long display cases stacked with CDs and videos. It hadn't changed much in fifteen years. One wall featured death metal music and the usual posters of skulls and hollow-eyed clown bands. On the other side was reggae, hip-hop, R and B and rap. An eclectic mix, welcoming anyone and everyone with a taste for music.

It was there Colby and I had discovered Nick Drake, a brilliant but little-known British musician from the seventies whose brief rise to stardom was curbed by his debilitating depression. After a few years of obscurity, he took his own life at the age of twenty-seven. His music was a revelation to us with its rippling guitar sounds and gorgeous orchestrations, not to mention the singer's soft, plaintive voice. The fact that there was no known video of him only added to his cachet. We were hooked and Toonz had rare copies of his few albums.

I remembered that I'd kept them when I left my apartment and made a mental note not to dispose of that suitcase until I'd removed them to someplace safe.

Now I saw a couple of customers rooting through the display cases. It was a miracle the place had kept open this long when most people were pirating music now.

Fifteen years ago we all knew there were secret screening booths at the back of the store where – for a few bucks and proof of ID – you could watch porn videos in private. But when the internet came along and all the porn was free, the owner moved on to other income sources.

I found out about all that much later.

But I couldn't help wondering how the place was still going. Now that YouTube was here and CDs were on the way out.

This was a bad place in my history. I felt it deep in my bones. And like so many places, people and events from my past, I'd blocked some memories so entirely they'd almost been erased. Rachel Levine said it was one of the aftereffects of extreme trauma. Your life history becomes warped and twisted as you try to create and recreate the experiences that shaped you. And sometimes you're not sure if you're actually making up your own version of reality or whether it's actually true.

It was a tough way to live, but at the time I managed to keep going.

The moment I opened the door the years slid back. That musty odor like mildewed book covers and sweaty laundry lurking behind the musky scent of patchouli incense sticks. I'd bought incense there to remind me of Dennis.

The owner was sitting behind the counter talking to someone. I hid behind a tall stack of Disney movies and peeked round to see him. Fingers of heat plucked at my neck when I saw him; a golden-skinned, baby-faced guy with close-cropped red hair and cool, green eyes. Earl Rafferty. Record store owner, DJ, amateur filmmaker and God knows what else. The guy who'd promised to get Carla into modeling. A sweet-faced soft talker who offered vulnerable young girls free manicures, shoes, clothes, hairdos and food. But they paid a high price for his generosity.

This was the guy I'd seen at the nail salon.

I peered around the other side of the stack. All I could see was the back of a head of white, well-groomed hair that twisted sideways to reveal Peter Karrass's profile complete with chiseled goatee. That guy turned up everywhere like a bad penny. But I couldn't figure out how he was connected to Gord. And why he kept showing up in all these sleazy places from my past.

I watched from my hiding place trying to listen in on their conversation, but their voices were too low to make anything out. When my phone rang loud and clear into the silence, both of them turned to see where the noise was coming from. I ducked for cover behind a CD rack. It was Guy.

"We're done," he said. "Come over now. Mom's making supper."

"Okay," I whispered, peering over the shelves to see the two guys disappearing into the back room. That was my cue to get out of there. I'd had enough of that hole in the wall and its creepy owner.

I needed fresh air. The goddamn store was suffocating me.

—

Nancy, looking fresh and tailored in a crisp white shirt and jeans, slid a plate of herbed chicken garnished with rosemary and wild mushrooms onto the table. Guy passed round bowls of endive salad and roasted cauliflower. I heaped my plate up, realizing I hadn't eaten all day. Nancy kept a close eye out for any spatters and stains, wiping them up immediately with a clean cloth. Gord and Guy paid no attention, but I couldn't help wondering if she ever served red meat or pasta in tomato sauce. Maybe the thought of blood or tomato spatters across her pristine kitchen counter was too much to bear.

"Looks great, Mom," said Guy, squeezing my hand and smiling. His way of saying sorry. I smiled back. After seeing Earl Rafferty I needed to feel safe and get the balance of my life back to normal.

We ate in silence but I could tell that Gord was bursting to talk. He kept smiling to himself as if conducting a private inner conversation. Guy looked tense and apprehensive while Nancy's gaze bounced from one to the other. Then, when Gord had chewed up the last piece of chicken, his face broke out into a broad, beaming smile.

"So, Anna," he said, directing his hooded, blue eyes at me. "Guy tells me you're looking for an opportunity to broaden your horizons, turn a new page in your life – maybe get your feet wet in an exciting new venture."

I winced at the string of clichés, but decided to follow suit. "Yes, I'm definitely interested in branching out. Striking out towards pastures new."

"Good, good," he said, dabbing a napkin against his lips and leaning back in his chair. He really got off on those hackneyed phrases. Guy stared at me with raised eyebrows, a hint of suspicion in his eyes. "Well, as you may have realized, I'm a firm believer in family first. Family is the backbone of our society. More to the point, there's solidarity in blood."

My jaw ached. When was he actually going to get to the point?

"To that end, I'm happy to tell you that I'm the recipient of a very generous government grant, courtesy of my friends in high places who really came through for me yet again. It's earmarked for an important assessment project and I thought you'd be the perfect person to assist Guy in getting it off the ground. I know it means mixing business with pleasure, but you can be sure our Guy is a consummate professional and won't let personal matters interfere with the work. In other words, no shenanigans in the boss's office. No kissing in the copy room." He winked. Guy gave a half-hearted grin.

"I-I'm not sure what to say," I stammered. I should have been gloating.

After all this was exactly what I'd wanted.

"If I was in your shoes I'd say yes," said Gord. "You'll be doubling your salary. Not that it matters. What's ours is yours after all."

"Say yes, Anna," said Guy. "I can't wait to work with you."

"I should finish the semester," I said, my voice a little wobbly at the thought of leaving all my students. "There's only a month left."

Gord leaned forward. "Of course. Then I take it that's a yes."

"Yes," I whispered.

Gord pushed his chair away from the table and stood up. "Nancy, champagne's chilling in the fridge. Bring out the glasses and let's toast the newest member of our team."

Nancy set out the glasses on the polished tabletop, watching anxiously as Guy clutched a white tea towel over the neck of the bottle. When he pulled out the cork with an explosive *pop* I felt suddenly light and disoriented – untethered, as if my body would somehow spin off into the air. The school and Robin and all those kids had been like family to me for years, a steadying force – an anchor that had kept me stable and grounded. Now I'd agreed to become part of this perfect family and their successful business. I grasped the arms of my chair. Had I made the right choice?

Or had I screwed up everything I'd worked so hard for?

21

May sunshine streamed in through the window, throwing the lines on Robin's face into sharp relief and revealing the frayed collar of his shirt. I told him I was leaving at the end of the semester.

"I'm disappointed, Anna," he said, fingering the shark's tooth necklace. His nails looked yellowy, scored with deep ridges. His face had the caved-in beaten look of a tired old man. "You know I'm on the way out here and I harbored a faint hope that you'd take over when I left. I've always admired your firm, unsentimental approach to the kids. You never patronize them."

I studied the worn parquet flooring and the faded Persian rug, a relic from his pilgrimage to Marrakesh in the sixties. "I try not to."

"It seems as if you know them so well, which makes me wonder about you." He sipped his coffee and grimaced.

"I guess I won't miss that vile brew we call coffee," I said, but my poor attempt at humor didn't deflect him.

"Anna, I don't know much about your past, and I don't want to pry, but I could swear I detect some deep wounds there. I've worked for many years with troubled kids and I can sense hidden pain. If you ever want to talk, I'm always here."

That was my cue to leave. I could already feel him digging into my head, lifting the lid from my secret store of memories so he could peer inside. No way would I let that happen. That stuff was private. Guy didn't even know about it. About Birdie. I stood up and searched my lexicon of niceties.

"I appreciate everything you've done for me, Robin. I've loved working here. I'll miss you all and I'll never forget the things you taught me." All I could think of was how Gord would've been proud of the trite sentiments oozing from my lips.

Taken aback, he realized the moment of revelation was over. "Of course, Anna. Goes without saying and I'll be happy to provide an exemplary reference should you need it."

I backed out of his office muttering thank you and was almost clear when he stood up abruptly. His somber face lit up.

"Wait. Before I forget, I must thank you. Bringing Guy in for that in-service in February was a brilliant idea. For you and for us."

I stopped dead in my tracks.

"Come again?"

"You recommended him." His brows knit. "You told me you'd read some papers he'd written on education for homeless kids. Gave him a glowing reference. How could I say no when you were so persuasive? And now look. You're married to him."

I struggled to focus. The features of Robin's face became blurred and fuzzy. The springs on the wall clock behind me whirred and clicked. "It must've slipped my mind," I said, feeling my throat seize up. "I've been so busy with other things. Married life, you know."

"I'm sure you have," he said, attempting a grotesque wink. "After Guy's inspiring presentation I put in a proposal to the board and we're receiving extra funding for our street kids' outreach program."

"Good news," I said, trying to breathe deeply, to focus on Robin's moving lips and make sense of something I'd tried to shove to the back of my mind.

He sighed and knitted his fingers, resting his hands on his faded denim lap. "An old dog like me would call it romantic. Destiny. You two were meant to be together. You couldn't have planned it better, Anna."

"But I didn't," I said more firmly. "It just happened."

"Of course. I'm not accusing you of anything, Anna. I'm just kidding. Lighten up, luvvy."

Somehow, I got to my classroom, though the floor seemed to tilt under my feet. I thought he'd forgotten my little note about Guy, hastily shoved under his door. Just a casual hint – a nudge in the right direction.

Luckily, the kids had left for the afternoon, so I was alone. Nobody there to witness me fall into my chair and sweep the books and pencils aside to make space for my aching head. To collect myself.

To focus.

To think about Birdie and what happened at Patti and Lester Flatt's after the incident at the mall.

To picture her wounded gaze when she watched me clutch at my swollen eye. To remember how her nose was dribbling from the after-effects of glue sniffing.

Patti and Lester perched like two stone gargoyles on the plaid couch while Birdie and I stood in front of them trembling. A storm threatened outside the window, lighting the leaden skies with flashes of white sheet lightning. Sweat dribbled down my back underneath my sweatshirt and I felt giddy – lightheaded as I struggled not to breathe in the putrid mix of sweat and rancid bacon fat.

"You gave your sister a freakin' black eye?" Lester stared right at Birdie. He'd been toking on Patti's medicinal weed, so his eyes looked big and unfocused. He nudged Patti and giggled. "She goddamn knocked her own sister out. Can you beat that?"

Birdie shook her head. She was wearing a ripped gray T-shirt that had once been white. Her thin arms stuck out, her hands twisting the T-shirt hem into a ball. "I didn't do it. Loni did."

Lester's face turned purple. "Curb your wicked tongue, kid. You let your friend beat up your sister? That's worse. That's a coward's way out." He turned his eyes on me. "Is it true? Did she let them hit you?"

A small fist of anger bruised my heart. The more beaten she looked, the more I wanted to hurt her. Crush her like a paper doll. I nodded. "Yeah," I whispered, feeling a rush of vengeance so strong I had to bite my lip to stay quiet.

Patti held her arms out to me, her face fixed in a weird, twisted grin. "Looks like that eye hurts, baby. Come sit down next to Momma and I'll take the pain away."

I stood, rooted to the spot. She beckoned again. "Come, come, baby. Patti's not gonna hurt you."

Her voice was soft so I edged forward until she grabbed my hands and yanked me down onto the couch. I'd never been that close to her. She smelled like dried armpit sweat and skunk weed. I shuffled away to the other end of the couch.

"Don't be scared now. Get comfy," she said, patting the spot right beside her. "I'm gonna make you feel good and take the pain away. Lester, fire up that weed."

The click of the lighter and Birdie's heavy breathing were the only things I heard. A cloud of smoke drifted by my nose. A pungent, musky smell. Patti's hand appeared in front of my eyes, the nails covered in chipped purple polish.

"Take a drag, baby. Your eye won't hurt no more."

I'd only smoked once when Duane and Loni decided I could have the last toke of their joint. They'd all laughed when I choked my guts up. Now tears pooled in my sore eye. I shook my head.

"Go on, baby. It won't hurt. Take a hit. It'll make you feel real good. Relaxed."

I glanced up at Birdie. She motioned with her eyes as if to say *go along with it*.

"Don't look at her, baby. She don't give a rat's ass about you."

I took the joint and put it to my lips. The smoke tickled my nose as I inhaled deep, feeling the hot, dry hit and holding my breath so I wouldn't lose it. When my chest was about to burst, I let it all out. Its bitter taste crept into my throat and mouth and nose. I handed it to Patti and fell back against the couch, my eyes heavy, my heart throbbing in my ears.

"Hey, Patti, you got that kid high," said Lester in a weird sing-songy voice. "I'll have to report you to the author-i-ties."

"It's medicinal, Lester. Pain relief. No worries." She sucked back a long drag, her throat straining to keep the smoke down, then exhaled a billowing cloud of smoke. Lester grabbed the joint and took a long hit. We all sat back looking up at Birdie. Her left foot tapped on the floor. She chewed at her fingernails. The other hand plucked at the hair above her left ear.

"Now what we gonna do with this little bully?" said Lester.

Patti shuffled her leg up underneath her butt. "How 'bout medication? You got something to maybe knock her out a bit? Cos we can't deal with this kind of *ant-eye-social* behavior here."

Lester eased his ass off the couch and shuffled into the kitchen. I heard him rooting around in the drawers. Birdie shifted from one foot to another.

"Don't need nothing," she mumbled.

Patti stiffened up, her eyes bulging. I felt sick, scared and sleepy. "Did I ask you to open your filthy mouth, you little shit? Did I?"

Birdie shook her head. Nausea flooded my throat but I couldn't move.

Lester returned with a handful of pill bottles. "I think we got something here might work. Left over from the last kids."

He shook a couple of pills from each container into the palm of his hand and held them out to Birdie. "Here – take 'em."

She shook her head and edged backwards. But Lester was on his feet in a minute, his chin jutting out like a freaked-out bulldog.

I sat bolt upright. "No – don't make her."

Patti's arm locked across my chest like an iron barrier. I started to cry when he got Birdie in a choke hold from behind, forced the pills into her mouth and clamped his hand over her lips. Her feet pedaled underneath her like she was trying to run somewhere – anywhere – but she was stuck, her arms flapping liked a bird's wings.

"The glass," he shouted to Patti, pointing at a half glass of Coke on the coffee table. She reached it up to him and he pinched Birdie's nose and poured the liquid down her throat. He held a hand across her mouth for a few minutes of muffled sobs and moans. Her body heaved until there was no fight left in her. I tried to jerk myself away from Patti but Lester swung around, let go of Birdie and shoved me backwards. My head thunked against the back of the couch jarring my teeth and sending a wave of pain across my swollen eye.

When I opened my eyes again, Birdie was crawling along the floor, trying to pull herself upwards by holding onto a chair. Her body made weird, jerky movements like a half-dead wasp that you've batted enough to stun but is still trying to escape. She pulled herself upright and placed her hands on the wall. The wall with the flowery wallpaper. She was trying to climb up that wall, her legs jerky and splayed like a spider's. I cried so hard when she kept flopping down and getting up again as if those flowers were a pathway to some magic woodland world. To a place where there was no pain and no terror. She did that until she collapsed in a ragged heap, knocked out by the meds they'd given her.

I touched my tight, swollen eye that burned with tears while Lester and Patti shook with laughter.

22

I made an excuse to get out of the staff meeting so I could leave school early. Besides, I'd squirmed my way through the first thirty minutes, chewing my nails, tapping my fingers on the table, and scrolling through my phone. It didn't matter now I was quitting, I didn't give a damn what anyone said. I had to sort my head out and get control of myself before I went home to Guy. Had to come to terms with what I'd done to my sister. Betrayed her. Squealed on her. Let those junkies abuse her like that. And all because I was pissed off. Mad at her for letting Loni hit me. For choosing Loni over me. I was an evil bitch. Loni was right.

I grabbed my bag from the classroom and was about to leave when Sabrina strode into the room. She stood there, hands on her hips, blocking my exit. I needed to get out so bad I could've mowed her down right there and then, but I didn't. I swallowed my rage and stood there, silently seething.

"What's going on with you?" she said, moving herself into my path so I'd look at her. I couldn't.

"It's best if you just let me get by," I said, holding back the prickly, jumpy feeling that set my insides rolling.

"I hear you're leaving. How come you didn't mention it?"

I didn't need a heavy discussion. My body was about to burst open if I didn't get out of there. "Only told Robin today."

"I thought we were friends. You could've shared it with me, Anna."

Before I could stop myself, the hateful words spewed from my lips. "Then I guess we're not really friends."

I might as well have punched her in the face. She stumbled backwards, her fake-tanned cheeks sinking inwards. "You can be a nasty heartless bitch, Anna," she said, then slammed out of the room.

But I couldn't think about Sabrina right then. I had to stay focused on Birdie. What had happened to her at the Flatts' place. What I'd done to cause it all.

Once I got in my car I ran a couple of red lights and almost sideswiped a truck, so I was in a real state when I got to Linda Martin's office. Eyelids swollen from crying, head buzzing in confusion, breath coming in raspy gulps. I sat opposite her trying not to look at the stupid posters plastered on the wall behind her. The only thing I could focus on was her T-shirt. Another Gap clearance special. Navy with white polka dots that danced in front of my eyes.

"So tell me something I don't know already, Anna. I'm fully aware that too many kids in foster care are highly over-medicated. Don't you think we've tried to do something about it?"

I blinked and looked up at her.

"Huh? What's that?"

"The drugs. The over-medication. You told me you witnessed Lester and Patti Flatt giving Birdie a cocktail of prescription drugs."

I snapped back into the present and remembered why I was there. I'd had a breakthrough. Something that brought me closer to Birdie. "Yes – I finally remembered the place with the flowered wallpaper. Lester Flatt, the mall cop and Patti, his wife. They dosed her up for a week or more so she could barely stand upright, let alone get out of bed."

Linda rolled a pencil back and forth across her desk, scrutinizing its motion. "First, I already told you last time you talked about the Flatts. According to our records, Birdie wasn't at that particular placement. Second. Wherever you witnessed this – and it must've been somewhere else – it's nothing new, Anna. Statistics tell us at least one in four kids in foster care is taking psychotropic medication. Half of kids in residential care or group homes are prescribed these drugs. Sometimes multiple drugs with serious side effects. All of us front-liners have tried at some time in our career to get the matter taken to the highest level, but no matter what we do, there's always some total shit of a doctor happy to prescribe even red label drugs with only a five-minute consultation. Sometimes to kids as young as six. It's easier on the foster parents than trying behavioral therapy, and from the doctors' perspective, it gets those troublesome patients out of their hair more quickly. That's the sad truth."

"But I'm only concerned with Birdie. It might help us find out what happened to her."

Linda checked over her notes. "Anna. For the last time, there's no record of Birdie even being there with you. She ran away from the group home before you were placed at the Flatts' house. We do know for sure that you were placed there and they gave you drugs. Many drugs that messed up your memory of that particular time."

"But I remember every detail. I had a black eye. Birdie's friend hit me and I told on Birdie. That's why they drugged her."

Linda looked at me as if I was talking gibberish. "Anna, it's natural you feel some sense of guilt about Birdie. She was your twin sister after all."

I tried to hold back the urge to smack her smug face and kept my voice low and steady. "But I distinctly remember smoking weed. Patti gave it to me."

Linda folded her arms and bowed her head. Some major revelation was coming. I could hear her brain ticking, as she considered the most merciful way to frame her response. She looked up again and waited for a moment, absently rubbing the tip of her chin. Measuring my expression.

"Sadly, it was way worse than that, Anna. You were a severely traumatized kid. Removed from your family, bounced around from one home to the other. You lost Birdie, the only person close to you. That means you already had a high risk of developing mental and emotional disorders. You were given much more dangerous drugs that put you over the top."

I had to stop her. Tell her she was wrong. It was Birdie, not me who was drugged into oblivion. "You're all mixed up. Those notes are lies."

"Anna, you were injured physically, mentally and emotionally when you left there. And then – there's something much more important I need to remind you about…"

I stiffened up. Clasped my hands over my ears and shook my head. "Not now – please, not now."

"Okay," she crooned in a soft voice that sounded like air hissing through a crack in a window. A voice meant to pacify me, but instead drove me into a silent frenzy.

"I've always told you, you're welcome to go through the notes. But perhaps it's time for you to sit down again with a therapist. A trained psychologist or psychiatrist will help you deal with the tough details about your sister. To help you finally come to terms with the truth."

I placed both palms on her desk and tried to steady my voice. "I don't need a damn shrink. I just need to get the facts straight." My mind was racing, grasping onto ideas before they disappeared. "Oh, and there's something else. A guy who works for you. Peter Karrass. He's been hanging around the riverbank with some of my underage hooker students. He picked one up in his car. Then I saw him at Toonz. He went into the back office with the owner. Where the porn material is kept."

Linda was sitting bolt upright by this time, eyes flashing. She flicked the pencil between her middle and forefinger.

"Why are you hanging around that place, Anna?"

"What do you mean?"

A sappy look wiped across her face like grease on a windowpane. "When you were at the Levines the therapist told you to stay away from places that have negative associations for you. You become disturbed, agitated, confused. You need to put all that stuff behind you. It's over. Try to heal. Be happy. You're married to a good man."

She might as well have been telling a crippled woman to pull herself out of the wheelchair and walk or a blind man to open his eyes and just see. I felt a sudden urge to tip her desk over. Instead I balled my hands into tight fists.

"I can't. I have to get it straight. What happened to Birdie. What's still happening to all these kids. One of my students disappeared for days, then was picked up by a known trafficker. I think this man, Peter Karrass, is somehow mixed up in it all."

She ran her fingers through her cropped hair. "Anna – oh, Anna. You forgot."

My breaths were coming short and fast. I told myself *slow down, focus on the T-shirt – the photograph of Linda standing in front of the Arc de Triomphe. The cube magnet with the safety pins sticking to its face.*

"Forgot? What?"

She slid a sheet of paper towards me. "This is a memo written recommending your removal from the Flatts' home. Take a look at it."

The words buzzed in front of my eyes like tiny insects, blurring then coming into focus on the social worker's signature at the bottom of the page.

"Peter Karrass," I whispered.

She pulled the paper back, pressed her lips together and nodded. "Exactly. He made this recommendation and you were the only one removed from the home. Almost fifteen years ago. I have the full report somewhere here. You can read it if you like."

I stood up and yanked my handbag from the back of the chair. "Someone tampered with those records, Linda."

She shook her head. "Why would anyone do that, Anna?"

"God knows, but why don't you ever believe me, Linda? And for once in your pathetic career, maybe you should goddamn well look into it."

When I pushed the door open I heard Linda say, "I can't change the facts, Anna. There's no mention of

Birdie in the report. She wasn't there and what's more you already know that…"

I didn't hear the rest. I couldn't listen to lies.

-

I rested my arms on the edge of the Stone Arch Bridge and looked down into the Mississippi River. Dark waters swirled and twisted on their way from Saint Anthony Falls. Behind me, massed against the watery blue sky stood the tall towers of downtown. Multifaceted blocks of concrete and glass crowded together like massive beehives, housing all the tiny lives that fueled the grinding machinery of the city.

I always felt a crushing sense of insignificance when I played with that thought. That even those who are cherished by large, loving families, struggle daily with the idea of their own inconsequentiality. But when life becomes too burdensome and hopeless, they can retreat into the warm cocoon of family love until they get themselves back into fighting shape. Ready to face the stress and turmoil of the real world.

I had nothing left when Birdie pulled away from me. Nobody who cared. Only the overworked social workers whose solution was to shuffle the deck and concentrate on the neediest kids. As far as they were concerned, I already had a home with Patti and Lester Flatt. Even though I struggled for survival every day I was there. But every instinct – every feeling – told me that Birdie *had* been there. I *wasn't* imagining it. I *had* seen her standing in front of Patti and Lester, her leg twitching, her fingers twisting strands of hair. I'd felt the hard swelling across my eye as I watched the horrible scene unfold.

A cyclist skimmed by behind me and I was suddenly certain I'd been at this bridge with Birdie. Some time during our stay at the Flatts. I had to trust myself.

Linda's report was false – nothing but lies.

So I searched the water to find Birdie's face. To bring her back to me.

23

Right after the horrible wall-climbing night, Patti and Lester kept Birdie in bed by feeding her a daily cocktail of drugs. A cup of multi-colored pills before I left for school, and the same dose when I came home. I'm certain they gave her more drugs at noon. Every morning I tried to wake her, but she was so groggy she just turned over and fell back into a deep sleep. A couple of times she reached out to me and mumbled *bathroom*. At those times I dragged her out of bed and sat her on the toilet where she promptly fell asleep sitting up. In the dim, yellowy bathroom light her face looked ashen, her skin papery. I tried to feed her water, enough to keep her going. She got some down, but the rest dribbled down the corners of her mouth wetting the neck of her T-shirt. I told her not to take the pills – to spit them out, but she nodded her head towards the bed. I helped her back, tucked her in then spent the rest of the day at school worrying she wouldn't survive, that she'd end up a slobbering vegetable. Even Colby noticed my distraction.

After the incident at the mall our literature discussions had changed. The air between us was electric, charged with possibilities. While I talked about books I'd be looking at the way a beam of sunlight lit the curve of his lip or the way his lashes cast a shadow on his cheek. I could smell him all around me. The warm tang of sweat and soap drove me to distraction. Instead of worrying about Birdie I imagined his naked body in the shower. I felt him watching me, studying my every move, until he finally asked.

"What's eating you? I can tell something's up."

I put down my book. I'd read the same page of *Madame Bovary* at least three times. The part where Hippolyte's reeking, gangrenous leg is finally amputated.

I shrugged. "Just can't take this stuff right now."

"It's pretty screwed up that all this shit was going on in nineteenth-century France. I always thought those Victorians were supposed to be so prudish."

"I guess when you're trapped and everything seems hopeless it can drive you to extremes."

"Is that how you feel?"

I turned away from him. "Don't want to talk about it."

He leaned forward and touched my arm. My skin trembled. "Let's cut class. Go somewhere we can talk."

We walked through Mill Ruins Park along the river. Halfway through, his hand slipped into mine and my heart softened. That's when I told him about Birdie and the drugs. That's when he stopped in his tracks and clasped both of my hands.

"You have to get out of there. Both of you. I'll help you."

-

My phone buzzed in my pocket anchoring me once again to the present. It was Guy. I couldn't speak. The choked up feeling in my throat was for Colby. Another man. I'd forgotten about my husband. And then I remembered what Robin said earlier.

Thanks for bringing Guy into the school.

"Anna – I tried to call you at school. Robin said you'd left early and you seemed upset. Is everything okay?"

Robin was right. I *did* want to meet him. But I couldn't think of it at that moment, when Guy was questioning me.

"I'm fine," I said, watching a mother jog across the bridge pushing a stroller. "I told Robin I was quitting, so I needed a walk to clear my head."

"Hey, I totally understand. You've put in a lot of time there. Invested your heart and soul into those kids."

"It's tough to turn my back on it all."

"I know, I know, but you're doing the right thing. Those kids would suck you dry and you wouldn't have made one iota of difference to them."

"How can you be so sure of that?"

"I've met plenty of idealists who want to change the world. You have to work with the kids who want to improve themselves."

"Is that what Gord told you?"

"Anna, you agreed to join us. Right now you're just feeling sore about leaving, but you'll get over it, and besides, Dad wants to get together to talk about the project. Give you a head start. You'll feel better once you get your teeth into something. See the light at the end of the tunnel."

I shuddered. Now Guy was spouting clichés. But maybe I just hadn't noticed him doing that before.

"I just have to finish up at school," he said, "then I'll meet you back at home. We'll drive over to Mom and Dad's together."

Talking to Guy had left a flat, heavy feeling in my heart. I wandered down the steps towards the car park, but something drew me in the other direction towards the sloping road that led underneath the arches of the bridge.

Colby and I had walked this same path, hands clasped together, palms damp with apprehension, head fogged with possibilities. I trailed my finger along the metal railing until it ended at the arches. Clambering up the gravel incline I stood underneath the arch inhaling the river's scent of mud and rotting vegetation. The stones polished by years of rising and retreating waters. Maybe I could still find the place where Colby and I had carved our initials. I stood on tiptoe, running my fingers across the scummy gray stones. Surely there was something left to remember the place where he'd run his hands down my body, his head bent into the crook of my neck, his breath coming fast and warm on my skin, his hair tickling my face.

He'd looked into my eyes like couples do in movies. I pushed in closer to him as he fumbled with his belt. His breathing was raspy and fast. The sudden rush of air chilled my legs when he pulled down my sweats and thrust forward. Urgent. My body molded to his, warming me all over. His hand grasped mine and guided it to his erect penis. *Hand job. Do you know what to do?* I remember laughing and saying, *Yes, I think so,* even though I hadn't a clue. Then we were pushing and shoving against the stone until it scraped the skin from my ass, but I couldn't let go of him. I buried my face against his neck and moved my hand up and down until he reared and called *oh, oh, oh* when he came. Afterwards he kissed my face. Tiny, shivery kisses all over. And when he swept his hair back to look at me, I saw his whole face for the first time, rather than the half-shaded one he presented to the world.

It was beautiful.

Now fifteen years later I had to stand on tiptoe to read the letters scratched into the weathered old stone. He'd taken a penknife from his pocket and carved our initials. I saw the *CA*, Colby Anderson on one side of the heart but the initials on the other side blurred out of focus. I looked again at the letters. *BH*.

Birdie Holt.

Straining my legs to reach higher I studied the B. There was no mistaking it. The original *A* was clear but someone had scraped over it and changed it to a B. I swayed backwards, lost my footing and flopped onto the ground. A cyclist screeched to a halt nearby. A young guy in racing clothes.

"You okay up there?" he shouted.

I turned around, barely registering his face against the glare of streetlamps.

"Do you need help?" he said, more urgently.

Everything snapped into focus, as if a spotlight was shining down behind me. "I'm fine. Just lost my balance."

He nodded and sped away. I checked my watch. I had to meet Guy at home and I was already late.

24

Identical twins bond in the womb. As early as fourteen weeks after gestation they're reaching for each other. At eighteen weeks they touch the other twin's body more than their own. Scientific researchers have even filmed grainy videos of tiny swimming embryos, their transparent fingers lingering over each other's faces, gently caressing delicate eyelids, fragile noses and budding ears. Looking out for each other even before they're born.

I believe it was like that for Birdie and me. Even though we had our own amniotic sacs, we shared a womb. We sensed each other's presence right from the start. We were inseparable. Bound to each other.

Things went wrong much, much later.

According to Dennis he fought a twenty-four-hours-a-day battle to stop our mom from shooting up heroin when she was pregnant. Maybe in that watery uterine world, Birdie and I could sense the intensity of her hunger. But we had each other to keep away the danger. When we were tiny babies, Dennis said we wouldn't even take a bath alone. He had to put us both in the water and we'd cling on to each other, slick as a pair of baby seals, longing to be close again.

When I lost Birdie, I felt like half of me was gone. Like the limbs on one side of my body had been amputated. I had to find her to feel whole again. Had to believe in the jigsaw of memories and images that spilled into my head at random intervals, inspired by a particular place or person or maybe even a smell or color.

But Guy couldn't know any of this. How could he understand what it feels like to lose the other part of you? When you look into a mirror and realize half your identity has been erased and you have no idea where it's gone.

-

I changed into something smart but comfortable to go to Gord and Nancy's. My other clothes were covered with smears of mud and grass from the riverbank.

Pushing that part of the past into the back of my brain, I checked myself in the mirror. It was so much easier to think of clothes. To distract myself with the soothing details of a well-groomed professional appearance.

I dressed in slim, black slacks, a white shell top with a deep V neckline to show off my silver medallion, and a short, fitted houndstooth jacket. I tousled my hair and fastened on a pair of silver hoop earrings. Remembering Guy loved red lipstick, I applied it generously then stood back to gauge the full effect. I hardly recognized the glossy, well-dressed woman who looked back at me.

Success was at my fingertips. I should have been completely happy. And I was to an extent. Happy with Guy, excited at my new job, secure with money for the first time ever. So what was eating at me?

Birdie. Birdie was the missing piece.

Without her I was "*a walking shadow, a poor player that struts and frets his hour upon the stage*", as Shakespeare so aptly puts it in the words of the tormented butcher, Macbeth, when he muses upon the loss of his wife.

Guy's face lit up when I ran towards his car. I sat back in the seat, pushed my hair behind my ear and smiled. He was still staring when I leaned over to kiss him.

"You are the sexiest, most incredibly gorgeous teacher I've feasted my eyes on. I could eat you up." He traced a finger around my chin. "Let's do a little late-night detention duty tonight."

I pushed him away. "You're so cheesy. And while I'm at it, please don't talk in clichés when you're trying to sell me on Gord's project. I despise them."

He shot a pained look at me. "I don't. I'm just trying to be cooperative."

"Sorry, it's just that you're catching the cliché habit from your dad."

He pulled out from the parking spot. Traffic was heavy. "He does tend to get carried away sometimes. Then he falls back on hackneyed phrases. But the truth is he's really very insecure."

"You're kidding," I said as we pulled up at a red light. "He's the cockiest, most self-assured guy I've met."

Guy took a long, deep breath. "I know he's all bluster and bravado, but it's all a front. He comes from humble beginnings."

"So what's the problem with that?"

Guy ran a hand through his hair, the other tapped at the steering wheel. "You don't get it. Dad has to be the best at everything. It's hard-wired into him. But he's just a guy who scraped through a general degree in some state university and never made it any further. He built his business with hard work and raw charisma but he's embarrassed by his poor vocabulary. Tries to compensate by studying the dictionary and memorizing quotable sayings." He darted a worried glance at me. "Don't ever mention I told you that."

"Never," I said, pulling an imaginary zipper across my lips.

We drove past the Stone Arch Bridge. I turned my head away, those carved initials still lingering at the back of my mind. But I pushed the thought aside and tried hard to concentrate on the way the sun etched Guy's profile with light.

"So how does he feel about you and your doctorate?"

"You're too smart to ask me that, Anna. You already know the answer. So tell me."

The image of those carved initials kept reappearing at the back of my mind. How had Birdie's initial appeared on top of mine? But I sensed Guy had asked me something important. Something vital to his own self-image. I studied his face, the slight furrow scored between his eyebrows, the long lashes behind the glasses and the faint stubble on his chin. His vulnerability brought a lump to my throat. I wanted to lean against him. Tell him I'd support him whatever happened, so I ripped my mind back to the present.

"Okay. I'd say he's proud of you, but at the same time you're a constant reminder of his own inadequacy and that's what drives his engine. His need to dominate the upstart professor is in constant conflict with the guilt that he's competing with his only son. How's that?"

I could swear tears glistened in his eyes. "Right on the money," he said, reaching out to grasp my hand. "That's why he's always needling me – always trying to call the shots. If he has the upper hand then he feels he's less of a loser. So he goes on the attack before anyone else can fire the first missile and put him down."

"Why do you go along with it?"

He shook his head. "It's easier that way. When he's happy, everyone's happy."

"You mean your mom?"

"Especially her."

"But not you." I squeezed his hand. "You put so much into that street kids' outreach program. Why don't you just tell Gord you want to keep going with it?"

His eyes narrowed and he chewed his lower lip. "You mean well, Anna. I know you do, but you just don't get it. Going against Dad is like starting a mutiny. It's not worth the headache." He paused for a moment, then lowered his voice. "Our family has had its share of troubles in the past and now things have settled down. I'd like to keep it that way."

"What kind of troubles?"

He nodded. "Mom and Dad went through a rough patch when I was younger. A long time ago."

"What happened?"

He adjusted his glasses and cleared his throat. Concentrated on the road ahead. "I don't know. Other women, I think. It's tough to talk about."

"She left him?"

"She tried. But it's not easy when you have a kid and… *shit*…" The screech of brakes and blare of a horn shattered the moment. "I almost sideswiped that guy."

A truck squealed by. The driver gave Guy the finger.

"Can we talk about something else?" he said, lifting his glasses and pressing at his eyelids.

"But this is about your life and your ambitions. Not your father's. So what's the worst that can happen? He'll have a hissy fit and then he'll get over it. We're all adults, aren't we?"

"Sometimes Dad can be like a big kid. Mom and I know it's best to humor him at those times. Life runs smoother for everyone if we do." He sighed as we pulled up to yet another traffic light. "But I promise I'll think about keeping the project going. I'll do it on the quiet."

I remembered Robin's sad, puppy-dog face. "Robin's gung-ho about his street kids' outreach program. Thanks to you and Brian they got a grant for it."

We pulled away, following the slow stream of rush-hour cars on their way to the suburbs. A light drizzle fogged the windshield. "That was the luckiest day of my life, coming to your school." We pulled up at another red light and he dipped over to kiss my temple. "I met you."

"So what did you think when Robin first called you about the presentation?"

"Let me think. I should remember because his accent stuck with me. That weird Brit and US mix. He rambled on a bit then mentioned that I'd come highly recommended, by some talented teacher at his school."

My face flushed and I turned away to watch the drab brown freeway walls flashing by. I glanced back, hoping the blush wasn't too evident. From the corner of my eye, I could see him grinning.

"Holy crap – was that you? Were you the one who recommended me?"

I watched a homeless man wheel a packed shopping cart up a steep incline away from the freeway.

Guy persisted. "C'mon, Anna. That's sweet. I love the idea that you noticed me. I remember when I got to your school I had this weird feeling that something life changing was about to happen. I mean I don't usually believe in all that karma crap. But I was actually looking out for someone to walk up and tell me they were my secret admirer. And I was hoping like hell it wasn't the wiry female bodybuilder with the fake tan. Or the weird science guy with the bed-head hair. But all the time it was you. I should have known. The way you were hanging back but still checking me out. You had a hungry look in your eyes – sort of predatory and brooding. I couldn't resist you."

"I did no such thing," I said, playing with my silver medallion. "You were the one checking me out."

"I couldn't take my eyes off you. That wild, dark hair and those lips. It was all I could do to stick to my notes. And I was terrified I'd develop a huge hard-on and they'd kick me out for lewd behavior."

"Beast," I said, snuggling closer.

"I love you, Anna," he whispered. My chest tightened. I felt that old fear creeping in again, but somehow I felt more connected to the present – to the reality of what was actually happening now.

"I'm glad we met, Guy. So glad."

25

Gord was in a prickly mood. I could sense it as soon as I walked through the polished teak doors. The whole mood of the place was off. I had a nose for that kind of thing. When you move from one shitty foster home to another you become an expert at reading the mood of the people in a house, at sniffing out danger.

I've been in many abusive households. Seen it all. The way a woman jumps up from the couch when her husband comes in, because she doesn't want him calling her a lazy slut. Or the way she hovers round the dining table, not tasting a bite until he takes the first and nods his head or grunts to let her know it's okay for her to sit down and eat. The way members of a family touch or don't touch each other. When a father or stepfather's hand lingers too long on his daughter's hip or when a mother's fingertips dig into her toddler's arm leaving angry red splotches. The way the tendons in Lester's neck used to tighten up when Patti started moaning about her back pain. Or the way Lester walked past our bedroom in his raggedy boxers, stroking his crotch when Patti was passed out cold on the living room couch.

When you're immersed in all that, you learn to make yourself so small you're almost invisible so you can blend in with the furniture. That's the only way to survive. I was an expert but Birdie hadn't mastered the art of disappearing. Until later. When there was no other option.

The first hint of discord was Nancy's swollen eyelids. Either she hadn't slept or she'd been crying. As usual she was immaculately groomed and still greeted me with a kiss on both cheeks. But she was jumpy around Gord, as if she was deliberately trying to keep space between them. Her bright smile looked forced and weary and her fingers bunched up on Guy's shoulders as she clutched him just a bit too tightly. Gord, meanwhile, was on overdrive. He wrapped Guy in a fierce embrace that almost knocked the wind out of him, then he placed both hands around my waist and placed a long, damp kiss on my cheek. I pulled away, fighting the urge to slap him, but he was already on his way to the kitchen.

"Get some drinks together, Nancy. We need to celebrate the arrival of our newest team member."

She scurried by him but not before he reached out and grabbed her ass in his hand, squeezing so hard she cried out. I glanced at Guy who glared at his father with burning eyes.

"Dammit, Dad — Anna's here," he protested.

Nancy froze rigid to the spot until Gord let go, a mischievous grin on his face. "Chill out, son. My wife may be well past fifty but she's still got a great ass. I'm a lucky man." He delivered a parting slap to her rear as she scuttled out of the way, then glanced around at us. "C'mon — loosen up you two. Oh no. Have I offended the *professor*?"

"Cut it out, Dad," said Guy, moving away into the living room, but Gord followed like a hound scenting blood.

Gord filled the doorway, his face flushed with drink. His eyes fell on me. "Anna, you've got a sense of humor, unlike the other ghosts in my family. They wouldn't know a good time if it stood up and smacked them in the face. As the Brits say, they couldn't enjoy a piss-up in a brewery. At least I think that's the saying." He frowned as if searching for the right words. "But I'll bet you've seen a bit of action in your time."

I looked at Guy, trying to get a cue from him. What to say? How to respond? And what exactly did he mean by the last comment?

"Cat got your tongue, sweetheart, or has the professor briefed you already on how to deal with his vulgar clod of a father?"

Guy moved forward as if to shield me. "You said we were coming here to celebrate, Dad. You could at least be nice to Anna."

Gord reached for his half-finished drink and swigged it back. Then he held up a hand to his mouth in fake surprise. "Oh dear. Better show some penitence. Take a hundred lashes. Or maybe I might enjoy that too much."

A sudden, loud crash from the kitchen had Guy and me up and out of our seats. We rushed in to find Nancy on hands and knees trying to pick up shards of a broken wine glass with her bare hands. A pool of white wine was spreading across the floor tinted with the pale tinge of blood. Her shoulders shook as she struggled to contain the mess.

Guy swept over and pulled her up. "Mom. Stop. Get up." He cradled her in his arms.

I yanked some kitchen towel from the roll and wrapped her hands. Tiny dots of blood soaked into the white. "It's okay. Just minor cuts."

Nancy was almost hyperventilating. "So clumsy. Don't know what happened." Her eyes darted to the doorway. Gord stood there. Eyes widening in horror.

For a moment they stared at each other. The silence quivered.

Suddenly his big body seemed to deflate, all the bluster fizzling out of him like a burst balloon. Nancy pulled herself away from Guy and walked towards her husband. She reached for his arm, gently steering him to the couch where he sat, legs splayed, head bowed. We all held our breath, watched and waited until he finally raised his head, then held her injured hands and kissed them.

"I'm a bad drunk," he said, looking directly at me with baleful eyes. "Been under a bit of stress lately with all this funding bullshit. I hit the scotch too early. Nancy warned me to go easy, but of course I never listen to her. I should, I know I should. She's my guiding star. I just don't appreciate her enough."

He reached for her, nuzzling his head against her waist. I could swear she stiffened at first then took a deep breath and ruffled his hair. Peace was restored for now as Guy and I went to clean up the spill.

Supper went without a hitch. Gord sobered up, then slipped back into professional mode, outlining the data gathering techniques and focus groups I'd be involved with once I joined the project. Everyone was relaxed and loose until the coffee arrived. The cocktails and wine had loosened my tongue enough for me to blurt out, without too much warning, that Guy really wanted to opt back into the homeless kids' education project. Then all the goodwill fled, as if I'd wiped a whiteboard clean. Gord's face was tight with anger.

"So you've been whining about me behind my back instead of facing me like a man, son?" said Gord, his face contorted into an injured expression.

I gulped, feeling suddenly stone cold sober. "Actually I brought it up, Gord. I know how passionate Guy is about the program."

Guy was already glaring at me and Nancy's hand hovered in the air, holding the cream jug.

"I should get a refill," she blurted, but Gord's hand clamped down on her wrist and she sank back into her chair.

"Anna, my darling daughter-in-law. You must learn very quickly if you want to get along with this family that charity and passion don't pay the rent. Guy's condo, his import car and your designer wardrobe are out of reach on a professor's pittance. He knows and Nancy knows that you don't get all that from doing goddamn charitable deeds for deprived street kids. All this good stuff comes courtesy of my goddamn business savvy." He spat the words out as he jabbed at the side of his temple with his forefinger. "*Capiche.*"

My mouth was dry. I nodded. He wanted to own all of us. Guy and me included. Suddenly he reminded me of Loni who'd sunk her talons into Birdie and never let go until she'd dragged her away from me. I dug my fingernails into my thighs just to let the sharp stab of pain bring me back to the present.

"I put a lot of work into setting up that project, Dad," said Guy. "I just wanted to keep in touch with Brian – get some updates, that's all."

Gord glared at me, then reached for the Drambuie and poured a glass. As he sipped, the anger seemed to drain away. We all held our breath.

"Okay, I guess that can't hurt. But keep it at arm's length, son. Karrass advised us not to get in too deep with those kids. Too many problems. All kinds of liabilities and too many other do-gooders with fingers in the pie."

"Karrass?" I blurted, unable to stop myself. Gord glanced over at me, squinting as if to measure up what I knew.

"You know him?"

I shrugged. "Not really. But some of my students may be on his caseload. Down-on-their-luck teens looking to make money from unsavory characters down by the riverbanks."

Nancy's face almost went purple and Guy choked on his coffee. Gord's eyes flicked back and forth between them. He fixed a forced smile on his face.

"Please keep that to yourself, dear. Peter is a respected social worker. I'm sure he wouldn't choose to be referred to as *the old guy working the underage hookers*."

He winked at me and my stomach lurched. But I forced a fake smile and busied myself stacking dirty plates. Gord stood up, beckoning for Guy to join him in his study for a private word. Nancy silently cleared off the supper dishes, her bandaged fingers waving away my offer of help. I sat there wondering exactly what I'd stirred up with my impulsive comments.

Before swishing off into the kitchen she'd passed me the TV remote and curtly ordered me to put my feet up since I'd been at work all day. I guessed she was still embarrassed about Gord's ass-grabbing exploits and the kitchen incident, so I flipped through the channels unable to settle on anything but the Shopping Channel where someone was trying to push today's showstopper product – a ninety-four-dollar, nine-piece, skin hydration set.

I was just considering the idea of pulling out my credit card and ordering a set when Nancy bustled back in to collect the dirty serving dishes. She mouthed *everything okay* at me and I nodded. Leaning my head back against the couch I put the sound on mute and closed my eyes. Let my mind wander to thoughts about Colby and Birdie. Always Birdie.

–

Colby actually came through with a rescue plan in the end. Reid, one of his gamer buddies, had his own house with a spare room that he was willing to let Birdie and me stay in until we got ourselves sorted. All we had to do was find the right time to sneak out with our few belongings. Birdie said she was working on her own escape plan and didn't need my help, but I convinced her Colby and his buddy would come through with their promise. We just had to wait until Patti and Lester were both out of the house, which was virtually never, since Patti was a permanent fixture on that grungy couch.

She sometimes ventured out for medical appointments or when the two of them made a trip to the Treasure Island Casino just outside of the city. But the last time they'd gone, they must've lost a bundle because they came back yelling at each other, then slammed the front door so hard the walls shook. We ate instant noodles for days after that.

That entire week after Colby came up with the escape plan, I stuck close by Patti and Lester, listening in to their conversations by pretending to do homework at the kitchen table. I checked out the calendar on the fridge to see if Patti had scrawled down any appointment times.

By that time Patti had slipped into her usual lethargy and had lost interest in forcing medication down Birdie's throat. Instead she shoved the pill cup into my hand and told me to *give her the damned shit instead.* So I switched Birdie's pills for junior aspirins and vitamin capsules that I jacked from the drugstore. I wanted her alert when the time came. There's no way I could drag her drugged body from that apartment. So after a few days Birdie's head cleared, but it seemed like our plan was on hold until I could get Birdie to school with me and Patti and Lester wouldn't allow that.

I went to find Colby at the mall to tell him I still didn't have any idea when we could leave. But really I just wanted to see him and touch him. Since the incident under the bridge we'd acted like there was an electric force field between us. At school when our fingertips touched, jolts crackled across our skin. Our desire for each other was almost palpable, a shimmering wall of sweaty teenage hormones.

On the way to the gamers' store I spotted Lester who was working a lot of overtime – probably to fund their escalating drug habit. I caught him with his sweaty face pressed against the window of Toonz, his breath fogging a small circle on the window. Not wanting him to spot me, I hid around a corner. He checked to see both directions were clear before he slid into the store and made his way to the counter where Earl Rafferty was perched, chatting like a madman into his cell phone. Lester loomed over him, his shoulders hunched. Earl broke off the conversation and nodded his head towards the back room. Lester plunged through the curtain into the darkness of the cubicles. I was so focused on him I almost jumped out of my skin when two cool hands clamped across my eyes.

"Doing some secret surveillance?" said a familiar voice. I whirled round to find Colby grinning at me. My heart did a somersault. I was burning for those hands to be all over me, but all I could do was swallow and make lame excuses.

"Just checking Lester out. I think he's jerking off to porn at Earl's place."

"Perv. People like him should be banned from fostering kids," he said, digging his hands into his pockets.

"I haven't found a good time for the escape plan. Patti never goes out. But it needs to be soon so let's make it Wednesday."

Colby reached a hand out to twirl a long, ragged tendril of my hair. I'd just started letting it go wild. He leaned close and whispered in my ear. "I've been thinking that when you're at Reid's I can spend some nights with you. I sometimes stay there at weekends. Especially when my dad has people over. Imagine what it would be like to hold each other all night and wake up together."

Back then I thought this was true love. The warm, slow burn in my lower body that made me squirm with an urge to run round in ever-decreasing circles until all that excess energy was used up. Then the seedy mall became a magic place, its graffiti-covered hallways and grimy corners filled with the hiss of whispered promises and the memory of breathless groping.

I clung to Colby's hand. "I can't wait till Wednesday."

He glanced around. The mall was filling up with last-minute shoppers. Office workers dropping in before starting the long commute home.

He bent his head downwards and kissed me on the mouth. Our teeth thunked together and we pulled back laughing. I stood on tiptoe and kissed him softly, slipping my tongue into his mouth. The taste of gum and sweet saliva made my skin tremble.

"You're so hot, Anna. I can't wait until you're at Reid's house. In the meantime I got something for you."

He reached into his pocket. "Here. Read this," he said, taking out a dog-eared paperback. "It'll turn you on."

I checked out the cover. *Tropic of Cancer* by Henry Miller.

"It was banned everywhere when it came out. You'll soon find out why. Just don't show any teachers you have it."

Stashing the book in my backpack, I glanced through the window of Toonz to see if Lester had surfaced. "Must be watching a double feature," I said, pushing my hair away from my eyes.

"Maybe he couldn't get it up for the first one," said Colby, trailing a finger down my arm. "See you at school?"

I nodded. How could I tell him that wildfires, tornadoes, even alien invasions wouldn't stop me from getting there to see him?

That night I could barely concentrate on my homework. Just the idea of hatching a real plan to get away from Lester and Patti had me perched on the edge of my seat in a permanent state of readiness. As if I could spring up and run five miles without stopping. But I couldn't forget about Birdie. Somehow I had to be able to get her up and out of that house before Lester took those few steps across the bedroom threshold while I was away at school and took everything from her.

And I knew it was only a matter of time before he did.

–

"Do you take sugar in your coffee?" said Nancy. I blinked my eyes and snapped back to the present. Tuning into the past was becoming a habit. Images slid in and out of my consciousness until I barely knew what was real. And I had no idea how I appeared to other people around me when it was happening. Was I just sitting there staring into space? Was I was even talking to myself like a crazy person?

"No – thanks, Nancy," I said, taking a long sip. I could feel a jolt from the caffeine filtering into my brain.

Nancy sat on the edge of her chair occasionally glancing at the door. I recognized the posture. I'd sat opposite Lester and Patti that way, carefully monitoring their voices, gestures, tiny movements. Always watching, testing the mood, training myself to spot the first sign of trouble. My body was exhausted by the time they stuck a joint under my nose, forced me to take a couple of hits then said *get lost and go to bed and check on your sister.*

Correction. They didn't have to strong-arm me to smoke weed.

I was craving it by the time it got round to me.

The skunky sweet smoke was the only thing that took the edge off my constant state of tension.

"Don't let Gord get to you," said Nancy. "Most of the time he's pretty accommodating. He just has this need to feel like he's in control. Make him believe he's running things and he's like putty in your hands. Then you can basically get on and do your own thing."

"Is that what you do?"

She tilted her head. "Do what?"

"Let him think he owns you?"

She opened her mouth to respond but the office door burst open and the two guys strode out.

"Time to go, babe," said Guy. I tried to read his face but he wasn't giving me anything. What plan had been hatched in that office between father and son? And when would Guy fill me in on it? I wondered then where his loyalties really lay. If it came to some vital life or death business decision would he choose Gord over me? That familiar sense of precariousness caused me to stumble against the chair when I stood up. Guy's eyes flew over to me.

"You okay?" he mouthed.

I nodded just as Nancy stood up to immediate attention and Gord wrapped an arm around her shoulder. She didn't lean in towards him until he squeezed her close. It was like watching an intense war of wills that Gord inevitably won.

"So don't forget Thursday night," he said to Guy.

"What's happening Thursday?" I said.

Gord shook his head and grinned. "Just a guy thing, Anna. One of our programmers is getting married and we're having a bachelor party."

"I'm an unwilling guest," said Guy. "I'm not a fan of all that beer and male bonding garbage."

"What did I tell you, Anna? My son is a wuss. He's afraid of letting loose and enjoying himself. But you'll change all that. Help him man up. I have high hopes."

We drove home with Guy barely saying a word and later, when we tried to make love, he stopped halfway through and said, *I'm sorry, I can't*, leaving my frenzied body screaming for release.

I lay there staring at the ceiling, listening to the night sounds and wondering exactly what Gord was up to and how it involved Guy.

26

Noises at night are magnified. It's something to do with the darkness snuffing out your sense of sight. The clanking of rails cars shunting in the distance, the *flak flak* of a police helicopter circling overhead, the faint snuffling of Guy's breathing. Like a symphony I couldn't shut out. An hour later I was still awake, so I stroked the inside of my thighs and thought of Colby.

The day before the escape plan I stopped him at his locker once classes were done. He was shuffling through a deck of Magic Cards.

"I started reading the book you gave me. I loved that bit at the beginning, about the book being *a prolonged insult, a gob of spit in the face of art* but after that it just rambled on about men wishing they had bigger dicks to use on women. Why is Miller such a misogynistic jerk?"

He snapped the locker shut, pushed his hair from his face and sighed. "I thought you of all people would see beyond the words. Can't you see he's just denouncing conventional art and morality? Asserting his own personal freedom – distancing himself from the crippling tedium of mainstream society. It's like when you spell out the forbidden, you demystify it. Get it?"

For the first time we were on a different wavelength. But I couldn't tell him that when you live with someone like Lester Flatt who tries to grope you every time you pass by him at the kitchen table, or rubs his groin while he's sitting next to his stoned wife, it's tough to find subtlety and meaning in explicit sexual imagery.

I followed Colby towards the exit door. "Tell me something," I said, grasping his wrist. "If you're so keen to demystify the forbidden like Miller says, then why're you too chicken to go all the way with me?"

He looked scared. "I'm not. I just don't want to take advantage of you."

"What if I want you to?"

"Are you serious?" he said, stopping to look at me for a long, slow moment. "Then let's go to Reid's."

The place was empty when we arrived at Reid's house, breathless from running. "He's done around six," said Colby unlocking the back door of a tiny white stucco bungalow. Inside was a typical guy hangout that reeked of musty laundry and rancid cooking oil. He led me past a sinkful of crusty dishes and a kitchen table stacked with empty beer bottles and open cereal boxes. I took it all in, savoring the idea that this would be my first time. That someone cared enough to want to be with me. It was the closest thing I'd ever experienced to being loved by anyone other than Birdie.

"In here," he whispered, pushing me into a tiny room off the kitchen. Warm, dark and musty, it contained a narrow single bed covered with a faded blue bedspread. We never made it to the bed. Once the door banged shut he pushed me against the door and started to tear at my clothes. I followed his lead, yanking his T-shirt over his head and groping at his jeans zipper. Soon we faced each other naked. I'd expected his body to be pale and skinny but his skin was lightly tanned and silky. I pressed against him. Skin on skin. Slippery like silk. Every nerve end tingling when I touched him.

He nuzzled the side of my neck. "You feel incredible."

His warm breath tickled my ear and I kissed his cheek, his eyes, his mouth. Our lips were still pressed together when we stumbled towards the bed and fell back onto the sheets. I didn't know what to do next until he fumbled at his groin, pushed my legs apart and I felt a slight stab of pain that set my thighs tingling. He thrust hard against me until he moaned and shuddered to a climax. And though I wasn't transported into a state of ecstasy, the feeling of closeness – of being folded against his body – was worth the world to me. For that moment I felt I actually belonged to someone. That someone really cared.

"I love you," I gasped, knowing that my heart would burst open with joy if I just let go for once in my miserable life. "I love you, Colby."

–

An arm landed across my chest zapping me into the present and the sound of Guy's soft breathing whistling into the silence. I was warm and safe in this room. I'd experienced that same feeling when I clung to Colby all those years ago. We were two clumsy teens experimenting with sex in that rundown little room, but I'd spent years trying to recapture the same intimacy in the arms and beds of many other men. It had eluded me until now. Colby, my first, and Guy who I hoped might be my last lover, would always be the best, and that was something positive about my life that would never change.

I could never risk losing Guy. And that's why he could never know about Birdie.

Even though I was so close to finding her.

27

Summer break was looming on the horizon and I still hadn't summoned up the courage to tell the kids I was leaving. I was afraid I'd lose them. They'd see it as treachery or desertion. Not a simple career move.

I knew their way of thinking. It went like this. You start by trusting every well-intentioned adult who enters your life. You cling to them, believing they can actually help you. Then, one after another, they drift away or cast you off when they can't cope with the ton of messy baggage you're carrying. I'd lived that life. Always hoping that this time I'd land a permanent, nurturing home where good, kind people would cherish me and never let me down. It didn't happen for me. Until the Levines turned my life around and then Guy came along and adored me.

But the kids in my class, they'd poured out their hopes, fears and deepest, darkest secrets into those journals and I'd received them with a promise that we shared a bond of trust that couldn't be broken. How could I tell them I was packing up and leaving?

I'd already lost Carla. Hadn't heard a word about her since I'd seen her at the manicure salon. But Dane was actually close to graduating and I couldn't jeopardize that fragile situation. Especially when there was a faint chance he could go to college and make a better life for himself.

Robin always knocked himself out searching for scholarships, bursaries, awards – anything to keep the kids away from the streets. That guy was dedicated. Irreplaceable. Not like me. And though I convinced myself they'd easily find a replacement for me, I still felt guilty that I'd sold myself out for money and prestige.

But there was no turning back now. I'd come too far.

-

I stayed late at school on the day of the stag party, flipping through the journals, reading the same sentence ten times over until I looked up and almost jumped out of my chair. Dane was standing at the back of the classroom. He'd dyed his hair and now sported a cerise Mohawk cut. Along with his wire-rimmed glasses he looked like some half human, half goblin character from a Harry Potter movie.

"Got a question?" I said, beckoning him closer.

He shook his head. He usually talked in two-word sentences. "Tell you something?"

"Sure, anything."

When he dug his hands into the pockets of the ripped trench coat and hunched his shoulders, he reminded me of Colby. A stab of pain ripped at my heart.

"It's Carla," he murmured.

I leaned forward and spoke softly as if he was a bird that would fly away at the slightest noise. "Okay – tell me."

"She's with Rafferty. It's bad stuff."

"What kind of stuff?"

He shook his head. "The girls. He gives them stuff. Gets them high. Makes them work for him. Hires them out."

"For what?"

"That's all I know," he said, shaking his head. It was useless to push him any further. "I gotta go now."

I called after him. "If you find out anything else, Dane. I'm here."

He nodded without looking back at me, then was gone.

I stood up, my heart thudding. Rafferty. That sweet-faced bastard, that conniving prick. Fifteen years ago, I'd found out everything there was to know about Mr. Earl Rafferty and his *business*.

—

The night before our planned escape, Lester and Patti had a couple of friends over. Tray and Anita. Two wild-eyed junkies who'd stopped by a few weeks before and promised to bring along some quality meth.

Perched on my usual chair in the corner of the living room, I was trying to write an essay outline when I heard Patti in the kitchen jabbering like a fiend to Lester while he stirred up a huge pot of mac and cheese. Tray and Anita sat like a pair of shabby scarecrows at the kitchen table, a scrunched up brown paper bag in front of them. Tray was skinny with stringy, yellow hair. Every time Lester passed by, Tray's hand shot out to cover the paper bag.

I was just about to make a hasty retreat to the bedroom when, for the first time in days, Birdie dragged herself out of bed. She flopped down on Patti's couch, grabbed the sacred remote and began to flip through the channels. My stomach churned. I had to get her out of the room before Patti found her there. The late afternoon sunlight streamed through the window showing me how much Birdie had changed. Her body was so thin her shoulder blades poked through her skin, which was covered in pale peach fuzz. If Patti got pissed off she could snap those bird arms with one twist of her pudgy fingers.

"Come sit at the table," I whispered.

Birdie looked at me with blank eyes.

"Patti's gonna be pissed."

"Screw her. Wait a couple of hours. Then the shit's really gonna hit the fan, Miss Goody Two Shoes."

"What are you talking about?"

"How long do you think they can lock me up here like some sad junkie? Every day I have to fight off Lester the pervert while you go off to school like Miss Perfect Angel. I know you're in it with them. I know you're getting high on all their junk."

I knelt down by her chair. Her eyes blazed out from dark hollows. "You don't know what you're saying. I've tried to help you. My friend Colby – he's gonna get us both out tomorrow. We're gonna stay with his buddy. We'll be safe there."

"Too late for that," she said, slumping deeper into the cushions and hiding her face. "*Ew*, this chair reeks of armpits."

I grabbed her arm, shocked at the brittleness of her bones. "What do you mean too late?"

"You'll see," she said, hoisting herself out of the chair. "You'll see."

"Stick around, kid," Patti yelled as she, Lester and the two ghouls shuffled in from the kitchen. Lester had a piece of macaroni in his moustache. Birdie's shoulders dropped. She frowned.

"Cut the attitude," yelled Lester, holding out two bowls of macaroni. "Sit down with your sister and be grateful for the food we're putting in your stomach."

"Good on you, Lester," said Tray. "Kids today have no respect. You show 'em who's boss."

Tray's wife, Anita, sniffed and wiped her arm across her nose. She had wrinkled smoker's lips and hair so bleached it stuck out in fried, blonde wisps. "You and Patti sure have big hearts taking in kids nobody else wants. Too bad they're just trash, taking you for all they can get."

Patti shrugged and nodded her head towards me. "The dark haired one's all right, but the skinny one. She's a little witch. Can't trust her for a minute. She'd strip us bare and sell us for a few cents."

Birdie's whole body tensed until her sinews were two taut chords in her neck.

"I said sit the hell down," yelled Lester. "You look like a goddamn scarecrow. So eat."

I grasped her wrist. "Do as they say. Please."

Birdie's eyes burned into mine with such hate I wanted to retch. But she slowly sank down onto the chair, her head bowed. Lester clunked the two bowls down in front of us. I was famished but nauseous at the same time, so I dug into the noodles and shoveled them into my mouth. It was a rare occasion that food came our way without us scrounging through the cupboards for it. Birdie sat unmoving.

"Eat," I whispered. "Don't piss them off."

In slow motion she reached for the spoon, picked up one piece of macaroni and placed it on her tongue. A look of utter revulsion flickered across her face. I tried to remember when she'd last eaten something more substantial than a handful of crackers.

Lester and Patti settled themselves onto the couch while Tray and Anita fumbled with the brown paper bag, pulling out a plastic baggie tied with a twist tie and a hollow glass tube with a bulb at one end. Tray held the pipe like a sacred artifact while Anita tipped a tiny chunk of *ice* into the bowl. He reached into his pocket and took out a lighter. Flipping it on, he held the flame under the bowl. A fizzing, bubbling sound was followed by a sweet stink of burning plastic. Birdie's eyes tracked the pipe as it rose to Anita's lips. Her spoon hovered in the air. I wondered if she'd already tried it with Loni and was craving a hit.

Anita fell back against the chair back, a blissful grin cracking her face. Tray beckoned Patti who sprang forward and wedged her squishy butt on the corner of a cushion, then closed her eyes as he slipped the pipe into her mouth. The lighter clicked and flared. The meth sizzled, and all eyes followed the magic pipe as it rose through the air. Patti inhaled a lungful of smoke and sank back with a blissful grin on her face. Lester took his like a starving baby craving milk, and soon all four of them had blasted off to oblivion, chattering and blabbing about how great they felt and how Lester was going to get right up and whip up a batch of strawberry waffles from scratch, but maybe he'd wait till he had another hit.

"Stupid junkies," mumbled Birdie. "Look at them."

"Let's get out of here. Go to our room," I whispered. "They'll be out cold soon."

"I'm not moving from here. I got friends coming. Friends who're looking out for me. Unlike my dumb sister."

I put a finger to my lips and shook my head. "If we lock our bedroom door they won't notice. And tomorrow we're getting out for good."

"Too late, baby. Loni called this morning. She's got friends who'll get me out of this shithole. Connected friends."

I was cold and prickly all over. It wasn't supposed to go like that.

Loni wasn't included. It was just going to be Birdie and me like it always had been. I wanted to argue, to beg her not to go with Loni, but I stifled the urge and instead kept an eye on the crazy quartet who were struggling to their feet and trying to dance to 'More Than A Feeling' as Lester cranked up the music.

"When is Loni coming? When?"

Birdie barely glanced at me. "Any time soon. And she's gonna teach these losers a lesson when she gets here. A big, fat lesson they'll never forget and I'll be laughing my fricking head off when it happens."

Sick apprehension clenched my stomach. The macaroni sat like a heavy lump in my gut. Birdie watched the door and cracked her knuckles. Watching. Waiting. For freedom and revenge.

—

I called in at the outlet mall on the way home. I knew Guy would be at some downtown bar having pre-stag drinks and I had a whole lot of time to kill. Besides, all this stress and worry had drained me and I needed a shopping fix. It was time to find some office chic stuff for my new job with Gord's company. Jeans, denim skirts and plaid shirts wouldn't cut it in Gord's upscale empire. Slim, tailored and sexy was the look I was after though not too provocative. If Gord attempted to touch my ass the way he'd done with Nancy, I'd waste no time plowing him in the jaw. To hell with his stupid ego.

After a major shopping binge for suits, little black dresses and a rainbow of fitted silk shirts and shells, I flopped down at a coffee shop table to sort through my stash. Carla's lingerie store was directly opposite but she wasn't there anymore. She was working for Earl Rafferty now. He'd lured her away from her one chance to make a decent life for herself. Promised her manicures, pedicures, beauty treatments and probably clothes. I imagined he'd come across as sweet and generous at first, easing her into trusting him. Only later when he had her under his thumb would he spring the real jobs on her. Maybe easy ones at first, then the unmentionable ones later. It was standard practice for jerks like him.

I was about to sip my hazelnut latte when I spotted a heavy-set, broad-shouldered guy standing outside the lingerie store. His white T-shirt stretched across his muscular chest, the short sleeves revealing a bold zigzag tattoo down both arms. But it was his face that made my hand shake so hard, I spilled the hot coffee down my wrist. I'd seen that face before. The broad, flat nose, reddish cheeks and narrow slits of eyes. A black baseball cap covered graying straggly hair. A phone rang and he lifted it to his ear with a hand as big as an oar.

I knew him. Jimmy "Mack" Durban, one of Earl Rafferty's henchmen and chief "talent" spotter.

How did I know that? He'd recruited Birdie and Loni when they were hanging out in the mall. And he was there that night Birdie got her revenge. For that she owed him and Earl Rafferty big time.

–

Lester twitched his scrawny hips and tried to drag Patti off the couch to dance to their rubbish music. Her face glowed crimson from giggling when she gave one, huge tug and pulled him on top of her. He struggled for a moment like a fat turtle, then said, *To hell with it*, and started necking furiously with her. Tray and Anita just sat smoking as if that pipe was the only real thing that existed in the world. They were old hands so it probably took a whole lot more hits to get them high. Birdie's eyes glanced over at the clock with the knife and fork hands. The look on her face was so cold and cruel I couldn't think of what to say.

"I'm coming too," I mumbled.

She shrugged. "Depends."

"On what?"

"If Loni lets you."

"You can't leave me here on my own."

"You left me here for weeks while they stuffed me full of drugs. What's the difference?"

I leaned forward and grasped her wrist. "I helped you. Gave you food and water. Looked after you."

"You went off to school so you could make out with that nerdy guy."

"How do you know Colby?"

"That his name? Figures."

"You've never met him."

"I have so. He's a lousy lay. Saw him at the mall. He was so easy. A genuine man-whore."

I heard a loud buzzing in my ears. "Where? When?"

"Under the Stone Arch Bridge. It was freezing out – a crazy wind chill. He came so quick I barely got started."

"You're a liar," I said, loud enough that Lester's head swiveled like a chicken's.

He creaked to his feet and lunged towards me, probably to give me supreme shit, but a loud banging started up at the front door.

"What the hell...?" he gasped, bashing his knee on the coffee table.

Patti and the two others stopped their babbling to gaze around in a shell-shocked stupor.

"Did someone call the freakin' cops or something?" said Tray, stuffing the meth paraphernalia into the bag and tearing it in the process, while his wife licked her finger and gathered the stray dust, not missing a grain.

Patti's bloodshot eyes finally came to rest on me. "Lying sack of shit," she hissed. "Creeping around here like a freakin' owl and watching everything. Lester," she squealed. "It's her. She's sold us out. I told you she was trouble. Both of them ain't worth shit."

I shook my head and looked down at Birdie whose eyes were fixed on the locked door.

The banging escalated to such a point that the neighbors would soon start to complain. A call to the cops might follow and neither Lester nor Patti wanted to risk that happening. Panicked looks flew between them.

"Ungrateful bitches, the pair of you. Sit tight and open your books. Patti, answer the door," said Lester. "Tray and Anita are gonna leave out back."

The two ghouls vanished like a puff of noxious smoke and Patti, launched from her meth fog into a grim reality, shuffled to the door and grasped the handle just as it burst open, knocking her flat against the wall. Loni swept in, her spiky hair standing up as if her entire body was plugged into an electric socket. She spotted Birdie and flounced over to her, ignoring Lester's sweaty red face.

"Who the hell are you?" he bellowed. "Get out of my..."

Loni was taller than Lester by almost a head. She towered over him, her eyes burning into the top of his freckled head. "Or what, you pervert piece of junkie dirt?"

"Or I'll..."

"You'll call the cops. I doubt it. You been hot-icing it in here and you call yourself a foster parent."

"Better than a crazy punk dyke."

I crept behind the table as the door swung open to reveal Earl Rafferty and a square-shouldered man with a shaved head and flattened nose.

Patti and Lester retreated to the couch while Loni gathered Birdie into a bear hug. Birdie was sobbing, her whole body heaving while Loni whispered into her ear. "I'm gonna get you out of here, baby. Get you healthy again. No more Lester the sick pervert. You'll see, baby. Earl's gonna take care of him."

Earl and Jimmy hovered over Lester who'd shrunk into a shivering, quaking mess. Earl cracked his knuckles, dragged Lester up onto his feet and snapped a sharp right hook into his face, demolishing his nose and sending a spray of blood across Patti's face. She yelped like a puppy as Jimmy punched him deep in the gut. Earl followed up with a thudding kick to his side. Jimmy let go of Lester's shirt and let him double over into a heap on the floor, sobbing like a baby, his nose streaming with blood.

Loni guided Birdie towards the door. My legs were frozen. I could barely move. "I'm coming. Take me too," I called above Patti's whining.

"What did you ever do for her?" said Loni, hand on her hip. "You let them dope her up till she was a freakin' zombie."

My legs loosened up and I ran to the door past Earl and Jimmy who were at the sink washing the blood off their hands. "Birdie, tell them I fed you. I looked out for you. Always."

"Seems like I'm always telling you to get lost," said Loni. "So do it."

Tears streamed down my face. "Birdie, don't leave me. I can't stay here."

She stared at me from the shelter of Loni's arms, her eyes swollen and red. "You left me here alone while you went to school. And what do you think Lester was doing while you were out? Made me jack him off or give him blow jobs every other day while Patti was sleeping on the couch."

I ran to her, grabbing at her T-shirt. "I didn't know, Birdie. You never told me. Why? Why didn't you say anything?"

Her cheeks were wet from sobbing and her eyes so weary I wanted to crush her in my arms and comfort her. I'd always promised to protect her but I'd been so busy with Colby and school and my own miserable life, I'd forgotten about her pain and left her alone to fend for herself.

"I'm so, so sorry, Birdie. I'll never do that again. I'll stay right beside you like always. Like it used to be. Say you'll forgive me. Please."

I waited for the magic words but she just nuzzled her face against Loni's chest.

"Guess you got your answer, bitch. Let's go, Birdie." When they vanished through the doorway I wanted to throw up. Lester lay on the floor moaning so Earl and Jimmy delivered a couple more kicks before leaving just to shut him up.

I scanned the chaos. Smashed coffee table, scattered cigarette butts. Patti crouched over Lester, bawling her eyes out.

I knew Birdie wouldn't be back this time. I had nothing. Nobody in the world.

"Call the cops," whined Patti. "I think he's dead."

I couldn't hear anything but a weird gurgling sound coming from Lester's nose as I handed Patti a Kleenex, picked up my coat and walked out the door.

28

Grief is like anesthesia.

You become numb and disembodied. A random mass of cells suspended in the ether. Your senses shut off from the to and fro of everyday life.

When Birdie left for good, I had no purpose left.

Protecting her had been my driving force – my reason to survive one nightmare home after another. Without her I was a non-person with no direction, no family, no identity. And with such a weight of sorrow on my shoulders it would crush me like an insect.

When I left the Flatts' apartment and slammed their battered front door, I half-slid, half-ran downstairs to the street only stopping to flex my fingers and touch my face and body to reassure myself I still existed. I tried to settle my breathing – tried to erase the image of Lester's bloodied face, and Birdie's head nestled against Loni's shoulder like a child reunited with her mother.

The street was deserted, Birdie, Loni and friends long gone. A bright moon shone behind ragged clouds, and I stood still for a moment to let the night sounds engulf me. A dog howled in a back yard, traffic hummed on a freeway bridge, then a siren sounded, its high-pitched whine edging closer. Patti had cleaned up the drug paraphernalia and called 911. The urge to escape jolted me into action. I ran, the damp air slapping at my face, until I shuddered to a stop at the corner of the block. Nighttime traffic flashed by. My head spun. Which way to go? I had no home. Belonged nowhere. I stood, temporarily blinded by the glare of headlights, and rested my hands on my knees, bent my head and gulped in chilly mouthfuls of air.

I had no home.

So I started jogging in the direction of the mall, my only sanctuary. I ran, the tears sticky on my cheeks until I reached a patch of grass near the mall entrance.

I flung myself down on the ground and rolled over and over in the gritty grass. Pulled my hair, ripped my clothes, howled until my throat was raw and my face covered in snot. Then I lay there, burnt out and hollow, staring up at stars that shone like silver pinpricks in an infinite black expanse of sky.

I'd already made my mind up to jump off the bridge into the river. The stars were just pointing the way. It would be so easy to let the muddy waters close in over my head and fill my lungs until they burst. Nobody cared anyway. My death would be insignificant – less impact than a fly smudged over a windshield.

I got up again and ran towards the river. Exhausted I stumbled down the bank towards the Stone Arch Bridge. The place where Birdie and I had eaten hot dogs and watched the tourists go by. Envious of the bright, laughing faces of those happy families. We didn't know the truth then. But now I was wiser. Now I knew that families were just collections of disparate individuals thrown together by nature. Parasites who sucked the life from each other while trying to promote their own miserable, selfish needs.

I grasped the painted metal railing, hiccupping and retching at the same time. I howled into the night like a stray, unloved dog. The river lapped and sloshed below me, its muddy brown water flecked with golden coins of light from the streetlamps. All I had to do was hitch myself up onto the parapet. No problem. Wipe myself out.

I was done with everyone.

With every careless person who'd treated me as less than human.

I hoisted my body upwards and leaned over the parapet, when a hand clamped down on my shoulder. I froze.

"Don't move," said a soft voice. "Stay absolutely still."

I turned round to see a gray-haired man with a silver goatee. A hand with pink, manicured nails grasped my arm so tightly I couldn't move.

"You might think things are so bad you don't have a choice, but you can't throw your life away."

My head swam. The man's face blurred in and out of focus, like a picture taken too closely. I jumped down and for a split second he loosened his grip. That's all I needed to yank myself away from him and sprint away in the opposite direction.

-

"Are you okay, ma'am?" said an urgent voice. Someone was shaking my arm. I blinked my eyes and focused on the crushed coffee cup lying on the table. I glanced up at the red-haired barista. I was still at the outlet mall. At the coffee shop. I'd sat down at one of their tables after spotting Rafferty's henchman, Jimmy. A puddle of brownish foam leaked over the edge of the table and soaked into my jeans.

"I-I'm okay," I said, grabbing a handful of napkins and dabbing at the mess. Then I stuffed the whole lot into the garbage as I left, slamming the exit door open so fast I almost took out a middle-aged woman on the other side.

I could barely remember driving home, but somehow I got back to the empty condo, stripped off my coffee-stained clothes and poured myself a stiff shot of brandy. Afterwards I lay back on the sofa, trying to collect my thoughts and orient myself.

Guy was late because he'd gone to some stag party with Gord. I glanced at the pile of bags arranged in front of me. I'd been buying clothes for my new career with Gord's company. And somehow Gord was connected with Peter Karrass, the man I'd remembered from the bridge the terrible night Birdie left me at the Flatts' place. I hadn't imagined his face glowing like a half moon in the darkness. Karrass. The man who stopped me from jumping into the raging waters. He was at the wedding celebration at Gord's house. Now memories of places and people were melting into each other, blurring the lines of what was real. The past was bleeding into the present.

My phone buzzed with a text from Guy.

> Rescue me. I'm too drunk to drive.

The address followed. Some swish area, about three miles away. I texted back.

> Be there in 20.

Traffic would be light so it shouldn't take me long.

To calm myself I unpacked all my new clothes and threw them onto hangers, slotting them into place among the silks, cashmeres and fine cottons. From the back of the closet I extracted a stretchy red and black dress. It was tiny, with a plunging neckline. Strange how small items from the past kept reappearing. Like Birdie's ring.

I shuddered and snapped off the closet light.

The dress fit like a second skin, hugged at my hips and ass even though I hadn't worn it in years. But the underwear had to go. Panty lines were a no-no in micro-dresses like this. A pair of red strappy sandals and a slick of scarlet lipstick and I was ready to deliver Guy from the bachelor party.

I drove along the tree-lined shore of Lake Calhoun. On the other side, the downtown towers twinkled like magic boxes, their lights reflected in the calm waters. The house Guy had directed me to was a grand three-story detached mansion, partially obscured by trees at the top of a sweeping driveway. Every light in the place was blazing. Silhouetted figures moved back and forth across the windows.

My stomach gurgled. I couldn't remember when I'd eaten last, so I texted Guy, told him I was waiting outside and asked him to grab me some food on the way out. I waited a few minutes. No response. Texted again and still nothing. Either he was too drunk to reply or he'd lost his phone. Neither were great options. I didn't want to drag him out in front of Gord and a bunch of leering revelers and I also didn't relish the idea of rooting through someone else's furniture looking for his phone.

The air was cool and goosebumps prickled my arms and legs. Why the hell had I worn this skimpy dress? Some logic had directed me to unearth it from my old suitcase. Had the address jogged some lost memory? Some association with this house?

I edged around a vine-covered wall and peeked in through a side window to a circular white vestibule.

Inside, a speckled marble floor and a sweeping oak staircase led upstairs to a darkened space from which the swell of laughter, chatter and voices rose and fell. A small sitting room lined with white couches was off the hallway. Inside I made out the shapes of couples embracing.

A tall man in tan slacks and a white shirt open to the navel, padded down the stairs holding the hand of a thin slip of a girl. She couldn't have been more than fifteen, her eyes ringed with dark liner, her feet bare. She stopped for a moment to take in the crystal chandelier, the Baroque mirror and the white Rodin knockoff on the walnut occasional table, but the man tugged her towards him and led her to the room beyond where the other couples writhed and squirmed on couches and chairs.

I knew there'd be girls there. This was Gord's kind of place. Alpha males on the prowl for tail. Young tail. As young as you could get. Younger than your botoxed wife sleeping soundly under her goose down duvet.

Slipping through an open side door, I padded into the vestibule, my shoes dangling from my hands. The lights were dimmed in that small sitting room but the sound of moaning and heavy breathing was like a weird chorus. Glancing up the spiral staircase with its heavy oak bannister and cream and black carpet, I weighed my options. Either thread my way through the bodies in that dark sitting room and hope Guy was slumped somewhere in a corner or venture upstairs into the party proper.

I decided to go upstairs – more chance of blending in with the crowd. As I climbed upwards, the din of laughter, voices and muddled music grew louder until it became so deafening the bannister vibrated.

It was pitch-black at the top of the stairs, the massive room lit with flashing lights that bounced off walls and bodies and faces. The place reeked of cigars, booze and male sweat. I figured if I kept to the periphery of the room, I could go almost unnoticed because it was packed with men of all ages eating, swigging beer, playing cards in the far corner. A young girl lay stark naked on a nearby table surrounded by pastries. Men crowded around gawking and cheering as one after the other placed cannoli pastries in strategic positions on her body and attempted to eat them without using hands.

Young girls with makeup-slathered faces sidled up to them and bared their bum for a slap, a feel. Some girls wore cowbells draped round their necks. I watched as drunken men took their hands and led them upstairs or down to the lower sitting room. These were the freelancers. The ones who offered special services to make extra money on the side. Money that came in handy for kids' clothing or college tuition or just more swag.

Guy was nowhere to be seen, so I continued around the edge of the room, dodging the hands that slid my way. Someone started chanting up ahead where a knot of guys had gathered around another spectacle. As I came closer I made out the back view of a familiar young girl. I edged round for a front view and my heart slammed in my ears when I saw her face. It was Carla, her eyes squeezed shut, her half-naked body thin and pale as a child's. A drunk old guy who could've been an accountant or bank manager groped and kissed her while the others egged him on. Without another thought I lunged forward and yanked his stiff gray hair. He yelped and let go of her. Seizing the opportunity I grabbed her arm, jerking her away from the crowd of wide-eyed men who stumbled backwards in shock. I shoved her behind me, noticing how her head lolled onto her chest and saliva dribbled down her chin. She was high.

"Goddamn animals," I hissed. "She's only fifteen."

"Who let this crazy bitch in?" yelled Bank Manager. His buddies edged forward, their eyes hungry, eager to teach me a lesson. "Where's security?"

I squared off with them and held up my cell phone. I hadn't totally forgotten life on the streets. "I'm recording all this. Come any closer and I'll scream bloody murder and phone the cops."

They paused, weighing up my threat. Considering their options.

"Maybe there'll be a nice spread in the paper so your wives and bosses can see what fine family guys you all are. Just let me out with the girl and everything's cool."

Palms held upwards, Bank Manager held the other guys back. "Okay, cool. No worries. Take the girl and get the hell out of here."

A loud wave of music drowned my voice out. Bodies swam in front of me lit blue, green and red by the dancing lights. A tall girl with pneumatic breasts waltzed by and Bank Manager and his cronies turned tail to follow her.

A bald guy wearing a black silk shirt, turned back to me and whispered, "I'd get the hell out of here if I were you. Earl doesn't take kindly to anyone that messes with his girls."

I realized I'd have to leave Guy here, since he was nowhere in sight, but across the room, surrounded by a sea of faces I spied Karrass slugging beer from a bottle, standing behind Gord who was bent over the cannoli girl, head bobbing as he struggled to lick the cannoli cream from her thighs. Things began to blur and for a moment I forgot Carla was still hanging onto my arm. Bald Guy tapped my arm and I sprang backwards like an electric volt had charged through my veins.

"You okay?" he said. "Only you look like you're gonna keel over."

I shook my head and backed away. Carla whimpered behind me, coming down from whatever drug she was on. I grabbed a cloth from one of the food tables and draped it around her shoulders. Across the room the door to the spiral staircase glowed like a magic portal and I slithered around the edge of the room letting the lights and music swallow us into blessed oblivion.

–

After five minutes of driving, Carla moaned that she wanted to throw up so I pulled up onto the grassy roadside and helped her out. A stream of booze gushed out of her skinny body until she was dry heaving. I stopped at a gas station and bought her a bottle of cold ginger ale and made her drink it. By this time she was giving me furtive sideways glances.

"Why were you there, Anna?" she murmured, clinging onto the neck of the old sweater I'd found in my backseat.

"My husband was at the stag. He asked me to pick him up."

She leaned back against the seat and closed her eyes. Tears leaked from beneath her lashes. I laid a hand on her bony wrist. "It's okay. You don't have to go back. I'll take you home."

When she shook her head, her whole body moved. "He'll come and find me. It's too late."

She lifted the tablecloth and turned sideways. Tattooed in stylish, looped script across her buttock was a signature.

Earl J. Rafferty. The car swerved to the right, almost hitting the guy in the next lane. I tried to collect myself. Grasp the wheel tight with both hands.

I'd seen that signature before.

The night I almost killed myself on the bridge I kicked the gray-haired guy in the crotch before I ran away. I didn't like the way his manicured body invaded my space, hated the clammy pressure of his fingers on my wrist.

He yelped, doubled over clutching himself as I ran past the dark stores and cafes, to the mall – the only place I could think of. Maybe Birdie would be there. She'd take pity on me. Let me sleep on a couch somewhere. Even the floor of some motel room would do, but then that sharp knife twisted in my heart again. She'd left me for Loni. She screwed the only guy I'd ever cared for. She despised me now. I'd seen the hatred burning in her eyes when she went off with Loni.

The stores were five minutes from closing, so I wandered around in a daze trying to figure out where I could go. Alone, unwanted, and scared, the world closed in on me and hope was a distant dream. I drifted towards the gamers' store. There was no more rescue plan. Colby was my only hope.

I slept on the couch in Colby's basement for two days until Birdie showed up with Loni. Supposedly to check up on me to see if I was okay, but I knew she just wanted to hit me up for food or money to buy drugs or even piss me off by making eyes at Colby. Her hands shook so badly I almost felt sorry for her. Especially when I could see she was freaking Colby out.

He didn't know she'd told me about their little session. I figured I'd forgive him for it. But when his mom came back from her job at the hospital and found Birdie and

Loni rooting through the fridge, she said she'd had enough and told me to go back to my social worker. Said she was really sorry but she couldn't take on the cost of feeding all these extra mouths, or risk having junkies and trouble-makers in the house when she had her grandchildren to look after three days a week. Birdie was long gone by that time, though I knew she'd be back when she was hungry or needed money. She'd never leave me alone.

I hoped Colby would stand up for me, plead my case with the same cool logic he'd used in all our literary arguments. But faced by his mother's demands he became a tongue-tied kid. Not the enigmatic, shadow boy with the cool intellect and sexy whisper.

"Reid went ahead and rented his spare room out," he said, a sheepish look on his face. "What will you do?"

I shrugged. "Maybe hook up with Birdie and the other kids at the Capri Motel. The workers there are so slack they won't notice another body sleeping on the floor and it's near the mall so I'll have something to do after school."

Of course I had no intention of going with Birdie as long as Loni and Duane and all her druggie loser friends were around. I had other plans of my own.

Colby touched my cheek and bent to kiss me. I turned away, my heart frozen. "I didn't mean to do it with your sister," he said, his eyes limpid with tears. "I wish I could take it back now."

"Don't matter anyway. Not like we were gonna get married or anything."

"But I like you. You're smart and interesting. Not like the others. There's something special about you."

Words come easy when you're kicking out someone who has no place to go. You hope it softens the blow. Dulls the edge of the pain. But I wouldn't give him that satisfaction. I wanted to make him suffer. Stick in my own knife and twist the blade.

"You of all people coming up with a cliché like that," I said, picking up my backpack, the only thing I'd taken from Lester and Patti's place. I was done with garbage bags. "I really thought you were more of an original thinker. The truth is you're totally derivative. You plagiarize your ideas from Google and pass them off as your own. The good news on the other hand – you were a great first lay."

He stood at the door of his miserable turquoise painted bungalow looking utterly defeated and was still watching as I turned the corner. I thought I'd loved him.

Poor sucker.

I stuck my hand in my pocket and felt the comforting edges of his dad's rare baseball card collection. *Shit will hit the fan when he realizes they're gone.*

I reckoned I'd sell them for enough to keep me in food and clothes for a couple of months until I figured out how I'd survive.

And I *would* survive. I was sure of that.

30

Recent scientific studies have shown that identical twins aren't as identical as we previously thought. And fraternal twins are often the total opposite of each other.

Like me and Birdie.

Birdie could be smart if she put her mind to it, but she didn't use her brains like I did. She was way too trusting. When she was a kid, she'd knock herself out to make people laugh and be happy. Dancing, singing, playing tricks – a happy kid, always trying to spread joy. Later she changed. As a teen, she had the attention span of a two-year-old. She was edgy, impatient – a wrecking ball set to shatter the harmony of a moment. Always restless, searching for the next great thing to appear, to the point where she could barely enjoy the present.

Things became worse with the drugs.

She was also a sheep, preyed on by anyone that promised to lead her to that golden future. The paradise place where she'd finally settle and enjoy the *now*. I, on the other hand, was way more cautious. Weighing out every miniscule move I made and calculating the consequences.

Only now do I understand the deep differences in the way we handled the grief that comes with the loss of a family – of being cast away and unwanted.

I closed up. Became numb and cold. Shut myself off to deal with the rejection.

But Birdie needed attention like a junkie craves a high. She'd do anything to get it, and most often it was something risky. Shoplifting, casual sex, drinking, toking up, selling her body to anyone who was interested. Too bad the drugs opened the door for all the other reckless behaviors that shaped her life after the age of fourteen.

That's why I started to try and differentiate myself from Birdie after the Lester and Patti incident. She bleached her hair and flat-ironed it until it was silky blonde. I kept my natural black waves and let them grow wild. She wore blue contacts and plucked her eyebrows to a slim arch. I got into the habit of wearing granny glasses and burying myself in baggy hoodies. Other kids called me *the hippie*. I sprayed myself with patchouli oil and thought a lot about Dennis. He was my history, my only relic of the past, so I immersed myself into anything that reminded me of him. Old Grateful Dead music, books by Jack Kerouac and the beat poets, I combed thrift stores for tie-dyed T-shirts. One rainy Saturday I got the "D" tattoo behind my knee. A psychedelic D. I wanted to carve the memory of him into my body so that I too could claim I once had a family that cared for me. That's also when Birdie got another kind of tattoo. Like the one Carla showed me after the stag party, just before I took her back to her mom's house.

–

Guy finally showed up from the stag at four o'clock in the morning. I heard the hiss of frantic whispers and the sound of someone fumbling with the lock. He wasn't alone. At that moment I vowed that if he was with a woman I'd cause such a scene he'd wish he'd stayed out the whole night. Guy had no idea how fast I could escalate – how many objects I could throw at him before he made it out of the door. I sped through the darkness of the bedroom into the kitchen and found some paunchy old guy in a windbreaker rifling through Guy's pockets as he lay, limbs splayed across the couch. Grabbing a heavy silver candlestick I flicked on the light.

"Who the hell are you and what do you think you're doing?"

The old guy pulled his hands away and held them up in surrender, his bloated face sagging with fear. "Ease off, lady. I'm just the cab driver. Your husband's so loaded he threw up in my cab. Messed up my carpet. Now I gotta get it cleaned before I can work again."

I lowered the candlestick. "How much?"

He ground his teeth together. I could tell he was wondering if he should risk hardballing me.

"Make it an even hundred and I won't say another word."

"Stay right there and don't move," I said, reaching into Guy's pocket. He moaned and clutched at his stomach.

"I'd say that guy's gonna toss his cookies right about now," said the cabbie.

I lunged for the garbage can just in time to catch a projectile of vomit.

"I guess you're thinking all men are pigs now," said the cabbie as I wiped off Guy's mouth with a kitchen towel. "And you'd be right. Shouldn't tell you this but you might wanna ask him about that party he just came from. I've seen it all in my time, but these rich guys are something else. Messing round with kids. I have a granddaughter same age as some of those girls at that party and I tell you, I'd slit the throat of any guy that interfered with her, and that's after I broke both his knees with a baseball bat."

Guy's wallet was empty except for his ID. I breathed a sigh of relief and nodded at the guy. "Wait here."

I came back from the bedroom with a wad of bills. "Here's three hundred. Thanks for your trouble."

He flipped through the bills and looked up with a smile. "Mighty generous of you, lady. And don't forget. You ask him about that party and then you tell him to stay the hell away from that house. I know that place and nothing good happens there."

When the cab driver left, Guy stirred again, his face ashen. I turned him onto his side, spread a large bath towel under his head, covered him up with a blanket and left a big glass of water on the table beside him. I didn't want him in my bed until he'd washed every vestige of that filthy house away.

He was still sleeping when I left for work the next day. I didn't have the heart to wake him up before he'd slept the booze off. Besides, I had important business. I needed to get to school early so I could convince Robin that getting Carla into a teen support program might be the only way to extricate her from Rafferty's clutches. It had to happen before he destroyed her like he'd done with so many others in his miserable career. That guy was a verminous creep who should've been stamped out long ago. Too bad he had friends in high places. Wealthy, influential customers who made sure the cops stayed away.

I could barely start the car. My hands were so sweaty I couldn't grip the ignition key.

My mind raced, slipping from one event to another, then back and forth in time. I knocked my forehead against the steering wheel.

Take a deep breath. Slow down. Don't think so much. Stay focused on just one beautiful thing.

Ruth Levine's calming words slid across my messed-up mind like balm on dry skin.

Snap out of it. Control yourself before Carla becomes Birdie and the past sucks away the present.

Whenever that happened to me, I was borne back in time by a current so strong I feared I'd never return to Guy and the new life I'd carved out for myself. That's why I'd loved *The Great Gatsby* so much. When Nick tells Gatsby *you can't repeat the past*, I wanted to shout along with Gatsby, *why yes of course you can*. The past never leaves you. It just lies in wait, sneaking into your present like an unwelcome guest at your party who refuses to leave even after everyone's gone home. And though you try to shut it out, it shows up over and over again until you have to finally face it. Deal with it. And then erase it from your life.

When the door to the underground parking garage swished open, the sky was leaden and a shower of spring rain slapped at my windshield. But something in my gut told me that was only the beginning.

In the distance a thunderstorm was brewing on the horizon.

31

The first few nights after I left Colby's were rough. After a sleepless night huddled behind the door of an unlocked storage closet, I decided to quit the mall and head to the Capri Motel. I'd met a couple of decent kids on my way to the ice machine the night I was there after Donna's house. Whole families lived there. Worn out single moms with bleached nests of hair who pinned up their kids' school drawings or put special *Star Wars* or Disney Princess bedspreads on the beds to make those bare cubicle rooms look a little more like home. But no matter how hard they tried, they were still stuck in a grungy hotel room, buried in a mess of diaper packages, no-name cereal boxes, empty chip packets and baskets of musty laundry.

I thought they might welcome me in if I offered to babysit, but then I'd be just another mouth to feed. They didn't need me, a sullen fifteen-year-old, if their skinny, uncomplaining nine-year-old was perfectly capable of feeding the baby and looking after her toddler twin sisters.

I ended up moving from room to room. A night here and a night there on someone's floor or couch – if I was lucky. I'd look for the next party, hand out a few free beers and soon I was everyone's welcome guest. Sometimes I even scored a spare blanket to lie on. I spent the day at school, the evening at the library or the mall, then went back to the motel to sleep and shower.

Just about every night was party night. Starting around ten and going on till dawn. It was tough to get a decent sleep, but I managed a few hours once everyone was so hammered they passed out or someone called the cops. At those times I hid in the closet or bathroom because I was a runaway and I didn't want them to take me back to my own social worker.

My mornings were precious. At six when everyone was still comatose, I took a quiet shower and slipped outside to sit on the wooden bench seat by the drained pool, a cup of coffee steaming in one hand and a book in the other. I imagined the world had stopped just to let me enjoy a silent hour of reflection before school. Unlike the other kids who came up with every excuse in the book to get out of going to class, I cherished my time there. I had a single purpose – to watch my marks climb upwards. It was my only chance of an escape from the dead-end life I was living.

Colby transferred out of all my classes. When I passed him in the hallway, I pulled my hoodie over my face. I was sure he knew about the baseball cards, but he didn't say anything. I figured he owed me a favor and selling them had given me enough money to buy food and favors for at least a few months. Beyond that I had no plan.

I soon found out which motel rooms housed the prostitutes and junkies and avoided them in favor of the rookie party animals. Everything was working out until Birdie showed up again with Loni in tow and ruined things.

At the time I was staying with three girls who'd been caught shoplifting and were ordered by the court to attend school, but instead they spent their days painting their nails, dying their hair and calling up guys to join a party that never seemed to end.

We'd just finished the extra-large pepperoni pizza I'd bought when the door flew open and Birdie burst in followed by Loni. I barely recognized them. Birdie had transformed into a painted doll, her sleek, blonde hair expertly cut into long, choppy layers. She sashayed into the room like a model in her white crop top and matching skinny designer jeans. Loni followed close behind, a deep mahogany loop of hair hanging over one eye and the rest cut short and spiky. With her black spandex tights and pierced eyebrow she resembled a villain from a superhero movie.

I huddled deeper into my hoodie, to hide from their scrutiny.

"Get the hot wax out," shrieked Loni. "Your sister's got a unibrow."

"Don't tease her," said Birdie, standing over me. "Ain't her fault she got no money and no style."

"What do you want?" I mumbled, clutching my book. I was re-reading *The Great Gatsby*.

Birdie tapped her foot and tried not to look me in the eye. "You never went back to Lester's place then?"

"You guys almost killed him. What am I gonna say? Sorry, Lester. They didn't mean to smash your face in."

"Oh but I did mean every bit of it," said Birdie, her hands curling into fists. "I wanted to make that dickhead suffer."

Loni loomed up behind her. "Damn right. Some foster parent. Couldn't keep his miserable little prick in his pants."

"Okay, so what do you want?"

Birdie placed her hands on her hips and posed like a model, turning this way and that. "You like? All this cost more'n three hundred bucks."

I glanced through my raggedy bangs. "Looks okay for turning tricks. Where'd you get the money?"

"Wouldn't you like to know," she said, tapping the side of her nose.

"You working for that Earl guy?"

"Might be."

"Earl's our buddy," said Loni. "He done some favors for us, so we do favors for him. Get dressed up. Go to nice parties. Act friendly. Meet some real nice guys."

"In other words," said Birdie with some emphasis, "we get paid to have fun. Something you'll never understand."

I shrugged. It sounded like the worst job in the world. "I guess. If you like that sort of thing."

Birdie flew towards me. Feeling the heat of her anger, I tried not to look up. "You're such a snob. Always judging me. Think you're better and smarter than everyone else. All you do is sit in a corner and read about life. You never tried living it."

I slammed the book down. "You came here to give me shit?"

"You're wasting your time, Birdie," said Loni. "Let's get out of this toilet and go to the Martini bar."

I glanced up. "You're not old enough to drink."

Birdie looked smug. "Earl got us ID. We can go to any club we want because he knows everybody. Not like you, still drinking your Burger King pop and milkshakes. Anyway, I came to make you an offer – one time only. I can pay to get you cleaned up so's Earl might be interested in hiring you. I'll take the money from my own pocket."

I shook my head. "I'd rather have all my teeth pulled without freezing, than work for that pimp scum."

"Suit yourself, I guess you got your reasons." Her painted lips drooped at the corners. For a moment I caught a glimpse of the old Birdie, the wacky kid with skinny spider legs and a fragile heart. A thick wave of emotion flooded into my heart, but I turned away before she saw the tears welling in my eyes. "But I really mean it. You're my sister after all."

"You said your piece, now let's get the hell out before some fat-assed social worker comes and takes you in," said Loni, grabbing her shoulder.

I looked up through my hair at Birdie who still hadn't made a move. "You don't have to do everything she says. You got your own mind."

Loni elbowed Birdie aside and stood in front of me, legs planted firmly apart. I thought of Ursula the sea witch from an old Disney movie. "Bitch – you lost your say in her life a long time ago. She's someone else's now. Tell her, baby. Tell her."

Birdie closed her eyes and shook her head.

"Come on, sugar. Tell big sissy what you done."

Blood rushed in my ears, like the sound the wind makes when you lean out of the window of a fast-moving car. "What did you do, Birdie? Tell me and we'll fix it."

"Ain't no fixing now, baby. Now you made a promise," said Loni in that saccharin voice.

Birdie pursed her lips together. Her eyeliner was smudged.

"Check this out," said Loni, lifting up Birdie's tiny shirt and exposing her bony back. Written in large flourishing loops across her skin, on either side of her nubbly spine was a name, *Earl J. Rafferty.*

I jolted upright. "It's not too late, Birdie. We can get out of here. Find Dennis. He'll take us in. I have money."

Loni tried to hook her arm into Birdie's but she shook it away, her eyes fixed on mine. Daring me to jump up, grab her and not let go. "It's too late," she said.

"Damned right, Birdie," said Loni. "You don't break promises with Earl."

Birdie reached into her purse. "I gotta go."

"I mean it, Birdie. I'll look after you. We'll be okay." I scrambled to my feet and caught her wrist in my hand. Suddenly Loni was in my face. Her green eyes glowed like alien cat eyes.

"Bitch don't get it. She ain't going with you. And if you try and take her, I'll send Earl's man to mess you up so bad nobody will want you. Now c'mon, Birdie."

Birdie stuffed a wad of bills into my hand. "I can look after myself, Anna," she whispered. "Don't worry."

I stuffed it back into her hand. "I don't want your whore money. You sold yourself to a pimp."

She shrugged. "It's just a job. I'll do it until I save enough money to go to Vegas. I can be a dancer there."

I grabbed her skinny wrist so hard I could almost snap it. "Idiot – he'll never let you go."

Loni's hand was on my throat so fast my arms flew upwards, releasing Birdie. "I could end it right here," she hissed. "Just say the word, Birdie."

Tiny white dots of light danced around in front of my eyes. Birdie shook her head. "Let her go."

And before I could stop her, they were gone, leaving only a cloud of cheap perfume behind them.

–

After a productive day at school helping Robin fill in the paperwork for Carla's teen support program, I dropped by Linda Martin's office to find her in a flurry of activity sorting papers into piles and stashing them into a filing cabinet.

"I'm off to Cancun tomorrow. A week in the glorious sun sipping on margaritas and lying on the beach. Can't wait to leave this behind," she said, glancing out of the window at the overcast sky and the thin curtain of drizzle that blurred the outlines of buildings and trees. I shivered, imagining her lumpy body in a bathing suit. Would she choose one of those floral types with a little skirt at the thigh or maybe a tankini with a loose flap to disguise her pudgy midriff? I chastised myself for being so superficial and slumped into my usual chair. She fidgeted with her stapler and hole punch, shifting them from one side of her desk to the other. Easy to tell only half her mind was on work.

I leaned forward trying to catch her eye but she transferred her attention to the paper clip magnet. "I'll get right to it, Linda. You need to get the cops onto Earl Rafferty."

Her eyes snapped open in surprise. Dreams of golden beaches shattered for the moment. She exhaled deeply. "Anna, I told you it's in your best interest to stay away from those downtown places. They're bad karma for you."

I placed both hands on her desk and leaned forward. "I don't want to ruin your holiday, Linda, but I'm done playing games here. And by the way, I'm recording this entire exchange."

She leaned against the back of her chair squinting at me. Her face flushed with scarlet streaks. "What exactly do you want?"

"Yesterday I dragged one of my students from a stag party. She's underage – barely sixteen years old – but she was drunk, high, almost naked and in the process of being assaulted by men old enough to be her grandfather. She also has Earl Rafferty's name tattooed in bold script across her back." I sat back and took a deep breath. "And your esteemed colleague Peter Karrass and a number of other so-called respectable members of our community were willing spectators to the entire proceedings."

I could almost hear Linda's heart thumping. I'd presented her with something way too big for her to handle, but I wanted her to suffer. To worry about me every time she lifted a frozen margarita to her lips.

"You're sure about this?" she said in a small voice.

I nodded. "Damn sure. And Birdie had the same tattoo fifteen years ago."

A grin twitched at the corner of her lips. She covered her mouth with her hand. "Sorry, Anna, but you're doing that transference thing."

"What the hell are you talking about?"

"You had me going there," she said, smirking as she busied herself with her pencil holder. "But now I realize you're just confusing Birdie with this girl that you say you rescued. Another thing – why would you, a respectable teacher, frequent that kind of party? I believe the school board might have a few questions for you."

I flipped her pencil container over sending pens and highlighters rolling across the desk. "You stupid bitch. You wouldn't know the truth if it slapped you in your dumb face."

Her fingers flexed into claws as if she was trying to restrain herself from scratching my eyes out. "What's that saying? You can take the girl out of the street but you can't take the street out of the girl. I believe our meeting is over, Anna. I have places I need to be."

She stood up and began to pack her briefcase, but I wasn't done.

"Make the most of your holiday, Linda. It'll be your last. Because when I take Rafferty and Karrass down, I'll take you with them. You and all the others who screwed up my life and Birdie's. You'll be lucky to find a job flipping burgers for minimum wage."

She clicked her bag shut then pushed her face towards me, her cheeks puce with anger. "Get the hell out of here, Anna, and don't come back until you've checked in with a psychiatrist and completed a course of treatment. I can't deal with you anymore. You won't accept the truth."

"You mean your version of the truth. Just watch yourself, Linda. I'll be back when I can finally prove you're being paid to lie."

"I'll call security," she said, picking up the phone. Her hand shook.

I stood by the door and looked back. "You'll need security when I'm done because you'll be looking over your shoulder to see who's after you."

"Out," she screamed.

I swept down the hall as if my feet were barely touching the ground. Time to set the wheels in motion.

I'd been waiting fifteen years for this chance.

32

Guy's face was still sickly-white when he came back from work. I'd bought takeout sushi but he took one look at the seaweed salad and slumped down onto the couch, head in his hands.

"How about a chilled club soda?" I said, clearing the containers up and stacking them in the fridge.

He nodded and groaned. "I'm hungover, but worse than that, I feel like crap about last night." He flopped back against the cushions, his face the color of plaster. "Why do I let Dad talk me into these things?"

"Okay, what happened?" I asked as innocently as I could. I wasn't about to tell him I'd actually witnessed the whole disgusting debacle *and* had rescued a minor from the marauding clutches of some of the city's most upstanding citizens. I wanted to hear it in his own words from his own mouth. To test his honesty.

"It was pathetic. All these old guys leering at kids. Touching and interfering with girls who could've been their daughters or granddaughters. And they acted so *entitled*. I was ashamed to be there among them."

I perched on the arm of the sofa. "You were drunk. I got your text."

He scraped his fingers through his hair. "I was wasted. Lucky I passed out before I tried to punch the crap out of some of those perverts. I'm glad you didn't end up coming there."

"I stayed late at school. An emergency." I chewed at my lip, hoping he hadn't spotted the lie.

He grasped my wrist. "Anna, I want to be honest with you. I don't want any secrets between us."

"Okay," I said, tilting my head and wondering what was coming next.

"It wasn't just a drinking party. There were girls there. Strippers, prostitutes. Underage girls. I couldn't tell how young. Selling themselves to men who should have known better. I wanted to get out but Dad kept feeding me drinks and like an idiot I drank them. I can't believe I was so spineless. I should've left but I stayed like the dutiful son. I don't want to be that kind of guy. I detest them all."

"So I don't need to worry about what you were up to all night?"

"Anna, I love you so much I can't think of anyone else. I'd never cheat on you. You have to believe me. Things I saw last night were so disgusting, it sickens me to even think about them."

I stroked the top of Guy's head. "So why don't you talk to Gord? Tell him how you feel."

He looked up at me with hopeless eyes. "He'll just blow it off. Say it was just guy stuff. Accuse me of being soft."

"If the girls were underage, then it becomes a crime. Doesn't he get that?"

He nodded, wiping his hand across his eyes. "I could lose my job if someone had seen me there. But he'll say I'm exaggerating. Claims it's all harmless stuff. That nobody's going to snitch. It's like some weird old boys' club."

"All the same, you should have a word with him. I work with kids who are exploited. I know how they get trapped and can't get out. You don't want to be a part of that."

He took my hands and smiled. "What did I do to deserve you, Anna? You're the best thing to ever come into my life. I swear I'll talk to him. Just for you."

I never found out if Guy followed through with his promise. And Gord must have laid low that night because he didn't make his usual daily phone call. Instead we stayed home and spent a quiet night drinking wine, eating pizza and watching *The Sixth Sense*, one of Guy's favorite movies of all time, though when the kid cowers under his blankets and says *I see dead people*, the buzz in my head grew louder with each sip of wine.

Later, when Guy was passed out, sleeping off the last remnants of his hangover, some strange impulse drove me to clear out the old stuff I'd brought from my apartment. When I flung the first case open the stink of rancid cooking oil and musty closets had infused all the cheap clothes I'd brought. A black lacy blouse with diamond buttons, a white linen shirt with a mustard stain on the elbow, a pair of designer jeans with glittery embroidery on the back pockets, a cropped white top stained with brownish makeup around the neckline. I held it up to the light and remembered Birdie wearing it that time she came to the motel.

But how did I come to have it?

Stuffed underneath in a ball of tissue paper was a tiny knitted hat. A baby cap. Pink, white and blue crochet.

With the tag still on. I shoved it back into the case together with the white top and slammed down the lid.

I wouldn't open this case ever again. There were things inside that were lost to me. That I could never explain. That I didn't want to explain.

I dreamed the baby dream again that night. Couldn't remember when I last dreamed it. I was at a carnival pushing a stroller round. A small baby sat inside dressed in a yellow romper suit. I wasn't sure if it was my baby or if I was just looking after it. *It* because it wasn't clearly a boy or a girl, neither did it seem to matter. I entered a large theater. On stage was an important man who I knew was my lover. Hot with desire to see him, I worried about the presence of the baby and how he'd feel about it.

The audience sat at round tables talking and drinking wine. I parked the stroller to watch the show, only to turn back again and find the baby was gone. I ran through rooms pushing that empty stroller crying *where is my baby*, then *where is the baby* because I was suddenly sure it wasn't mine. I knew I was just watching it for someone else. Finally I came upon a table of old people playing cards. One of them looked familiar. A woman with a broad face and cap of mousy hair. She reminded me of Linda Martin, but older. I was sure she'd taken the baby. *Give me the baby*, I screamed. *I know you have it. Give it back*, I screamed again, clamping my hand round her throat. Here's where it got weird. She'd hidden it behind the stove. It lay on the floor in that tiny, cramped space, in its lemon-colored romper, sleeping.

She shook herself free of my hand. *I took this baby because you weren't looking after it*, she said. *That baby is soiled from head to toe.* And when I picked up the tiny, warm body its diaper was wet and heavy.

I'm going to love it and take care of it, I said, placing it back into the stroller. *I will. I will.*

I woke up still whispering *I will. I will.* The room was stifling, Guy snored lightly and my eyes wouldn't shut. It was 3:00 a.m. I tried to breathe but my throat was still choked with guilt, sorrow, grief.

The dream was all about Birdie. I knew it.

33

I saw Birdie again. When I was still living in the motel, dodging the social workers. After all I was still only fifteen and legally too young to be living alone. The baseball card money had dwindled to just a few bucks, so I'd resorted to my old habit of shoplifting and selling the stolen stuff on the street. But I was terrible at it. I looked like a deadbeat with my matted curls and baggy sweatshirts. Store detectives zoomed in on me as if I was wearing a sign on my back that read *amateur shoplifter right here*. Strangely I did my best stealing around perfume and beauty counters. Those painted ladies in the crisp white coats didn't expect the scruffy teen slouching around the sparkling glass counters to have any interest in cosmetics, and so I stole lipsticks, brow pencils, eyeliners, anything I could get my sticky hands on.

One rainy Wednesday afternoon after school I ventured into Dayton's for nostalgia's sake. Hadn't been there since the Donna era and I felt the need to look at pretty, clean things. Four months of sleeping on motel carpets leaves a layer of sleaze and grime that can't be removed using threadbare motel towels and cheap soap.

At first, I started with a squirt of Narcisco Rodriguez hand cream, the black one with the hint of sandalwood and musk. I rubbed it on my chapped hands, imagining that one day, when I had money, I'd bathe in the perfume, then rub the cream all over my body. Having money meant being clean and fragrant. Meant sleeping under crisp white cotton sheets instead of a stained towel or old sweater. Rows of lipsticks gleamed in open display cases, and I was just considering how to transfer a few into my pocket when someone yanked my hood down. I almost jumped a foot into the air and whirled around, expecting the grim face of some mean store cop.

"You still couldn't jack a raindrop in a thunderstorm," said Birdie, grinning, her mouth glossy with scarlet lipstick. Dressed in a tiny suede bolero jacket and form-fitting jeans, she glowed. I'd never seen her so beautiful. "And what's with your hair? It looks like a plate of leftover spaghetti."

"I like my curls," I muttered, twirling the ends of one around my finger. "Easy to look after. And the bathrooms are lousy where I'm living."

"Where's that?"

I shrugged. "Still at the motel. You know. Hiding out."

"You're sleeping on floors?"

"Yeah."

She took a pen from her Louis Vuitton purse and scrawled something on a piece of paper. "Here's my address. You can come in the afternoon, around three, when Loni isn't there and get cleaned up. I'll lend you some clothes."

I stuffed the address in my pocket. "You still working for Earl?"

She shrugged and chewed at her index finger, flaking off the tangerine polish. "Kind of. Except now I got myself a regular. A special boyfriend. He's loaded and he's crazy about me. And I'm clean – off the junk and all that. It's been three months now."

The cosmetician glared at us, her heavily penciled brows knit into a frown. Birdie shot a *screw you* look at her and pulled out her wallet, fat with bills. I watched in awe as she peeled a few off and slapped them on the counter. "We'll take the biggest Narciso Rodriguez gift box. And you can wrap it for my sister."

The deflated woman disappeared behind the counter and busied herself with pink paper and black ribbon.

"Does he know how old you are?"

"Doesn't care. Says he loves me for my spirit. And I make him happy. He's going to leave his wife. She's frigid. A real witch. He promised. Just as soon as he gets the balls to tell her."

"Sounds like something from a lame soap opera."

She flipped a wing of her hair to the side and looked away as if she wished she hadn't told me. "I know it sounds cheesy, but he's different. He says he wants me to have his babies because he knows they'll be beautiful."

Her eyes were glassy – her expression trancelike. As if she was poised on a cliff edge above a turquoise ocean, gazing towards a sun-tinged horizon and the happy place where dreams finally come true. For Birdie this fantasy of luxury, a family and babies of her own was so real nothing else mattered.

I moved around to face her. Make her see sense. "You must be high or something. How could you have a baby? You're still a kid. You don't even know what it takes to be a mother. We never had a real mother."

She finally looked at me, her tear-filled eyes furious and defiant. "What do you know about what I want? What did you ever know?"

I staggered backwards, her words knocking the breath from me. She was so wrong. I'd always had her back

– always put her needs first when we were kids. Then Loni came along and trampled over the life we'd built and the memories we'd shared. Broke the bonds that held us together.

"Your package, miss," said the sales clerk, breaking the tension between us. She presented the pretty wrapped package to Birdie who shook her head.

"Jeez, can't you see she's the one who needs it?" Birdie said, her voice raspy and sharp. "Oh and keep the change. Get yourself a donut and coffee."

She swept away from me in a cloud of perfume. I clutched the beautiful package, my head filled with the certainty that she was heading for another massive betrayal. Then I thought of supper and wondered how much I could get on the street for this extravagant gift my sister had just sprung on me. I decided instead to return it the next day, when another sales clerk was around. I'd had the presence of mind to grab the receipt just as Birdie flounced off in a huff.

A couple of weeks later I looked Birdie's place up. Her directions led me to a concrete and glass downtown tower block with a security system and real plants on stone tables in the front lobby. Pretty good for a fifteen-year-old high school dropout, I thought as I schlepped my plastic bag of dirty clothes across the polished marble tiles towards the elevator.

That same morning I'd just made it down the motel's rear fire escape as a pair of social workers in beige trench coats and shades descended like enemy agents to scour the rooms along our hallway checking for runaways like me who'd slipped through the cracks in the system.

My options were running thin. Soon I'd have to go back to sleeping in the mall or even check out the homeless shelters, though they usually asked way too many questions and all for the dubious pleasure of sleeping on a sleazy mattress recently vacated by some old drunk with a leaky bladder and night sweats. No way I'd ever stoop to that.

Birdie met me at the door of her apartment wearing a fluffy pink housecoat, her hair wrapped in a towel.

"You stink like a toilet," she said, grabbing the bag of clothes from me. "Strip off in the bathroom and I'll wash everything before it pollutes the place."

I couldn't figure out why she was acting so civil to me. But I was glad to be back on semi-friendly terms with her. And where was her bodyguard, Loni the lioness?

The bathroom was clean and modern. Black granite and white cupboards. Through the open door I heard Birdie humming like she used to when we were kids playing in Dennis's backyard. A wave of optimism washed over me. Suddenly my grim world seemed beautiful again, if only for that moment.

Whenever I felt that way I'd run over all the good things in my life as if I was flipping through the pages of a Sears catalogue. I was young, free for the time being, and still likely to graduate high school. The sun shone through the bathroom window and the prospect of a hot shower in a bathtub without a hair-encrusted scum line, was the most wonderful idea in the world.

I stepped inside the spotless shower enclosure, drew the ruched white curtain and stood under a steaming spout of water to wash off every trace of filth from my body. I scrubbed until my skin was raw and tingly. Fluffy, thick towels hung from hooks on the door. I guessed this was where Birdie entertained Earl's important customers, including her new sugar daddy who was probably bankrolling the entire place. But I didn't even care if some guy had wiped his ass on them. I was just happy to be clean.

I rooted through the cupboards looking for scented body lotion and found some lavender rosemary organic stuff that smelled okay. My head was buzzing now. After I left Birdie's, where would I go? Maybe she'd let me stay with her. I was just about to shut the door when I spied a stack of small photographs shoved into a corner. Straightening up I listened for Birdie, but all I heard was the sound of water running in the kitchen. I grabbed the pictures and flipped through the fuzzy images.

The first few were of Birdie posing in pigtails and skimpy schoolgirl costumes. So her special guy liked them young – really young. She pouted, sucking a huge lollipop and spread her legs to reveal lacy panties, in another she flipped up her skirt to reveal her skinny bare bum. The last few featured a man. Only his dark hair and husky shoulders were visible since he never faced the camera. Someone had snapped a pic of Birdie on her knees in front of him, her head down between his legs. On another she lay across his lap while he brandished a leather whip. His head was cut out of the shot. Too bad. I'd hunt him down and scratch his evil eyes out if I found the bastard. But I couldn't figure out who the hell took these pictures and why this guy would want them. Unless he got off looking at them afterwards. I shuddered at the thought of Birdie with this creep and suddenly I was really, really scared for her.

In the last photo he'd been careless and in his haste to mount a naked Birdie, he'd allowed his blurred face to drop into the frame. I slipped the photograph into the folds of the towel. Something told me it might come in handy later. For what, I had no clue at the time.

I emerged from the bathroom to the aroma of toast. A plateful of it next to jars of peanut butter and jelly. Birdie's hair hung in soft tendrils around her bare face. She looked like a twelve-year-old kid who'd just plucked her eyebrows for the first time.

"Feast?" she said, a grin spreading across her face.

I settled myself onto the white leather stool at the breakfast bar and shoved a whole piece of toast into my mouth. "I am so sick of Twinkies from the Seven-Eleven," I mumbled, my mouth stuffed with food. She pushed a massive glass of chilled orange juice towards me, which I gulped down and set to work on the next slice. Birdie nibbled at the corner of a piece of toast and stared at me.

"You need to pluck your eyebrows."

"I like them this way. Nobody bugs me."

"You mean guys?"

I nodded, helping myself to another slice. Wonder Bread had never tasted so good. "Some real sleazy types hang out at the motels."

"You gotta get out of there. I told you," she said, pouring coffee into two Hello Kitty cups.

"You always did like Hello Kitty." I remembered her nose pressed up against the window of a souvenir store, her big, sad eyes lusting after a Hello Kitty cookie jar.

"Now I can buy things whenever I want," she said, slugging back the black coffee. I helped myself to sugar and cream, not knowing when the next fresh cup would come along.

"Doesn't come free, I guess."

Her eyes narrowed as she fidgeted with the teaspoon. "Meaning what?"

"I mean what do you have to do to get all this?"

Her cheeks flushed. "None of your business."

"Play naughty schoolgirl? Is that what you do?"

She stood up, spilling coffee across the counter. "Have you been snooping?"

"Didn't take much effort to find your little porn collection."

I expected an all-out screaming match but she was silent, pressing her lips together as she tore off loops of kitchen towel and mopped up the mess.

"You know the law would call this jerk a pedophile. And you're only fifteen, so it's statutory rape."

She wiped and wiped until the paper towel disintegrated. "You don't know anything. He loves me. He takes care of me."

"That's why he takes those pictures? Because he loves you or because you let him get off on sick schoolgirl fantasies?"

I shoved the plate away. I wasn't hungry anymore. I looked around the place. At the pink, fluffy beanbag floor cushion, the candy pink and blue striped rug, the white futon stacked with rainbow pillows, the posters of Zac Efron, Leonardo DiCaprio, and pouting models in skimpy bikinis. It was like a pre-pubescent girl's hangout. A real turn-on for this guy.

"Does he chant *Daddy's home* when he comes to visit?"

Birdie gnawed at her nails. A sure sign I'd hit a nerve.

"What does Earl Rafferty get out of this, anyway? Did he set you up? Does he get a weekly cut?"

She shrugged again. "Maybe."

I wanted to take her and shake her by her skinny shoulders. The pounding started up again in my head. "Don't you get it, Birdie, or do I need to spell it out to you? They're all using you. Earl's a pimp, your sugar daddy is a pedophile and you're nothing more than a whore. And an underage one for that matter. They took you when you were only fourteen." I could barely breathe. I wanted so badly to drag her out of that stifling dollhouse of an apartment.

She slumped down on the stool again only this time fat tears oozed from her eyes. "I'm pregnant," she whispered, placing her hands across her tummy.

I curled and uncurled my fists until they hurt. "You mean that creep didn't use a rubber?"

Now her shoulders were shaking. "He says it's like screwing someone wearing pantyhose. He can't enjoy it."

"And you allowed it? Does he know?"

"About the baby?" She shook her head. "I'm gonna tell him."

"And what about Earl? What do you think he's gonna say?"

"About what?"

"You're more stupid than I thought. What's he gonna say when his big investment is out of action for a year or more?"

She was sobbing now, with big, heaving gulps that made her whole body shake. "It'll be okay. He says we'll live together and have the baby. In our own house. He promised."

"Who? You and this creep?"

She nodded, looking up at me with wounded child's eyes. I remembered a poster on the bedroom wall at the Penners'. *Bear the cross and wear the crown*. I'd always thought Birdie would be the princess with the crown, but now I realized it was about me. She would always be the cross I'd be forced to bear. A cross that would eventually crush me under its colossal weight. I felt cold and shaky and sweaty at the same time.

"Where's Loni?"

Birdie wiped her hand across her runny nose. Another old Birdie habit.

"Gone," she said in a small voice. A phone rang from somewhere. Birdie sprang to attention. We both looked towards the bedroom.

"Gone where? She left you?"

She shook her head. "Not exactly."

The way she was gnawing at her fingernails, I knew something was up. I caught her wrist. "Tell me. I mean tell me everything."

She reached for a cigarette pack with shaking hands, fumbled, then dropped it.

"She pissed Earl off, so he sent her to the boats."

"Which boats?"

"Up north. Duluth. At the port. She's working the ships."

I thrust my face into hers. "Doing what?"

"You service the crew. But it's not as bad as it sounds. You get to cruise the lake."

I stood up so fast I knocked the stool over. The ringing started up again.

"I have to get that," she said, looking up at me with puppy-dog eyes that kept darting towards the phone.

I scanned the room. "Where are my clothes? We have to get out of here. You don't understand what kind of danger you're in, Birdie. You're coming with me. We're gonna find Dennis. It's not too late."

By that time I was crying. Tears streamed down my face as she ran into the bedroom to get the damn phone that wouldn't stop ringing. I slammed closet doors open to find my clothes, until the last door smacked against the wall revealing a washer and dryer. My clothes were still damp but I ripped them out and stuffed them into a plastic laundry bag. I needed to get away from there but I had to find something to wear. I stormed into the bedroom to find her perched on the edge of the bed talking in a little girl voice to someone.

"Yes, I'm waiting for you, baby," she crooned. "Can't wait for your hot bod."

She swung around, saw me and covered the phone. "Get out," she hissed.

"I need clothes."

"Just help yourself and leave. He's coming over."

She watched as I pulled the mirror doors open. Flowery perfume wafted out of the closet, one side taken up with a row of lacy baby doll pajamas and frilled little girl dresses. I yanked them off their hangers and threw them to the floor. Birdie strained her neck to see what I was doing then went back to talking in hushed tones. From the other side I grabbed the white crop top and embroidered jeans and struggled into them, amazed they actually fit. A knitted tan cardigan was roomy enough to cover my midriff, so I took that too. For good measure I snatched a dress – a red, clingy one – and a denim shirt. Then I spied it. Her secret dream. On the floor in the corner a Babies R Us bag. Filled with bibs and toweling sleepers, tiny bootees. I took the pink and blue knitted hat from the top of the pile, stuffed it into my pocket, then backed out of the closet with my stash.

Birdie glared at me angrily, but she was a prisoner to that phone.

"Tell your pervert boyfriend I'm going to the police to report him."

She threw the phone against the bedspread but he must've heard me. "Shut your mouth," she screamed. "Just get the hell out of here and don't come back."

"I'm gonna do it," I yelled. "Tell the asshole I'm really gonna report him. You'll see."

Her hand flew out to the side and grabbed the ceramic Hello Kitty jar from her night table. She hucked it right at me. I dodged but it glanced off the side of my head. I lunged towards the door.

"You don't deserve me, Birdie," I screamed but she slammed the bedroom door shut with her foot.

I swept the jam and peanut butter and coffee cups off the breakfast bar on my way out.

I never made it to see the cops because the social workers were waiting for me at the motel when I got back. Never found out if Birdie's pimp or sugar daddy had ratted on me. She was the only one who knew exactly where I'd been staying. I still can't be sure who told them because everything that happened next was a blur.

Down at the social worker's office a dough-faced woman with a lisp told me how fortunate I was that the Flatts had agreed to take me back, which was truly selfless of them considering what Birdie and her friends did to Lester's jaw, but they'd both assured the authorities that there were no hard feelings and, since I wasn't the troublesome one, I'd be better off without the influence of my delinquent sister. In other words, the income from one foster kid was preferable to none.

The words they threw at me suddenly merged into a blur. I fixed my eyes on the mustard yellow walls that pressed in on me, squashing me into a two-dimensional cutout. I thought about Colby and school and the mall and how I was always fighting to eat and sleep and learn.

And how Birdie would try to have a baby and the kid would live a crappy life as well, with a brainless kid for a mother and I couldn't save her from Earl and her own stupidity. Then something snapped inside me. Twanging like some fraying thread that'd held me in check for the last six years of neglect and abuse, but now was stretched to breaking point. It came apart so fast I swear I heard it *ping* in my ears, sending shock waves across my brain.

That's when I let it all go, buoyed by a tidal wave of anguish and rage. I screamed, kicked, thrashed, swept pens, pencils, staplers into the air. Watched orange fire flare from their edges. I screamed and yelled every curse that came to me – every piece of filth I could muster until my head rang with the sound of my own voice. Then someone with hairy arms grabbed me from behind and I felt the sweet stab of a needle in my shoulder. Purple clouds rolled across my eyes and my limbs went numb and woolly as the sun was finally blotted out.

34

At breakfast Guy reminded me we were invited over to his research assistant, Brian Metcalf's place for supper, but I barely registered the information. My mind was stuck on Earl Rafferty and Birdie and my meltdown in the social worker's office.

How things can change so drastically in fifteen years.

This was my life now. Friendly but casual dinner parties, reading the papers in bed on Sunday, a bowl of fresh fruit balanced on my lap and fresh-ground coffee steaming on the night table beside me.

My thoughts drifted to Brian's place, and I imagined a quaint one and a half story craft style bungalow complete with Dad, Mom, new baby in eco-friendly hemp or bamboo cloth diapers. A front garden filled with lavender bushes and Spot the dog prancing around like a trusted old friend. No snarling pit bulls or hissing feral cats ready to carve your eyes out if you messed with their territory.

I knew I'd have to get to the mall at some point that day to calm myself down, but there was no need to dress up in a fancy new outfit, with the likelihood of a rancid stream of baby vomit on the shoulder. Instead I'd scour the stores for lovely baby gifts. Guy beamed at the mention of it. He tossed the rest of his coffee back, leaned over and stroked my hair.

"Maybe it'll give you some ideas," he said.

The sun broke through a cloud and lit up the kitchen. "Meaning?"

He shrugged. "You know, baby stuff. The maternal instinct."

My mind went numb. Like cold water had trickled into my head. I shrugged. "Maybe."

"No pressure," he said, backing off. I wanted to hug him for his sensitivity, but I dug my nails into my palms instead. He stood up. "See you back here at five. I'll get the wine."

"Thanks," I said, my voice husky with the tide of emotion I was holding in check. He was so good to me and so good *for* me. I didn't deserve him and all the loveliness he'd brought to my life. The sun on his hair, the gleam of the orange juice jug, the velvet mounds of peaches in the bowl. All now so familiar to me, I could've burst out in song right then. Instead I reached up and caught his fingers, traced the smooth edge of the wedding ring, took in the calm contours of his mouth.

"See you at five," I said, relishing the certainty of it.

–

At school I went to see Robin again. Asked him what was being done about Carla and Rafferty and the whole sickening mess. He shook his head and gave me a bloodshot, mournful look.

"I've talked to the cops, Anna. They assured me they're looking into it. Seems they've had their eyes on this sleaze, Rafferty, for a long time now, but they can't get anything concrete on him. Every time they get close enough to flush him out of his rat hole, all their witnesses clam up. He's got too many friends in high places. Probably has so much on them, they won't spill a thing."

I studied the crêpey pouches under his eyes, the thinning strands of hair plastered across his crown, the frayed collar on his faded plaid shirt. Maybe I could pick up a couple of new shirts for him. Get him a haircut. Spruce him up a bit then the cops would take him more seriously. I'd learned long ago that appearances count for a lot in our screwed-up society.

He shook his head, scratched at his wrinkled ear. A tide of sympathy washed over me. After all these years of dedication he deserved to be sitting on some California beach soaking up the sun for this last chapter of his life. Every ounce of his energy had been drained trying to fix a corrupt, screwed-up system.

"I wish I could do more, but I'm only one voice in the grand scheme of things and I'm afraid it carries very little weight. So I offer a Band-Aid to a bleeding system. If I save only a few kids I'm happy. I've done my bit."

I left his office so agitated I almost forgot how to get to the exit doors. Then I reached my car without even realizing how I got there. Thoughts cranked through my head like an endless film reel. Nothing was being done about Rafferty, which meant I had to do something. And besides, I'd made a promise years back. At night on a bridge – streetlamps throwing cones of light onto the sidewalk, river foaming beneath me, freeway traffic roaring by in the background, the concrete trembling underneath my feet. I'd be the one to take Rafferty and all his cronies down. God only knew how I'd do it, but I would.

For Birdie. For my twin sister. Who'd vanished from the face of the earth.

I'd screw them all over and destroy their miserable lives.

–

I didn't shower for weeks after I went back to the Flatts' place. I woke up in that beige bedroom with the two single beds, my head foggy from the drugs they'd given me to calm me down. I lay there looking at Birdie's empty bed, its poster of Zac Efron tacked above the headboard, and realized how she'd felt all those days she was a drugged-up prisoner in this same room, while I went off to school and flirted with Colby. Guilt stabbed at my gut and I curled into a ball until the pain subsided.

The stink of leftover Chinese takeout and boiled hot dogs seeped through the space under the door and the spiderweb of cracks spread across the ceiling like a living fungus. I squeezed my eyes shut. Rules didn't count in that house. Expect the unexpected at all times. The Flatts were opportunistic beasts disguised in sagging bodies, who'd successfully fooled the authorities into believing they actually cared about the lives of vulnerable children.

I squirmed onto my stomach and pressed my face into the pillow, vowing that Lester would never touch me like he touched Birdie. The only way I could be sure was to become so unkempt – so disgusting he'd steer clear away from me.

As it happened, I needn't have worried. Their crack buddies, Tray and Anita, had become regulars at the house, so Lester was occupied in a downward slide towards addiction. Hence the urgency that I return to the family fold to help fund his growing habit.

At first I missed a few days of school. My brain was so blurred from the drugs they fed me, recommended by the helpful social workers who'd managed to check off another prickly client from their caseload. I didn't speak. Just shuffled around in my hoodie and showed up at the kitchen table. Patti, now thin, courtesy of her cranked-up meth-fueled metabolism, usually slid a plate of burnt macaroni and chopped wieners towards me.

Her stained yellow fingers twirled a lock of her stringy hair. "Eat – don't want you wasting away. Myself, I'm not hungry," she said, placing her hands on her hips so I'd notice her skinny waistline. "But I wanna say, I'm glad to see you back on your own. Your sister was one big mess of trouble."

I nodded and tried to eat. It was easier just to go along with her.

Lester and Patti fought a lot more. Seemed he wasn't getting so many shifts at the mall. Not surprising considering the way his hand shook when he handled his revolver. No doubt some paunchy supervisor got panicked imagining the aftermath of a mass shooting at the mall. Emergency workers bagging up innocent victims, the whirling lights of cop cars and ambulances flashing in his eyes and some blonde news anchor shoving a microphone into his face while he blubbered to the cameras that he'd always thought Lester was a decent family man until he got into the drugs.

Lester screamed that his fucking boss had always been on his ass only now it was way worse and Patti should get a fucking job instead. See if she could handle the day in and day out of it. She yelled back that if she was out of the house he'd be shooting up from morning till night instead of waiting till after six.

"What difference does it make when I shoot up? I'm gonna do it anyway," he said.

But when he suggested getting another foster kid I almost threw up my noodles. Patti was surprisingly astute for once and soon put him straight that they'd never qualify for a new kid. They only got me back because nobody knew what to do with me.

At night Tray and Anita showed up, more decrepit than ever, their faces pocked with sores, their eyes vacant and bloodshot. They'd graduated to shooting up rather than smoking. Lester and Patti were headed the same way but hadn't registered that they too would be walking skeletons if they kept up with the junk.

When Lester wasn't working they slept most of the day, so I usually smoked up a bit of their spare weed to prime myself for the outside world. Then I let myself out to go to school. I'd given up socializing there. Just soaked in all the lessons, did my homework in the library and if any do-gooder teacher tried to collar me and get me to *open up about my problems* I gave him or her the evil eye, pulled my hood over my head and clammed up. I got good grades so they all backed off eventually after three minutes of silence. Besides I probably stunk of days' old sweat and in those heated, stuffy offices the stench soon spread like a pestilence.

After school some days I found my way to Birdie's apartment to watch the comings and goings from behind a cedar bush on the opposite side of the street. I wanted to see if she was showing yet – make sure she was safe and maybe even catch the sugar daddy creep who'd screwed up her reasoning until she couldn't think straight. Sometimes I brought a book with me.

One hot May afternoon when the sky was so blue I wanted to fly right up among the clouds, I cut school early and went to Birdie's.

I was sprawled out on my hoodie in the clearing behind the cedar bush reading Zola's *L'Assommoir*. I was totally blown away that someone in another country, living in

287

a distant century, could capture the abject misery and squalor that addiction brings. I threw myself, full tilt, into a Zola phase. I vowed to work my way through every book he'd written. They made me feel I wasn't alone in my misery. That other human beings had lived lives of endless suffering and Zola recorded it all in graphic detail.

A car pulled up and stopped outside the block. I flipped the book shut and craned my neck to see. I'd already watched a stream of people come and go but I had a gut feeling this one was for Birdie. Something about the way the car, a prowling BMW with tinted windows, purred to a gradual stop then sat there, its motor throbbing like a heartbeat. When the door finally swung open, a man with sleek reddish-brown hair, shiny cheeks and wearing a sharp navy suit hoisted himself out. He straightened his shoulders, adjusted his shades and checked around him like he didn't want to be seen in that dumpy street.

He slammed the door shut and with a quick glance both ways, hopped up the steps and pressed the buzzer. The pink curtains on Birdie's window parted for a moment revealing the pale flash of her face. *Bingo, this was my guy.* I heard the faint twitter of her voice over the intercom and then he was inside. My cue to check the car out and maybe key its brilliant black flanks. Carve out in crooked letters, *I am a sick pedophile.* My hand itched to get started.

I waited a few moments then picked up my hoodie, now dusted with dry grass and leaves. The air was stifling, heat shimmered like a curtain. But I still pulled my arms into the sleeves and flipped the hood over my curls, then shoved my hands into the pockets to touch the rough edge of my locker key. Sidling up to the car, I checked out the street. It was quiet enough. The busy cross street was way up ahead and late afternoon traffic din would drown out the screech of my key on the paintwork. I placed both hands on the smooth flank of the car, still warm from the journey across town. He must've really gunned it in his haste to get to his naughty little schoolgirl, led by the forbidden urges that scrambled his brain and coursed like a fever through his flabby, middle-aged body.

The key was out in the open now, its sharp edges poised above the slick shellac of the paintwork. I breathed deeply, almost afraid to defile its beauty. After all, I too lusted after something this gorgeous. I rubbed the sharp tip on the rear panel just enough to hear a scraping sound so high-pitched my teeth ached. A sudden *swish* made me jump backwards and shove the key back in my pocket.

"What do you think you're doing?" said a clear young voice from the passenger window. "I'm calling the cops."

I spun round, prepared to escape down the street and over the bridge when the door snapped open.

"I saw you," said the voice. "I'll call my dad. He'll report you. You'll go to jail."

I was looking at a tall young guy about my age – wearing a navy school blazer with a crest. A rich snob with rosy hairless cheeks and a snow-white shirt. Did he know what his creep of a father was up to? What fake line had he given this kid to get him to wait like an idiot in the car?

"Your dad is a freakin' john who diddles underage girls," I screamed from the other side of the street. "Tell that to the cops."

His face fell. The hand holding the cell phone dropped to his side. "Say what? Come back and say that to my face," he screamed, his new man's voice cracking into a girlish shriek. I glanced upwards to see the pink curtains shift and his father's face look out onto the street. *Who'd harassed his precious, shiny son?* But I'd disturbed his sleazy session with Birdie and I hoped to hell he wouldn't take it out on her.

"I said come back," the boy shrieked again. So I gave him the finger and ran down the street, my hair flying out behind me, my body drenched with sweat under the hoodie. Away from that car and away from the poor little rich kid with the sicko dad.

35

I'd never set foot inside the baby store at the mall with its pale blue sign above the window and the rows of sleepers, dresses and pants so tiny they'd fit Esther Penner's perfect dolls.

I ran my fingers across display cases of baby booties and smiley-face bibs and hairbands for bald baby heads. I'd neglected to ask if Baby Metcalf was a he or she, but yellow or mint green would work for either sex so I loaded up my cart with one of everything in those colors.

Moms with strollers and Dads carrying babies in snugglies milled around the aisles laughing and chatting. Pastel colored posters of smiling cherubs beamed down on me, reminding me of Birdie's broken dreams.

Shoving my purchases towards the pink-cheeked sales clerk with the blonde ponytail and unicorn-covered smock, I paid cash. Threw out a wad of fifties and tens and fives so she had to sort through it, glancing up at my frowning face every couple of minutes. I could sense her confusion. *Why aren't you happy? A baby brings joy to a home. You should be brimming with hope for the future.*

"Just put it all in the same package," I said, unnerved by the polished gloss of instant happiness that exuded from the place.

"I'm going as fast as I can, ma'am," she said. Finally I grabbed the bags, stumbled through the door into the mall and breathed in the tropical scent of air freshener. My shoulders instantly relaxed. I headed towards the coffee bar and promised myself a fat, sticky pastry. A sugar fix was exactly what I needed.

–

I saw Birdie a month or so after the car incident. The last week of school before summer break.

An early heat spell had charred the grass to a dull brown and polluted the air with dust. Sizzling heat pressed down on everything, blanketing me in sweat. It got so bad I actually caved in and showered in Patti and Lester's moldy tub. Patti had given up housework months ago so the place was rancid.

The air conditioner was bust so they lay on the couch most days, a creaky fan whirring around in front of them, barely stirring the heavy air. Patti usually shoved a couple of bills into my hands and told me to go to the store for slushies and hot dogs. That's what I lived on those weeks before the summer break. The fridge was empty. Nobody bothered to go shopping any more. Any spare cash went to Tray and Anita and a troupe of other junkie scarecrows who showed up wherever a good time could be had.

Birdie left a message shoved into my locker to meet her in a diner just a couple of blocks away from the school. I was starving and hoped she'd buy me supper. Two months of leftover noodles warmed up day after day had left me craving a fat, juicy burger and hot fries with ketchup.

I barely recognized her when I walked in. She sat at a window seat. Sunlight blazed through the blinds casting a shadow of slats across her bony chest. Her face was so thin the skin looked transparent. A network of bluish veins spread like a web around her temples. Her eyes were sunk into dark sockets. She chewed on her nails and I noticed a bald patch above her ear where she'd been pulling her hair out.

"What's up?" I said, sliding into the seat opposite noticing how she persistently drummed her knee on the underside of the table. "You look like shit."

"Screw you," she said, twirling a piece of hair between her fingers.

The waitress, a lumpy fortyish woman with spiked burgundy hair swept up to the table. "You have to order. It's not a drop-in center."

Birdie looked right through her, reached into her purse and slid a couple of fives onto the table. "Two coffees. One black and..."

"One with triple cream. And an order of fries," I added.

Burgundy-hair shuffled away mumbling to herself and I looked at Birdie. I wasn't going to ask again.

"The baby's gone," she said, staring vacantly out onto the street.

I breathed an inner sigh of relief. "You lost it?"

She shook her head. "They made me kill it." Her eyes brimmed with tears. She wiped her arm across her face and I handed her a napkin. Next thing she'd be blowing snot bubbles like she did when she was a kid.

"Who made you do that?" I leaned back as the waitress placed the coffees onto the table. She glanced at Birdie but I glared up at her. Didn't want any of her fake concern.

"That guy I was seeing. Said he'd changed his mind and couldn't deal with the responsibility. And his wife would make his life hell for him if he left her. She'd take more than half his money and business. Then Earl found out and told me I had to get rid of it. Just like that. They sucked my baby out in a few minutes."

"Did your guy tell Earl about the baby?"

"I don't know and I don't care. I loved him. He said he wanted me to have his babies because together our kids would be the best. So I didn't take my pills. I thought he loved me. He told me over and over again."

"Don't you know he was lying to you, Birdie?" I grasped at her skinny wrist and tried to get her to look at me, but she just shook her head and stared down at the table, jabbing at her paper napkin with a fork. "There's no way he'd let some teenage whore's brat pollute the happy family home."

She looked up at me with wounded eyes, but I had to keep going. Had to make her see sense. I remembered the fine-skinned boy in the BMW. "He has a kid already."

"How do you know that?" she said, tears running down her cheeks and a tiny dribble running from her nose to her lip. I felt as if some evil hand was clawing at my heart, squeezing the breath from me.

"I saw him."

She glared at me with bloodshot eyes. "So it was you sneaking around out there. You scared him off."

"You're crazy. You think that guy would leave his fancy wife and kid for you?"

Her eyes drifted back to the street again. I couldn't tell what she was thinking any more. That connection between us was long gone.

She looked back at me with those sad, puppy eyes. "I knew about his son, but he said the kid was going off to college and wouldn't need him anymore, so he'd be free."

"And you believed him?"

"He said I was the best thing that ever happened to him."

I asked myself which soap operas this guy had been watching to come up with bullshit lines like that. "Did he tell you that when he had his hand up your schoolgirl panties or when he was spanking your bare ass?"

She doubled over and retched into her napkin. Burgundy hair flew over so quick her feet barely touched the floor. "You need help, honey?" she said, hovering over Birdie then glaring at my wild mane of hair, which was tangled and greasy after a year's deliberate neglect.

"Fries and ketchup?" I said, realizing she'd probably spit on them before she brought them to me. I didn't care. I'd eaten worse at the Flatts' place.

"Now he's gone. Finished with me. And he won't return my calls. And Earl's pissed," whispered Birdie, her eyes darting to the door. "I mean really pissed. We're not supposed to contact the clients. He says I'm becoming a pain in the ass."

My skin felt cold and prickly despite the hum of heat. I reached out to her. Clasped her hand. "You don't have to go back to him. We can leave here."

"What can I do? Go back to Lester's hellhole?"

"We'll run away," I said, my body feeling suddenly lighter. I'd been waiting for this chance to get Birdie alone to talk some sense into her. But I had to make sure about something first. "What about Loni? You still hanging with her?"

Birdie picked at a dried spot of ketchup on the table. Eased it off with her fingernail. "Haven't seen her in months. Don't know where she is. Nobody knows. She never came back from the ships. Earl says she got sick, but I haven't heard a word."

"And I guess there's no search parties out looking for her?"

"Why would they? Nobody cares. You don't either. You're probably glad she's gone."

I couldn't lie to her, so I said nothing. Just waited until she was calm again.

"So there's just the two of us again. Like the old times. We'll run away somewhere. Get the hell out of the city. Hitch a ride up north. Maybe even ride all the way up to Canada."

The fries appeared and Birdie actually ate a few. Dipped them daintily into the paper cup of ketchup. I tried to hold myself back from stuffing them down three or four at a time. I was so hungry I couldn't fill my mouth quickly enough.

"Could we really get there?" she said, a smile twitching at the corner of her lips.

I nodded in between bites. "I bet we could find Dennis if we tried." The food and the idea of being with Birdie were making me dizzy.

She shrugged. "I have money and we can sell some of my stuff. There's enough to keep us going for a while. Until we get a job."

"We could be waitresses," I said, a spark of hope crackling inside me.

She rested her elbows on the table and smiled. "Maybe I could work in a clothes store. Or do makeup at Dayton's."

She grinned and we clasped hands. Suddenly I knew she was back. For real.

"We're gonna do it tonight," I said. "I'll come back to your place with you now. Make sure you're okay. Then we'll head out on the road. Maybe even get a bus."

A cloud passed over her face. "Remember Esther and her dolls?"

I nodded.

"I dreamed about my baby. How beautiful she would be." Tears oozed from the corners of her eyes. "She was perfect. Like those dolls. But so soft and pretty. She smelled like soap and powder and I held her in my arms. I sang to her and told her I'd always be there to protect her from all the bad things no matter what. She was so small. I touched every tiny toe and counted her fingers. When I cuddled her she looked up at me and I knew she loved me. More than anybody else in the world. She'd always love me."

Birdie had always ached to hold Esther's dolls. She'd even pressed her face to the glass so hard, Esther had to push her aside and make me polish away the smudges left by her sticky nose and mouth.

"I love *you* like that, Birdie," I whispered. "We'll be okay together."

She smiled through tears, and our hands clasped so tight I felt the old electricity again. The charge that bonded us together. Sisters. Forever. "I love you too, Anna, and I'm sorry about Loni and the way we hurt you."

"I forgot about that already," I said, my heart so big in my chest I thought it would burst.

"But you gotta wait here for now," she said, getting up. "Don't want anyone getting suspicious. I'll be back in an hour."

I pushed my chair back. "No. I'm coming with you. I'll stay hidden just to make sure you get out okay."

She smiled at me with real love in her eyes. Again, like the old times. "Always looking out for me, Anna. You never change. But this time you'll have to trust me."

My heart thudded so hard it seemed deafening. I couldn't let her out of my sight. She'd never come back. I knew if she walked away it would be the end.

The diner door swung shut and I watched her disappear down the street, walking with that awkward pigeon-toed limp. She crossed into a shimmer of heat that scrambled her figure into a thousand wavy lines until she was gone. As if she'd never been there.

My sister. My Birdie.

Gone from the empty chair across from me. The faint scent of cigarette smoke the only evidence she'd been there.

Birdie was here.

Only a minute ago. Wasn't she?

I picked at a cold fry, dropped it back into the bowl without even touching it to my lips. It felt cold and heavy like a dead finger.

I waited there until burgundy-hair threw me out a couple of hours later. Then I hung around outside till it was dark. I left just after ten.

Back at the Flatts' place, bodies were passed out on the couches, chairs and floor. Six of them stretched out, the pipe lying unguarded on the table. I lit the tiny crumbs of meth left in the bowl and inhaled deep, waiting for the smoke to blast me into oblivion. To a place where there was no image of Birdie cringing under a sweating pig of a captain in the stuffy cabin of some rusty tanker up north, while the rest of the crew punched, cursed and jostled each other into a lineup outside her door.

-

A couple of weeks later I pulled myself up from my stupor. After a few days without a hit I saw the grime in every crack on the ceiling, every spore of mold that spread in damp patches down the wall and I couldn't turn that dark feeling off. I knew eventually I'd have to get myself up and out of that prison.

One evening Lester and Patti actually went out. Made the effort to drag themselves to Tray and Anita's dump of a place two blocks away. I'd seen them there before, with a crowd of deadbeats slouched on the steps outside, drinking beer, smoking and waiting for the next hit.

I ate a hasty supper of leftover hot dogs then walked to Birdie's apartment building, avoiding Tray and Anita's place. Once there I sat by the cedar bush to watch for her.

The pink curtains were gone, but someone moved across the window. Hope soaring in my heart, I raced over to the door just as a guy leading a chocolate lab stepped out. I slipped around him and into the lobby before he could protest.

Birdie's floor was silent so I sat by the elevator, waiting for her door to open. I didn't want to knock and get her in trouble so I stayed still like a zombie, my head reeling because I needed a hit of something but I had no way to get it. I must've been tired because I fell asleep. When I woke up, the moon was full, like an orange disc in the hallway window. I gazed at it, hypnotized, as if I'd somehow slipped into another life. Someone had placed a bottle of water and a bag of chips next to me. I wolfed them down, cramming handfuls into my mouth even though I tasted nothing but oil and salt. Then I remembered Birdie. Maybe she'd left them. Maybe it was a sign that she was okay.

I scrambled to my feet, ran to her door and smacked it hard, slapping the wooden panels with the flat of my hand.

"Birdie, it's me. Open the goddamn door!" I screamed over and over.

Nothing. Not even the sound of breathing. I smashed at the door again, this time with my fists, calling for her, my voice cracking with the pressure of tears. The door next to Birdie's smacked open, bouncing off the wall. A guy in a plaid robe stuck his head out.

"Nobody lives there, so stifle the noise or I'll call the cops," he yelled, slamming his door shut again.

I fell to my knees and flopped forward onto my stomach. If I could only look under that door I might catch her making tea or doing her laundry or painting her nails. But all I saw was the moonlight streaming through her window and all I could feel was the bone crushing, choking sadness that comes when you realize you're totally and absolutely alone in the world.

36

As I'd expected, Brian Metcalf's place was cute as a doll-house. A tiny white stucco bungalow with two triangular peaks on the brown shingle roof, neat beige timbers cris-scrossing the exterior, a mini glassed-in porch complete with two cedar rockers and flower boxes stuffed with pink and white petunias below the front window. Two manicured globe cedars stood on either side of the front steps and a brass mailbox with matching carriage lamps gleamed a cheery welcome.

"Brian's pretty frugal when it comes to investments," said Guy, opening the car door for me. "Said he picked this up for a hundred and ninety grand, sunk twenty into it and now he reckons it's worth two seventy-five at least."

Brian's house was the exact opposite of Gord and Nancy's. Small and cozy, with eco-friendly bamboo floors, leaf-printed calico drapes and natural cedar furniture. Brian and his wife Judy welcomed us inside with a whispered *hello*, index fingers plastered to their lips. Seemed baby Scout (*who actually called their kid Scout?*) had finally decided to take a nap, so we tiptoed around the woven straw bassinette into the living room. I glanced at the rosy-cheeked baby. Perfect, peachy and untouchable, she reminded me of Birdie's dream baby. I turned away, anxious to forget the episode in the diner and the words I could never say to Birdie, that her baby wouldn't have stood a chance if it had lived. That it was better to get rid of it than risk another baby condemned to a life with a mother who was still a child.

Swathed in cream organic cotton, baby Scout would be pampered, protected, fed lactose-free soy milk and peanut-free, vegan organic food. Dressed in reused, recycled, non-toxic, organic clothes. Its life would be dust-free, additive-free, germ-free, danger-free and possibly fun-free until it grew into a timorous child whose sheltered life was dominated by a long list of food-borne and household allergens. I could see it all by scoping out the kitchen and the assortment of boxes and jars scattered across the counter.

And Judy looked like she'd just blown in fresh from the set of a kids' show. Makeup-free with scrubbed apple cheeks. Even, white teeth behind pink lips. Tousled shiny curls never tainted by color or charred by the heat of a flat iron. Bold, dark eyebrows and baggy jeans topped with an embroidered white cotton smock, easy to flip open at a moment's notice for an emergency breastfeeding. And so sweet she set my teeth on edge.

I wasn't good with women like Judy. They threw me off with their unfailing kindness and sweet, doglike patience. I could handle Sabrina and her hard edges, but Judy was infinitely more threatening when she tilted her head, radiated maternal bliss, and listened with such interest to everything I said, or rather mumbled to her.

Under her gaze I felt like an imposter. As if sooner or later the ten or so years spent bricking up my shameful past would turn out to be an utter waste of time and those monstrous secrets would force their way through the crumbling wall of lies and denial. Then the real, monstrous me would be revealed.

Women like Judy had a way of teasing out those demons. They'd shake their glossy curls, win your trust with an intimate smile and try to wear down your guard until you blurted out every appalling secret in the vain hope of friendship and acceptance. I'd always got on better with men who could be distracted with sex or tantalized by the mystery of my shady, secret past.

We settled down at the kitchen table with our ginger and goji berry tea, which Judy assured me was a deep detoxer and bowel cleanser. I'd have preferred a large glass of Pinot Grigio but she probably would've pressed a burning crucifix to my forehead if I'd mentioned alcohol around that baby. I'd already sinned enough by not checking the labels on the baby clothes for chemical contaminants, and though she'd unwrapped our gifts with the required bursts of *oohs* and *aahs*, she couldn't hide the slight downward droop of her mouth and the tentative way she handled the little dresses and jackets with thumb and forefinger, then placed them immediately back in the bag.

Brian served supper. *To give Judy a much-deserved rest*, said the ever-considerate husband and father. He carried out a clay casserole dish of eggplant lasagna made with brown rice pasta. Too bad it turned out to be a steaming mush covered with a layer of sticky goat cheese that would've been better eaten with a spoon. Smiling and nodding at appropriate times during the hum of conversation, I plowed my way through the large, chunky pasta island and its accompanying beet greens and arugula salad. Meanwhile Judy kept popping out to *do some more expressing*. When she left the room, Brian explained that her milk production was so high it made her nipples leak even through the special pads. I had trouble with the melted goat cheese after that, especially when Brian kept eyeballing me in a shifty, corner-of-the eye way all through supper.

Sometime in between the apple cobbler and the nettle tea, he placed his hands flat on the table and drew in a long breath. *Something's coming*, I thought. *Did I have anything to worry about?* I reached for Guy's knee under the table. Squeezed it. He was real. Flesh and blood sitting right next to me. Wouldn't fly away like some gorgeous dream in the hot rays of the sun.

"Anna, it's been bugging me ever since I saw you at school. But I know we've met before and I couldn't put my finger on it."

I shook my head, then turned and smiled at Guy who'd tilted his head as if waiting for me to confirm Brian's hunch.

"Unless I'm suffering from early dementia, I talked to you a few months ago. You came to ask questions about Guy's research. I thought you were a journalist writing a feature."

Judy had just arrived back to find us all staring at each other in a kind of stalemate.

"What's going on?" she asked, hugging her breasts and easing herself onto her chair. Wet milk patches spread across the front of her smock.

Guy grinned. "Brian thinks Anna was scoping me out months before I actually met her."

Now they were all looking at me. Waiting for me to spill the goods.

"Maybe I checked him out for a presentation," I said. "But I never claimed to be a journalist."

A small frown flickered across Brian's face. "I could've sworn — but with the baby's arrival it's been a sleep-deprived few months, so my mind is mush."

I was just about to redirect the conversation when a piercing wail echoed through the kitchen. Baby Scout was awake. It was like battle stations to the ready. Brian and Judy swept into immediate action ushering me and Guy politely out through the front door. Not soon enough for me. The moment we were in the car, I sighed, closed my eyes and leaned my head back against the soft leather car seats.

On the drive home I nodded off. In that state between consciousness and sleep I pictured myself searching Guy's number online, then actually making that call to Brian. My heart lurched a little at the sudden memory.

I'd known exactly what I was doing. I just didn't want to admit it.

I stayed quiet for the rest of the drive, just mumbled in monosyllables while Guy prattled on about the happy Metcalf household.

Later, in bed, he traced a finger across my stomach. "Were you really stalking me?"

"Just doing my homework," I said, turning my face away from his scrutiny.

"You little predator. You know the idea of you watching me, itching to get your hands on me really turns me on."

"You are so impossibly vain," I said, propping myself up on my elbow and trying hard to look disapproving. "But how could I not lust after you? You're perfect."

"So are you, Anna. Perfect for me," he said, pulling me close and wrapping his arms around me. I closed my

305

eyes and breathed in his scent, marveling that he really was mine.

Much later, I lay awake staring at the ceiling again. Sleep was so elusive those nights. I couldn't slow down my thoughts enough to relax. I was barely getting by on four hours a night. No wonder I spent the day in a semi-hallucinatory state.

I really had sought Guy out. Deliberately engineered him into my life. Lured him. Seduced him. And now we were an item.

Only I was in deeper than I'd intended.

He'd caught me off guard with his gentle devotion, making me unsure of my next step. How could I hurt him?

But I'm a person who always likes the last word. I never forget when I've been wronged. Because then I have to exact some kind of payback.

You could call it an obsession with revenge. Like with Lester and Patti in the final days I spent with them.

37

Financially strapped, Lester and Patti moved onto manufacturing their own meth. That was the darkest time for me. Can't remember too much about it. Only that I barely made it to school much for a month or two, preferring to hang around the apartment sucking up the remnants of any junk the Flatts left when they crashed out of their meth high. Anything to deaden the ache of being completely alone. To stop myself asking *what's the point of living?* I'd smoke to get jacked up with enough energy to do homework, make crazy plans to change the world, find Birdie and whisk her away. I don't remember sleeping or eating then. My reality was a buzz of voices and color and twitching limbs that jerked and flickered in a fast-forward motion.

My world was in chaos, but I do remember what happened before the explosion, though my memories are always blurred at the edges and colored with a yellowy tinge. Like old home movies over-exposed to the sun.

Linda Martin said I was there. I must have been. But Birdie wasn't.

Where was she? Selling herself to the highest bidder? Screwing crewmen on a cargo ship in Duluth? Working a strip club in Vegas?

By that time I didn't care. Time slipped back and forth. One day overlapping another.

I remember old rock music blaring in the background. Janis Joplin. Me sitting against the hallway wall, crouched on the edge of the action. I imagined I was her. Shook my long, crazy hair. Tipped back a beer. *Fuck the world and everybody in it.* Lester and Patti and friends were in top form, all hell breaking loose as usual. The place reeked of burning plastic, everybody jerking around like crazy old puppets.

Then some old crone with a drooping stomach and skinny legs decided to mess around with Lester. Patti caught her straddling his lap, legs twined around his back like a fleshy vine, so Patti grabbed a handful of her hair and dragged her backwards onto the carpet. Thumped her in the ribs once she was down. Called her a *two-bit whore.* Everyone yelled. *Cat fight, cat fight.* Then another guy, Todd with the glass eye, flipped out on Tray, claiming he was hogging the pipe. Elbowed him in the throat, wrestled him onto the floor next to the crone who was sucking in air like a fish out of water. Wrapped himself around Tray. Chewed on his ear then spat out blood.

And I thought to myself how weird that this was all going on next to the counter with the boxes of macaroni cheese and the spoon collection on the wall and the framed picture of Elvis against the wallpaper with its sickly orange and yellow flowers.

And Janis screamed. *You say that it's over baby.*

It's never over.

That's when I planned to get myself out the next night.

Put an end to being stuck in this miserable hellhole with these dangerous, useless people. My plan was drastic, but in my frenetic state seemed totally reasonable and logical. They'd graduated to using the "shake and bake" method to make their stuff, so next day, all it took from me was to convince them to use a heat gun to dry out the meth in a plastic water bottle.

I had the sense to throw myself behind the kitchen door before sparks shot up. Three – four – five blasts of scorching light, like fireworks on the Fourth of July. Patti screeched to Lester, *Don't throw it, shake it* and the bottle blew up like a bomb in their scabby faces. They were rolling on the floor, their clothes blazing with toxic chemical flames when I called 911. I jammed a dishcloth into my mouth to keep out the smoke, and crawled back to the bedroom in time to curl up under the blankets like an innocent victim.

The firemen burst in and hosed Lester and Patti down until they blubbered like mad chimps. I covered my eyes when the paramedics led me away through the smoke and burning stench of flesh, though I squinted at my soon-to-be ex-foster parents through gaps in my fingers on the way out. I heard their moans and saw their swollen, bloodied faces and arms, the tatters of clothing still sticking to their blistered skin.

Outside it was raining. A fine sheet of drizzle soaked my hair. I tipped my face upwards to taste the clean, fresh droplets. Dew from heaven sent down to tell me I'd never go back to the hell I'd left behind. Ever.

So the Flatts were the first to pay for their sins, but I wouldn't forget the others who wronged Birdie. Like Earl Rafferty, his henchman Jimmy and, worst of all, the main man, the rotten piece of scum that robbed her of her innocence and all her dreams, then took her away from me.

I'd pay him back. I'd take him down – destroy him by taking everything he had.

38

We always dressed up for our school grad. Just the same as if we were teachers in some ivy-covered prep school in the suburbs. Robin dutifully trotted out his one and only suit, a navy, double-breasted, pinstriped number with shiny, bare patches under the arms. Probably a genuine vintage piece straight from the streets of sixties Carnaby Street in swinging London. From before his beach bum hippie phase. Everyone else did their best.

I'd shopped long and hard for my dress. Spent nights at the mall trying to calm the turmoil inside me. Walked around sucking in the fruity, tropical scent that reminded me of everything clean and safe. That's how I'd felt as a kid. Sloping around the polished hallways in my hoodie, chewing on my hair, breathing in the aroma of clean and happy and bright things. The scent of possibility, of what I could be if I just kept my head down and pushed forward. If I could graduate then I'd have the key to all the glittering secrets the mall promised me.

That's what I hoped for Dane and Carla. Dane would actually graduate from my class along with Hailey who'd been accepted into a nurses' aide program, Clarence who'd start auto mechanics at the local tech college and Viola who'd already applied to become a cop. I'd convinced Dane to check out some graphic design schools and he was floored when he heard back from a couple.

I found the perfect dress after four hours of wandering. Just right for afternoon tea. Acceptable at even the swankiest college prep school. A fifties-inspired flared white cotton skirt printed with brilliant blue cornflowers, topped with a white, glazed cotton shirt, with starched wing collar and three-quarter sleeves – all tied together nicely with an indigo cotton sash. I scraped my hair into an Audrey Hepburn pleat, slipped on some pearl earrings, applied a final slick of scarlet lipstick and twirled around in front of the mirror. The tulle petticoat rustled and crackled underneath the cotton glaze. I felt beautiful. I'd achieved success in my job and I had a beautiful, safe home. A wonderful, gentle man loved me and I loved him back in my own limited way. My heart swelled with joy.

If only it could always be this way, but it wouldn't. Birdie was always there in the background. The memory of her needling at me like an itch that couldn't be scratched. The vengeance still to be exacted thrumming like a discord in the harmony of my new life.

"You're a vision," said Guy sweeping into the room. "Did you ever consider a modeling career?"

I snapped out of my dream. Adoration burned in his eyes. I could barely look at him.

"You could say I was a late bloomer."

It was a crevice, a crack in the armor, enough to entice him. He caught my hand and kissed it. "Tell me what you were like as a kid. I want to know. Did you have a dumb hairdo or zits on your chin?"

The drawbridge clanged shut. All entries barred. "There's nothing to talk about," I said, turning away. "It's all in the past now."

He touched the stiff points of my collar, a playful smile on his face. "You know I'm a patient guy, Anna. I'll wait and whenever you're ready you'll tell me."

I wondered what I'd ever done to find someone like Guy. Then I remembered. I'd made it my business to find him. Why pretend to myself I hadn't? It was time to be honest with myself. To quit the lying and self-deception.

"You're a good man," I said, kissing him on the lips. "A good guy. Guy."

He caught me around the waist. "I always feel so happy around you. So complete. Something about you is so real, so familiar. As if we've met in another life."

"Don't get all cheesy on me," I said, looking at my reflection in the mirror next to his. If only he knew.

We *had* met in another life.

On a day when two very different lives collided on a street. Me tracing the sharp edge of a key with a nicotine-stained finger, the stink of days' old sweat on my clothes. Him standing by a gleaming BMW, shiny hair and clear skin like a young prince. The look of panic in his eyes. *Tell me what you said*, he screamed as I ran down the alley, away from the scene of my sister's undoing.

"Maybe we did," I said, wiping the smudge of lipstick from the corner of his mouth. He smelled like lemon and shaving soap. I could have lapped my tongue into the crevices of his neck. He was mine. All mine now. What would his father say if he knew? It would tear him up inside. Make him sweat a little at the thought of someone so close knowing all his dirty secrets. But I caught sight of the time and remembered Robin's obsession with punctuality. "Gotta go. It's grad day."

"Dinner tonight. Somewhere special," he said, catching me around my waist.

"A rare steak and some blood-red wine by candlelight," I whispered.

He kissed behind my ear. "Then I'll bare my neck to you, my favorite, sexy vampire."

"Promise? You know I'll suck you dry," I said, tearing myself away to grab my purse. My face was so flushed I'd need a full blast of air conditioning to settle down.

–

Robin had invited a group of local musicians to the ceremony. They played a folksy version of 'Pomp and Circumstance' as the graduates filed in. Scented candles burned on the front table next to bowls of bright yellow daisies. We sat in a circle in the multi-purpose room, my skirt rustling with the slight trickle of air conditioning that blew from the aged wall units. The light tinkle of the tambourine and the heady, floral scent of candle smoke made my heart ache. For some strange reason they reminded me of my mother. For the woman I'd never known. When she was young and hopeful and full of life.

I wished I could have seen her then, but I rarely touched that hollow place, barely thought of the shadowy figure that was always out of reach, closing a door before I got to it, turning a corner when I was too far behind. I'd never know when and why she lost her way. But then the sounds and scents lulled me into a daydream and I found myself slipping back in time again to think about another graduation day. My own high school grad.

–

After the explosion at the Flatts' place, the medics rushed me to hospital. Social workers, doctors and nurses flitted in and out of my room, discussing, conferring, trying to figure out why on earth I'd landed back at a known meth house.

I was malnourished, anemic, and I had a raging chest infection. I was also suffering withdrawals from a whole smorg of drugs. I lay in that cool, white bed and willed myself back to health. My body was so weak they had to feed me an iron-rich diet and pump me full of vitamins and antibiotics.

When I left that place, I was physically healthy but my mind was still a nest of dark, angry confusion. I could barely focus long enough on a thought to sort out what was real from what I'd imagined. Enter Rachel Levine. The first human being, after Dennis, to show me love, patience and real kindness.

Dealing with me at sixteen was like approaching a snarling dog. Stay back, hold out a hand, let the creature come to you. Don't impose yourself. Wait till she's ready. And Rachel waited. Sweet-faced, soft-voiced and firm. Always there. Just like Guy and Dennis – at the beginning.

I enjoyed two blissful years with the Levines. Their home became an oasis of calm. Birdie had disappeared from my life, sucked back into that nightmare world I'd narrowly escaped. I was free to concentrate on my studies, graduate with honors, win a bunch of scholarships and buy a sky-blue tulle prom dress. I'd finally let Rachel take me to a hairdresser, who struggled to get a comb through my tangled hair, then gave up and promptly cut it into a pretty, face-framing bob. After that I'd shrugged the hoodie off and emerged from my chrysalis to also discover it was okay to be pretty, to show my face and be proud, now the perverts and predators had been banished to the margins of my new middle-class life.

I didn't think about Birdie again until my high-school grad.

Rachel and her husband were in the audience. I smiled at them as I crossed the stage, palms sweating, teetering on heels too high for comfort. I grasped that diploma like a talisman, beaming when Rachel pressed a bouquet of roses into my arms then steered me into the common room among the dizzy swarm of eighteen-year-olds feasting on party sandwiches, dainties and fruit punch. Hugs from school friends, breathless promises to stay in touch and plans for the summer made my grad day feel almost normal. Until I thought I glimpsed Birdie.

Outside the window.

A flash of denim and skimpy crop top. Bleached hair and hollow eyes, pushing a stroller. Inside a baby sucked on blue Kool-Aid from a bottle. She stopped and stared at me. Her eyes bloodshot, her mouth slack and drooling. I blinked and she was gone. Dropping my plate on the floor, I ran over to the window, placed my palms flat against the glass and searched for a sign. A plastic soother. Wheel marks in the dirt. Nothing.

"You okay?" said Rachel, taking my arm.

"It was her. I saw her."

"You mean Birdie?"

I nodded. Rachel's face was calm. Her voice soft enough to quiet every raging demon inside me.

"It's natural that you'd want to see her here. To be proud of you today."

I accepted her explanation and let her soft arm wrap around my shoulders to guide me back to the coffee table.

I told myself I must have imagined it.

I've often lied. Stretched the truth. Made things up. I've done it a whole lot of times. Like telling the cops it was Patti that told Lester to *shake it, don't drop it*. Not me.

I didn't think of Birdie again until my first year in college. I still went to the mall then, but to buy things rather than find shelter. I'd discovered guys. Found that I could actually be attractive if I dressed up and made an effort. Their sudden attention was a revelation to me after years of hiding behind a hoodie.

In my first year I went on the pill and slept with three or four guys. All of them had money. I made them buy me stuff. Drinks, food, college T-shirts, school binders with gold crests, writers' journals with gorgeous covers – and books. So many books. I impressed them with my reading list. Burroughs, Proust, Wallace, Melville, Munro, Atwood. I read them all. Even tried to discuss them, but none of them held a candle to Colby who, for some reason never made it to college. I heard from one of our ex-high school buddies that he'd taken a carpentry course at some community college and lived out in the sticks making garden chairs and kitchen cabinets.

So once they'd bought me enough gifts and I'd eaten my fill, I slept with them. Strange, they all seemed so grateful. And so persistent afterwards. But after I'd bared my body to them and abandoned all control, I couldn't bring myself to look them in the eyes again. Then I hightailed it back to the mall in search of familiar ground and a new outfit to lure the next sucker. I'd become a slightly different version of Birdie. More educated, more respectable, but way more sly and calculating.

One afternoon I went there I used the back entrance. Walked by the benches where the deadbeats and junkies hung out. That's when I saw Loni.

Or at least a cartoonish, used-up version of her. Caved-in mouth, broken nose and fried clumps of hair sticking up from her scalp. She was hunched over a bottle, pushing away some old drunk who was whining for a shot. She yelled at him and shoved him off the bench. I stood a few yards away. Far enough to bolt inside if I had to. Far enough to get to mall security if I needed them.

"Loni," I said. Very calm. Very confident because of my shiny shoulder-length hair, nice jeans and Hollister hoodie.

She looked up and grinned showing yellowed stumps of teeth. "Well, if it ain't the bitch sister."

"Charmed to see you again. Where's Birdie?"

She shrugged. "Hell if I know."

A necklace of purple hickies adorned her neck. Who would kiss her now?

"Oh, but you do know," I said, despising her as much as I always had. Maybe more.

"Could be up in Duluth on the ships. Can't say. I got out before it killed me. Or maybe she went to some pussy palace near Vegas. I heard they like 'em young there."

"She still with Earl?"

She squinted up at me like I was an idiot. "You're a real dumbass. Earl never lets go. Until he don't want you no more. I guess he's done with me. Can't blame him. Nobody wants me now."

That was when she started to cry. Big, gulping sobs until the old drunk nuzzled at her neck while she took a long swig from the plastic bottle. She handed it to him and he kissed her full on the lips. Told her he loved her.

I'd seen enough. I left.

Sabrina, who'd forgiven me for my bitchy comment about our relationship, nudged my shoulder and I came to just in time to see Dane cross the stage to receive his diploma. My eyes were misty. He'd taken the first step in a long journey towards a good and decent life. When he passed by my seat, I held out a bunch of red roses.

"You did it," I whispered, daring to hug him for the first time. "I knew you could."

He wiped a sleeve over big, teary eyes and said, "Thanks, Anna. For everything."

After a long burst of applause, he gathered himself up to walk back to his seat.

Carla looked shell-shocked when she walked across the stage. Like she didn't belong there wearing that mortar board and gown. And when I pressed the flowers into her arms she blinked and said, "It's so unreal. All of this."

"Believe it," I said, letting her go. "It's the beginning of a new life."

She was set to take culinary arts at the nearby community college, then go to live with an auntie in the country who owned a bakery. She was safe. Every year it was like this. I lost a couple, saved a couple. But it was all worth it. Maybe it made up a little bit for not rescuing Birdie.

But it didn't.

With all my education and reading and scheming I couldn't save the one person who mattered to me the most. What kind of sister was I? A failure. That was the real story of my life. I couldn't tear my sister away from the man who ruined her. Who blew the whistle to Earl. I imagined his call.

Hey this little whore gets pregnant and expects me to play happy families with her. What kind of game are you playing, man? You expect me to pay premium dollar for this kind of trouble?

So Earl takes care of it. Gets rid of the precious baby and exacts a punishment.

You belong to me and you don't mess around with VIP clients. They don't give a damn about you and your baby and your dreams. I bought you. I sell you. You're a product. I have to protect my clients.

His client.

Not a man. A coward. A predator. A monster.

I cursed him until my head ached.

The man who led Birdie on with false promises, who sucked the life from her then threw out the carcass.

I cursed him until my blood burned. Go back to your shiny house and wife and son.

I will find you.

I have found you.

39

The first official team meeting to mark the beginning of my new career in Gord's empire fell on a scorching Monday in late July.

It came as a bit of a shock to actually work during the summer months. My last few years teaching had meant long, lazy summers spent traipsing around the mall, maybe trekking further afield to the outlets at Albertville. Meeting for cocktails, swimming in Fran Kuzyk's condo pool, or soaking up the sun on a Lake Calhoun beach. One summer I'd even hopped in the back seat of Sabrina's SUV to tour casinos up north in lake country with two of her buddies. I'd never taken a real trip, mainly because I barely had enough money to pay the bills and fund my shopping habit. But I'd loved those summers for their laid-back laziness. Idle sunny days would turn into hot summer nights. I had no plans. Just slept in, ate takeout, washed my hair a lot, and tanned. If I met a guy, I usually slept with him, made him my summer romance, then ditched him when school started up again. It was sweeter that way. No ties meant no complications.

My first official meeting as Gord's employee was scheduled for three at his suite of offices two blocks away from the university. Guy said he'd join us a little later when he could get away from school.

I parked near the university so I could take a walk by my old alma mater. Past the gray stone columns and the burgundy sign emblazoned with gold letters that spelled out University of Minnesota, and beyond that gate, the white colonnades and brick façade of the library and lecture halls. I'd missed the place so much I decided to start taking my morning jogs around the campus. How many times had I walked through these gates, feeling a surge of pride and gratitude that almost bowled me over? I'd survived the horrors forced on me by an uncaring system, and only I knew the magnitude of that achievement. I felt in control for the first time in my life, but many mornings I'd wake shaking with terror that my new life was really a dream that could suddenly end and I'd find myself in a drug-induced stupor back in the Flatts' house of horror.

After five years of recovery – two spent with the Levines and three at college – I'd thought I was finally normal, my mind lucid. The demons gone from my life, the drugs cleaned out of my system. Five solid years not thinking of Birdie or hearing from her. Then I saw him again. The man who'd used her and thrown her away. The man who liked his girls young. Nubile. Childlike. The man I hated with a passion that terrified me.

Towards the end of my third year of education I attended a guest lecture. The speaker was billed as Gord Franzen, a leading expert on student engagement and author of a string of successful titles, all standard texts in university. But the moment he walked onstage it was as if a bolt of lightning slammed into the top of my head and seared through my body.

My eyes took in the figure at the podium. The sheen of his dark suit, the smooth swath of reddish hair combed to the side and set with hairspray. Like a glossy TV news anchor, the words flowed from his mouth, sending a fine spray of spit into the microphone. I could barely focus. My fingertips danced on the arm of my chair. Those Polaroid pictures flipped through my head like a porn catalogue, with fifteen-year-old Birdie as the fantasy sex toy. If I'd had them in my pocket I'd have fanned them out like a winning poker hand, shoved them into his face and said, *What do you have to say about this, you creep? What would the cops say if they knew it was you? What if your precious family knew?*

But I didn't have them with me. I had no ready evidence at hand to pin him to the crime. Only my junkie sister's word and now she was gone. Who would believe her anyway? I had to be patient. Wait for the right time and place. The right way to make him pay.

Now that time was really close.

–

Despite the warm sunlight, I shivered at the memory. But this was no time for distractions. I grasped my briefcase and marched further up the street, away from the university. Gord's offices were situated in the top floor of a glass and brick building. I stood outside to get the feel of the place even though I knew it already. Had been there years before. Stood outside that brick facade many times in my student days. Watching for signs of Gord. Maybe even a glimpse of his son. Violent scenarios ran over and over in my head. What I'd do to Gord if I confronted him. A gunshot to the chest. A vial of acid thrown in the face. A knife thrust just under the ribs. I'd imagined them all.

I passed through the plant-filled lobby, hummed as the elevator took me up to the fourth floor and stepped into a modern suite of offices. Nancy was already there. The smell of freshly perked coffee and warm cinnamon rolls told me she'd been busy preparing. I found her in the ultra-white kitchen cutting up pineapple and adding it to a tower of fresh fruit. In all my thoughts about Gord I'd tried to put Nancy out of my head, but watching her bustle about in that kitchen I found myself wondering about her. Had she known about the girls? Did Gord ever force sex on her? Bully her? Degrade her? Why the hell did she stay with him? Why didn't she slit his throat while he slept, his mouth gaping open, the pale swell of his Adam's apple quivering, begging for the edge of a blade? And what about Guy? Did he suspect anything or had Nancy always protected her darling boy?

"Nervous?" she asked and I almost jumped out of my skin.

I shook my head. "Just bummed I can't sleep in anymore," I said, reaching for the coffee. "I need this so bad."

She ushered me into the meeting room. "Gord's on a call. Make yourself comfortable."

I grabbed a warm cinnamon roll, sat back and took in my surroundings. White walls decorated with twisted wire and glass sculptures, shiny black conference table surrounded by white leather chairs, pale wood-grain flooring. Typical Nancy décor. Pristine, almost sterile surroundings. Maybe her way of coping with the dirty mess of being Gord's wife. And now I was Gord's daughter-in-law as well as his employee. Couldn't get any closer to him. My palms tingled, my temples ached, my heart thrummed in my ears. I wished Guy would come. I'd never been alone with Gord and I hoped to hell I could hide my loathing and disgust when I saw him. After all, he was street-smart, like me. Perhaps he was already onto me and wasn't letting on. But I had one major advantage over him.

I had nothing to lose.

Unlike Gord who had everything at stake.

As if he'd read my thoughts, he appeared, larger than life at the door. My hand jolted the coffee cup, sending a pool of brown across the white tabletop. I jumped up to grab a napkin.

"Relax, Nance'll get it. *Nancee*," he yelled. "Cleanup needed."

I mopped at the puddle. "No need to bother her."

"She'd be hurt if I didn't," he replied as she swept in with a spray bottle and wad of paper towel.

As she bent across the table to wipe away the mess I caught the slight movement of his hand on her ass. Patting it. Proprietary. As if she were a chattel he'd bought and paid for. Her whole body went rigid. I bit my tongue. Checked myself from calling him a slimy piece of garbage, turned to glance out of the window, wishing, hoping Guy would show up so I could tether myself to the present again.

"So Guy tells me you've no family," he said. A bolt totally out of the blue.

Nancy chewed on her lower lip. "Gord, you could be a bit more diplomatic. Maybe ease into the personal questions."

He glared. "I think Anna would appreciate a fresh cup of coffee, dearest heart."

She glared back at him, drew her shoulders back and swept out of the room. The door swung shut leaving me to face his question. He stared straight at me, clearly awaiting a response.

"My parents passed away a long time ago."

"Brothers and sisters?"

I thought I detected a hint of rancor on the word *sister*, but decided I'd imagined it.

"None. I was an only child."

He tilted his head and narrowed his eyes. "So who raised you?"

I tried not to blink or look away. "My gran, Rachel."

"Alive?"

"Dead."

"No cousins, aunts, uncles?"

Shaking my head, I tried to focus on the open sky beyond the glass wall. "I prefer not to talk about my past."

He raised his palms, tipped his head back, checked out the ceiling for a moment, then slapped his hands down on the pile of folders in front of him. "Fair enough. I can respect that. Let's get down to business then."

He shoved a pile of folders towards me. Something to focus on. My heart rate immediately ratcheted down to a level I could control, allowing me to spend the next half hour chatting about innocuous matters like focus groups, interview questions and data collection, even though I loathed the very air he breathed.

–

Thankfully the first week I barely saw Gord. I spent my time conducting discussion groups with teens, teachers and parents in the meeting room on the third floor, a comfy blue room with soft couches, oceanscapes on the walls and pots of ferns and ivy. It was easy work and I established an effective rhythm in my discussions. Only once did I forget to record the first half hour of a session and had to go back to do it again. Guy looked in once in a while, smiled and gave me a thumbs up. At those times I felt like part of something normal. Something so comfortable I could've forgotten those old promises made in a moment of crushing guilt. I'd tell myself to pretend it didn't happen. Move forward. Suppress it all. But then the memories came flooding back at night and I'd toss and turn so violently the sheets wrapped themselves in a tangle around my legs, then Guy woke up and stroked my back until I calmed down.

I was heading towards the toughest part of my life story. The part where I'd find Birdie or lose her completely and I wasn't ready for either.

40

Before Linda Martin was assigned to my case, I had a temporary social worker. Martha was sixtyish and retired, returning to fill in for a maternity leave. I was in my final year of education when she called and asked me to meet at her office.

At first I thought she had news about Birdie. I raced to the meeting with the sun blinding me and my stomach rolling with nausea. The childcare people had left me alone since I entered university, so I was shocked to find myself in that yellow-walled office again, sitting in a chair across from a big, bustling woman with blunt-cut bangs and a brightly flowered top who'd somehow worked her way through every detail of my life history, yet she barely knew me.

After the usual formalities and introductions, she placed both hands flat on the table and leaned forward. I noticed every finger was adorned with a ring. Silver swirls, turquoise stones, copper bands. I couldn't take my eyes off them.

"I know. I'm a sucker for handmade jewelry," she said, leaning back in her chair. "Every damn craft fair and artisan stall – they can see me coming."

"They're pretty," I said, hardly daring to breathe.

"Look, I suppose you're wondering why I called you," she said, a brief smile flickering across her face.

I nodded.

"I've been checking your files," she said, crossing her arms over her ample bosom.

I shifted myself to get more comfortable in the metal chair. I remember wondering why the authorities were so reluctant to spend some money and buy decent furniture.

"Why me?"

She shuffled the pile of folders in front of her and opened one. "I received a phone call that I think you should know about. It prompted me to check your file and I found some grave irregularities."

I leaned forward. Now this was interesting. Maybe someone was finally interested in me and my case. "Who called?"

"Someone who claims to be your father phoned yesterday asking about you and your sister."

I blinked twice as if the light would suddenly change and I'd find myself somewhere else. Somewhere real. "Dennis? Dennis called?"

She nodded. "Yes. That's the name he gave. But then I looked through your files to verify the information he gave me and I discovered that he'd called before." She flipped through the sheets, tracing her finger along rows of numbers and words. All about me. My life summed up in a slim, brown folder. "It seems the calls began over ten years ago. At least three times a year. But if I'm reading this correctly you were never notified and he was never granted access to you or your sister."

So Dennis hadn't forgotten us. He'd tried to find us. Maybe even wanted us to come home. My eyes ached. Tears pressed at the back of my eyeballs. But I wouldn't give anyone in that office the satisfaction of seeing me cry. "Where is he?"

"I can give you that information but I need you to confirm that you were never notified," she said, fixing me with a quizzical look.

"I never heard a thing about him. Why?"

"That's exactly what I'm going to find out," she said, smiling. "Your file is incomplete. Undocumented gaps of time, especially around the time your sister went missing."

"Did they just forget or did someone take information out of the folder?"

"I can't say yet, but I've found other clients' records that look like they've been tampered with. And two of them are girls we know have been missing for years."

"Why would anyone take the time to do that?"

"Maybe someone wants us to forget about these young women. I can't say for sure, but perhaps the person who's doing it knows what happened to them and wants to make it difficult for us to trace them."

She put on a pair of reading glasses and studied the papers in front of her. I leaned forward and whispered.

"Martha, does it say my sister was sexually exploited by a wealthy, respected member of the community and nobody lifted a finger to help her? She was fifteen years old."

She flopped back in her chair and shook her head, her eyes magnified by the glasses. "I didn't see anything about that, Anna. I'm so sorry. The system failed you both. But I'm onto this now and I won't let go until I have some answers."

I was so choked, I couldn't think of anything to say except, "I want to see Dennis. Give me his contact info."

She nodded and slid a piece of paper towards me. "Be cautious. Start with a phone call. It's been a long while since you talked to him and you can't be sure what to expect. People change but not always in a good way. You may have built up unreasonable expectations of him."

"Dennis was... I mean is a good man and was a good father."

"You might remember him that way. Children of abusive parents sometimes paint a glowing fantasy picture in their memories that has no relation to reality. The truth can be a massive shock to the psyche. But I do believe you're mature enough to handle this now. My question is why it was ever withheld from you."

I left that office clutching the address in my hand. I wasn't ready to act on the information but three weeks later, when I called the office again to ask Martha more questions, I was alarmed to discover she was no longer there. *Reassigned* was the official word, but after checking through all the social work departments I found no trace of her again. Like I said before, people around me tended to disappear. Maybe she knew too much for them to keep her around.

I kept the piece of paper in my wallet, waiting for the right moment to call, to think of the right thing to say. What could I say to my father after fourteen years? We'd both failed Birdie and I dreaded telling him she was gone.

A year later, one frigid night in December, in my first year of teaching at the alternative school, I rolled out of a cab so drunk Sabrina had to drag me to my front door.

"I hate to leave you alone on Christmas Eve," she said, blowing on her hands. "But I have a plane to catch in a few hours and I haven't even packed."

I fumbled around for my key, dropping it into the snow then crawling around on hands and knees to dig it out. I was stone cold sober by the time I got inside the house. And frozen to the core. The frigid wind had whipped the ends of my hair into icicles and I could barely feel the tips of my fingers. When the door slammed shut, I looked around at the bare room with its floor cushion and TV. Loneliness was a weight crushing down on me with such force I felt like I'd disappear. Every cell of me pressed into the floor. Gone without anyone knowing or caring. I needed a friendly voice to tell me that life was still worth living, so I ripped Dennis's number from my purse and dialed before I could change my mind.

I imagined his phone ringing somewhere. Far away. Echoing down the years until it reached the man I remembered as Dennis. Dad. The man with the long hair and broad shoulders. The man who read me stories.

A sudden click and I held my breath.

"Hello. Hello?" The voice was scratchy. "Who's this?"

"Dennis?" I said in a small voice. The long silence was punctuated only by the sounds of our breathing. The voice waited, maybe for further proof. "It's me, Anna."

And then the sound came over the wires and cables. In waves that ebbed and flowed. The sound of an old man crying. Soon I was sobbing along with him. Pouring out all the hurt and pain.

"I reckon we both needed that," he said, when we paused for breath.

I held the phone as if it was made of gold. "I feel better."

He coughed. Blew his nose. I tried to match the man from my memory with this older, more vulnerable man. "I've never stopped crying since I let you two girls go. I thought it would just be for a while, till I could get my feet on the ground. Then they wouldn't let me see you. Said it was best for the both of you that you went to a good, solid family."

If he only knew.

"Where's Birdie?"

The question I'd been dreading was finally out. The question I'd been asking myself for so long now.

"Gone." The word echoed. Took on a life of its own.

"Gone where?"

I tried to explain but how could I capture years of pain in a few minutes over the phone?

"Promise me you'll find her," he said after I was done. No comment on the drugs or the abuse or the pimps. Just *find her.* "Find her and let her know where I am. I want to see both of you. Make up for everything. If I can do that, I'll be able to rest easy at night."

I made that promise to him though I hadn't a clue where to start. First, I scoured the net for Las Vegas *bunny ranches.* Pages and pages of curvy young girls in frilled bikinis and thigh high boots posing outside wooden ranch style nightclubs or gathered around bloated, bald guys in red silk shirts and cowboy hats. *Starlight Bunny Ranch, Moonlight Pussy Palace, Hot Love Junction*, all lit up in pink neon, shining down onto the pumped-up boobs and bulging buttocks of a thousand nameless young girls.

I didn't find her there. Earl Rafferty was probably too cheap to put out the bus fare to Nevada.

So one frigid March weekend I took the bus up to Duluth.

41

Lake Superior was still partly iced over. Rivers of free-flowing water ate their way through rough sheets of slate colored ice, shattering them into a rubble of dirty chunks that piled up against the shoreline. I stood on the harbor front clutching Birdie's picture and watching a thick bank of ice fog roll across the lake. Above it a watery sun rose, an opal disc in a colorless sky.

I ate breakfast in a little diner by the harbor. Warm and cozy, it smelled of toast and browning sausages. Huddled on a blue vinyl bench seat, I finished off a plate of bacon, eggs and all the fixings in record time. I'd never felt that kind of nervous hunger before but then I'd never traveled so far away from the city, and in this unfamiliar place I felt a thrill of adventure and hope. Now I understood why all my college friends set off on summer-long backpacking trips to Europe or Thailand. To recreate themselves as someone carefree, open, even joyful. A person who embraced change, not dreaded it. I came to that understanding while I chewed on rye toast and watched the sunlight finally bleed through the mist.

After an hour of scoping out the docks and getting more familiar with my bearings, I summoned up the courage to approach dock workers moving crates, and laborers leaning over the rails of freight ships. All morning I traipsed up and down, talking to as many as I could.

Nobody had seen her. In the afternoon I switched to the bars, chain restaurants, family diners, beer parlors until I narrowed my search down to a couple of places – seedy hangouts where hookers drifted through like tired ghosts and wild-eyed guys searched for cheap sex.

I pulled up my hood to cover my hair, shrank into a corner seat, ordered a beer and waited. I repeated the routine in all three places, but by late afternoon I was checking my watch. It'd soon be dusk and the last bus was in less than two hours. I'd just drained the final dregs of beer when a bartender sidled up to my table. He had a thick beard and a shaggy ponytail and kept checking out the front door as he talked.

"You Anna?" he murmured. I could barely see his lips move underneath that beard.

I nodded. "Who wants to know?"

"Some woman outside. Says she wants to talk to you."

My heart leapt. This was classic Birdie. She wouldn't approach me directly. Always left a note or sent a message. Gave you options. As if she wanted to be sure you were actually interested in talking to her. I stuffed a couple of dollar bills into the guy's hand and raced outside.

A woman stood in the street, her back to me, shivering, hands stuffed into her pockets, shoulders hunched against the cold in a thin denim jacket. An icy wind blew off the lake, whipping her hair into a shaggy halo. She turned. Through the ice fog I saw her nose was running. As long as I could remember, Birdie's nose was always streaming. My heart hurt so bad it knocked the breath from me. I offered her a Kleenex. Looked closer and knew it wasn't her.

"Heard you're looking for Birdie."

"Who are you and how do you know her?" I tried to stop my voice from cracking. This girl's nose was different to Birdie's. Instead of a slim, delicate nose, hers was a flattened-out bulb, the bridge crooked and knobbly, like it'd been broken and healed wrong. Her top lip was scarred and swollen.

"Name's Tara. Birdie was — I mean is — my friend."

"Where is she?"

"She was here," she said, her voice rough and scratchy — a smoker's voice. She reached into her pocket and took out a pack. Her hand shook so bad when she tried to light the cigarette, she dropped her lighter. I swooped down and picked it up, held it to her trembling hands and cradled them while I lit her cigarette. She took a long drag then sighed and released a cloud of smoke into the frigid air. "But we ain't seen her around for maybe a year or more."

My voice was strangled in my throat. I'd wanted so badly for it to be Birdie, but Tara looked twenty years older. Skinny, sallow-faced, dull-eyed. A middle-aged face on a scrawny kid's body. All the light and life gone from her.

I pulled up the hood of my parka. The wind cut through the opening.

"You'll freeze," I said as she dug her hands into her pockets. She shrugged.

"Don't matter. I'm a tough old whore," she said, cackling then doubling over into a wet, hacking cough that caved her cheeks in.

I waited until she wiped her mouth with a paper napkin. Her face appeared almost ghostly in the light. "So how d'you know my sister Birdie?"

She bent her head down against the wind and started to walk. I followed her along the waterfront away from the ships until we came to a pier. The lake water shimmered through the gaps netween the planks, its black surface pocked with ice floes. Beautiful but deadly.

"How many times I walked along here with Birdie and she talked about jumping right in," she said, gazing downwards. "Ending it all."

I looked into the frigid water. "Why – why did she talk that way?"

"Our life here is worth nothing. It's like hell on the boats." She grasped the handrail, her breath blowing out in icy plumes as if her life was sapping away into the night. "You're nobody. Not even a person. They punch you, cut you, do stuff I can't even talk about. And Birdie was too young. Not like the rest of us. She was a good kid. Always acting crazy, trying to make us laugh."

That sounded exactly like my sister. My heart was sore thinking about where she could be. "How d'you know about me?"

She flicked the live butt into the water. Coughed and spat over the rail. "She always talked about her sister Anna. Her bodyguard, she called you. Said you were the only person that loved her. Said she planned to make enough money to get away from here and find you."

I cursed myself. *Why hadn't I come to look for her earlier?* "You think she ran away?"

She shook her head and took out another cigarette. Lit it, sucked back a drag and wiped a sleeve across her frozen nose. The smoke billowed in small clouds as she talked. "Nobody leaves here. 'Specially Earl's girls. Maybe she's hiding somewhere. Maybe she met up with a bad guy. Maybe she did jump. Thought it was her only way out."

My mind raced. She wouldn't give up. Not Birdie. I shoved a piece of paper with my number into her hand.

"Call me right away if you hear anything. Gossip, rumor, talk, I mean anything."

She nodded and tapped her cheap red purse. The chain strap cut across her chest. "I got something for you. From Birdie."

I was dizzy. From the biting wind belting against my cheeks, and the ships' revolving lights playing like strobes across the water. I held out my hand.

A ship's horn boomed into the evening as she pulled out an envelope. "She told me if anything ever happened to her, to open it. Or better still, if you came looking for her, to give it straight to you. And now here you are. Like she knew you'd come."

"What is it?" I said, holding out my hand.

"I don't want no trouble. Best you deal with it."

I stuffed the package into my backpack. "Anybody call the cops to report her missing?"

"You know how many girls like Birdie disappear? So many it'd make your head spin." The wet, gut-wrenching cough returned. When she looked up her face was bleached like damp paper. "And the cops. They're worse than the crewmen. Can't tell the good from the bad."

Her phone rang so I left her at the dockside. Tara. A shrunken, huddled figure. Shoulders hunched, porcupine hair prickly and static from the cold. She reminded me of Birdie and how she'd be in twenty years. Beaten up and sucked dry.

My Birdie.

Gone. Disappeared. And nobody knew where. I was no further forward and I had no idea where to look next.

42

After my initial briefing, I only saw Gord once a week for Monday updates. During those one-hour sessions, I'd watch him, nails digging into my palms, until the face of the man who ruined my fifteen-year-old sister, became a blur. Indistinguishable from the objects around it. And while he rattled off a series of instructions, relayed information about future plans, then listed the week's tasks, I'd study the crêpey skin under his eyes and hate him with a passion that would have seared the skin from his bones.

Afterwards I'd go back to my office to settle down. I'd gaze around the blue room with its simple, white furniture and sweeping view of the park and try to become someone else. A busy, focused person. Not someone with revenge eating away at her insides.

When I wasn't thinking about Gord and how I'd make him pay with every fiber of his being for what he'd done to Birdie, I worried about what would happen to Guy.

He met me from work most evenings and took me out for supper or to the theater or a concert. We sat over drinks, holding hands across the table and talked about his homeless outreach project. His plan was to bring me in on the front lines when Gord's project was over. I gazed at his honest, open face as he talked about our future. Together. A team. And it tore me up inside to know this would likely never happen. Not after what I was about to do. I loathed myself in those moments. Hated that I was lying to him every minute of every day.

But still I listened. Smiled. Nodded. For Birdie.

"You're great with those kids, Anna. We could work together on something really meaningful. Something that makes a difference. Then I'd cut down my time with Dad's company. Make a break."

He'd already envisioned a future that didn't include Gord. A battle raged inside me. I could tell him. Maybe he'd understand. Maybe we could both be free. But who was I kidding? Gord was his father. And he'd never desert Nancy. He couldn't turn his back on family.

When things got really bad the nights Guy was at work, I'd miss him so much I'd slip into his closet and press my face against his clothes, searching for his scent on shirts and sweaters. Another time I did a load of laundry and tried to arrange his socks in his drawer just the way he liked, but I was left with three odd ones. I undid all the neat pairs, and threw them in a pile on the floor to sort through them again. I made a long row of socks stretching from the drawers to the bedroom door. Then I placed each one with its matching partner, but still three different odd socks remained. Panicking, I tried again and again until I sat back against the bed, beaten and utterly exhausted. I didn't even hear Guy come in. He found me clutching a huge ball of socks to my chest and sobbing my heart out.

"What's wrong?" he said, squatting on the floor beside me. "Anna – talk to me."

For a moment I thought of telling him everything. I could just unload the whole messy story. Share the burden with someone who cared for me. It could be that easy. I opened my mouth to speak but my jaw was paralyzed. All my resolve simply drained away. The moment passed. I shook my head.

He sat down and put his arms around me, held me for a long moment, then loosened the silly clump of socks from my grip. "I know something's been bothering you, Anna, and I don't want to pressure you to tell me. I told you I'd wait until you were ready. Didn't I?"

I looked up at him and nodded.

"And I'm not mad about the socks," he said, smiling. "But I'll tell you a little secret about them."

He shifted around until I was lying against his chest, calmed by its steady rise and fall. "When I was a kid and things got really bad at school or when Mom and Dad were fighting, I'd empty out all my drawers and arrange everything – underwear, socks, T-shirts, sweaters – in perfect rows. If something was even a fraction out of place I'd start over again. I'd soothe myself into a trance state where the only thing that existed were those stupid pieces of clothing and their uniformity. It was something in my life that I could totally control. I guess it sounds weird for a kid to obsess about something like that."

I turned to look at him. "Did your parents ever find out?"

He shook his head. "I was a quiet kid and Dad monopolized Mom's time with work stuff in the evenings. So I was left to my own devices a lot."

"You were a lonely kid?"

"It was good for my grades. Paid off in the end. I mightn't have been a prof otherwise."

I took his face into my hands and kissed him hard on the mouth, then pulled away. His eyes were wide. Liquid. "Can I ask you something, Guy?"

He perked up instantly. "Anything. Fire away."

My heart lurched. This was the moment. I held my hand against his cheek and took a deep breath. "Do you love your father?"

He turned away from me, then pulled himself up. "I'm not sure I want to talk about that right now," he said, throwing the socks onto the bed. "Think I need a drink."

I sat there. Alone. Confused. More conflicted than before.

—

Things came to a head one Monday in the fall when I left work. A young man in a dark coat was waiting outside the door, leaning against a streetlight.

"Anna," he called to me.

It was Dane. He still sported traces of the goth look but the long, black overcoat was gone, replaced by the greenish parka and backpack of a student. I rushed over to hug him.

"Great to see you," I said, stepping back to take a good look at the transformation. He swept the hair back from his face and smiled self-consciously. "Are you taking classes round here?"

"I'm at the College of Art and Design," he said, a grin twitching at the corner of his lips.

I held onto his arm. "That's incredible. I'm proud of you."

He stared down at the sidewalk, grinding his toe into the concrete. "It's pretty good there. I like it."

"Everything's okay?"

He nodded. "Great. My mom's all crazy about it. She packs me lunch every day."

He chewed on his lower lip.

"Something's up, Dane," I said. "Spit it out."

He looked at me, his eyes wide and vulnerable under the caked-on eyeliner. "Carla's gone. Left her auntie's house. Nobody knows where she is."

"But she loved it there. She was more settled than she'd ever been."

He shifted from one foot to the other. "Everything was going okay, then she made a big mistake. Came up to the city for the weekend. Didn't get back to her auntie's place afterwards. That was last week."

Suddenly the noise of the traffic was a din in my head. The stink of car exhaust made me sick. "You asked around?"

He nodded. "Nobody knows anything. As usual."

"You go to see Robin?"

He nodded. "Says he's gonna look into it."

I reached out and touched his arm. "I know he will. He really liked Carla. Had high hopes for her since she turned her life around. I'll call him too. But come back here in the next few days and let me know if you hear anything from her."

I gave him my number then watched him go, his shoulders hunched. That's when I knew the past would never leave Carla alone. And now she was going the same way as Birdie. It had to be stopped and that meant sacrificing everything I had for the sake of my lost sister. After all, I could never forget what was in the package Tara gave me on that frigid night in Duluth.

43

Dennis called me again the day after I got back from Duluth.

I saw his caller ID and let it ring. How could I answer it when I hadn't found her? It rang for almost a minute, and I ached to pick it up. But there was nothing to say. When the noise finally stopped, I sat down at the kitchen table, poured myself a half tumbler of rye and placed Birdie's envelope in front of me. I knocked back the drink, reached out my hand and slit the seal.

The first photographs were similar to those I'd found in Birdie's apartment. I flicked on the kitchen light to see better, then held them up to the light. Birdie lay on a bed, her frilly little girlie dress hiked up, her bare, skinny legs spread wide, a handwritten sign on the headboard read *Birdie 15*. Three men stood at the side of the bed staring down at her. Gord's flushed face was clearly visible next to a shorter blurry-faced man as well as a silver-haired guy with a goatee. Had to be Karrass and Rafferty. The other pictures featured just Gord and Birdie and were far more incriminating. In the pictures, it was like Birdie's mind was somewhere else – anywhere else – her expression vacant like a doll's. Smacking the pictures face down on the table I screamed and howled until my voice cracked then I ran to the washroom to throw up.

"Visitors from your old school?" said a voice from behind me. I blinked and realized I'd been standing alone, lost in thought. A statue in the middle of the sidewalk. Gord walked around to face me, smoothing back his hair.

"Looks like you were reminiscing about the good old days. You missing your old job?"

"Oh… no… it's not like that," I said, scrambling to separate the past from the present. "That kid graduated this year. He's come a long way."

A chilly breeze ruffled my hair. Gord buttoned his overcoat. "I can always smell the fall," he said, scanning the golden leafed trees. "It's my favorite season."

"Busiest time in teaching," I said. "New beginnings and all that. Well, you'd know about that, wouldn't you? I mean…"

His brows knit as I blathered on, terrified to allow even one moment of silence between us. I was still mumbling about something inane like putting up inspirational posters on classroom walls when he checked his watch, stepped out onto the road and glanced down the street. "He's late."

"You expecting someone?"

He nodded as a familiar silver SUV approached, swishing to a halt beside us.

"You'll have to excuse me now, Anna. My ride's here," he said, opening the passenger door. Karrass's silver head craned forward to look at me. Past and present collided. I staggered backwards on the sidewalk as the car swished away.

It took me a few seconds to realize they were gone. Leaving me in the terrible present. Me, Anna. Teacher.

Educational researcher. Respectable woman. Beloved wife of Guy Franzen, son of a monster.

I glanced up at Gord's office. The windows were dark except for one that glowed with a night security light. It was as good a time as any to take a look inside his inner sanctum up on the penthouse floor. After all, I'd waited a long time for this moment. But my insides coiled in on themselves at the thought of the task ahead. I checked the street in both directions. It was dark, deserted. Guy was in class. I had at least three hours to kill and I was ready.

-

The day after Duluth, I hid Birdie's pictures somewhere safe. Dennis kept calling me but I ignored him. I'd done without him for so long I didn't know how to be around him again. Better to let him stay in my memory like he'd always been. Didn't want to spoil it by seeing some broken-down old train-wreck of a man. Besides I hadn't found Birdie yet. Couldn't explain how hard I'd tried for so many years to cling to her, protect her – the princess wearing the crown. I saw her now in every kid that walked through my classroom door. Broken down, hungry, rejected, tattooed, pierced, scarred, angry. I tried to save them all, but none of them were Birdie.

I ignored him for three, maybe four years. Until the phone call came. The call I'd waited for but dreaded.

Linda Martin, her voice echoing from the other end of an infinite tunnel.

"Anna?"

"Yes. It's me."

I took the call in the staffroom, a cup of stale coffee in my hand. The sun shone through the barred window and a robin perched on the tree branch. Nice. Normal. Happy springtime. *Tweet, tweet.*

"You still there, Anna?"

"What's up?"

"I have news."

"Is it Birdie?"

"I need to see you."

"Did you find her?"

Tweet, tweet. Why doesn't it goddamn shut up? It's messing with my head.

"I'm coming there to see you."

"Tell me. Tell me now."

"I'm on the way."

But she couldn't tell me because she didn't find me there. I left so I didn't have to see her lumpy, saggy ass under the faded Gap jeans. I shut myself in my apartment kitchen and wouldn't open the door so she came around to the side door. A uniformed cop was with her. She let herself in. I couldn't hear because I pressed my hands to my ears and backed away from them.

"We found her body, Anna."

A weird sound like a child's wailing came from my mouth. I slid down the wall to the floor and sat there rocking back and forth. Linda squatted down, put her arm around me and held me.

"Rachel Levine's coming in from the country. She'll be here soon. Don't worry."

All I could say was *Rachel, Rachel.*

I sat like that for maybe two hours until Rachel showed up and put her soft arms around me. She was the one who took me to the cop station, who held me up when my legs buckled under me after they showed me Birdie's green ring and her little denim jacket and asked me if they were hers. She was the one who cradled me like a baby when the sweet-faced cop with the photo on his desk of a toddler in overalls, explained that dental records helped identify a decomposed body found buried on a farm outside Duluth as Birdie's.

Birdie's was the sixth body unearthed in a nightmare harvest of missing women at the home of Arliss Stroud. He was a local handyman and carpenter who'd hung many a door and framed numerous barns for people in the neighborhood. Seemed he made a whole lot of trips to Duluth in his spare time and rarely came back alone.

It was all over as quickly as that. My search. Finished.

Half of me was finally gone.

Forever.

I was off work for a year after that.

A good part of it was spent in a hospital where I slept all day and gazed out of the window at night trying to think of nothing. Pills dulled the edge of feeling until I was ready to come home. After that I endured six months of therapy. Long days made bearable by many trips to the mall. Always the mall. The scent of cleanliness, the sparkle of lights and nice things. Guaranteed to take the sting of pain away.

Robin welcomed me back like the father I never had and the very next day I called Guy Franzen's colleague, Brian. I'd already vowed to hunt down the bastard who ruined Birdie. But I decided to do it through his precious son, Guy.

44

Gord's office reeked of Axe. The sweet, flowery stink reminded me of a funeral home.

I flipped his laptop open. Careless and arrogant, he'd left a screen saver without password protection, so it was easy enough to open the history and find the chat rooms. I took out Birdie's note from my purse. The one that came with the envelope of photographs. I never could figure out what she meant by *ToXicBoy* and the string of numbers listed on the torn-edged scrap of paper. But I had a hunch. I typed it into the login column and *click* – a long string of talk bubbles. ToXicBoy and his friends PaiN, ScAndal, DriLLer and CatAStrophe shared fantasies with each other as well as photo and video files. A real community of sickos. ToXic described how he took a little girl's clothes off and made her scream and her slut of a mom knew about it too. Then PaiN sends a file swap. Fresh pictures. *So hot you'll explode.*

The file was nowhere to be seen. Even they weren't that stupid.

I spent the better part of two hours combing through folders on the desktop. Nothing. Gord was too smart to leave them somewhere they couldn't be permanently erased. I sat back in his chair trying to figure out how his mind worked. I knew they'd be in the office somewhere. It would be a turn on to know he could have them under his nose. At the center of his empire. Immediate gratification at his fingertips. One minute he'd be in a well-lit lecture theater lecturing earnest academics on the best way to cultivate young minds, the next minute he'd slither away to the dark confines of his office to feed his sick fantasies. It must've given him a real buzz jacking off after hours in the pristine comfort of his well-appointed office.

Somewhere, a USB was hidden. It had to be.

My phone buzzed. It was Guy. I couldn't talk to him at that moment. Couldn't associate him with this crap. Guy was a victim too. Just like those kids. Gord and I had both screwed him over and he didn't know it.

I went through the drawers. Nothing there among the pristine, obsessively ordered paper clip containers, tape dispensers, pencils, erasers, and file tabs. I stood in front of the bookshelves and scanned the spines. On the bottom row were all his books. A lifetime's work based on a framework of lies. On the top shelf a row of novels. Thrillers, murder mysteries. The usual junk.

In the middle were two copies of *Lolita*. It seemed too obvious a hiding place, but then I remembered the scope of his vanity. This guy thought he was invincible. That the rules weren't meant for him. He destroyed people's lives without a second thought.

I pulled the books down. One was real, the other revealed ripped out pages and nestling inside, a silver USB. On the page, two lines were highlighted:

> *Lolita, light of my life, fire of my loins. My sin, my soul. Lo-lee-ta: the tip of the tongue taking a trip of three steps down the palate to tap, at three, on the teeth.*

I plugged in the USB. Blinked once and images flooded the screen. A gallery of young skinny bodies. Splayed out, twisted, their faces turned away. Thin wrists secured to bedposts. Gord was in some of the pictures with girls like Birdie. It was enough to incriminate him a hundred times over. And then I couldn't look any more.

He was loathsome. Vile. An addict. I'd read about people like him.

My heart raced and my hands shook as I downloaded the contents of the USB onto the desktop. I glanced up at the clock. Plenty of time left to finish the job off. I waited as the bar inched along to completion. Car headlights swished by on the street outside. I prayed that Gord hadn't forgotten something and had to come back for it. That the door wouldn't slam open to reveal Gord, Nancy, or worse, Guy standing there wondering what the hell I was doing.

My mind was working overtime so I concentrated instead on the screen. So many videos and images took a long time to download. *Fourteen minutes remaining* it said. I told myself that was normal. It would probably only take five. Once it was safely on the desktop, I'd hide it in a secret place. I'd learned the trick from a student last year. A veteran hacker of corporate computers. Only I'd know where it was hidden but Gord would have no idea it was even there. It would stay concealed until I told the right person exactly where to find it after they'd seized Gord's computer. After I'd handed Birdie's photos over to the cops, and told them her story. Then everyone would know the truth about Gord and his sick buddies.

Finally the authorities would have all the ammunition they needed to put an end to Earl Rafferty, Karrass and Gord. To lock them away for a good, long time. Throw the keys away if I'd had my way. No doubt many other respectable pillars of the community would be caught up in the sting as well. Maybe it was too late to save Carla, maybe not.

The electronic *ping* told me it was done downloading. I did my secret hiding trick, closed the laptop lid and put the books and everything back exactly in place. On the way out I spat in his water glass and shut the door.

Out on the street I felt calm.

Peaceful for the first time.

My phone rang. Guy again. I clicked the receive button and spoke before he could say a thing. I had to protect him. Get him away from here when it all came crashing down.

"Hey, sweetheart. I was just thinking. We don't need to wait a year. Let's celebrate our six-month anniversary in Vegas. It's coming up next month."

45

Las Vegas, November 2019

"If he's any kind of a man, he'll understand why you had to do it," says a voice from behind me. The hand squeezes my shoulder. Comforting. Warm.

If breaking Guy's heart was part of Gord's punishment then why do I feel so empty? Why do I want to run after him, throw my arms around him? Tell him I never want to hurt him.

"He made a home for me. I love him for that."

The person hands me a cold beer. "Drink this. You'll feel better."

I take the bottle and press it against my forehead. The cold feels so good I turn around to take another look at the gaunt-faced man behind me. I can't believe he's here. After all these years. I'd never have recognized Dennis if he hadn't sent a photograph to prepare me for our first meeting. He's shrunk in height and in girth. Stooped, sinewy, sucked-in. Not the husky, long-haired hippy of twenty years ago.

"I mean when the shit hits the fan you might be the last person they'll want to see. At first, anyway. You'll be like a turd in a bakery." He starts to chuckle at his own joke. He's lost a few teeth, but his eyes are still young and lively. "Nobody likes it when you mess with their family.

Ask me. I'm the expert. I nearly decked a few of those do-gooder social workers when they wouldn't let me see you."

Dennis has chin length choppy gray hair now. He told me he cut his long hair when he found out about Birdie.

"You've got real family now, Anna. Your mother's folks. They're up in Fond Du Lac. A whole bunch of them waiting to meet you when we bring Birdie home. Aunties, uncles, cousins. Maybe even a couple of little bastard half brothers and sisters I don't know about," he says, winking.

But I'm not laughing right now. The thought of all those strange people I've never met scares me, and right now the only person I know that loves me is about to get up and leave. Guy looks so helpless. He's a gentle, good man. He doesn't deserve any of this.

"Just kidding," says Dennis, the smile leaving his face. "I'm clean now. No booze or drugs for eight years. Your mother's people helped me out. Rented me a two-bed log cabin on the riverside and gave me a whole lot of family love to make me feel human again. I do some hunting, fishing, cut the grass at the local golf course. Clear the snow in the winter. I'm set. I thought I was all alone in the world just like you do now, but there's no need to be lonely when there's people who love you. I know it'll be a bit strange at first but these are good people. You'll see."

He tugs at my sleeve. We have a flight to catch.

"Just give me another minute, Dennis," I say. I can barely see Guy now through the tears that turn everything hazy. It's like tearing off a Band-Aid. I should rip it off quickly so it doesn't hurt.

My body aches for Guy. And then I remember something I read on the internet. About this couple who'd been married for sixty-three years. When the wife was dying with cancer, the husband sat for days beside her bed and massaged her callused old feet because it made her feel good. That's the kind of intimacy and devotion Guy promised me.

I'll never find someone like him again. And it kills me to think of all the pain he'll endure when his family is destroyed. How will he cope? What about Nancy? I can't even think about it.

Now the cops have the file and Gord will be arrested, the story will soon be all over the news, and the empire will crumble. Any time now Guy will go back to the hotel and find the note I left him. I feel like a coward explaining it all in a note. Maybe he'll get the call. From Nancy. Maybe from the cops.

In the note I said I love him and I'll be there to support him if he cares to find me. I also told him about Birdie and Gord and how this was all about justice for the sister I loved and lost. If he's really the man I fell in love with, he'll understand. He'll be on my side.

Then I told him I have to go away for now and do one last thing for my sister.

I have to bring her home to a family that will honor her memory, then lay her to rest somewhere peaceful and untouched. Somewhere clean where trees grow and snow falls, where the sun shines and rain cools the ground. Where life is treasured.

And I already know what the headstone will say.

A kind and gentle soul
Who gave the world so much joy
And only asked for love in return.
My sister.
In body and spirit.
Birdie was here.

Dennis lays his hands on my shoulders again. "Listen to me," he says, turning me around to face him. "I have to live every day with what I did to you and Birdie. Abandoning you like that. Maybe if I'd tried harder, stuck around, she'd still be here. But I didn't. I let it go. I let *her* go. If you love him, maybe you shouldn't run. Maybe that's taking the coward's way out."

Guy's on his phone again but he's not calling me. He stands up, clasping the phone to his ear for a few moments, then his arm falls loosely to his side. He flops onto a nearby bench, his arms splayed out at his sides. He knows about Gord.

I look back at Dennis. His eyes are moist and weary looking, the lids wrinkled and drooping at the corners.

"Maybe you can save him, Anna. Make something good of your life. I'll wait here for you. I'm not going anywhere this time."

He squeezes my shoulder again and I lean in and hug his bony shoulders, then I step out from the shadows into the glare of sunlight.

"Come with me," I say softly, reaching my hand out behind me. This feels unfamiliar – a show of weakness and vulnerability. And yet this is Dennis, my father. Father. I roll that word around on my tongue. It's sweet like candy.

He follows as I move out from the cool of the alleyway into the blazing wall of heat in the plaza. Guy spots us, his brow wrinkling at the sight of this shrunken old man padding along behind. I put a hand to my face to shield my eyes from the glare. Guy lunges towards me.

"What the hell's going on?" he gasps, catching my arm. "I thought I'd lost you."

I turn to Dennis who's pulled a ball cap low over his eyes.

"This is my dad, Dennis."

Guy pulls back, his brows knit as he glances from me to Dennis. "I don't get it — you didn't say anything."

"Remember, you said you'd be patient and when I was ready, you'd listen."

He rakes a hand through his hair. Beads of perspiration glisten on his forehead. "I know — I did, but now's not the time. Something terrible has happened and…"

I stroke a dampened curl of hair away from his eyes and hold my index finger up to his lips. "I know all about it."

"How — how's that possible?" He holds onto the arm of the bench and steadies himself.

I stroke his shoulder. Try to reassure him. "Will you come back to the hotel and let me explain?"

His eyes are wide and startled. He pulls back like he's trapped. "I don't know — I mean, you're scaring me."

Dennis moves to my side, his body resting against mine as if to shore me up. "My daughter has a good heart, son. She's got quite a story to tell you, if you'll listen."

Guy chews at his lip. I reach a hand out to him. He studies the wedding ring now glinting in the sunlight, then reaches out and, with the tip of his finger and thumb, lightly turns it so the stone is centered.

"No more secrets or lies?" he says.

I clasp his hand and shake my head. "Just the truth, and it starts with my beautiful sister, Birdie."

A Message from M. M. DeLuca

Thank you so much for reading read *The Secret Sister*. I hope you enjoyed reading it as much as I enjoyed writing it! If you'd like to keep up-to-date with any of my new releases, please click the link below to reach the sign-up form for my newsletter. Your e-mail will never be shared, and I'll only contact you when I have news about a new release. Sign up using the link below!

https://www.marjoriedeluca.com/thrillers

If you have the time to leave me a short, honest review on Amazon, Goodreads, or wherever you purchased the book, I'd very much appreciate it. I love hearing what you think, and your reviews help me reach new readers – which allows me to bring you more books! If you know of friends or family that would enjoy the book, I'd love your help there, too.

You can also connect with me via Facebook, Goodreads, Instagram and Twitter. I'd love to hear from you.

Instagram:
https://www.instagram.com/mmdelucaauthor/

Facebook:
https://www.facebook.com/marjorie.deluca.3

Goodreads:
https://www.goodreads.com/author/show/20984340.
M_M_DeLuca

Twitter:
https://twitter.com/DeLucaMarjorie

Thank you again, so very much, for your support of my books. It means the world to me!

M. M. DeLuca

Acknowledgments

My sincere thanks to everyone who read and commented on early drafts of *The Secret Sister*, particularly my sister, Janet, and friends, Leslie and Kay. Their enthusiastic feedback was invaluable to me.

Many thanks also go to the amazing publishing team at Canelo, most notably my editor, Leodora Darlington, whose unflagging optimism and passion, as well as her insightful sense of story and structure inspired me to produce the best work possible. Also thanks to the other team members who helped make this an incredibly smooth and exciting journey: copyeditor, Jane Eastgate; proofreader, Claire Rushbrook; designer, Lisa Horton; sales and publicity, Francesca Riccardi, supported by Claudine Sagoe; marketing, Nicola Piggott; production, Micaela Cavaletto.

Thanks also to my family: brothers Trevor, Ken and his wife, Linda. Your interest and unwavering support have spurred me to keep on writing. To my son, Mike, and daughter, Laura, your imagination and creativity amaze and inspire me. To my husband, Fausto, thanks for supporting my work and putting up with the hermit in the office!

Thanks also to the beautiful city of Minneapolis where I've spent many happy times.

Finally, a huge thank-you to all the readers out there. It's your love of reading that keeps me striving to produce the best work I can. I couldn't have done this without you!